NIGHTMARESCAPE

. . . Soon enough the sounds were decipherable. Curse could not believe his ears.

"The time has come for you to awaken from your slumber and follow your pastor into battle. There are those that would have us destroyed and eradicate the blessings granted to us . . . to stop us from fulfilling our legacy that has been destined since the dawn of creation!"

A strange sloshing sound caught Curse's ears. A sense of horror washed over him as he looked down at the pit and learned what had been lurking beneath the dark water. Emaciated and rotten bodies were climbing up the ladders and onto the stone. Gangling, atrophied limbs stuck out from under the surface as more of the corpse-like Plague Faction creatures crawled from the water. The scene was one of true repulsion. More and more bodies crawled from the water. They dragged the filthy dark liquid onto the stonework with them as well as detritus from the pit. The voice from overhead intensified as the chains descended. Curse looked up and observed a grated metal platform attached to the chains with several shadows on it.

NIGHTMARESCAPE

NIGHTMARESCAPE

T. S. Dann

MORBID
PUBLICATIONS

Morbid Publications
Atlanta, Georgia

Second Edition

10 9 8 7 6 5 4 3   1 0 0 7 1 4

ISBN: 978-0-9854370-0-8

Printed in the United States of America

Cover Art by Robert Taylor

♾ This paper meets the requirements of ANSI/NISO Z39.48-1992 (Permanence of Paper)

This book is dedicated to the memory of
Paula Dennerline and Luke Gregory.

PROLOGUE

In our restful state known as sleep we sometimes find ourselves locked in unreal situations that seem temporarily inescapable. Our fear reaches its zenith just as these unimaginable circumstances are about to play out on us in their disastrous fruition, but then we wake up and find resolution in our conscious minds once more. We feel relief in the fact that we have been returned to a sense of reality that is somewhat safe, where no imminent dread is about to destroy us. This is not always the case however. In certain instances, we find ourselves happier in our unconscious realms and have feelings of rejoicing and relief crushed upon re-entering reality.

Sometimes we get stuck in an area between the reality we live in and the realms our unconscious create for us during slumber. At these times, we struggle to discern what is real and what is a delusion, what can be done and what is no longer possible, and maybe even how to wake and revive ourselves…if possible.

From the unconscious however springs the conscious, a state of perception that exists from sensory information. Information from the world enters our brains through our nerves, where it is processed through our neurofibrillary bundles and strained against our latent feelings. It is from these processes that we form our view of what is around us. Not all situations are kind enough to allow the time for the complete run of such processes however.

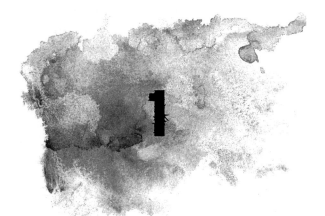

1

He could feel what was happening around him, but he could not see or hear anything. His mind could not make sense of what was occurring, for he could neither think nor tap his senses to realize his situation. He felt himself drifting in the dark purgatory along hidden currents and appendages as he was jostled through the abyss. Within a few moments, his ears were beginning to pick up sounds, although they were indistinct and melded together into a cacophonous mess. It had to be a dream. Reality seemed to be bordering on the threshold between consciousness and a dream state. That was the first thought that actually seemed to process.

Floating in a dark abyss without senses can turn several moments into an eternity. He had no concept of time, but it felt as though days were passing as the world around him seemed to carry on in tempestuous fashion.

His hearing began to hone itself somewhat, and the sounds came to him with a little more clarity, although they were still undecipherable. All around him, voices were speaking and whispering to one another—some loudly yet some very softly—while over the voices a wind blew, seeming to carry some of the voices with it. Everything was insubstantial. As he pondered why this may be, his eyes sluggishly observed several indistinguishable shapes moving about. Light and dark were clearly separated from one another, but nothing was definitive about the strange shapes swirling over him. His field of vision shifted violently due to their constant movement, for they clearly were holding him and tugging at him; it seemed certain ones were actually trying to take him from the others.

His eyes focused. A torrent of shadowy beings was jerking him around. Helplessness overcame him as he attempted to will himself to resist them. Movement was a remote possibility as he realized that his limbs were not functioning. His senses slowly began to give shape to the world. The voices around him were distorted in a sense that they seemed slow and lingering; the pulling of his body also did not seem in concordance with the physics of their tugging.

It was in this state of forced passiveness that he had to remain until he felt that he could move his body under his own power. Had he ever been able to move at all? His senses were becoming more alert as the shadows' clamoring intensified. The sounds were becoming clearer, and his perception was starting to keep pace with the world around him.

Suddenly the sounds around him were shattered by a clear and distinct booming noise. Almost as if on cue, the shadowy beings promptly scattered, letting their quarry fall to the ground. An impact shook his body as he landed on his back and was reminded of pain as a stimulus. He lay on the ground staring up at a pale gray sky with his senses not completely intact. The world around him crawled along in a state of slow motion.

Wind blew over his body and echoed through his ears with elongated howls and bellows. Another boom shook the ground under him, and with the boom, his senses suddenly sped up; he became totally aware and lucid in his surroundings. He could shift his vision and see, but to his terror, he realized that he could not move the rest of his body.

With his senses returned, he became aware of a new sound with the wind. Gone were the whispers of the shadows; they had been replaced with the sound of footsteps running toward him. He attempted to move his eyes to see who or what was coming next but could not find anything in his field of vision. A sense of shock ran through him as the footsteps came closer, and he looked up at their owner.

2

Reflexively his eyes shifted. No sooner than he had looked up, he saw a being standing above him. A horrific visage stared down greeting him. A truly indescribable being is hard to come by, but this one seemed to fit the bill. Towering over him, its muscular frame was adorned with black overalls that hung down over a pair of rugged boots. Its body was covered by an unnatural whitish gray skin. The skin stretched taut over a pair of toned arms that ended in bony hands wearing ragged gloves and holding an archaic shotgun. After surveying all of this, he looked at the creature's face. It was what truly made the visitor so horrific. It was unlike anything that he had seen at any point in time, real or fictitious, seeming to be described loosely as an amalgam of flesh and bone. The lower part of the face seemed to lack flesh, exposing the teeth in a skeletal grin. Above the teeth, a nose was absent, showing an empty nasal passage. The missing nose was framed by protruding cheekbones that had skin tightly drawn over them. The cheeks were covered in a viscous black ichor that bled from the sunken eyes, while the eyes themselves were white orbs floating in what seemed to be sockets full of the dark fluid. A strange presence lingered in

Nightmarescape

those eyes . . . they seemed unpredictable and wild, infused with a certain degree of insanity. Above them, a strong bony brow line stuck out, hanging slightly over the eyes. This was joined by the forehead, which stretched back into a scalp that was predominantly bald except for a thin, scraggly horseshoe line of dark hair surrounding the head.

How such a thing could exist biologically weighed heavily upon his mind as it spoke to him from above. "You all right down there?"

He found himself frozen now . . . not necessarily because he had not regained his ability to move, but from the horror that this being exuded.

"C'mon, son, I scared 'em off, but they might be back real soon . . ." At this point, the being reached its hand down to help him up. Still in a state of shock, yet relieved at the seemingly helpful presence, he found his hand unconsciously reaching up to meet a strong grip that lifted him up to a sitting position and then helped him to his feet.

"What's your name, son?"

He stood silently for a moment, trying to remember but unable to recall anything. In fact, he could not recollect anything about his existence. A name, a memory, a relation . . . it was all absent. Did he have amnesia?

"Guess that means you're nobody, huh?" The being's voice was slightly humorous in tone, which was angering. "Well, nobody, Larry Spectre's the name and shootin' folks is my game!" The being was studying him for a reaction.

"Obviously, Larry, if I'm standing in front of you, I have to be someone."

"WELL HOT DAMN, YOU CAN TALK!" Larry exclaimed excitedly. His comment was followed by a peal of hearty laughter. The sparkle of insanity in his eyes had not been deceiving. His inappropriate affects were testament to that.

Larry continued: "Wanna know how I got my name?"

"Enlighten me."

"I gave it to myself."

"Okay . . ."

"You don't know nothin' about yourself, do you, son?"

"No . . . I don't . . . but how would you know that?"

"HAHAAAAAA! Cuz I was just like you once . . . I just kind of showed up and didn't know anything . . . I basically took up here and created myself. I think I have a name for you . . ."

"Now what might that be?"

"Curse!" Larry thrust his left hand skyward with his index finger pointed as he exclaimed the name as though he were christening a newborn to some unseen audience above them.

"It has a nice ring to it . . . but why that?"

"You haven't seen yourself yet . . ."

"I'm sure I'm not the prize you are . . ."

"HAHAHAHA! You haven't seen yourself in a mirror yet!" At this, Larry let loose with another blast of laughter and began slapping his thigh. After several moments, he calmed down and returned to conversing. "Ah, I'm just yankin' your chain; you're as pretty as they come around here . . . although I don't mean that as . . . well, you know"—Larry's eyes shifted from side to side as he leaned forward and dropped his voice—"questionable . . ."

Ignoring Larry's comments, Curse thought about the new name he had just been given. He liked it. It was strong and intimidating. This thought was short-lived, however, as hundreds of questions began flooding his mind. He turned from Larry and looked out at the vast landscape that stretched before them. They stood in a field of blackened grass under a stale gray sky. Leafless trees shot up from the ground in a few places, but everything looked dark and dead. Whether it had ever been alive was something to be pondered . . . it looked to be in a strange limbo of decay that had never played out in full cycle.

"Where in the hell are we?" Curse stared out at the strange place.

"Been here a long time myself and I don't quite know still . . . but I damn sure love it!"

"It's always like this?"

"You're darn tootin' it is!"

"The sky never changes?"

"Gets a little darker sometimes, but always stays gray. Not really a night or day here . . . stays like this most of the time."

"And the plants never grow back?"

Larry giggled a bit before responding. "Are you shittin' me, boy? Never grow back, but never go away either."

"How is that possible?"

"Best not to think about it and just try to live with it, son. You know you're the first one like yourself to come this way in a long time . . . I know you're not here to grow plants and plot the farm."

"What are you talking about?" So far Mr. Spectre had not really been of any help in giving information about where they were. The only information he had offered was providing a name where one was not remembered before.

"Come with me and I can explain what I know to you. Those shady folk are liable to come back at any moment." Larry reached out and slapped Curse's shoulder before turning around and starting to run off into the sickly landscape. Curse had no choice but to follow his unlikely mentor. His legs began to work themselves, and he sped off behind Larry with the wind whipping against his body and shrieking over his ears. Somehow the cold wind in the deathly landscape seemed invigorating to him—but not only invigorating . . . somehow familiar too. It evoked strange connotations in his mind, all of which seemed alien to him.

Ahead of him, Larry was charging at a blistering pace across the deadened grasses, his legs bounding in great strides as he hurled on towards a destination that was known only to him. Curse surveyed Larry from behind as he kept a strong pace. Larry was not as tall as Curse had initially thought him to be. His frame hovered right around six feet while Curse believed he had been several inches taller. Curse actually reckoned that he stood a few inches over Larry. To him that meant that he should be the one running faster. His legs picked up the pace as he built momentum and bounded forward, gaining on Larry bit by bit. Within moments he had surpassed him.

"HEY, BOY, SLOW DOWN!"

Curse slowed his pace as Larry caught up to him and grabbed his shoulder, jerking him back and stopping him in the middle of his run. Larry's humorous demeanor had disappeared, and he took a tone of total seriousness now.

"Son, you can't be reckless here . . . just yet. You need to stick with me, and I'll teach you a thing or two . . . get you properly equipped . . . then we can be reckless and run around like Injuns, but the thing is this place is dangerous for you. I'll get you set up, and then you can be the one who starts hurting others rather than being hurt." At this point Larry suddenly snapped out of his seriousness and lapsed into another moment of insane laughter. "Really though, let's get you fixed up and then you can get wilder than a barmaid with a bunch of coal miners! HAHA! Follow me!" Larry sped off again, and Curse refused to let a stretch of ground exist between them.

The gray and black landscape sped by as they ran across the empty plains. Among all the deadened vegetation and gray skies, mystery engulfed the seemingly dismal world. Curse felt himself energized by unseen electricity. He knew something was going to happen very soon. However, he pushed all thoughts out of his head as he ran, his newly recovered senses taking in the landscape. Before too long, a huge old house loomed into view.

The house was dark and colorless just like the rest of the world. The achromatic aesthetics were cold to the eyes. Curse found his thoughts drawn back toward the strange air of familiarity he felt for this place; everything was surreal, almost like a dream, but dreams are good things usually . . . this felt more akin to a nightmare . . .

Nightmares are things of fear and anxiety; the house seemed to be the perfect setting for a nightmare. It was a crumbling old building reminiscent of something constructed in the late 1800s. The way it sat on the fetid ground made it look as though it jutted up out of the earth itself. It was of solid construction but incredibly ramshackle in appearance. Curse imagined that the building could have been constructed below the surface and then forced up through the ground.

"There's us, Curse!" Larry pointed towards the dilapidated building and picked up his pace a bit. Curse was not far behind. Their footsteps thundered as they charged onto a beaten path of black packed dirt and then ran up the wooden stairs and onto the porch of the brooding house. Larry went to the door and stood to the side as he reached into his overalls, pulled out

Nightmarescape

several keys attached to a small chain, and then unlocked the door.

Curse turned to survey the stark surroundings in front of the house. The path that they had just been on began abruptly about fifty yards from the porch. Miscellaneous features dotted the yard before the house. A crumbling brick well sat off to the side of the path, with a smaller less-trod path worn into the dead grass. Leaning against the well sat some corroded metal pieces, possibly from an old disused plow. Behind that scenery sat a bush reduced to nothing more than black sticks.

"CURSE!" Larry's exclamation caught Curse off guard.

"What!?"

"Don't step on that welcome mat; step over it."

Curse looked down and saw a large mat sitting in front of the door. It looked more like something that would belong in an industrial setting to prevent slipping than a welcome mat.

"Trapped?"

"HOHO, YOU BETCHA!" Larry lifted up the mat and momentarily tossed it aside as Curse peered down into a fairly deep hole that extended below the porch and several feet into the ground. In the dark pit, Curse made out several large wooden spikes shaved from tree branches sticking up from a small pool of black water.

"Has that ever worked?" Curse inquired.

"Has that ever worked? HAHAHAHA! SON, YOU'RE TOO MUCH! HAHAHA! Long story short, yes. Now let's get on in here," Larry said as he jumped over the hole and across the threshold of the door. Curse reached down and placed the mat over the hole again before taking his own leap into the old house.

As he crossed the threshold, darkness consumed everything. Remembering the terror of not having his senses just a little while ago, Curse paused for a moment to allow his sight time for adjustment. As he stood looking back and forth, he noticed light coming in through the many holes and cracks in the exterior of the building. As he looked on, the dark gave way to shapes of what he believed to be furniture and other such paraphernalia. He didn't know what to do or where to go . . . Larry had disappeared into the rotten guts of the house.

"Larry, where the hell are you?" Curse's voice echoed off into the darkness to join the indistinct shapes as an indistinct sound. *I'll probably hear him laughing in a moment,* Curse thought to himself as he took a few steps forward.

He strained to make out the shapes in the darkness as he moved closer to them. What kind of furniture and decor would an obscenely grotesque madman use to adorn his broken-down home? Curse inched forward and pondered this, but suddenly a shadowy form flew out of the darkness and landed heavily in front of him.

Reflexively, Curse set himself into a strong defensive stance as a familiar voice hollered from the form, "HEY, SON, LET'S HAVE US A HOOTENANNY!"

Curse was still surprised, but let his guard down as he realized this visitor was none other than Larry. Light beamed through a hole in the roof to reveal Larry's form; he was holding a fiddle in one hand and a bow in the other.

"Ever hootenannied before!?"

"Afraid not . . ." Curse held his stance, unaware of what Larry might do next.

"Well then let me show you how . . ." Upon these words, Larry dragged the bow across the fiddle, creating a high-pitched shriek that reverberated off the walls around them to fill the house with a horrid sound. As the piercing note echoed its last sound waves, Larry broke into a strange dance where he moved around in a circle, kicking his heavy booted heels against the floor while jerking the bow across the strings of the fiddle and sounding off more piercing wails of high-toned cacophony. During all his movement, Larry continually bellowed at the top of his lungs, "HOOTENANNY, HOOTENANNY, HOOTENANNY, YEEEEEEEEHAAAAAAAHAHAHAHAHA!"

Curse thundered back in a voice just as loud, "What the fuck are you doing!?"

In response to the question, Larry stopped mid-stride with his fiddling arms frozen in midair, the bow across the fiddle's midsection, and his legs positioned so his upper body was hunched over. One of his feet rested flat on the floor while the other stood up on its heel in mid-kick. He remained motionless in this fashion for a moment until just his head turned to look at Curse.

For the first time, Curse detected something on Larry's face that he had not yet seen. The skeletal features on the lower part of his face sat stuck in their grin, while the upper part of his face had contorted itself into a twist of pure anger. Curse studied this briefly until his eyes met with Larry's. Larry's eyes were too easy to read. He had a playful twinkle in them, and just as Curse realized this, Larry hopped up from his frozen position and immediately broke into one of his peals of laughter.

"HAHAHAHAHAHA! Boy, you should have seen your face," Larry cackled, as he tossed the fiddle aside, allowing it to crash off into the darkness with a resounding twang. He then bounded over to Curse and exclaimed in a manic tone, "Hey, you wanna see the rest of my fort? Follow me!"

In an instant, Larry had turned about-face and was charging off into the darkness. Curse found no challenge in keeping pace with him as they rushed off to a new part of the house. The first room they had occupied was the decrepit living room. It was very dark, but as Curse's eyes adjusted, he could make out a room that was adorned with Victorian-style furniture that had fallen into rancid condition. Paint was peeling off wood, rips in cushions let the stuffing stick out, and the walls were pockmarked with holes of different depths. Some of the holes showed the skeletal slats that rested within the walls, while others went straight through the building and allowed small slivers of gray light to intrude from outside. There was a hint of moisture and a mildewed scent that pervaded the room.

"Beautiful, eh!? This here's my sittin' parlor! You can sit in there and read or pull up a chair to the gaming table and play backgammon or faro!" Larry spoke of the place with pride as though it were a high-class center of relaxation.

"Have you ever considered cleaning it?" Curse wondered aloud.

Larry's head slowly turned until his eyes were locked with Curse's; he then said, "And rob it of its character? Are you batty, son!? HAHAHAHAHA! No, you know I'm just kidding. C'mon, there's more to see here . . ." With this, Larry turned and started to walk out of the room, giving Curse a wave over his shoulder indicating that he should follow.

The next room they entered was a kitchen resembling a broken-down abattoir. This room was better lit due to a large window that sat at the far left side of the room letting in gray light. Opposite the window was a large door made of heavy planks of black wood. Dark metal bands stretched across the door, holding the planks together. Large rivets were crudely shot in through the metal into the wood to provide anchorage. The no-man's-land between the window and sink was filled with various instruments and surfaces that could be used for butchering. The central cutting surface was a large table that created an island in the center of the space.

"Slaughterhouse!" Larry summed it up in one word.

Curse looked around and noticed thick pools of dried dark liquid on the surfaces around the room. The cutting tools, which looked old, rusty, and barbaric, seemed also to be coated with a similar dried discoloration.

"What's behind that door?" Curse inquired.

Larry's eyes opened a little wider, and it seemed as though his grin grew with them. "We'll come back to it. Soon. In the meantime, speculate if you must." Larry turned and quickly walked out of the room. "Come on."

Curse followed Larry back out to the living room. As Larry walked down toward a corridor that had been hidden in the dark before, Curse shuddered from an unseen force. His body trembled momentarily as he attempted to keep stride with Larry. It seemed as though Larry was getting farther away, but he knew that the distance between them was not increasing by much. He reached his arm out and attempted to call out to Larry as his perceptions began to fade once more, and he fell to the ground with a heavy thud. Curse lay on the ground looking forward as Larry turned to see what had happened. Helpless to give Larry any indication of what was going on as his vision disappeared, he was once again consumed by darkness.

The unsettling darkness brought him back to the abyss of helplessness that he had found himself in only a short while before. *Don't let yourself go again.* He echoed the thought in his mind over and over in an effort to retain consciousness. The attempt was futile, however, and within moments he had slipped into oblivion once more. How long he lay in that torpor was anyone's guess. He drifted upon the waves and eddies of the abyss indefinitely. No thoughts came to his mind to keep him company or lend insight to his predicament. There was nothing. Not being able to think or feel once again, the emptiness was not terrifying—it was just there. Floating indefinitely.

After a long while in this abyss, he noticed a sensation against his chest. Someone was touching him. The soft touching was accompanied by a sweet and distant voice. The voice was subtle and gentle in its approach, clearly addressing him, although he could not decipher how just yet. His vision began to pick out a shape in the dark. A silhouette in the shadows. His eyes adjusted as an entire image formed in front of him. A woman. A natural, living being. One that was human in every sense of the word. He realized from other physical sensations that she was sitting on his hips, straddling him while resting her hands upon his shoulders. Loose and delicate blonde hair descended from her head and caressed his chest as she hovered over him. Curse gazed up into her face. To him she was the most immaculate thing he had ever seen.

She was immaculate not in the sense that she was flawless, but in the fact that she was so natural and alive compared to the world he had endured.

"I've missed you so much; after all my hopes and prayers, you've finally come back to me!" Her face beamed with happiness.

"Where have I been?" Curse asked.

She moved her hand from his shoulder and pressed it to his lips. "Shhhh, we can get to that later; right now I just want to be here with you." Her happiness with his presence was obvious, and he got a strange feeling of belonging from the situation and her face, even though he may have not known whom this woman was.

Not questioning the momentary good fortune, Curse reached up to her and placed both hands on her cheeks. The reciprocation for this action was a warm smile that accentuated her beautiful face. Something inside him stirred knowing that he was the source of her happiness. This feeling also carried a strange air of being intimate yet alien at the same time.

As he looked at her face, he took notice of his own hands on her cheeks. Something seemed off about them. They were quite ashen, and the blood vessels showed very dark and pronounced through the skin . . . almost as if pooling of the blood had occurred. As he noticed this, the epidermis instantly began to crack, peel, and rot away, exposing terrible black viscous tissue beneath the skin. Whereas normal muscles would be red and covered in blood if the skin were suddenly removed, his were black and covered with a substance reminiscent of oil. Bones of the fingers protruded from beneath the mass of tissue. Some of the wretched fluid splattered on the girl's face as the skin ruptured. She leapt up from him with a start, threw her hands over her eyes, and began thrashing around as if the substance was burning her face. Reeling, she fell backward and hit the floor hard before scampering into a corner and emanating a shriek of pure fright.

Curse sat up. He had been lying in a bed. The current surroundings were that of a contemporary bedroom . . . one that rang with a familiarity of some sort yet not one that he could place in his mind. Without a further thought to the matter, he sprang up from the bed to aid the girl. Upon standing and walking almost halfway across the room, he froze in the crippling grip of his own terror. Opposite him was a vanity mirror mounted on top of a dresser.

Standing before him in the mirror's glass was a horrendous sight to behold, that of a being conceived of the cruelest design. Skin was in short supply over the thing's tattered body; what did remain was a dusty, desiccated, gray layer of ruined tissue that hung loosely over more of the black muscular tissue that secreted the dark liquid vileness. The face was a horrific blend of rotten pieces of flesh draped over a skeletal structure with bits of the gray skin hanging on in small clumps here and there. The eyes were missing from jagged sockets that looked as if the bone around them had been chiseled away. In their place, two small, blue lights emanated from deep inside the skull. How such a thing could exist baffled Curse.

The appearance reminded him of Larry to an extent, but not as clean. The black substance coating the muscle tissue was quite similar to the fluid constantly dripping from Larry's eyes. Even Larry was a tad more presentable than this. In an attempt to possibly dispel the image, Curse lifted one of his arms and was hit with a stark wave of horrific reality when the thing in the mirror followed his movement.

"My God . . . ," he whispered. The girl screamed again.

Curse turned to her. Moments ago, she had been above him, a beautiful siren that was professing her bliss at his mere presence, but she had been reduced in an instant to a screaming wretch on the floor. The familiarity he felt in her presence was overwhelming. What was she to him? He to her? *What* was he? Obviously he hadn't always been like this. He moved and knelt beside her to inquire.

"Calm down, please," he spoke. The girl gripped her head tighter and began to tremble violently. "How do we know each other?"

"Get away!" At this exclamation, she shot one of her feet out and struck Curse hard in the chest with her heel. The blow knocked him backward onto the floor. He knew that he would not be able to ascertain any information from her in this state. Standing, he examined his new self in the mirror once again. The dread at his own visage had left him and was now replaced with a profound sadness. What kind of abomination had he become? So many questions raced through his confused mind. The blistering pace of contemplation and frustration quickly turned his sadness into anger. An anger that he had never felt before, one that was beyond harnessing by any extent of willpower. In an act of blind rage, he slammed his corroded fist into the mirror, sending shards of slivered glass flying in all directions.

"Don't hurt me . . ."

In response to this, Curse threw his head back and let out a scream of his own. It boiled its way up from his gut and burst forth from his mouth like a thunderstorm bellowing from the throat of a savage beast. The girl's screams sounded once more and raised a piercing accompaniment to his bellow. As he continued to roar, his body was suddenly thrown into violent convulsions and his mighty expression of anger deteriorated into agonized yelling. He seized and contorted on the floor as his surroundings began to go black once again. The girl's screams became a distant echo until they were no longer audible. He became aware of the fact that he was convulsing on a hard surface. His arms and legs kicked against the floor as a dull thumping echoed throughout the space. He was still yelling and thrashing uncontrollably as his sight returned to him. The convulsions stopped, and he lay on the floor looking up into more recognizable surroundings.

Pain blazed through his body as well as his mind. He lay there staring up into the darkness, trying to make sense of what just happened.

"Curse."

Curse turned his head in the direction of the voice and realized that he was in Larry's living room once again. Larry sat in a rocking chair, his elbows resting on the armrests and his hands raised slightly with his fingers folded together as he studied Curse.

"What did you find?" he asked.

At first, this question took Curse by surprise. How did Larry know what had happened? With the idea in mind that maybe Larry could shed some light on what was occurring, he felt obliged to tell him.

"There was a beautiful girl . . . on top of me . . . said she missed me . . . then I turned into something . . ."

Larry nodded. "Stand up and look over there," he commanded with an outstretched hand. Curse stood as he spoke and followed Larry's hand to reveal a full-sized mirror against the wall.

With trepidation, Curse moved toward it to see if he was still the disgusting being from his recent experience. As he moved into view of his reflection, his fears were confirmed. He was the exact same creature. A heavy sigh escaped his mouth as he took a good long look at himself.

In this setting, he was able to garner a little more detail about his features. He looked at his new face again. The same bony face stared back at him, peppered with the vile black tissue and the dusty skin. Around his mouth there were small tears which revealed teeth encrusted with dried residue of the black liquid. Jagged and broken eye sockets with their cold, blue light sat under a large bony forehead. The top of his head was mostly bald. Looking down, he noted that his frame was tightly muscled. Gray skin covered his torso, but patches of it were torn open with the black muscle tissue oozing its secretion. Following the image down further, he noticed his legs were covered with a pair of black jeans that had rips and tears in them here and there but were still in fairly good shape, while the legs of the pants rested over a pair of worn combat boots. It struck him as funny that he had not been aware of the sensation of clothing before. This was not a priority in his mind so much as explaining why he had become what he had become.

"Larry . . ." Curse felt his anger rising again, and his fists involuntarily clenched.

He controlled himself this time and avoided breaking Larry's mirror. "Why? What am I?" He growled the question.

"Get used to that face. That's you now, son. None of us are pretty here."

"And just where the hell is here, Larry?" Curse inquired with a tone of increased aggravation.

"I haven't quite been able to figure that out yet."

"Is this Hell?"

Larry's permanently affixed grin seemed to widen somehow at this inquiry. "If it is, I sure enjoy it."

"What is there to enjoy . . . I don't know who I am, I look like a damn zombie . . . I can't remember anything."

"Oh you will remember . . . bit by bit, through the seizures and convulsions." Larry leaned forward and dropped his voice. "The real question is . . . do you want to remember?"

Curse was perplexed further than he had been since this whole sordid experience began. "What do you mean by that? Do you know something about me?"

For a moment Curse fought back an overwhelming urge to lash out and attack Larry. His questions and demeanor seemed to hint that he knew something that he did not want to share. Such an idea was torturous . . . was Larry holding something back just to cause him pain?

"Larry, do you know anything about me? Tell me if you do."

"I don't. You're a mystery to yourself, but keep in mind . . . I went through it once too."

"How long does it last?"

"HA!" Larry threw his head back and laughed. "The hell if I know, son. I don't even know all of my own saga yet . . . don't know if I'll ever know it . . ."

"Fucking great . . ."

"Let's get outta here. You haven't seen upstairs yet," Larry offered in an attempt to lighten the mood.

"Fine by me; lead the way." Curse wanted to direct his mind away from the realization of what he had become. Maybe seeing more of Larry's "fort" would give him time to calm his thoughts and let things sink in.

Larry strode out of the room as Curse followed closely behind, wary that another seizure could strike at any moment. The house felt different. Whereas before it had just been old and musty, it now felt cold as phantom drafts seemed to permeate the structure. Although discomforting, Curse pushed these new stimuli out of his mind as Larry guided him up the stairs to a second level of the decrepit building.

Catching sight of Larry a little way up the hall, Curse quickened his step to keep up. Moving to reach Larry, he noticed a single doorway in the middle of the corridor that seemed to emanate a soft light from inside, reminiscent of the gray sky. Abandoning his mission to keep up with Larry, Curse turned into the room as though he were drawn by an unseen wire tugging at his chest. The sight of a small spiral staircase greeted him. A great deal of light poured in from above. Curious as to its source, Curse hurried his way up the rickety set of stairs and found himself in a large empty room that was completely missing a wall that should have been facing him. Broken remnants of old boards bent outwardly, hinting at the idea that something had occurred at some point in time that completely destroyed the wall. From his current vantage point, Curse noticed that the sky had darkened into a foreboding shade between black and gray. He also noticed that this was the highest point he had stood at since awakening in the new world. Unconsciously, he stepped forward and brought himself to where the edge of the floor gave way to open space. From here he gazed out at the deathly landscape before him.

The rotten vegetation rested under a sky that had grown dark yet still emanated a fair amount of light, very similar to a sky that would appear before a sudden storm, enveloping the sun and clouds. Upon stepping to the edge, almost as if just for him, a strong wind began blasting into the room. For once, the inanimate landscape was suddenly alive with the wind pushing the stalks of ruined plants to and fro. Curse breathed in the air that came with the wind. Cold and musty yet energizing. Gazing out, he thought that the landscape was reminiscent of dead farmland with a forest of ash-colored trees surrounding the plains. He worked his diaphragm to suck in the essence of the world now flowing around and into him. The air he breathed in was soon forced outward as his chest resonated with a bellow of rage and triumph.

Triumph? But he had not conquered anything. Or had he? This landscape was his now. This wretched wasteland. As he looked at it, he realized that he found a strange beauty in his new world. It was what mattered now. Whatever he had been before coming here was gone. What existed now was what was in front of him. He had become a creature of this realm, and therefore this realm was his now. That made it beautiful to him. There would be time for all the questions later; right now, he had a new world to explore.

6

Expending the remaining air from his lungs in another forceful bellow, he slammed his fist into a stray board sticking out of the ruined wall. The result was a sickening splat that shot the oily ichor from his hand in several directions. It didn't hurt now. In the grip of an excited frenzy and lust for this new place, he hurled himself against the wind and leapt out into the air in front of him. His body parted the cold air beneath him as he dropped downward for what seemed like an eternity. At the end of the flight, he crashed down heavily into a patch of hard ground. Amazingly, the fall did not hurt the slightest, and he was able to quickly reposition himself in a standing posture. From here he dashed forward, abandoning all caution and pushing himself ever farther into his new world.

Once again, it was all passing before him, the landscape and the sky. His feet pounded the ground harder as he pushed himself to hurtle forward into the unknown. He had covered a large amount of ground in a seemingly short amount of time before his charge came to a skidding halt.

There, not more than a few meters in front of him, he saw a being nearly as horrific and disfigured as himself. Tattered bits of gray wrapped loosely around an emaciated frame. The

Nightmarescape

thing's hair stood dark and wiry around a face that was as repulsive as his own. The eyes were missing as well, with small, blue lights burning coldly in their place. Taking in a bit more of the thing's body, Curse realized that it was a female. The remnants of a white dress hung over her gaunt frame, providing a small bit of cover for her body. After standing and looking at her for several moments, Curse became aware of something. She seemed more pathetic than terrifying.

There was something about her . . . something that reflected Curse's own inner turmoil. Gazing upon another lost being seemed to magnify his own sense of being lost. This confusion quickly succumbed to a blind rage that began to burn within his chest and trembled out into the muscles of his appendages. His flesh tightened as his fists clenched, and the world suddenly disappeared around him as the anger surged forward from his body in a bestial howl that shook the ground around them. And with this, his legs began to pound the ground once more as he propelled toward her, swinging his fist on approach and connecting with the side of her head.

She never made an effort to move. Perhaps she had been too scared to move, or perhaps his onslaught had occurred too fast for a reaction to make its way from her brain. At any rate, she lay on the ground before him, stunned from the impact.

A predator had awakened within Curse, and no mercy would be shown to this wretch. Her skull was cracking, giving way to all sorts of fluid and soft matter as his fist hammered into her head over and over again. How long had he been hitting her? The lights in her eye sockets began fading rapidly, and after several more blows, they disappeared entirely as her body disintegrated into dust.

The sudden disintegration surprised Curse enough to snap him out of his berserk rampage and afford a few moments to examine the dust that had once stood as a semi-living thing in front of him. His first kill in this forsaken place was almost as perplexing as his own predicament. For, in the blink of an eye, he had obliterated another being's existence. Why had that happened . . . why did he attack and kill her? The anger faded from his body and was replaced with a profound sadness. His fists clenched harder. Harder. Harder. Pain from his bony fingertips digging into the flesh of his hands. *Why? What the hell?* It didn't make sense . . . nothing did; would it ever . . . maybe not. What good did thinking about it do if he did not have any knowledge to go on? He wanted to cry but lacked the lacrimal glands to do it, so he made himself content with sitting on the ground next to the pile of dust that had moments ago been a sentient presence. Almost falling from his spinal cord, his head dropped to hang itself low. Time ground to a standstill as everything grew silent around him save the wind, but even that seemed to be fading away. He found his behavior an indecipherable enigma.

In truth, he had not wanted to kill the female, but it just happened, seemingly the consequence of a series of natural events. The action had even felt natural, automatic almost, yet it still bothered him. His actions were lacking any form of context. His feelings of regret were not for her; they were grounded in selfishness. The destruction of another being wasn't what was eating him so much as that he could not fathom the reason for why he felt the subconscious urge to kill. He could not understand anything that he felt.

And so it was that his mind began to swirl into its own shade of gray, resembling the landscape around him, as his consciousness slogged groggily from gray uncertainty and into a black oblivion once more. The darkness surrounded him and paralyzed him into a state of total numbness.

7

Time and existence became inconsequential as everything disappeared. It was an odd state of being that seemed nonexistent yet somewhat sentient though devoid of any awareness, a state of forced nihilism, dark space, emptiness, a hell unto itself. After an indecipherable period of time, a scene became visible in the dark. Suddenly there was awareness, but it was not entirely conscious.

Curse was watching events unfold through his own eyes. Here it was, another memory.

His mind showed him something from the past as he shouldered a shotgun and began stalking across a yard toward a small suburban home. There were shouts and yells behind him, but they warped into an unintelligible noise as he continued his advance. He was fully aware of the situation now, mentally and physically, yet he still did not know why he was performing the actions nor could he control his body to change his course. The only thing to do was watch and learn.

His advance slowed as he closed on the door. In a fluid motion, he angled the shotgun down as he inched ever closer and then delivered a load of buckshot into the area surrounding the door handle, blowing out the wood and taking the handle to the ground. On reflex, his leg raised before his foot flew forward, connecting with the door and sending it swinging back to open the house to him. He racked another round into the chamber.

His unchosen path led him into a room where several people were scrambling from his unexpected entry. Two males and a female. He had seen one of the males before, but at this point he couldn't recall where. The one that bore recognition began reaching to his backside. The shotgun locked onto him reactively, and an uncontrollable impulse gave a quick squeeze to the trigger. A number of small, bloody explosions erupted from the man's torso as he was thrown back from the concussive force of the blast. The retort of the firearm was the perfect soundtrack to the man's falling body. The blast was strong at first, but began to fade as the body fell closer to the floor. Upon hitting the floor, a heavy thud rang out to serve as the crescendo piece to the dying echo of the blast. The deadly symphony soon had another sound: the female's scream of horror and sadness tinged with a hint of shock and disbelief.

Curse's perception shifted to her now; she stood from where she had been on the floor and began screaming between broken sobs, "YOU KILLED HIM! YOU MOTHER-FUCKER—HE'S DEAD!" In addition to her screams, she began to rush toward him. He didn't need to exercise lethal force on this one. The other male in the room was already standing with his hands up, and the girl was small and probably wouldn't offer much of a fight; besides, backup was behind him. He had just been leading; the others would be in soon . . . what others? He knew someone was with him, but he didn't remember who. That was fascinating. He didn't have to kill her, but it was impossible to stop the shotgun from leveling with her head as another explosive retort rang out and half of her face flew away in its constituent parts.

She seemed to fall faster than her male counterpart, with blood trailing from what remained of her head and face. It was impossible to look away from her fall. The half of the face that remained seemed to be trying to communicate an expression appropriate of what was happening, but the effort was lost as she fell to the floor. The look on her face solidified into one of shock and fear as the life ultimately left her body before it hit the ground. And hit the ground it did—hard. The impact knocked a splatter of blood, brain matter, and bone tissue out of her head and onto the floor. After the initial impact, the blood came freely from the gaping hole in her head. It seeped out in a puddle at first, a sickly red upon a white carpet. As the carpet absorbed it, the blood spread farther, stretching out in red tendrils across the floor until they coalesced and crossed one another as though the floor were growing arteries itself. The blood grew darker and eventually blackened and turned hard while the carpet turned a stale shade of gray. Through some strange twist of perception, he was looking up now at blackened veins stretching across a gray sky—black tree branches overhead from the dead trees spreading before the cold sky of his stark reality.

So that's it. I'm a cold-blooded killer, his mind echoed to him.

Was that all there was though? As true as the perception felt, it felt somewhat hollow and lacking, that there was more to it than just murder. There was little to do but think, as his body seemed paralyzed once again. Just as it had been when he supposedly materialized in this place. *Murderer.*

The word hung heavy in his mind and stuck to his brain, but it just didn't feel correct at this point. Maybe that was part of the story, but probably not all of it. How much time had passed since he faded out? How much time was passing as he meditated on his thoughts? How long would it be before he could move again? Did any of that matter? No, it was really inconsequential given the circumstances.

Looking up at the tree limbs stretching across the gray sky filled him with a sense of isolation and death. He had not really noticed it since he had been here, but he was cold from the inside out. He knew he was dead, but he didn't know how simultaneously he was still alive in some form. The thoughts were interrupted as the black branches and gray sky were suddenly replaced with Larry's ugly face.

Ah, shit, here we go again . . . déjà-fucking-vu . . .

Larry helped him up again, just as he had the first time. Upon standing and looking at Larry, Curse noticed it subtly over the course of a few moments, but he noticed it nonetheless . . . something was different this time. The world was cold—very cold. It was the first time it had bothered him.

"When did it get so cold?"

"It's always been cold . . . that's not important right now though . . ." Larry was looking at Curse as a scientist would examine a specimen that they not only were captivated by, but also in which they saw some sort of great potential . . . for better or worse.

8

"What did you do before you came here . . . what were you?" Larry inquired, his face twisted into an expression of total delight.

"I can't remember . . . do you know?"

"HAHAHAHA, son, I wouldn't ask if I did. You have some skills though . . . I've never seen anyone kill anything with their hands like you did. HOOWEE!"

"That still doesn't explain anything . . ."

"It explains something about who you were. Admit it . . . splattering that bitch's brains all over the place came right and natural, eh?"

"I suppose it did . . ." Curse's bony fingers dug into the skin of his scalp. Damnation if he didn't have an excruciating headache at this point.

"Heh heh heeeeehhhhh . . . you've killed people before . . . in cold blood, boy. I can see that much about you. You have an anger set deep in your head, and you've just been dying to let that son of a bitch out for a long time."

"I'm more perplexed than anything, as usual." Upon peeling his fingers back from his scalp, Curse let his head hang.

"Not for long, son . . . you'll tap that there root soon and then . . ."

Looking up, Curse was startled by something in Larry's face. For the first time, he had become completely serious about something. Such a situation seemed highly eerie in its own right. Curse stood, trying to make sense of the bizarre being before him, but before he could muster any thought, Larry startled him by letting loose another one of his ludicrous peals of laughter. Larry would not shut up. He just kept laughing and hooting and pointing to the spot where the female had crumbled to dust. Almost all of her had been carried away on the wind by this point.

"I can't stand this!" Immediately following Curse's exclamation, a hard, right-handed blow flew into Larry's mouth and knocked him off of his feet.

At this point, Curse ceased paying attention to him and was concentrating on the fact that his head was throbbing. Was it due to Larry's annoying laughter? Perhaps his reentry from the dream state? The cause did not matter so much as the fact that it was the first real pain he had felt in some time. All the confusion was getting to him . . . in addition to the splitting headache, the world began to tremble and spin around him as he lowered himself into a sitting position on the ground and held his head. He squeezed . . . the harder he squeezed, the more bearable it seemed. He scratched as well . . . there was something itchy under his dead skin. The bony tips of his fingers slipped through the skin and muscle tissue and allowed him direct access to his own skull. He applied more pressure there; it all ached horribly.

Perhaps I could just crush my skull now and end this whole fucking thing, he thought to himself.

That seemed like the best idea. Whatever kind of reality he had entered was not worth staying in. Not for all this. What had a short while ago been an inspiration to him was now a source of misery and vexation. His hands dug further into the skin and muscles around his skull, prying them up from the bone with a sickening tear. Oh the pain from this was excruciating, but no pain, no gain. When his hands were under his skin, and black ichor oozed out from the displacement, pressure, and the ripping of his own flesh, he finally felt as though he had enough leverage. At this point, he pushed inward as hard as he could, the bones of his palms grating against his temples. A tremendous amount of strength and willpower surged through him as he let another roaring bellow out from his throat. With the sound, his skull's structural integrity gave way, and his hands pushed inward as the bone cracked. His head caved in from the sides, and for a few moments he was stunned. His perception had shifted; he looked out at the world now from the new shape of his head. His eyes looked in different directions than normal, and he could feel the unreal pain of his skull bones being fractured. The pain was short lived, however, as he became aware that it was steadily disappearing while his head was reforming itself. Within mere moments of crushing his own skull, the bones had entirely reformed themselves, and his head was as complete as it had ever been.

"CURSE!" Turning, Curse saw Larry standing before him once more, a heavy trickle of black ichor pouring from a split on the side of his mouth, right where Curse's blow had landed. To his astonishment, the substance was disappearing, and the wound was steadily closing as Larry stood and faced him. At this point, Curse slid his hands out from under his skin and muscle, and they promptly returned to their previous condition as well . . . the open holes closed, and the pain subsided.

"I KNEW there was something real special about you! Sure we're all fucked up here, but not many of us are that indestructible!" The grin that Larry's face always seemed to carry looked as though it were about to stretch off his face and carry on for miles to either side. However pleased Larry was, Curse only found himself sinking further into a lost sense of desperation.

"And what else . . . how strong are you!? I've never seen anything crack its own skull before . . . well except for this one Indian fellow back in . . . that's not important . . ."

Curse could only shake his head. The psychotic idiot really did not understand that this was not a pleasant experience for him.

"Larry."

Larry's revelry in Curse's newfound abilities ceased as he realized that it was important to pay attention now.

"I do not enjoy this. What are you so damn happy about? I still don't know anything . . ." Larry only stood and looked at him. Curse's hands reached out to grab Larry and found his fingers digging deep into Larry's flesh right over his collarbone. Larry barely winced at the sensation.

"What in the hell is going on here? Who am I? Who are you? What is this hellhole, and why do I keep having these hallucinations?"

Larry looked thoughtful for the first time and pondered the questions momentarily while attempting to formulate the best answers.

"I don't know who you were."

"Were?"

"Yes, son, you're dead. That I know for sure. The hallucinations are memories from your prior life."

Well, that made sense. Curse thought that he had found Hell. It was different from the typical conceptions, but it was painful enough.

"Is this place Hell?"

"Not quite . . . I dun got me a theory about it, if you care to hear . . ." Larry's eyes grew so large with his statement that they could've swallowed Curse then and there.

"Go ahead. Ramble."

Keeping the perpetual drama that surrounded him, Larry began his professing by turning and raising his hands toward the empty landscape as though he were addressing a crowded auditorium.

"You see folks from all over time and wherever occupy this place. The woman you killed—I didn't get a good look at her, but she could've been from any time. What's more . . . the more you remember your past . . . the more you remember this place . . . does it seem familiar at all to you?"

Curse thought back to his previous feelings on the world being so alien yet holding an air of familiarity at the same time and acknowledged the question with a nod.

"Well," Larry continued, "the thing is, I remember this place from before I came here too. I used to have dreams about it . . . dreamed about it and all the fools in it." He abruptly turned to Curse with his hands outstretched and his eyes wider than usual. "YOU SEE . . . my theory is this . . . this place—I call it the Nightmarescape—is a world created of conscious psychic residue . . . all the negative feelings humanity has had since the dawn of time have poured themselves into creating this place. Now, see, I call it one thing, but there are very few rigid rules here, and many call it different things.

Some call it Hell like you said; some call it Purgatory; a select few call it Heaven! Others just don't know what to make of it. Anyway, when you're alive, somehow your dreams can get in touch with this place . . . and then it has you. When you die, it wrangles you in, and you manifest once more into a rotted and twisted version of your former self, not knowing anything about your former life."

The crazy bastard is making some sense finally, Curse thought as he nodded his head along with Larry's speech.

"Those facing a great deal of negativity and adversity often find this place easier than others. I look at the folks here . . . lots of soldiers, warriors, sufferers, from all across time. They are knights, western jerks, samurais, tribesmen, savages, soldiers of later wars, people who have just been hurt, violent folk, insane folk, motel folk, abused folk, killers and, believe me, lots of 'em, victims of all sorts, folks who got screwed over . . . they're all here. They're all here, and this place found them before they got here. Their negative emotions were a beacon or something of that nature for this place to get into their heads. Once it got in, they were damned. Regular nightmares about this place and all the malicious souls in it haunted them until death . . . and then here they are. Just . . . like . . . us . . ." After finishing the speech, Larry fell silent for a spell and stared at Curse with his wide eyes and his forehead furrowed.

It made sense. The place did seem familiar, and while not consciously registering his dreams just yet, the idea did not seem too far from plausible given the specific circumstances. The more Curse thought about it, the place seemed more familiar with each passing moment. It was becoming comfortable, almost as if he had resided here before and had come home after being away for some time. The place was

Nightmarescape

different, but as he took more of it in, his mind processed that it was somewhere he had been before.

His thought process was derailed as his consciousness was snapped to attention by a familiar noise . . . a gunshot—where had it come from?

"A fight!" Larry exclaimed.

Another shot rang out over the dead landscape.

In unison, Larry and Curse turned and sought cover behind the trees. Curse's vision struggled to decipher who was firing. For a moment, he scrutinized the land in front of him before settling his vision on several forms charging towards their position.

9

"Why are these guys shooting at us?" Curse asked.

Larry was quiet for a moment before he answered. "You see, I'm a visionary . . . not everyone cares for the fact, and it's earned me a few enemies here . . ."

Curse peered out into the landscape as Larry finished aggrandizing. It was fine for Larry to have enemies to fight on his own accord, but the attackers were coming after Curse due to affiliation. Maybe . . . perhaps they were just lost souls consumed by bloodlust . . . either way, they were coming for him, and they would pay. He assessed the attackers as their long-coated forms galloped surreally over the gray landscape—gun-toting wraiths issuing a steady volley of fire in his direction. There were five in total; four of them carried bolt-action rifles that shot supernatural ammunition in gray and black bursts. Gas masks concealed their faces, unsettling as any grim-faced resident of the realm. The last one wore a tattered military cap over his mask and carried a primitive submachine gun that belched forth the same ghostly flare in rapid bursts. Through the filth-encrusted masks, red lights burned out of hollowed sockets. If Curse remembered his history correctly, their uniforms looked to be those of German soldiers from the Second World War. Who they were became of little consequence, however, as they charged toward him with their weapons blazing.

Curse fell back behind a tree and pondered the contrast to the glowing, blue lights in his own skull. A volley of bullets found its mark on the tree, sending dark petrified matter in all directions. The tree was not terribly wide, and what cover it afforded was rapidly disappearing. Curse looked over to see Larry aiming his shotgun at the assailants.

Another volley of fire struck the tree, and petrified matter flaked onto Curse's back just before the first bullet followed into his shoulder, sending him falling forward onto his hands and knees. His head began to pound with rage once more, and the pain radiating from the wound quickly subsided to the rush of aggression. It was time now to fight and ask questions later. The wound was already sealing itself. Black necrotic matter sealed over the opening before coagulating into a layer of gray fetid flesh. Muscles flexed all over his body before the familiar boom of Larry's shotgun sent him leaping into action. He carried himself fluidly from behind the tree in a roll to find that the enemies had closed a significant amount of ground. Being unarmed, that would serve him well.

The closest wraith looked stunned, his rifle hanging by his side, and fresh holes seeping black ichor from his torso. Larry's shot had hit home. Curse was upon the soldier like a feral predator on wounded prey. Desperately, the wraith attempted to raise his rifle and mount a melee attack, but Curse ducked low and launched himself up into his enemy's midsection before lifting him and bringing him to the ground in a crushing body slam.

The soldier was quick upon hitting the ground, however, and raised his rifle to place a barrier between himself and Curse. It was then that their eyes, or sockets rather, met, and Curse became aware of the raw essences that both of them were radiating. The soldier's red, baleful eyes seethed with hatred as he attempted to dislodge Curse. His hatred was also single-minded, which made him strong in his focus, but Curse was aware that he was being charged with his own visceral rage. The soldier was focusing only on deflection, while Curse was focused on destruction. Bullets were flying at him in volume now as Larry's shotgun sounded once more, and then the hail of bullets seemed to lighten. The superior strength of Curse's vindictive rage and more advantageous position allowed him to hold the rifle with one hand as he used the other to deliver a crushing blow against the masked face. The first blow seemed to do little to phase the grounded warrior, but a successive pummel yielded the concussive feeling of splintering bone. A third blow saw the head cave in under the gas mask, the lights of the eye sockets disappearing as the body beneath Curse lost its shape and melted into dust.

The sound of gunfire around him was deafening as Curse steadied himself after defeating his enemy. Larry's shotgun boomed again, and it seemed as though more of the gunfire quieted just as something long and sharp punched through the back of Curse's shoulder. A flare of pain ripped through him as he let out a cry coupled in rage and agony. In a hasty act of strategy, Curse leapt forward, the force of his movement ripping his body free of the bayonet while simultaneously creating a gaping wound in his left shoulder. A stagger and several seconds of tearing pain later, his wound was resealing itself, and his nerves were no longer screaming. Curse wheeled around to face another soldier readying for a second attack.

Military drilling paid off for the new attacker as the soldier faked a low attack at Curse's legs. Curse took the bait and leapt back as the soldier made a deft move and swiftly brought the bayoneted rifle up and impaled it into Curse's abdomen. Tearing pain ripped through him as his flesh was rent by the blade, but as he screamed in pain and an agonized tremble shook him, he saw his attacker's error.

With the length of the bayonet lodged in his belly and rifle between them, Curse still had a longer reach than his opponent. In a moment's space, he focused through the pain and lashed his arms out to grab his enemy's head before bringing his opponent's skull forward to meet his own. The impact dazed him momentarily as the pain of the bayonet in his belly continued to tear through him, but he saw that his opponent was staggering backward, holding his head with both hands. Curse reached down and with a howl of agony ripped the bayoneted rifle from his own gut. A thick stream of dark ichor followed and spilled on the ground in a steaming, black puddle.

The wound was resealing itself as another attacker charged Curse. A quick reflex sent the butt of the rifle into the assailant's chest, knocking him from his feet. Curse racked the rifle's bolt and readied the archaic war device that he held. Just in time, as the rifle's original owner regained his awareness and was preparing to claim his weapon once more. Curse raised the weapon and felled his opponent with a squeeze of the trigger. An explosion of dark fluid and brain matter erupted from the back of the soldier's head from the close-range impact as his body went limp and began to dissolve. It was nothing but dust by the time it hit the ground.

In no position to waste time, Curse racked the bolt again and fired it into the midsection of the remaining soldier. The wound caused the soldier to stagger back, but he was able to keep a fighting stance, trading a bullet that grazed Curse's left bicep. Curse barely acknowledged the flesh wound with a grunt as it was beginning to seal itself almost as soon as it had been torn.

Getting shot and impaled was quickly getting old to Curse. He bellowed as he lurched forward, stabbing the bayonet into the other's neck. The soldier gurgled on his own fluids as the weapon tore through the tissue of his throat. In a desperate ploy for survival, he jabbed his own bayonet at Curse but failed to cause more than several small cuts. Curse chambered another round in the rifle before pulling the trigger and sending a bullet through the soldier's neck. Muffled gurgles sounded from behind the soldier's gas mask as dark ichor poured from the wound. Curse racked another round into the rifle and repositioned the barrel so he could destroy more tissue. The soldier's head dropped to the side as the remainder of the spinal column was destroyed and replaced with a fountain of black fluid and a shower of necrotic flesh.

Momentarily robbed of nervous control, the body crumpled to the ground. The soldier's head hung from the body, connected only by sickly wet tissue. Curse could see that the tissue was beginning to regenerate and that the soldier would be on his feet again within minutes. Curse loaded and fired the rifle into his enemy's head at point-blank range. The fallen body dissolved, and the soldier's rifle dropped from his disintegrating hands. Curse slung the rifle he held across his shoulder and picked up the fallen soldier's gun before charging to join Larry's firefight.

As Curse approached, he observed that several trees had been whittled down to little more than splinters, and Larry was diving for a thicker trunk as the officer's heavy stream of submachine-gun fire followed him. Curse took aim with the rifle in his hands and fired a round into the officer's side. The hardened officer was barely phased by the heavy projectile and calmly turned to bring his weapon to bear on Curse. Curse ducked low while reloading the rifle as a hail of bullets whizzed over his head. The officer's momentary distraction gave Larry an opening in which he delivered a pulverizing shotgun blast. A blast of such force was capable of removing anyone from their feet, and the officer was no exception.

Seizing the opportunity, Curse quickly closed the ground between himself and the downed officer before plunging the rifle's bayonet into his sternum. The officer thrashed about and began wildly firing rounds from his weapon. In his desperate struggle, he swept the weapon across Curse's lower abdomen and several of the small-caliber bullets tore through Curse. Curse screamed as he fired the rifle into the downed officer's chest. The injury from the bullet pushed the officer down as the submachine gun fell from his hands. Then Larry was beside Curse. They took turns pumping shot after shot into the downed enemy until the officer's upper body and head were decimated, and his physical being crumbled to dust. Curse reached down and snatched the submachine gun from his crumbling hands.

"That was some rousing sport, eh, boy?"

Infuriated at Larry's question, Curse turned and screamed at Larry. "Who the hell were they, visionary?" he demanded. "You can have your enemies, but don't expect me to get killed because of something you've started!"

Clearly not bothered, Larry began rambling. "You, son, are indestructible, what did I tell you . . . sure, gettin' shot all over still hurts like hell, but you ain't goin' nowhere!"

Curse was starting to fume again, so Larry attempted to explain. "German soldiers from the Second World War . . . an affair you might know more about . . . it was a little after my time. Still, though, they couldn't get through us!"

Curse's anger was suspended momentarily at the incredulous statement. "German soldiers from World War II!?" he yelled. Even though he thought that the uniforms bore a strong historical resemblance, he found the confirmation of such an incredulous proposition hard to believe.

Thinking back on the heat of the battle, he remembered struggling with one of the downed warriors and seeing a black and white swastika armband on the soldier's sleeve. In the heat of the fight, such a detail was overlooked, yet it was very relevant now. So Larry was not just a raving lunatic after all; this realm was actually populated by presences from all eras of human history.

"You're dead serious." Curse looked down at the weapon in his hands. Sure enough, it was an MP40. "German soldiers . . ."

"Damn right, boy! Now you've seen it! German Nazis, knights, pirates, Yeomen, Injuns, warriors, tribesmen, chiefs, lords, cowards, mass murderers, executioners, preachers, rustlers, samurai, varmints, all here!" Larry was clearly excited to share this with Curse, but his delight could not be concealed as he shoved his face forward and screamed "We're gonna shoot 'em all!"

Larry's spirit was infectious. Curse forgot the rage of being attacked and hefted the new weapon in his hands. He felt the lust for violence again. It took him over, and he realized he was trembling in excitement. With a smile, he turned to Larry.

Nightmarescape

"Well, then let's get to it." The loneliness and isolation were starting to fade as he had bonded with Larry through combat. "Take me to more of them."

"That won't be hard! There's fightin' folks everywhere!"

Larry threw his hands out toward the landscape, almost as if the entire world was crawling with adversaries. Curse welcomed them, the cold inside him melting away into anger and a desire for battle. Whereas moments ago, he was angered at being fired upon, he had remembered the rush of combat. Suddenly it seemed as though all of the combatants in the Nightmarescape could not satiate his bloodlust and pent-up rage.

"Bring them on," he breathed just above a heated whisper.

In preparation for fights to come, Curse found the magazine catch on his gun and removed the magazine for an ammunition check. Much to his chagrin, the magazine was empty. In disappointment, he made a movement to toss the empty magazine away in frustration. A firm hand on his wrist stopped him as he turned to see Larry grinning as insanely as ever.

"Put it back in the gun, boy," Larry ordered. With a bit of vexation, Curse humored him and did as he said. Larry indicated the landscape behind him. "Now pick something and fire, son."

"But there's no ammo . . . ," Curse began to protest.

Larry reached down and racked the action before giving him a wink and stepping back. Curse depressed the trigger and unleashed a small hail of projectiles into the empty land. Curse's belly and chest shook with laughter as he fired another burst.

"How is it possible?" he asked Larry.

At first Larry shrugged. "Got a theory about that too," he said simply.

"Then let's hear it, you marvelous psychopath," Curse intoned.

Larry looked thoughtful for a moment before he began speaking. When his thoughts were gathered, he began his dissertation. "The way I see it, items and objects that manifest here along with folks retain their original purpose and continue to function. With this in mind . . ." Larry raised a finger and gave Curse a quizzical look. "A firearm still functions even though it has no ammunition in it. Why? Because you remember how the item functioned. There are vehicles here that people have been driving for eons, and they still drive on without needing to be refueled. It's sort of like your body. It's not what it was in life. It's a composite that this world created out of psychic residue. We're energy of sorts given a physical shape. So are the objects here."

Curse nodded as he considered Larry's words. Wrapping his fingers around the weapon in his hands, he turned to stare out at a desolated plain, once more wondering whom he would encounter next. Something that had been absent since he arrived in the place began to stir within him. He was unaware of it at first, but noticed that Larry had begun smiling once more as the sound of his own laughter fell upon his ears and shook his abdomen. He was beginning to remember. He had been there before, not in the exact same spot, but in his dreams, he had found himself in the realm of the Nightmarescape. Flashbacks flooded his mind as memories of dead and colorless landscapes, old crumbling buildings, sinister artifacts of times past, and items marking the suffering of others raced through his head. He remembered the place all right . . . not in a coherent capacity, but he had definitely been there before. He remembered the place for sure, but more than the place, he remembered the restless souls inhabiting it.

In his dreams they had come to him. Some screamed for his help, while others threatened and assaulted him. Memories of waking from night terrors had clung in his head after the attacks. In one, a crippled, old, rotting female specter lurched towards him from a small farmhouse before grabbing onto him and screaming a strand of gibberish into his face. In another, he had attempted to cross a dilapidated rope bridge while trying to escape from several angered souls that clawed and tore at his legs while he clambered across, kicking into their skulls and bodies. Another memory and he saw the interior of a decrepit stonework room where a figure in medieval garb was hunched over a table, prodding something that continuously screeched. After several moments, the figure turned and confronted Curse's dreaming self. Immediately the thing charged, its eyes burning a baleful red much like those of the soldiers Curse and Larry had dispatched. Memories of fear came back as the thing grabbed on to him and started to scream about destroying him, but he had been able to steady himself and put up a fight, the two of them locking into a furious combat as they tossed around the room slamming into stone walls and medieval instruments of torture. In a burst of strength and resolve, Curse had been able to pin the thing to a table with one hand as he reached down and removed a small bladed instrument from the thing's belt. In the throes of combat, Curse raised the implement and brought it down hard into the thing's necrotic flesh. Over and over again he raised the blade and stabbed it into his assailant. Now the screaming thing on the table was complemented by the screams of its tormentor as

Curse remembered passing into consciousness once more. Immediately another memory took its place. This one began with Curse making his way through a forest of black and gray vegetation towards the sound of a mechanical cacophony punctuated by yelling. Whatever he heard he wanted to see. He slowed his pace and dropped to conceal himself as he inched forward on his belly towards the commotion. After some time of stealthy movement, he found himself at the edge of the vegetation looking onto a true sight to behold. An assembly of archaic tanks and soldiers from many periods of time was formed before his eyes. As he looked he identified original tanks and trucks from World War I, half-tracks, Sherman tanks, and cannons from World War II, as well as artillery and soldiers that could have been relics of the American Revolution and Civil War. Curse was taken aback by the incredible sight before him and began picking out vehicles and uniforms that he had seen in books before passing out of the dream.

So this was a world of misery and fighting, a place for those who died in the throes of pain and suffering. Some found this realm out of condition; others found it out of their own negative trappings. Curse knew not where he fit in just yet, but his being in this place seemed appropriate.

He knew that he carried a great deal of pain and suffering of his own, he just needed to figure out the rest of his story in order to place everything together and understand his circumstances. He felt in touch with the reality around him and knew that this world could turn into his own in due time. As Curse regained himself from his reminiscing, he turned to Larry once more.

"Perpetual conflict and suffering . . . I think I can make it work here . . . ," he mused.

"That's the spirit if I've ever seen it, boy!"

Curse's fingers gripped the weapon in his hands. It was nothing but cold metal. He was happy to have it because it was something that was real. Nothing had really seemed to exist in a context just yet, but things were starting to make sense, and the realizations were grand. Curse began to laugh, thinking about the dreams that had plagued him during his life. At present, he could not remember exactly when they had started, but he was sure the memories would return in due time.

10

"Tell me, Larry, what brought you here?"

Larry shrugged and then threw his hands out in an exasperated manner. "The hell if I know! It was like this . . . it was back in the days when The Union was pushing westward! You see, good years were those when a man could move out toward the open frontier and make his fortune with nothing but what he had on his back . . . I was a doctor! I got my start working as a psychotherapist on the east coast . . . one of my patients was a young woman by the name of Maylene. You see, Maylene was a contemptible bitch, and she would come to me with all sorts of crap about cheating on this man and taking something from another until one day she came to me crying and claiming that she had 'finally done it.' I listened to her story, and she spoke to me of how she had recently been engaged to marry a suitor from her father's company.

"You see, her father was a high roller who owned several mills that had really gotten a kick at the start of the industrial revolution. He was also a blue blood who couldn't see his little bitch marrying anyone who wasn't rich! So long story short, he arranged for her to marry some business jerk so she could be taken care of and have rich babies. BUT! Being the beguiling whore she was, she went behind his back with one of the machine workers from one of the mills, and he found her out! She came to me crying that her life was over and that she had ruined it. She asked my advice . . . I told her that she had caused enough trouble in her short lifetime and that she was beyond self-control . . . therefore, the only logical solution was to end her own life. She not only listened, she agreed! So she went home and hung herself from a chandelier in her bedroom. They found her after she had hung there for several hours, and the weight got to be too much and brought the chandelier down! HAHAHAHA! Swingin' from the chandelier!"

Larry was enjoying his rant from the past and as always it was accentuated with his theatrical gestures and punctuations. Curse wondered to himself where this story was going. The seemingly one-dimensional lunatic's tale was becoming very interesting.

"All would have been well and good, but the bitch left a letter behind! Her father found it and came for me immediately, but I had something for him! My revolver put two bullets into his belly, and he fell down like the fat bastard he was! I convinced the police at the time that he had come for me, but the letter was convincing to them. I fled under the cover of night and headed westward. You see . . . my original name was Lawrence Crandall, but I assumed the name Larry Spectman upon my departure. I hated to leave my old life, but investigation into my case studies would have revealed that I had led several patients to commit suicide and murder."

Larry stopped and took a heavy breath before continuing his rant, his arms flailing wildly in all directions as he spoke.

"They said it was madness, but I thought it was common sense! Someone's making your life hell? Get rid of them! You're making your own life hell? Well, then get rid of you! Our benevolent Christian empire didn't see eye to eye with me on such things. But anyway, I had money when I left. I intended to go westward and work as a druggist in a frontier town, but I ran into a little more trouble on the way."

This is going to be good, Curse thought to himself.

"I was riding the railroad west. One night I stopped in a town somewhere on the way and went into a saloon. Mind you, it was a seedy hellhole, but there was this one whore who would not leave me alone, so I shot her! A huge brawl ensued, and I ended up killing a few more folks too. I made my way out and headed back toward the railroad where I found my trunk. I'd squared a few things away in there . . . two more handguns, one a revolver, one an early automatic . . . my shotgun . . . and a small amount of dynamite. I loaded up on the guns and headed out, walking the railroad by foot. There was a posse rummaging through the cars, so I began to move in the darkness following the tracks out of town. In my good fortune, the tracks happened to lead over a river by way of a trestle . . . I began to rig the dynamite to the trestle in the dark, but as fate would have it, a shock from my hand set the dynamite off and threw me for yards. I regained consciousness and started wandering dazed in the desert . . . dehydration finally got the best of me and I fell. A pack of vultures had been watching me and saw their meal fall to the sand . . . I remember them pecking at my eyes . . . that was the last thing I saw as I tried to fend them off in my weakened state . . . next thing I knew . . . here I was. I can't say I miss anything . . ."

Curse ruminated momentarily on the story that he had just heard. He knew that Larry was an honest madman, but the background story to his existence gave his insanity credibility.

"So, what makes you love this place so much?" Curse inquired.

"You already know." Larry winked.

"I might . . . but I want to hear it from you."

"You see, I've been here for a long time . . . when were you alive?"

Curse had to think for a moment . . . it was near the turn of the century . . . an exact date escaped him. "It was sometime soon after the year 2000."

"*Two thousand*?" Larry's eyes widened in his now-trademark inquisitorial expression. "You mean I've made it here over a hundred years!? HA!" Larry broke into a small dance, clicking his heels on the ground. "Let me tell you what I love about this place. It is something eternal . . . the archetypes of Heaven and Hell that men forge and chase . . . I can't speak for them, but this place is real . . . and what it is . . . the cure to what humans have struggled with since the dawn of their consciousness."

Larry was not only a doctor and a lunatic, but he was apparently a brilliant philosopher in his own right. Curse listened intently as a student would listen to a master.

"Why do I bring up Heaven and Hell? Death is the great goal of all life. Human beings have sentience that is not matched by any other species. This sentience is its greatest gift and greatest damnation. Animals live their lives mechanically feeding, fighting, and fucking, but not knowing why. Humans, on the other hand, know why they do what they do, and they also know it will end. This fills life with a permutation of fear . . . you see, humans realize that they are but worms in the gut of a rotting corpse . . . attempting to survive as long as they can until their corporeal selves inevitably give out. The Nightmarescape takes the essence attained in life and gives it new life in another realm. I've seen them from many periods of history . . . here as long as that essence can survive, the new life can survive. You see, this is a realm of despair and destruction, but only if you allow it to be . . . for me, it is a realm of immortality and greatness!"

Curse responded without thinking about his words. "And what about immortality? Can it in and of itself be a damnation as well as a blessing?"

"My dear boy, you miss the point, yet I know of what you speak . . . you left something behind, and you want to go back to it, do you not?"

"I'm trying to remember her . . ." Curse strained, trying to think of the woman from his earlier vision . . . he knew that she had been his, but he could not remember . . . what was her name? He remembered the wondrous feeling of seeing her face and feeling her touching him, but he could not remember anything about her beyond what he had seen in the vision.

"It will return in time. It took me a while to remember my life . . . but I know what you are thinking . . . how can you be here pressing for immortality when she is in another realm and destined to die and rot as most others do? You are in a realm of forever, and she is in a realm of the temporary. How can you press on knowing such a thing?" Larry pondered aloud for Curse.

Curse could feel his temper welling again at Larry's musings, but he kept himself in check. "For someone who barely knows me, you know me quite well . . ."

"Head doctor, remember, boy? Pay attention. I do not have an answer for you on how you can regain her. I was fortunate in that I never had a wife or children, so I felt as though I left nothing behind. Many here rage against the very fabric of this realm for the same feelings that you are holding right now. People go through their lives and build up a group of other people that gives them comfort and solace. To some it's a family, to others it can be a military unit, to some it's just acquaintances, but to all it's for the same purpose. Don't get me wrong, I had friends and people to care for me, but just not in the traditional sense . . . I didn't feel bad to leave them behind either though. I'm more of a loner than most, you see. You, however . . . you need folks."

"Apparently so." Curse listened and deciphered Larry's words through his own mind. What he was saying made Curse feel trapped. Surely many in this realm felt the same way . . . reborn into a new plane of existence while their old lives went on in another one. He wanted to go back . . . he wanted to find her . . . he wanted to know her again . . . he wanted to remember . . . the present reality was hurting him.

"Curse, let's go; more soldiers are going to come if we just keep standing out here. I can blither about this more later."

11

Larry began to disappear into the dead trees. Curse clenched his jaw and followed him. *She is in another realm and destined to die and rot as most others do . . .*

The words played in Curse's head like a tormenting broken record. On one hand, he had to hand it to Larry, he did know how to look into people. On the other hand, he really knew how to create a double standard. Living a life of immortality versus letting everything he'd ever known or cared for rot away in another reality . . . damned either way. Larry's lecture had deflated the sense of excitement for the new world, and Curse could feel himself slipping back into melancholy.

Larry was far away now, his frame growing more diminutive as he charged through the dead forest.

Do I even want to catch up with him? Curse wondered to himself.

So far Larry had been the only one he had found to be somewhat helpful and knowledgeable. Curse's thoughts were derailed as the sound of more gunfire erupted in the distance ahead of him. Although Larry was far away, Curse observed him leaping into the air as the ground began to explode in

Nightmarescape

small geysers around him. Almost as if performing some strange ballet in a weightless state, Larry's body spun almost a complete one hundred and eighty degrees. As soon as his feet touched the ground, he was barreling in Curse's direction once more.

Curse gripped his weapon and readied himself for another fight. His eyes darted about the wood as Larry charged in his direction, hooting and laughing all the way. More rifle fire . . . a small eruption of earth sprouted behind Larry. Curse took the cue to find cover behind a nearby tree. The first soldier came into view, another Third Reich German. This one wore no helm but was easily identifiable by the rifle he carried and the swastika emblazoned on the sleeve of his greatcoat.

Behind him came another soldier; Curse was taken aback by this one's appearance. Upon his head sat a large-plumed helm. His uniform resembled something from the late 1800s. Black riding boots encased the lower half of his legs, while a shirt covered in buttons and adornments clothed his torso.

"What the hell . . ."

Not willing to give the new arrivals any chances, Curse took aim and loosed a burst of gunfire. The soldier with the plumed helm was knocked back as several impacts struck him in the torso. As soon as he hit the ground, the soldier was already using his rifle to push himself to his feet once more. Curse readied his weapon and drew his sights upon the other pursuer. Once Larry was clear of his line of sight, Curse fired. An explosion of black liquid blew out from the back of the soldier's skull as the round tore through his head. The impact jerked him off of his feet. Not waiting to see if he stayed down or not, Curse found the Napoleonic soldier in his sights and let off another burst. This time the shots went high, but a single round struck his target in the throat. The soldier stumbled, removing one hand from his weapon to reach up and grab the wound. If the shot had not killed him, it had at least caused him a great deal of pain.

Larry skidded to a halt near Curse and turned around to survey his pursuers. One was on the ground and had not risen to his feet; the other was staggering and grasping a hole in his neck. Larry raised his shotgun and found the Napoleonic soldier in his sight. A moment later, the weapon resounded, and the soldier's head exploded into its constituent parts. The body fell to the ground and crumbled to dust.

Just as soon as one threat was alleviated, the Nazi was up on his feet again. The wound in his head was sealing, but he was still clutching it. Curse noted that his wound was taking a while to close. In order to keep one hand on the wound, the soldier had dropped his rifle and drawn a Luger pistol from his hip. Unsteady on his feet, the soldier lurched toward Curse and Larry while shooting the pistol indiscriminately. One round struck Larry in the shoulder, jerking him back.

"Damn!" Larry's wound began sealing over quickly, and he steadied his shotgun for another blast. Curse also took aim with his weapon, and together they fired into their adversary. Curse's spray of rounds tore a large part of the soldier's head open, while Larry's shotgun blast finished the job, causing the rest of the cranium to disintegrate in a hail of buckshot. Several stray balls of buckshot found the neck and upper torso, scoring eruptions of flesh and ichor. The body immediately began to crumble into dust and was nothing within moments.

Curse walked over toward where the soldier had been standing. His rifle and pistol were still laying on the ground. Already possessing rifles, Curse leaned down and picked up the pistol. He held the archaic weapon in his hand, feeling as though the piece belonged in a museum rather than a battlefield. Being in such a surrounding with people and relics of other time periods was quite an interesting predicament. Curse raised the weapon and aimed off into the landscape. He surveyed the sights and passed them over several things in the distance. A tree, a small embankment, a small clump of dead brush. Even though the sights were primitive by modern standards, they were still pretty damn good. It was interesting for him to think of what had changed and what had not as time crept along.

He let the sights drift back onto the tree, and his finger squeezed the trigger, letting loose a single shot into the rotten wood. The pistol had a nice snap to it as the round left the barrel. The kick was notable but not unmanageable. For a nine-millimeter pistol, it was not a bad make. Curse stuffed the pistol into his waistband and hefted the submachine gun into his hands once more.

"Like that one, eh?"

Curse had briefly become so enamored with the weapons of another period that he had forgotten Larry was standing next to him.

"Huh . . . oh yeah . . . it's good . . ."

"I got me a couple of them. Nice pieces . . . I remember when designs like that were coming out . . . only a few in the Union, but they were top of the line back then . . . had me a revolver when they got all that fancy stuff. You probably had all those fancy automatics and slides and whatnot."

Curse found himself laughing at Larry's ramble about guns.

"Shit, I remember . . . I had a couple of nice pieces. I had a shotgun that was a lot different from yours, several automatic pistols, a more modern revolver, and an AR-15."

"HAHA! I have all that stuff back at the house! Remember that room that you couldn't get into next to my kitchen? That's where I keep the weapons I've found. I've got all sorts of nutty stuff but . . ."—Larry turned his double-barreled shotgun over in his hands—"you've got to stick with what you know and love!"

The sentiment gave Curse a slight chuckle. "I'm trying to remember what I know and love," he mused.

"Well, 'til ya do, son, let's make do with what we've got!"

"Yeah . . ." Curse surveyed the landscape with a sweep of his weapon, straining to see if any stragglers were waiting to come forth. There were none that he could see, but that did not mean that they were not out there. Curse lowered the weapon and let the barrel hang toward the ground. Several moments later, a crack resounded far off in the distance. He did not understand the sound until after the impact and pain. Curse felt himself first being knocked off of the ground, and then his head splitting as the rifle round struck him in the face. His visual perception was split again.

He was lying on the ground—one half of his visual field was peering straight up into the gray sky; the other was staring off into the earth.

12

He was stunned. His perceptions slowed to a crawl. The pain radiated throughout what was left of his skull. It was the only thing that was real. He was floating in a choppy sea of agony. The edges of his skull hung open like the limp jaws of a mighty fallen beast. Pieces of dark tissue held the skull in place like broken and atrophied muscles. There was little he could do to take his mind off of the horrendous agony. He wished that he would mercifully be taken into one of the fainting spells that randomly overcame him. There was no unconsciousness to slip into or any respite to be found. What was left of his head was beginning to throb like an overexerted heart. The rest of his brain felt as though it would boil out through the splintered pieces of his skull. He wanted to scream . . . the motor centers of his brain strained to force a scream from his throat so that the sensation of screaming may alleviate the pain. It took several moments to register that he was already screaming. As he screamed, he felt that the pain was subsiding into numbness. Where once there had been sensation, his nerves were beginning to go dead and cease functioning.

He had to be dying again . . . experiencing final death in the Nightmarescape. In moments, his body would begin to crumble to dust, the same as those he had killed . . . the irony struck him. He had been given a second chance at a new life in a new existence, but it was being taken away as fast as it had been granted. Pain slid away from his nerves as he realized that his field of vision was returning to normal . . . his head was reforming itself . . .

The next sensation he could feel was the whole of his body being dragged across the ground in a frenzied manner.

"Damn motherfuckin' hicks ain't got no class . . ."

Curse's vision was fixed on the sky as his body was scraped and bounced across the gritty land. His faculties were returning . . . he became aware of Larry's bony fingers digging into his legs and tugging him along. It was good to be feeling something other than dying.

"You're gonna be okay, son!"

The tugging continued as Larry dragged him across the landscape. Curse felt his motor skills returning; he pulled himself from Larry's grasp, rolling over onto his stomach and pushing himself to his hands and knees. Larry slapped his shoulders and pulled him up to his feet.

"Good to have you back! Let's get away from this snipin' jerk!" Larry turned and skittered into the wood line. Curse pushed his legs into the ground and propelled himself after Larry.

Another round from the sniper's gun exploded rotten wood chunks and plant tissue beside him. They kept moving. The faster they moved, the harder it would be for a stationary sniper to acquire them in his sights.

Larry apparently knew where he was going, so Curse stayed locked on his heels as he plowed along deeper into the woods. The vegetation grew thicker the farther they pressed. The dead plant material intertwined on itself, creating leafless thickets.

Downed trees laid out an obstacle course through the thick brush. Under branches and over the logs they went, Larry still leading. Curse realized that his hands were empty. He must have dropped the weapon he had been carrying after the sniper's bullet struck him. He also noted that the rifles were no longer slung over his shoulders. The bulge in his waistline from the pistol felt absent as well. It was too late to go back and look for the weapons. Larry had said he was going to "fix him up" with a few things anyway. They just had to get back to the farmhouse . . . wherever it was.

Curse had no sense of direction in the foreign territory. Everything was on Larry at this point. Hopefully he had some sort of plan as to where he was going. Then again, Larry was a chaotic creature. He seemed to work best when operating on the spur of the moment. Maybe a plan would be more hindrance to him than help.

A deep thicket appeared in front of them, and Curse watched as Larry slid to the ground and crawled under a layer of desiccated brush. Upon reaching the mass of dead plant matter, Curse did the same. Offending branches and sticks found his skin, pricking and pulling pieces of it off as he forced himself over rough ground through the dead vegetation. His arms pushed the plants aside, pulling him along the ground through the jagged mess. After thrashing through it for a few minutes, he felt the vegetation thinning out and was able to pull himself into the open. Larry was on the other side to greet him, tugging him out from under the brush.

"Stay low, son," Larry advised.

Curse followed his advice as he worked himself into a crawling position, surveying what was ahead of him. He was rather surprised by what he saw. Before them lay a small settlement. It was in ruins . . . ancient ones, even by the standards of the Nightmarescape. Several small, ruined walls of stone surrounded the perimeter of what was once a building of some sort. The floor was nothing but bare earth for the most part, a few loose stones that may have once served as flooring dotting the ground here and there. A small set of stairs climbed its way out of the earth to a weathered stage-like platform. Curse looked at the walls a little more and was able to observe the outlines of what had once been windows. Windows were not a necessity now that the roof was gone. Curse's eyes continued to travel, focusing on a wall behind the stage. Up the wall about nine feet or so, several bricks had been left out of the construction, leaving the shape of a small cross that allowed light from outside.

"An old church," Curse said to himself as much as Larry.

"A really old church," Larry replied softly.

Larry had adopted a stealthy approach in lieu of his usual noisy and flamboyant demeanor. This was unsettling because it meant that the lunatic was cautious of something in the area. Larry used the walls as cover, making his way over to the stage. He ascended the stairs on his hands and knees toward a small hole near the bottom of the wall bearing the cross. Here he peered out for a moment before reaching back and beckoning to Curse. Curse made his way to the hole. Taking his turn to look, Curse saw more ruins outside. They varied in size from small houses to what may have been inns and taverns. The buildings were clearly medieval in style, consisting of dark stonework and some bearing wooden roofs.

"Is anyone still here?" Curse asked.

"Sometimes . . . just wanna see who's here now before we go further in; maybe there's friends, maybe there's foes." Larry nudged Curse out of the way and took another turn looking out of the hole. This time he craned his head from side to side to achieve a limited panoramic view. "Ahhh . . ."

Curse heard the approach before he saw anything. Heavy footfalls of marching feet sounded from outside the wall.

"Right then, let's move that gun over here!"

Curse was struck by the heavy English accent he heard from outside. Larry turned back to him, grinning wider than usual.

"Let's definitely call these boys friends!" Larry beamed.

Larry stood and stepped through a collapsed portion of the wall. Curse followed him. Larry strode confidently toward the sounds of activity. Looking past Larry's back, Curse saw several more soldiers. This time their regalia spoke of the First World War—British infantrymen if he had to guess. An officer was striding back and forth as several others were positioning a howitzer gun behind a makeshift gun emplacement.

"We haven't got all day here with this thing now! Put your backs into it!" The officer continued to chide his men.

Larry slung his shotgun across his shoulders and worked his arms so that his hands hung from it as though he were in a crucifixion pose. Curse moved from behind to beside him as they approached the soldiers. They were clearly not worth noticing as the soldiers busied themselves working the gun into its emplacement. What a gun it was. Curse found himself wondering what kind of carnage one such as Larry might inflict if he got a hold of such a thing.

"You limey bastards!" Larry exclaimed as he stepped toward the soldiers.

At once, the soldiers turned toward him; those on the gun did not take their hands off of it and continued trying to move it as the officer swiftly turned to brandish a saber at the new presence.

"Well, I'll be damned . . . if it isn't the bloody ol' lunatic himself! And what's this—you brought a friend this time?" The officer regarded Curse with curiosity.

Curse found himself taken aback, interacting with a presence from such a bygone era. The officer had not officially greeted him yet. Curse simply stood there, looking at him blankly. "What brings you boys to these parts?"

"Some of your Axis buddies ran across us a ways back . . . I think they're still unhappy with me. You blow up one train full of crap, and your reputation is soiled! Soiled, I say! Ah well, fuck 'em. I got this!" Larry shrugged the shotgun on his shoulders.

Curse's hand reached for his waistline and met with nothing but frustration as he remembered that the Luger was laying out in a field somewhere. Upon being reminded of the weapon's absence, Curse vented his frustrations.

"God damnit, I can't keep any of the guns I find here!" Curse blurted. The officer seemed to perk up and straightened his posture as he heard Curse.

"What's all this now? Your boy can talk, Lawrence! I thought he was going to sit there starin' all day!"

"HAHA! Oh yes, lovely speaker that Curse. Oh, the sermons he'll give if you let him! Nice talker . . . but he still doesn't know how to hootenanny . . ." Larry trailed off.

"Curse, eh? Got a good sound to it, and you sure look the part, dear boy," the officer offered. Curse looked up at the gaunt face with empty eye sockets staring out at him from under the officer's cap. He felt as though those eyes were inspecting him, seeing if he would make a worthy warrior or not. The inspection did not last long as the officer quickly made up his mind.

"You've got some meat to you; let's say you help us with the gun, eh?"

"Why not?" Curse found a place amongst the men struggling against the weight of the gun. They made room for him as he found a grip and good footing.

"All right then, lads, on three! One! Two! Three!"

Curse felt his muscles tighten as he strained against the massive piece of artillery. The others were straining just as hard. Their effort was pronounced to the point where it seemed as though their strength was permeating the air around them and their muscles were all tightening together at once. Against the strain, Curse could feel the carriage of the howitzer sliding along the ground. He pushed his weight into it and used his legs to propel himself forward with the hefty piece. Together, he and the men maneuvered the weapon into a makeshift emplacement that the soldiers had set.

"Right then, hold!"

Curse and the soldiers allowed their muscles to relax at the officer's order.

"Who are you going to be shooting with this thing?" Curse inquired of the nearest man. Several of the soldiers began putting braces under the carriage of the weapon.

"Not sure yet . . . trying to hold two fronts, we are. We've got the Axis teaming up with the plague blokes right now. They're trying to move in on us, so we were sent out here to set up a small welcome committee for 'em," the soldier informed through a hearty Cockney accent.

Obviously the Axis had to be the Axis of Europe and Japan from World War II. "The plague blokes," as the soldier had put it, were a little more mysterious.

"Who are these 'plague blokes'?" Curse inquired.

"Plague Faction, they call themselves proper. They're a disgusting lot what died of diseases and things. The bulk of 'em come from the death toll of the Black Plague. Rest of 'em are tons of people from throughout time what's died of all kinds of poxes and infections. Most of 'em got no minds really. Diseases must've eaten 'em away 'fore they died. They're led by a guy callin' himself Pastor Nox. Big fella, wears a doctor's mask from back then and carries a scythe to cut people down with. They say he was a doctor back during the Great Plague, but then he began worshippin' the plague, sayin' it was sent from Heaven to take the righteous ones off the sinful earth. History forgot him really. The Church denied it had ever happened, even though he had won over a good lot of plague victims. They said it was madness and whatnot that caused it and took it outta the records." The soldier coughed and spat a dark gob of phlegm out of his mouth.

"So now there's a whole army of disease-ridden morons running around out here?" Curse found it hard to believe he had actually asked such a question, but at this point it did not seem to be the most far-fetched concept.

"Afraid so. Like I said, they basically got no minds and just do what the Pastor tells 'em to. They ain't got a lotta weapons either—primitive stuff like knives and clubs, usually bare hands—but once they get goin', it's hard to stop 'em even with a good round. Funny thing is, they want to give everyone their diseases, but we don't get sick out here . . . they believe in it so strong even after all this time though that it keeps them going."

"And what are they doing with the Axis?" Curse inquired further.

"Don't right know just yet, but the fact that the two of them are together is enough to make us want to stop 'em. Jerries and plague-ridden zombies cannot make a good combination."

"Interesting . . . let me go speak to Larry."

Larry and the officer were talking. Crazy eyes rolled around in Larry's sockets as though he were frantically pondering points the officer was making. His unsettled eyes swung up to see Curse approaching.

"Curse! We might have ourselves a good ol' hootenanny to be a part of here!"

"Is that so?"

"Well, the rubes that we ran across are part of a bigger force of jerks that are moving this way, and they're allied with some plague-worshippin' clods. I say we get stuck in on this for a moment, how about you?"

"Why are the Axis powers allying with plague victims?"

The officer intervened. "Well, nothing is confirmed, but hushed rumors would have it that there is a device floating around that can split the fabric between this world and the one we all came from. The theory is that these bloody fools want to capture it and spill back into the other world. As a soldier who has been fighting for nobility and right for my entire existence, I cannot allow them to do that. Imagine the carnage the bastards would wreak! The Axis would be back up to their scheme of world domination, while the Plague Faction would be spreading rampant infections across the globe. If they were allowed to succeed, they could very well destroy everyone in the living world."

Larry pulled Curse aside.

"Ya hear that, son? A device that takes you back to life . . . imagine what we could do with that!" Curse could tell that countless schemes and scenarios were running through the madman's head. "We could even get you to see that girl you like!"

Now there was a possibility. The dream from earlier flashed back into his mind. Curse thought of her. She had been so beautiful, and he had been a man once, but then before her eyes he degenerated into an abomination. A heavy sigh breathed its way out of his chest. He felt his fists clenching, the skeletal ends of his fingers digging into his palms. It hurt to think about being removed from his life and tossed into an existence where he was lost.

"What's bothering you, boy? This gives us some fun to be had!"

Larry was right. If this thing existed, he could find it and use it to return to the world of the living to see his lover. If nothing else, he could just check on her. The proposition made Curse's body feel heavy.

"Let me sit down for a few." He walked past Larry and settled himself against the side of one of the ruined buildings.

He sat watching the soldiers scurry through the ruins, preparing for a possible assault. His body felt heavy, his mind ethereal. His perceptions melted into those of a conscious dream, somewhere in between being awake and falling asleep. Instead of sitting against the ruined building, he was sitting on a bed with his back propped against the wall. He looked down at his body and observed he was human again.

14

His body was only covered by black jeans and boots . . . the same thing he was wearing in the Nightmarescape. His hand was holding a large-frame .357 revolver. Chaos swirled through his mind, and he became conscious of several thoughts that had belonged to him at a point in his life. He was thinking of the woman . . . she had just left him.

She had said he was too volatile . . . that she could not live with him anymore because of what he had done. She said that she would never tell anyone what he had confessed to her as long as he let her leave. She had told him that she feared him. That even though he had never been violent toward her, his anger was getting out of control. That he only had two emotions anymore—anger and depression. This turn of events had certainly not helped. He felt neither angry nor upset at the moment; he only felt numb and exhausted.

Curse sat inside the body and listened passively as his mind experienced feelings and thoughts that had once been his own. They hit him as though he were landing on concrete from a high fall. Thoughts of his lover passed through his mind as he made the determination that he could not live with himself any longer. He knew what was going to happen.

Even before he felt his arm move, he knew that he was raising the gun to his temple. He focused his last conscious thoughts on the woman who had meant so much to him as his finger began the long trigger pull. The explosion of the cartridge followed, and his head was thrown to the side with the impact. His ears and his head rung for what seemed to be an eternity until his vision returned to the Nightmarescape. He was lying slumped on his side as he had after he shot himself.

So that's how I got here, he thought.

The soldiers were running around screaming now. Ringing from the gunshot echoed through his head. Scanning the area, he observed that the howitzer's barrel was smoking. Its firing must have coincided with the gunshot in his flashback. The soldiers moved quickly and took cover positions, sighting their rifles on a foe that Curse could not yet see. Nerves screamed through a sludgy haze that he needed to move. Slowly, sluggishly, he willed himself to move again. This flashback had decided to come at a rather bad time. Curse could feel his senses and body returning to normal. His right hand sent him a signal that he had not perceived earlier, for it did not feel like part of his body. Something was sitting in his hand. He looked down to see what he was holding, and a wicked smile crossed his face. His fingers were clenched around the frame of his .357 revolver.

Gunfire and screams now permeated the air. Curse was in full control of his body once more and leapt up into a sprint toward the soldiers. Bounding through the air, he landed beside the soldiers at the cannon as they were slamming another shell into the breach.

"Fancy of you to join us, lad!" One of them chirped at him.

The soldier's comment was quickly drowned out by the crack of rifles and the cries of charging enemies. Their screams were unearthly, raspy howls issuing forth from ruined throats. Emaciated bodies charged across the earth on atrophied and bony limbs. Even against the common rotten visages of the Nightmarescape, these creatures were hideous. Some showed large boils and pustules on their rancid frames, while others bore festering sores on their flesh. Gray froth poured over dry cracked lips and left slimy trails on the ground as the creatures ran forth. Creatures. Whatever minds or semblance of humanity these things once had was eroded away. They ran and lurched with labored gaits, some just stumbling. Some fell and crawled as they attempted to upright themselves. Many were trampled under the frail legs of their comrades.

Soldiers ran on the flanks of the diseased mass, firing at the position. They were herding the Plague Faction as though they were cattle. It made sense. The things had no mind left, so the soldiers had simply corralled them and pushed them toward their foes in an onslaught of disease-ridden bodies. Whereas the former soldiers had worn iconography of Nazi Germany, the current soldiers showed the image of the rising sun and wore Japanese uniforms. The officers wielded samurai swords and Nambu pistols.

The soldiers screamed in Japanese as they herded the afflicted toward Curse and the British soldiers. Their screams were drowned temporarily as the enormous gun belched forth another explosive retort. Curse had been in a strange mental fugue when the last blast had sounded. Although he was right next to this one and he was temporarily deafened, the blast served to energize him. He was in the fight now. The soldiers around him unleashed a volley of rifle fire and several of the decrepit bodies were knocked off of their bony legs. Moments later, the shell fired from the howitzer landed in the midst of the running plague-afflicted. Another explosion shook the earth as a cloud of dust and debris sprouted from the ground, and the air was littered with atrophied bodies and limbs. The Plague Faction and their pieces fell back on the ground in a macabre rain.

A cheer erupted from the soldiers as the last echoes of the explosion resonated. Such a burst of enthusiasm encouraged Curse to fight with them. He steadied himself, being armed with only his revolver, and waited for the rush of bodies to pile in so he might have a better shot. Once the charging undead broke upon the position, he would only be able to loose several aimed shots before being stuck in brutal hand-to-hand fighting. Even though the enemy appeared to be atrophied and weak, he knew that they would attack voraciously and with possessed determination. Numbers were definitely on their side, and even though most of them lacked weapons of any kind, a sea of biting mouths and snatching limbs would overwhelm a smaller force. Such a proposition combined with the might of the Japanese soldiers on the flanks made this horde something to be reckoned with. Voices sounded around Curse as he prepared himself for the onslaught.

"One more round from the big gun before they'll be too close!"

"Hit those Japs on the flanks!"

"Just kill the freaks! You'll hit a bunch wherever you shoot!"

Sporadic rifle fire accompanied their yells as the men attempted to fell any enemies they could before their position was reached.

All the sounds were briefly drowned out as the howitzer fired again. This time the shell erupted right in the middle of the horde, tossing limbs and bodies in all directions. The gun crew had chosen wisely when picking their target, for the majority of the plague-afflicted were clumped together in a large cluster, clamoring over each other. The shell had landed right in their core and taken down a large amount of charging adversaries. Not all of them would be destroyed, but even knocking them down would buy time as their uncoordinated bodies would take precious moments to get back up. That time could be focused on the armed soldiers.

Curse stretched his arms out in front of him and sighted his revolver. He would hit something wherever he shot. There were still too many for him to miss yet. His hand kicked as he fired several rounds from the weapon. He could not tell who had been hit or what damage had been done; the press of bodies was too great. Some lurched and fell forward under their own volition, not even struck by gunfire. Their stumbling movements were simply too unbalanced. Those that fell were trampled into the ground as the seething afflicted sought desperately to close the distance and dig their fingers into their prey.

Curse fired several more rounds and realized his cylinder should have been empty. He remembered what Larry had told him about guns in the Nightmarescape however. Reaching into his mind, he felt rage and hatred for the ugly things surging toward him. He focused that energy within his mind and unleashed a grating scream that passed as a battle cry while he leapt from behind the gun emplacement, firing his weapon wildly. The soldiers at his side followed suit and leapt forth as well. Their rifles issued sharp snaps as they poured fire into the enemy at close range. Once the enemies were on top of them, the bayoneted rifles turned into spears that were plunged into abdomens and chests. Black ichor poured from decrepit bodies and soaked the ground. Members of the Plague Faction were falling rapidly, but few were crumbling to dust upon hitting the ground.

The soldiers swung the butts of their rifles in wide arcs and some slammed home into the frail skulls of the attackers. Heads cracked open under the impact, and some began to disintegrate as the psychic centers of their beings were destroyed. Others simply snatched and grabbed from the ground, weighing the soldiers down.

Curse charged into a mass of rotten humanity with his gun blazing. Several of the bodies fell back, and one even disintegrated, but as soon as those hit the ground, more were surging forward to take their place. He met them head on and crashed into one with his shoulder. The momentum carried him and the rotten thing back into several more of its number. He tumbled down on top of them and began pounding the hilt of his pistol into the first head he could find. Beneath the crushing force, a gibbering creature spat out a howl of pain through a mouth full of froth. Its cry filled Curse with battle lust, and he let another hail of blows rain down into its head. The thing's skull thoroughly crushed and its brain destroyed, it crumbled into dust and ceased to exist.

Bony hands now clutched onto Curse from many angles. They dug into his flesh and grabbed onto his pants. Even though they lacked strength, their numbers were coming to bear as he had known they would. Curse gritted his teeth as they pulled at his flesh. He felt a froth-laden mouth sink its teeth into his right forearm. Adrenaline surged through his body, and he jerked his arm away from the bite as well as several bony fingers that had dug into it. The biting mouth tore a chunk of his flesh away while the fingers broke from the brittle hands of their owner and continued to dig in for several moments before melting into black ichor. Members separated from bodies in the Nightmarescape did not seem to last long and either melted or crumbled to dust as the bodies did.

With his arm now free, Curse unleashed more shots into point-blank targets. Several of the creatures holding onto him crumbled into dust as the destructive blasts disintegrated vital parts of their heads and brains. Even though he was killing many, more kept coming. His legs kicked and sent mandibles clacking upward. He wrenched his other arm free from the grip of skeletal fingers. His head slammed forward into the skull of another rotting attacker. Still, they pressed toward him. He fired the gun and then followed it with wide swings, connecting metal with brittle bones. His free hand lashed out and caught a long beard filled with rabid froth. The poor wretch he had grabbed struggled to get its hands into him, but he lifted it and with a mighty sideways swing hurled the afflicted thing into a charging mass of its own. A heap of boil- and sore-stained bodies collapsed in front of him, and he capitalized on the advantage to unleash more blasts from his pistol into the pile of flailing limbs.

All around him, the plague-afflicted creatures hissed and howled. The soldiers he fought with were holding their ground well. Each one had cleared a fair deal of space for himself despite the circumstances. Curse saw the officer wading into the fray, firing an automatic pistol and slashing in wide arcs with his saber. Plague-ridden bodies fell with each movement of the sword. Several of the soldiers had amassed piles of the atrophied creatures at their feet and were feverishly hammering at them with the butts of their rifles. Larry danced amidst the carnage, whooping and laughing all the while issuing a constant stream of rants and taunts that was punctuated by the boom of his shotgun. All things considered, the battle was going fairly well so far, given the disparity of numbers. From what Curse could tell, his allies had not suffered any casualties. The chance that they would fell the foe with all of their numbers intact was put to the test as Japanese screaming and gunfire began to come from within the charging mass of shambling bodies.

Curse took aim with his weapon and fired as a screaming Japanese soldier rushed toward him with a bayoneted rifle. The rounds struck the soldier and slowed his momentum but failed to stop him. Distance closed between them, and the soldier's weapon now stabbed at Curse. Not having dodged many bayonets in his time, Curse adopted defensive tactics. If he could wait for the attack and then get in along the shaft of the rifle for a close counterattack, his enemy would not have much chance to defend. The soldier screamed fanatically in his native tongue and stabbed at him several times. Each time Curse was able to escape backward, but the soldier was fast with his weapon, and Curse could not find the opportunity to move in on him. In frustration, the soldier fired his rifle at Curse from short range. Curse dropped himself downward and to the side as the bullet whizzed past. As the soldier still held the weapon up on his shoulder in a firing position, Curse stayed low and fired several more rounds from his pistol into the soldier's midsection. It was enough to knock the warrior back and break his momentum.

Curse flung himself forward and slammed his body into the soldier. The man fell backward from the impact, but Curse had hit him with enough force that the man's fingers let loose of his rifle, and it flew into the air. As Curse caught the weapon, he allowed rage and bloodlust to wash over him. His veins pounded as his mind screamed for violence. Quickly he placed the revolver in the waistband of his pants before descending upon his adversary, striking the man with the butt of his own rifle. The soldier attempted to throw his arms up and move himself backward, but Curse's ferocity was too great. Several times the wooden stock of the weapon smashed against the soldier's upper body and head.

The uniform he had been wearing was gray in color, but Curse's blows turned it oily black as the corners of the stock impacted with flesh and opened large crushing wounds. Black ichor poured profusely from the soldier's head, and Curse slammed the weapon down into his adversary's cranium several more times. The soldier lay on the ground, making a sound somewhere between a groan and a scream. Curse raised the rifle and brought it down one last time, shattering the warrior's forehead. This had killed most of the afflicted creatures he had fought already, but he watched the soldier and saw that the man's head was reforming itself just as all of his wounds had earlier.

Curse removed the pistol from his pants and aimed both it and the rifle at the man's regenerating head. Two explosions sounded simultaneously as Curse fired the weapons in tandem and reduced the man's head into nothing. Now with the center of his mind entirely destroyed, the man's body became dust, and he was no longer a threat. Curse had little time to admire his handiwork as several more plague-ridden bodies lurched toward him with their arms outstretched. Curse raked them with pistol fire before stowing the revolver in his waistband once more and charging into his attackers with the rifle swinging wildly in all directions. Seething creatures fell as the rifle crashed into them and knocked them to the ground. Almost immediately upon knocking them over, Curse was upon them, stabbing and smashing. After several strokes downward with the bayonet, it became lodged in the skull of one of the wretched things. The creature hissed and yowled as it still attempted in vain to reach out and get its decrepit fingers into Curse. He prevented that from happening by blasting the thing's head while it was still attached.

Wrenching the rifle from the dust pile, he returned to his voracious assault. Another creature crumbled as the butt of the rifle met its head and destroyed it. The others still grabbed and snatched. Curse surveyed the carnage briefly. The soldiers he had been with were still faring well. He honed in on one warrior who was attempting to break free from a group of the creatures that were grabbing onto him. It was probable that they would overwhelm him.

Curse left his pile of plague-afflicted and bounded over to the soldier's aid. He speared one of the creatures with the bayonet and threw it to the ground. Upon jerking the blade out of the creature's flesh, the butt of the rifle met with the head of another. The overwhelmed soldier steeled his resolve at Curse's arrival and attacked the creatures with renewed vigor.

He followed Curse's lead and slammed his own rifle into the mass of bodies in front of him. Some fell while some simply staggered. Curse added his efforts to the soldier's. His own rifle slammed into skulls left and right. Some of the strikes caused their victims to crumble out of existence. Caught up in delivering his furious assault, Curse suddenly realized his movement was compromised. Moments later, searing pain burned throughout his chest. Looking down, he observed a thin silver blade impaled through his ribcage from his backside. Curse snarled in pain and then howled as he forced himself forward and fell off of the blade. Agony still raged through the open wound as he stumbled away from the weapon. The wound began sealing itself over as Curse turned around to face the new attacker.

One of the Japanese officers stood before him, a pistol in one hand and a samurai sword in the other. The sword dripped with black liquid that had come from Curse's torso. The officer held the sword in a challenge and spoke in Japanese. Curse bellowed and moved to meet him in combat. The officer swung his sword at Curse in a downward motion. Curse brought his rifle up to meet the blade. Sparks flew as the blade collided with the barrel of the rifle. Curse slammed the butt of the rifle into the officer's belly and sent him stumbling back. The strike left Curse little time to press an advantage, for the officer was preternaturally quick on his feet and swiftly rebounded with another slash from his sword. Curse threw himself back as the edge of the blade slid just slightly enough along his abdomen to open a wound. While not deep, Curse felt the hot kiss of the blade licking through his skin. Backing away, Curse raised the rifle and fired a hipshot into the officer's midsection. The blast threw the officer back and set him off balance momentarily. Not willing to let the officer recover, Curse took a firm grip on the rifle and shoved the bayoneted muzzle upward. The officer was unable to react in time as the bayonet pierced through the flesh on the underside of his jaw and punched upward into his cranial cavity.

The officer tried to scream, but the sounds were drowned out by the sickening gurgle of ichor bubbling into his mouth. Curse gripped both hands around the stock of the rifle and raised the officer off of the ground. Having bounced from kill to kill so far with no showboating, Curse wanted to savor the existence he was about to extinguish. Ichor showered on him from above as he held the officer aloft. He was still trying to scream. Curse bared his teeth in a sadistic grin as the vital fluid of a body in the Nightmarescape splattered all over him. Through it all, the officer was still trying to move his mouth and make a legible sound. The bayonet stuck through his jaw and upper palate prevented him from doing so. Lost in the moment and the carnage, the raw pain of another, Curse felt his muscles flex and strain to keep the body in the air. The strange choked sounds of the officer filtered down to his ears as he enjoyed the moment. After the sounds fell as unintelligible garble for a brief period, he realized the officer was articulating through the blade in his mouth.

"No no no no no no no no no no no no no no no!" Over and over again the once-proud soldier begged for relief from the agony. Indeed not all wounds were immediately fatal in the Nightmarescape, but pain was as potent as it ever had been in previous lives.

The officer had most likely been in the Nightmarescape longer than Curse had lived his life; before then, the soldier had experienced the battlefields of World War II's Pacific Theater. Curse felt power tripping through him as he held such a warrior at his mercy.

The officer's hands gripped the muzzle of the rifle just above Curse's. He struggled to get a grip on the weapon so he might push himself off of it. Knowing that if he could get off of the blade, the wound would reseal itself and the pain would cease, he attempted to summon all his strength. Curse held him at an angle that prevented any leverage from being obtained. Having enjoyed the suffering this long, Curse racked the bolt of the rifle once more. He stared up at the officer for the slightest moment. The single moment slowed to forever. Curse watched the man struggling, his mouth trapped between a perpetual scream and agonized scowl. Curse could not see the man's eyes. He did not know if they were blue, red, absent, or what. It did not matter. He could see the man's agony and knew that, while he enjoyed it, he had to return to the larger battle.

The screams stopped suddenly as the crack of the rifle split the officer's head, adding skull fragments and brain tissue to the rain of ichor. The officer's body fell off of the bayonet, for there was no longer anything to hold it in place. Within moments, what had been a howling and fighting man disintegrated into a pile of dust. The warrior's weapons sat on the ground. Curse quickly reached down to retrieve the officer's Nambu pistol before tucking it into his waistband along with the revolver. He lifted the samurai sword from the ground and held it in one hand, the rifle in the other. There was no time to savor the new finds; another wave of rotten bodies surged toward him.

Curse moved just in time to avoid a pitted butcher knife flying past his head. The wielder stumbled off balance, exposing its side to Curse. A quick swing of the samurai sword removed the creature's arm. Not knowing how exactly to use such a weapon, Curse resorted to slashing wildly. He sliced with an upward motion and cut through the creature's side and spilled innards and oily ichor onto the ground in front of him. The thing hissed, and Curse kicked its legs out from under it. As it crashed to the ground, two more surged from behind it, their corroded fingers outstretched toward him.

Another wild swing from the sword sliced right through the neck of one of the creatures and had followed through the shoulder of another then into thin air once more. The decapitated creature's head hit the ground with a fleshy smack. After several moments, the other creature's shoulder and head slid off of its body and fell to the ground. Both remaining bodies quickly crumbled to dust. The head rolled around on the ground momentarily as black ichor poured from the severed neck and began to solidify into a new body. Even though the miserable wretch's head had been removed from its body, the psychic center in its brain still tied it to the realm and allowed it to reform itself.

The other that still had a piece of upper body used its remaining arm to crawl around as its body began to regenerate. Curse brought his boot down on its skull and felt the bone fracture upon impact. Hard, brittle bone gave way to soft, squishy matter that crumbled to dust. He slammed the butt of the rifle down upon the head that was trying to regenerate a body. The wooden stock smashed the thing's skull and brain, thus snuffing out its existence.

In his feverish assault on the two afflicted, Curse had neglected the first attacker. He was sorely reminded of its presence as its knife entered his left side. His flesh ripped as the blade tore into his torso and separated his ribs. Now it was Curse's turn to scream in pain as the blade was embedded deep in his chest. Its wielder hissed and gurgled through its disease-ravaged throat. Curse had to drop both weapons in his hands as the creature pushed further into him. Unable to obtain a good angle on his assailant, Curse reached for his waistband and grabbed the officer's pistol. He spun against his attacker, breaking its grip on him. Curse fired several rounds into the creature's atrophied frame. It fell back, the impact of the bullets knocking its frail body away. With the thing out of arm's range, Curse took the moment to find a grip on the handle of the blade and ripped it out of his side with no small amount of pain. Black ichor splashed out from the wound that had been created. He attempted to suck in a breath and scream, but the air bled out of the gaping wound along with the ichor. His lung was collapsing. The pain radiated through his chest as though the knife was still cutting through him. Curse gritted his teeth and doubled over on himself, emanating a low groan through the pain. Despite the pain, his rage was still strong at having been dealt such a wound.

Several moments passed. In the throes of rage, Curse could feel the wound healing. He just had to let the Nightmarescape work its will on his flesh. Within a few seconds, the wound had sealed itself. He forced his lungs to suck in a breath of air to ensure that they were working before rejoining the fight.

The plague-ridden creature was steadied now and leapt toward Curse again. Curse leveled the pistol in his hand and fired a single shot right into the creature's forehead. It fell backward from the impact, and Curse followed without hesitation by firing several more rounds that destroyed the creature's brain. It became a pile of dust like the others.

Curse surveyed his surroundings again. The attackers were slowly being driven back by the efforts of himself and the soldiers. Superior weaponry and prowess were winning out on the individual level, but their attackers' numbers were still vast. A gaggle of slavering ghouls were charging toward him again already. The soldiers he was fighting alongside were holding their own, but they were just keeping the enemies from pressing their advantage of volume. He looked back toward the howitzer and observed one of his allies speaking into a primitive telephone. The soldier's head kept leaning out from the side of the gun emplacement and surveying the battle. Moments later the soldier was on his feet and charging back toward the fight. As he ran toward several of the other soldiers, Curse heard him screaming.

"Reinforcements ten out!"

Reinforcements were definitely welcome given the circumstances. Curse found his mind wandering toward what would come to meet them. He had seen such incredible things already from numerous periods of human history. Even though the thought of what he may see next excited him, he still had a fight on his hands until they arrived. He grabbed the rifle from the ground, racked the bolt, and fired it into the mass of flesh coming toward him. One of the wretched things fell, but the others continued their advance. Curse threw himself forward and charged into those that were still standing.

A brittle ribcage splintered as Curse slammed his shoulder into the chest of the nearest creature. It flew back from the impact, a stream of black ichor trailing from its mouth as its fellows leapt upon Curse. Biting and clawing, they scrabbled for purchase on his body. His flesh was rended by sharp bony fingers and rotten teeth as they attempted to hold on to him, but his strength was superior to theirs, and he was able to tear himself free. Those that had been attempting to get a hold on him floundered upon the ground momentarily before their atrophied legs could pick them back up. In the time it took them, Curse bounded away from them and retrieved the samurai sword. The first plague-ridden body was on its feet, stumbling toward him.

"Come on, you walking carcass!" Curse bellowed in challenge.

The thing merely hissed in return and staggered for him with its hands out. Thick strings of frothy drool dribbled from its mouth and over its sunken chin. Curse came to meet it and slammed the bottom of his boot into one of its kneecaps. The thing's leg buckled beneath it with a sickening crack. A desiccated screech sounded from the thing's throat as it crashed down to the ground on its ruined leg. Curse shoved the samurai sword through its chest, pinning it to the ground. The sword ripped flesh as the thing struggled to free itself. Another body crashed into Curse, and he swung on the momentum, hurling it to the side. He threw his elbow backward and struck home on another attacker's face, bones splintering from the impact. The attacker fell to the ground, its face a shattered ruin. Two more bodies fell on Curse. He was able to shove one away, but the other dug its fingers into the flesh of his neck. Pain lanced through Curse's head and neck, but he fought through it and forced his hand to retrieve the revolver from his waistband. A blast resounded from the weapon and the attacker's head exploded outward. It staggered momentarily before falling, its fingers ripping out of Curse's flesh. The body was dust upon hitting the ground. A shotgun blast sounded near Curse, and he turned to see Larry standing over a disintegrating body with his weapon lowered.

"Good fight, eh, son?" Larry was clearly enjoying himself.

Before Curse could answer, the retort of a machine gun cut him off. Swinging his head, Curse saw two enormous tanks rumbling toward the battle. One of them bore a fifty-caliber machine gun on top of its turret. The tank resembled a modern design, sporting a large turret and wide body. An American solider wearing a flak jacket and ragged BDUs laid a storm of fire from the weapon on top. The other tank was recognizable as a rounded Sherman body, but its body was covered in all manner of scrap metal plates and spiked protrusions. A mass of warriors from throughout time periods charged behind them. Some wore pitted armor and wielded swords and maces; others wore various military uniforms and hefted firearms from different ages; some even wore the garb of long-lost civilizations and carried weapons from eons past. Bronze Age swordsmen, Egyptian warriors wielding khopeshes, Christian Crusaders, Yeomen warders, and African tribesmen carrying shields draped with tattered skins charged alongside World War I infantry, American Civil War soldiers, and modern marines wearing full battle gear. The newly arrived host bore the signs of their times, but they were a gruesome sight being that the Nightmarescape had warped them just as it did all who came to it. They appeared in shades of black and gray with their flesh rotted and their former visages twisted into those of undead specters. Blue lights stared out of empty eye sockets just as they did in Curse's head; some wore helms and gasmasks over their faces, the lights shining out from behind them.

Curse stood momentarily dumbstruck by such a host, the fight briefly forgotten. He was reminded of it when a plague-ridden body smashed into him and took him off of his feet. The desiccated sacks of bones had not been much of an individual challenge when he was focusing on them, but this one caught him off guard and was able to press its weight down on him. Reactively he shoved his hands up and caught the thing by the sides of its head as it attempted to dig its teeth into his flesh. Thick runnels of frothy drool poured from its mouth and onto Curse's face. He could feel the foulness of the creature's being as the substance hit his skin. As the thing tried to get past his guard, he stared into its face.

While most denizens of the Nightmarescape bore blue or red lights in their eye sockets, these creatures simply had empty sockets. Nothing burned inside of them. Curse remembered the British officer's words that they were basically mindless, their conscious thoughts being eroded away by the diseases that had claimed their lives. At the time of their deaths, they had been living dead for some time. The thought caused an acidic sting in Curse's chest as his rage rose once more. He wanted to utterly crush the thing on top of him. Its mindlessness offended him to no end. While he was suffering and trying to understand, this simple thing existed now because a disease had eaten its mind to the point where it could not care any longer. In some respects he envied the wretch, but his jealousy was subsumed by hatred.

Steeling himself, he found a grip on the thing's head and dug his fingers into its flesh. Its mouth still snapped and struggled to reach him, but he was able to jerk the head from side to side. If he could get the right angle, he would be able to snap the thing's brittle neck. The chance to obtain that angle never came as the back of the thing's head exploded.

Curse hurled the body aside as it crumbled to dust. Standing, he found himself before what he could tell had been an African man. The man's skin was dark, and he wore tattered safari fatigues over his body. A smoking, big bore rifle rested in his hands. His eyes shone with an ice blue intensity.

"Well met, friend; Mr. Spectre asked me to help you," the new arrival said.

"Thanks for shooting the freak. Where is Larry anyway? He was right next to me . . ."

"Mr. Spectre is saying his good-byes." To prove his point, the man pointed over to Larry slapping the British officer on the shoulder and then running their way.

"He is not, how shall we say . . . in good standing with everyone . . ."

"You don't say . . . so what was your name anyway?" Curse asked of his new acquaintance.

"I am Warden Kitenge," the man introduced himself.

"Curse . . . I'm still trying to figure out the rest." He felt stupid saying it.

"Don't worry, it will come in time," Kitenge reassured him.

Larry was upon them now, his wild eyes filled with fervor.

"Warden, good to see you again!" Larry slapped Kitenge on the shoulder and then turned to Curse. "Boy! We have to leave this romp now!" With that, he began to charge away from the advancing force.

Curse nodded to Kitenge before barreling off after Larry. As he ran, he continually turned his head to check on the battle. The cavalry had definitely arrived and were making short work of the remaining Japanese soldiers and mindless plague creatures. Larry ran into a line of sagging gray fir trees. Curse followed as Larry led them through another decayed and dark forest. The terrain became jagged and rocky as they continued to run. A ways into the forest, they came to the base of a stone outcropping. Larry rounded the face of the bluff and rested himself on the other side. He craned his head out as Curse slowed down and walked over to him.

"I didn't think you got scared of anything," Curse goaded as he approached.

"There are many loyalties here," Larry began. "There are also many old grudges. The Axis and Allies guys hate each other because they did in life. In that regard, they fight whenever they find each other. Whether there is one or a whole bunch, they fight. They do it because that's how they remember it. Hatred can cross the boundaries of life and death. When I told you earlier that I think the whole place is made of psychic energy, consider this, my boy, we're all here because of negative psychic energy. Hate, grudges, rage, sadness, apathy—they all are prime examples of things that keep this place running at full speed. The more you have in you, the stronger a presence you are."

Larry was lecturing on the metaphysics of the world again. Curse prepared himself to take in whatever the madman had to share.

"That's why some folks regenerate and get back to it so quick, like us. Some folks are easier to be rid of, like those plague fools. If they don't have enough energy to maintain their presence, then you can get rid of them easier. It's easy to be rid of someone here once you destroy their head and brain. No way to generate the energy to keep you here—your body crumbles to dust, and that's it. When I told you that you were indestructible, it was true in a certain regard. You have a stronger presence than most, but not to say you can't fall to their fate as well. You took a bullet to the head and survived, but it did not destroy your brain entirely. There was enough to regenerate a body and mind. It kept you going, kept you in the Nightmarescape."

It made sense. Even through all his lunacy, Larry was incredibly bright. Bright or not, though, it did not reveal why Larry had fled the battle.

"I understand your theory, but that doesn't explain why you ran," Curse intoned.

"As I started saying about hate and grudges and all . . . back in the days when I was able to shoot up cathouses . . . I went into one and killed a couple ladies of easy virtue and their company. Well, one of the company that I shot was the son of a Union colonel. The colonel knew it when he was alive, and he remembered it when he showed up here. Being a military guy in high standing, he gravitated toward the Archaic Front and built up a large group of cronies. You see, he recognized me and has been looking for me for a good while . . . how long have I been here . . . over a century, you said? He's been on my tail about that long. I make friends with each new generation of folks that shows up, but so does he."

"What is this Archaic Front you speak of?" Curse asked. It was something that Larry had not mentioned yet.

"Ah! They're a group of military guys from all periods of time. That was part of their number that we ran across back there. Usually the people who gravitate toward it are folks who were soldiers in life; therefore, it gives them a largely military presence. They adopted the name Archaic Front because so much of their weapons and equipment are out-dated by the standards of new generations that arrive here. The colonel that I'm not fond of has some friends in high places in the organization," Larry explained.

"And now whenever the Archaic Front moves in people you don't know, you fear they might be in league with this colonel," Curse completed for him.

"Yes! Your logic makes me proud, boy!"

"Why don't you just kill the bastard?" Curse's voice was flat and cold.

"I tend to work on my own . . . most people don't know that I have such a vendetta. Well, it's his vendetta, not mine really, but it's directed at me. It's not a fact I make known to those I hold contact with. Could be dangerous, you know? You never know whose loyalty lies where. Those English guys and the African guy back there, I know them. I'll help them fight, but by the time the reinforcements show, I'm gone. I never know if that grizzly fucker might be with 'em!"

"And you have some connections, but he has more with that group." Curse spoke for him again.

Larry nodded his bony head. "Exactly, my boy."

"What if you took care of the colonel, though? Would they still be on you?"

"That I don't know. His people might still have a sense of vengeance in mind. I will kill him eventually; he has pestered me long enough chasing after his revenge. I don't know . . . he probably has a bunch of people he knew in life here. It's all politics. This is a place of chaos, and some try to hold an order in it. That irritates me because chaos is my element." Larry's eyes showed the cold rage that he was holding inside him.

"The lives we lived in the former world, that's where order should have stayed. Some have dragged their sense of order here with them. It's discipline for a lot of them. That could be changed though . . . we need that device . . ." Larry's voice trailed off, and he seemed to be focused on something far away, something that was not quite concrete, but something that he sought to obtain nonetheless.

Curse felt the hairs on his neck standing. Someone was watching them from out in the forest. He reached for his belt and removed the revolver.

16

"Someone's keeping an eye on us," Curse said.

"Yes, they've been watching since we passed the trees. I didn't see 'em, but I feel 'em lookin' too." Larry's eyes scanned back and forth behind Curse.

Whoever was watching was close at hand, but their presence was undetectable; they exercised amazing skill in stealth. Curse turned and surveyed the dead forest behind them. Decayed and gray vegetation obscured the view past a few yards. Remembering the sniper's bullet that caught him in the head earlier, Curse eased backward while scanning. He found another large rock near the base of the outcrop and squeezed behind it to make himself a smaller target.

"You see anything, Larry?"

"Nay, son."

Curse wished that he still had the rifle from the battle. He also wished he'd found a scope to put on it. He had left the sword pinning one of the plague-afflicted to the ground. It would have been a nice relic to have, but he simply did not have time to retrieve it. He had dropped the rifle after his last attacker had leapt on him. He had not tried to retrieve it when he ran after Larry.

Kitenge had a nice rifle. It was a big game rifle with a quality scope fitted to the top. No doubt Kitenge had carried the weapon on the plains of Africa as a game warden. From his brief glimpse of the barrel, Curse guessed it to be a 30.06. Whatever the weapon was, it was not with him now. He possessed only his eyes to scan with and two handguns.

That was it . . . the eyes. So many denizens of the Nightmarescape had the glowing lights in their eye sockets. Curse scanned the dead forest for any contrast against the black and gray. At first his search was frustrating. It was possible whoever was watching lacked eyes like the plague-afflicted, or had actual eyes like Larry's, or they may have concealed their face.

His view panned across the landscape. His focus strained from tree to shrub to tree. Frustratingly he focused against the gray, and dragged his field of view through the forest. He searched near the ground and in the trees. Whoever was watching them could be anywhere. He continued straining until his attention snapped back to an area he had just passed. Several feet behind a shrub, he noticed a tiny hint of blue light emanating from between the gray leaves.

"I see them," Curse whispered.

"Where?" Larry sounded urgent.

"Eleven o'clock . . . between the tree and that bush. You can barely see the blue lights." Curse kept his attention focused on the lights, daring their owner to move and expose their position.

Now Curse wished that he had a longer barreled revolver. The lights were possibly twenty yards away. Not a great distance, but a challenging distance to place a good shot with a snub-nose barrel.

"Think they're hostile?" Curse was unsure whether he wanted to engage the target just yet.

"They've had plenty of time to do something if they are . . . they could've killed us twice over by now." Larry seemed puzzled by their stalker.

"Do you think you could hit them with your shotgun at this distance?"

"Yeah . . ." Despite the circumstances, Larry smiled widely as he replied. "I see the heathen."

Curse was cautious about engaging the stalker. If it was someone who meant them ill, he wanted to destroy them before they could mount an attack or escape and bring others. If it was someone neutral or seeking to help them, then he wanted to know who it was. If he made contact with them and they angered him, he would kill them.

"Larry, I'm going to move up. Cover me, and if they move, go ahead and shoot."

Curse looked over to see Larry already had the shotgun trained on the spot. A huge grin was splayed across his face.

"I guess that means you're on board," Curse said softly as he began to move.

Keeping his knees bent and his body close to the ground, he kept the gun out in front of him at a low ready. Slowly he took one step after another and made his way to the next thing that would pass for cover. He placed himself behind a large tree trunk and peered out at his point of focus.

He could still see the lights. Curse was sure their owner was aware of his approach. He moved for the next piece of cover, a hollowed stump. While it would not provide much if bullets began flying, it would allow him a spot to reassess the situation. He craned his head along the side of the stump and observed that his target had not moved.

They were separated by only about ten yards now. This was where the situation became tense, for Curse was unaware of what weaponry might be aimed at him as he moved. He was close to the stalker, but he could not know their intentions. His hands trained the revolver on the set of eyes behind the shrub and moved again. This time he moved to the outside of his path slightly and took a position behind a fallen log. He was going to attempt to maneuver around his quarry. Hopefully Larry would keep them pinned down with fire if they moved.

For a brief period, Curse lost sight of the stalker's position, but he knew they would still be there when he finished sneaking around them. He moved quietly, his boots stepping on dead leaves. The forest was silent and still around him. Then again, the forest was dead, and this was the Nightmarescape. Larry had said it was a place created of human mental energy. That meant there were no bugs, birds, or animals to make sounds in a forest. He wondered briefly if the Archaic Front had cavalrymen, and if so, whether their horses reappeared with them. He quickly dismissed the thought and returned to focusing on the task at hand.

Rounding another tree, he finally saw what he was looking for. The stalker's back was turned to him. Their frame was thin but lean. A mane of dreadlocks fell over their back. He could not tell yet if he was looking at a male or female. He would need to get closer for a better look. Swiftly he began closing the distance between himself and the other. He was about five yards away. He had maintained a brisk and quiet pace, until he took a heavy step and snapped a small branch that was in his path.

The sound resounded throughout the forest like a gunshot. The stalker whirled around and aimed an automatic pistol straight at him.

"Damn," Curse growled to himself.

Cold blue lights much like his own shined out from empty eye sockets and froze him in his path. She was every bit as terrible looking as he was. Her face was also deathly and covered with pallid gray skin. Her body was lean and muscular. The dreadlocks he had observed from behind fell around her neck and shoulders. She wore a torn sleeveless shirt over her upper torso. It was cut around the end of her ribs and showed her bare stomach which bore several hideous puncture wounds. Black ichor from the wounds bled down onto a pair of pants that had been ripped off about knee level. Her legs and feet were bare below the pants. Curse looked at the weapon she held in her hand and noticed that her forearms were wrapped in barbed wire.

"Who the hell are you?" Curse growled at her.

"You answer that for me," she replied evenly.

"Why were you stalking us?" he demanded.

"What are you doing in my woods?" She was studying him, trying to determine what he was going to do.

Curse still held his revolver aimed at her as she held her pistol trained on him. Curse noticed Larry was moving up behind her with his shotgun at the ready. Curse hoped that Larry could remain stealthy enough to get a good drop on the female. Hopefully he would not start giggling the moment he was able to get close.

"What is your friend doing?" She asked as though she had been reading his thoughts.

"He's still covering me," Curse lied.

"You're a terrible liar." She smiled slightly for the first time. It seemed almost as though she was attempting to play with him. Not necessarily to enrage him and throw him off guard, but to disarm the situation.

He did not trust her enough to lower his weapon. She probably did not trust him enough to lower hers. Whether he lowered his weapon or not, Larry was still sneaking up behind her, and she knew it. Curse weighed his options. If she did turn her back to him so that she could confront Larry, he could grab her from behind. For some reason, he did not want to kill her.

He thought back to the first woman he had encountered in the Nightmarescape. She had been so wraithlike and sad. He had seen much of his own situation in her, and it angered him to the point where he lost control of himself and unleashed every ounce of violence within him upon her. This situation was different however. For one thing, he felt a higher degree of control over himself. While still prone to rage and melancholy, he had a better handle on how his emotions affected him. Larry's counseling had helped some and having been in battle recently and vindicating himself against the plague-afflicted helped also.

Curse could very faintly hear Larry's footfalls as he crept up behind the female. The smile left her face as she whirled around to train her weapon on him, only to find herself staring down his double-barreled shotgun.

"Really now, who do you think is going to win this one?" Larry grinned from ear to ear; he was just waiting for a reason to pull the trigger and snuff her essence out. Curse knew why he had not yet. He was watching Curse, letting him interact with her, studying him. Now that she was turned to Larry, he was waiting to see what Curse was going to do behind her back. If it had been Larry alone, he would have shot her long ago.

Curse did not want her shooting at either of them, yet he did not want to harm her. He placed the revolver in his waistband once more and charged toward the female's backside. She heard him coming and attempted to wheel herself around in time to do something, but her feet left the ground as Curse slammed his weight into her and wrapped his arms around her in a firm hold. At first she struggled to kick out of his grip. When she was unable to break his hold, she attempted to place her pistol against his torso. His grip held her arms down to where she could not raise the weapon. She resorted to firing several rounds downward in an attempt to graze him. He whirled her around and took her to the ground.

Curse pressed his weight against her back as she struggled with the weapon. Curse brought his fist down on her smaller hand and sent a shock of pain up her arm. Her throat unleashed an ear-piercing scream as her fingers dropped the gun. Curse quickly seized her free hand and pinned it behind her back. He did the same with her other arm and then hooked both of his arms through her arms to pin her down in a full nelson hold.

Earth flew out from under the female's body as she struggled on the ground against Curse's weight. The barbed wire on her forearms dug into the flesh of Curse's arms as she struggled against him. Curse endured the pain with a grunt and held his grip. She opened her mouth again and emitted another scream. The woods had been quiet save the sound of their struggle. Her scream resonated through the air, and Curse felt the vibrations in his own head and body cavity. Sound waves rushed through him, and he felt as though his head was going to explode. Despite the earsplitting shriek, he gritted his teeth and continued to press her down. She was trying to build the scream into a deafening crescendo. He felt as though his eardrums were going to burst against her sonic onslaught.

The woods fell quiet again, her scream becoming an echo before dying out as the sounds coming from her mouth were replaced by a choked growl. Curse turned his head up slightly to observe Larry standing over both of them with his shotgun shoved into her mouth.

"Perhaps you should be quiet now, my dear." Larry spoke with a threatening tone. Curse could tell that he still wanted to kill her, that he would love nothing more than to pull the trigger and turn her head into numerous fragments.

"Calm down," Curse snarled in her ear. "Don't give him a reason." His words struck a chord with her, and she rested beneath his weight.

"Larry, do you mind?" Curse asked. Larry pulled his shotgun from her mouth.

"Why are you doing this to me?" she hissed.

"You stalked us and trained your weapon on us—are you really asking?"

"Get off!" She struggled against the ground again, attempting to throw Curse from her back.

She was becoming panicked. He steeled his grip on her and squeezed her between his arms. Curse removed his left arm and placed his hand over her mouth before she could scream again. She struggled against him, trying to move, but was only able to free her arm to a point where there was little she could do with it. Larry reached his foot out and kicked away the pistol she had dropped.

"Let's be done with this one, my boy!" Larry was itching to kill.

Curse did not know what had happened to Larry in life, but he seemed to relish in murdering women. Perhaps the woman he had convinced to kill herself had moved him in some way he failed to realize. Maybe he had been hurt by a woman and simply turned his rage toward all of them. Whatever his reasons, the grand misogynist would have to cool his hatred for the time being. Curse knew that there was something special about this woman just as Larry had seemed to know he was special in some capacity.

"We ran from a fight that broke out a way back." Curse spoke to her firmly. "We ran into these woods and took cover behind the rocks, trying to figure a few things out. I noticed you were following us and attempted to investigate. So I ask you now, why were you stalking us?"

The female calmed and ceased her struggle as she listened to him. Upon completing his question, he removed his hand from her mouth. She paused momentarily as though she were trying to compose herself and speak. She seemed traumatized by his seizure of her.

"You came into my forest. I was watching you . . . you both came armed. I did not know what you were doing here," she exhaled as she finished. "Please get off of me."

"If I do, what will happen?" Curse inquired.

"Nothing . . . I'll tell you whatever you ask . . . just get off of me," she offered. With due caution, Curse removed his arms and eased his weight off of her back.

Lacerations stung his arms where her barbed wire had grazed him, but they were closing themselves as he moved away. The female scrambled from under him and placed her back against the nearest tree before hugging her knees to her chest and staring up to her captors.

"I saw the battle," she began. "I was watching from the edge of the woods. I saw the two of you running in here, and I didn't know who you were, so I kept an eye on you. You were armed. I thought perhaps you'd seen me and come looking for me."

Curse knelt down, so that he was face-to-face with her. She pulled back almost as though his gaze could touch her.

"We were unaware of you and did not come to you with hostile intent," he said. "As I'm sure you're aware, this is a dangerous place and trust is in short supply. You see, just a short while ago, a sniper hiding in a forest like this one shot me."

She seemed to digest his words before choosing her own to respond.

"I feel the same way. You freaked me out more than you ever could with the guns by holding me like that though . . ." She turned her head, letting it hang as though she were ashamed.

Curse reached out, placed his fingers under her chin, and brought her eye sockets back to his own. He felt her pain in that moment and knew that she would be crying if she still had eyes.

The empathy warmed him. Despite being a creature of negative energy, he could still feel like a human.

"I realize that now, but it was either that or shoot you. None of us were dropping our weapons," he rationalized.

She nodded in validation of his point, but she did not say anything further. Curse realized he was going to have to keep the conversation moving.

"What are you protecting back here?" he asked.

"The forest itself," she responded.

Now that was something that seemed strange. The forest was dead. Everything in the Nightmarescape was dead. Why she was protecting a bunch of rotting vegetation made no sense.

"I'm confused," Curse said levelly.

Behind him, he heard Larry's voice humming softly and booted footfalls in the earth. The female had craned her head and wore an expression of disbelief on her face. Curse turned to glimpse Larry humming to himself and dancing in the dirt.

"Hee haw, hee haw, hee haw." Larry spoke quietly to no one as his heels struck the ground. He turned his gaze down as they both looked at him. "Don't mind me, kids!" He continued the strange dance.

"Larry Spectre, my traveling companion," Curse said. "He might seem strange at first, but give him a chance, and his eccentricities will grow on you."

A hint of a smile crossed her face. "That's when he's not putting a gun in your face, right?" The slight humor from earlier had returned to her voice.

"He does that to everyone, don't take offense." Her smile grew at his reply. "If I might ask . . . what is worth protecting in this forest? It's already dead from the looks of things."

"I just protect it because that's what I did when I was alive." She looked regretful.

"Ah, yes . . . when we were alive as you put it . . . I'm still trying to remember my story."

"It will come back in time. My name was Rayna. I used to protect the environment . . . only my method of protection was a little different from most environmentalists." She smiled, taking pride in the statement. "I used to actually *do something* and that often meant attacking or killing the people who were hurting things."

"You can hurt an environment!?" Larry boomed from above them.

Rayna looked at him as though he were a fool.

"Pollution doesn't seem relevant here," Curse said it to her as much a question as a statement.

"From what I can see it's not, but I hold onto the ideals because they're what keep me going."

"Just how did you get here, Rayna?" Curse was intrigued by her story now.

He knew Larry's story and had been learning his own tale as it unfolded. Now there was another person for him to communicate with and potentially learn from.

She hung her head and sighed. He could tell that the memories would be painful for her to relive, but he needed to persist in order to understand her.

17

Rayna shifted her weight and looked up at them before beginning her recollection. "There was a deer population that the hunters were hitting really hard out of season. They almost wiped the poor creatures out. The wardens and rangers were being paid off to look the other way, so I went with some friends, and we began hunting the hunters to give the deer a chance. As you noticed, I'm not too bad a hunter myself, but that comes from hunting people. It was autumn, and we killed several hunters one day, but they were part of a larger group. The remaining hunters found me . . . one of my friends got away . . . the other two were shot and killed on the spot, but I was injured, and they were determined to make me pay for killing their friends . . ."

She trailed off and stared at the ground for several moments before raising her head again. Curse tried to look as reassuring as he could. She exhaled again and continued.

"I remember when they found me. I tried to run, but one of them had shot me in the back of my leg. I tried to drag myself away, but they were faster than I could be. They beat the hell out of me first with their fists and rifle stocks. There was a barbed wire fence, and they wrapped my arms in it so that I couldn't move." She shuddered and looked up to Curse once more. "One of them . . . he pulled my pants down . . . then he forced himself into me . . . I screamed and tried to pull away, but the fence held me. I tried to rip my arms from the barbed wire—I didn't care then if I ripped all of the flesh off . . . I just wanted to get away. Then another one took his turn . . ." She hung her head and screamed again. It was not the same as it had been before. Instead of an ear-piercing shriek that shook all around it, this one pierced the soul and sang her anguish.

Curse allowed her to force the emotion from her body. She looked up to him again and yelled, "Why am I telling you all of this! I don't even know you . . ." He placed a hand on her shoulder.

"Because you and I are similar; I knew it the moment I saw you. That's why I didn't try to kill you. My name is Curse, by the way."

"You're the only one who's truly spoken to me since I've been here . . . I've tried to stay to my own. It's so hard to trust anyone here." She was rambling now, the weight of her experience crashing upon her. Briefly she ceased her breakdown and looked at Curse in puzzlement.

"Did you say your name was Curse? What the hell kind of name is that? What was your real name?"

"I don't know yet . . . Larry named me Curse . . . sounds good to me . . ."

Larry imposed himself beside the two of them. "Yeah and now I'm gonna call you Banshee for that hootin' and hollerin' you like to do!"

Curse smiled at her, hoping to soften the mood. "Banshee . . . appropriate. How did you learn to scream like that anyway?"

"I've been able to do it since I woke up here . . . when those rednecks were raping me, I screamed the whole time . . . I could hear my own screams reverberating across the mountains. I can't remember how many there were . . . several more . . . I kept screaming . . . when they were done, they did this . . ."—her hand passed over the wounds in her belly—"and then they left . . . they left me trapped there, and I just kept screaming until my voice was ragged . . . I could feel the blood pouring out of me . . . I remember my consciousness fading as my blood left me. I passed out and woke up here . . ."

Curse rubbed a hand through her dreadlocks. The gesture was intended to be comforting. Curse felt a slight pang of guilt for having brought the experience back to her.

"Want to get them back?" he asked her.

"How?" The lights in her eye sockets burned as she asked the question.

"Larry might have a way, if we can get our hands on it," Curse said. "We don't know where it is yet, but there might be a device that allows passage back to the other world."

She looked at him skeptically. Curse was not even sure he believed it entirely either. Larry seemed committed to the idea that the thing existed though. Curse continued speaking.

"If we can get our hands on it, I can find my lover, you can have revenge, and Larry . . . well . . ." Curse turned and saw Larry grinning down at him in anticipation of what he might say. "Larry can see how things have changed over the last hundred years or so."

"What is it, and where do we look for it?" she asked.

"It's somewhere here!" Larry thrust his finger into the air.

"Well . . . even if we don't find it or it doesn't exist, my time would be better spent chasing something than guarding a forest that's already dead." Banshee stood with the statement.

"Now I have two young'uns to look after . . ." Larry trailed off.

"I have to get some things before I go with you though," she said.

Larry and Curse consented to go with her to retrieve her possessions. Curse picked up the pistol he had knocked out of her hand earlier and returned it to her. She placed it in the back of her waistband and led them off into the forest. After several minutes of travel, they came to an old barbed wire fence strung between several trees. They followed the length of wire until they came to a macabre nest of sorts. The strands of wire twisted down and wrapped around each other in the shape of a human body. Black ichor that would have been blood in their former reality stained the wire. Curse could tell that this was where Banshee had awoken. Banshee slid past him, trying not to look at the wire that had held her in death, and bent down to remove a small backpack and an M1 carbine from behind a tree.

"Larry, do you know where we're going?" Curse asked.

"I don't know this area too good; I want to stay away from the fight for the time being in case the colonel shows up. What's on the other side of this forest?" Larry asked Banshee.

She thought for a moment. "There's a crumbling old fort back that way." She motioned over her shoulder. "I've been back there several times, and I don't believe I've seen anyone there yet. Not to say they won't come back, but we could try to hide out there for a while."

"Interesting . . . what kind of fort are we talkin'?" Larry inquired.

"I don't know . . . medieval . . . it looks like a small castle. The only thing is we have to run through a stretch of war zone to get there."

"War zone?" Curse asked.

"It looks like somewhere in Europe from the forties," she said shrugging. "There are a few people in it that are still fighting, but they don't tend to stray out from what I've seen . . . they just stay in the same place, fighting the same fight over and over again."

"And they don't make their way to the fort ever? Sounds like some rubes to me . . ." Larry was as chipper as ever now.

"Like I said, I'm not entirely sure—that's just what I have seen of them. Sometimes I'll creep up to the edge of the forest and just watch them . . . it's the same soldiers. They shoot each other, fall down, get up, their wounds heal, they seek cover, and keep at it. I've never tried to make contact or anything . . . it's almost as though they're in their own world in the midst of all this." Banshee fanned her hands out at the world around them.

"Let's get going then and see what's ahead of us." Curse began walking.

The three of them fell into step beside one another. Curse stood in the middle with Larry to his left and Banshee to his right. Larry utilized the time to explain his theories about the Nightmarescape to Banshee in his typical grandiose fashion. She listened and thought upon his points. Banshee admitted that she did not find him to be the scientific type at first. Curse could tell she was still cautious of Larry, and he could not blame her given the circumstances under which she had met him.

When Larry was done with his lecturing, Banshee told them the story of her life in depth. She remembered more than Curse, which led him to believe that she had been in the Nightmarescape longer, and he would have guessed that she died before him. Her story was an interesting one. As she had told them earlier, she was an environmentalist who used destructive action to stop what she perceived as ecological wrongdoings. She had killed for the first time at seventeen and had met her own end five years later. As Larry postulated, she had begun having dreams about the Nightmarescape while she was alive and awoke within it upon the death of her corporeal self. Though she had committed numerous acts of violence for the benefit of her cause, the only time she was caught for any of it was when the hunters in the mountains had taken her life.

Curse shared what he had remembered about his own death with the two of them. He told Larry about how he had woken from the memory-driven dream with the revolver in his hand. Larry was overjoyed and began another sermon about objects in the Nightmarescape.

"Ah, your own revolver, the first material possession to materialize along with you, out of your own memory. You see, when you had that flashback, your sense of memory was so strong that in addition to your manifested body, you manifested the object as well. Most items that exist here were things folks had been holding onto or using at the moment of their deaths. This shotgun, well, I dragged it through the desert with me, even used it as a crutch a few times. Banshee's guns and backpack, those were most likely on her when she got caught by the jerks," Larry explained.

Banshee nodded in agreement.

Nightmarescape

"Now, as for that other pistol you have, boy,"—he indicated the Japanese officer's pistol that Curse still possessed—"that's an item you took from someone else. Ya see, they got destroyed, but you still had their item, so it became a part of your being. A lot of times weapons and stuff just end up disappearing sometime after their owners get killed. Sometimes they stick around a bit, but not forever. Now I have a bunch of guns and whatnot back at the farmhouse, but they continue to exist because I have taken them into my possession, and they are now a part of my being here. I remember them, and it keeps them here."

Larry looked to both Curse and Banshee who were nodding their heads. Satisfied that they were paying attention like engaged pupils, he continued. "Now, you have no control over the things you bring into this world, and they will only come from memory. Some people try to think of things that they did not have in life to try and manifest them, but it never works. The items only come from memories and occupied physical permanence at some point."

Another mystery of the Nightmarescape was explained to them. The three of them strode quietly for a time, Larry allowing Curse and Banshee to meditate upon what he had told them. The forest began to thin, and somewhere in the distance ahead of them a machine gun sounded.

"All right, we're getting close." Banshee ducked her body low to the ground, and the others followed her lead.

18

Up ahead, the woods cleared and revealed a small, war-torn village. It came into view as a collection of crumbling brick buildings and narrow cobbled streets. Curse thought it strongly resembled something from a World War II documentary. The buildings appeared to have suffered heavy bombing, and all that stood in some places were sections of brick walls with piles of rubble climbing up onto them. The burned-out shell of an automobile sat in the middle of an intersection. Remnants of war littered the ground between the buildings. Sparse gunfire rattled from behind the walls and between alleys. Shouts rang out intermittently when the gunfire was not sounding. Curse watched as several forms darted from one building to another and hid from sight once more.

"That should be our opening," Banshee spoke almost in a whisper. "Let's move up and follow along the right side of the town that they just moved from."

Bursts of furious gunfire from a short-range firefight exploded through the air as the three of them hurried down toward the village. As they ran, Curse looked up and observed that the fort they were trying to reach was on the backside of the settlement. Trying to see if there was a way around the localized arena, Curse observed that two steep cliffs surrounded the village on either side. They would have to move through the narrow valley in order to reach their destination.

The idea that the combatants in the village would not take up positions in the fort seemed preposterous to Curse. Perhaps it belonged to someone other than the two forces. How buildings and landscapes came to be in the Nightmarescape was still somewhat a mystery. It could be that they were like objects, just springing forth from the land that already existed as they were remembered. Curse resolved to ask Larry his opinion on the matter later when they weren't walking into a war zone.

Banshee led them into the village from the far right side as she had said she would do. Gunfire and shouting continued as they made their way around the first building and into cover. The trio ducked into a ragged hole in a wall and hid inside the building. They found themselves in a room that looked as though it had been a living quarters at one point. A dining set made of dark, rickety wood sat in front of a disused sink and counter. Banshee made her way to a window on the far side of the room and peeked out into the streets. Moments later, she returned to Curse and Larry.

"They're several streets up; we should duck back out and keep moving," she whispered.

None disagreed, and they were back outside and moving within seconds. Banshee now carried her rifle down at a low ready; Larry did the same with his shotgun. Curse only had the revolver in hand and another pistol stowed as a backup. He was slightly outgunned, but he had not let that stop him yet. If he could get close enough to one of the soldiers in the ruins, he could possibly get one of their weapons. For the time being, he followed behind Banshee.

She halted as they came to another alley that ran between two buildings and stuck her head out to observe what the soldiers were doing. Satisfied that they were not a threat at this point, she motioned for the other two to follow her. The sounds of fighting intensified as they ran across the alley and behind another group of buildings. They could hear the bullets zinging around on the other side. If they could hug the road on the outside of the village, getting to the fort would prove to be little trouble.

Coming to another alley, Banshee stuck her head out and shrieked as a stray round ricocheted up from the ground and grazed the side of her face. She fell back behind the building and bit back a scream. A gory, dark chasm had been opened just below her right cheek. The wound throbbed as black ichor overflowed the chasm and trailed down her face.

Curse watched her grit her teeth to avoid making another sound. Several seconds had passed, and her wound was slowly sealing itself. She did not seem to heal as fast as he did. Why that was seemed irrelevant at the moment. She was steadying herself and indicated to the other two that she was ready to move again. Whether any of the combatants had heard her cry out or not, none of them could be sure. They would have to exercise even more caution.

All three of them ran across the alleyway that had been the avenue to the stray bullet. Curse felt the violence building inside of him again. He wanted to join their fight. His rage was digging at his psyche, trying to claw its way through his superego and pirate his conscious mind. He told it to wait, that there would be more bloodshed soon enough, but his anger was making him impatient. He did not know where the rage had come from so suddenly, but then he realized it had begun to burn because he had heard Banshee scream.

It made sense. Even though he was prone to violence and bouts of psychotic behavior, he had come to care for Larry and, much more recently, Banshee. Larry had proven himself to be a father figure and mentor thus far. Curse knew that without his help and guidance, he would quite possibly be dust by now. In Banshee, he saw a kindred spirit, and even though he had not known her long, he would fight for her. While quite possibly not as explosive as he was, she was also a young presence in the Nightmarescape that had recently endured the things he was currently experiencing. He would protect them both as though they were his own because they were all he had. He remembered how he felt earlier when he touched her—human again. Despite the fact that they were twisted, undead mockeries of their former selves, they still had feelings on the inside. Curse was easily consumed by his anger, but he could still feel other emotions as well.

He put such things aside for the moment as he took a hold of his rage and focused on the task at hand. Banshee skidded to a halt in front of him as she came to yet another alley. She looked out once more and watched as several soldiers were fighting in the street on just the other side. The sounds of the fight echoed through the alley. She watched as two small forces of French and German soldiers fought one another. One of them would get shot, fall, and then stand back up and back out of the fight for a moment before returning. They did this over and over, continually repeating the process, trading shot for shot and blow for blow. It was almost as if they were replaying the same battle, never wanting it to end.

Seeing that the town's inhabitants were too busy focusing on their own fight, Banshee ran ahead with the others close behind her. They had reached the last building at the edge of the village. Now they would have to make their way up to the fort.

The fort itself sat on top of a large hill. A winding rock-strewn road had been cut into the side of the hill and led up to the fort. Together the three of them broke from the buildings and charged for the path. Several shouts erupted as they charged past an open part of the village, and the soldiers were finally able to see them. A French soldier was the first to spot the outsiders and make their presence known. The opposing German soldier shot him in the belly. Seconds later, the French soldier was up off the ground and fighting a fierce melee with his adversary.

Curse watched the fight with a craned neck as he ran behind the others. It seemed as though they were only concerned with their own small fight. Whatever their reasons for fighting the same battle forever, Curse did not really care. They had their goals to focus on, and he and his companions had theirs. The three of them continued at their brisk pace up along the road to the doors of the fort.

Upon reaching the doors, Curse wondered how long the structure had been left unattended. The doors were nothing more than huge pieces of dark, rotting timber falling off of enormous hinges. A strange sense of unease crept into him as he looked at the walls and found the stones to be loosely hanging in place, the mortar between them seemingly little more than dust. The whole place reeked of decay and neglect, even for a setting in the Nightmarescape. So far it made Larry's decrepit old farmhouse look like a luxury hotel.

The interior of the fort looked even worse. Filthy debris was littered across the pitted stone floors. Banshee seemed momentarily taken back by the conditions inside.

"It wasn't like this last time I was in here . . . it was just old . . . all this decay is new . . . it looks like the whole building is rotting away," she spoke quietly as if her voice would disturb the disgusting surroundings.

Curse and Larry simply shrugged and did not bother to ask questions. They would briefly search for anything of use and then seek refuge in the crumbling walls for a brief while.

Curse moved toward an old stone stairwell that led downward. Banshee followed close at his heels. Larry grinned and followed as well. They had no idea what they might encounter in this dank keep. Curse led the way down, and they were swallowed by darkness. There was no light on the stairs, but when they reached the bottom, a barred window let in a small amount of light from outside. It was all that the perpetually gray skies could offer. It illuminated a hallway flanked by doors on both sides. The doors were similar to the large entrance to the fort, dried and rotted.

Curse moved to the first one and tried the handle; it opened smoothly, albeit with a creak that scratched out across the air and sounded like a scream in the dead silence. Curse eased his way into the darkness. A tiny bit of gray light poured in through the doorway, and he observed a pile of wooden crates stacked against the back wall. He moved toward them and quietly pulled one of them down. Lacking any tools and not wanting to disturb the silence, he dug the bony tips of his fingers between the top of the crate and the box itself. He found the wood to be as rotten as that of the doorway, and the nails slipped away with no challenge.

Inside was an old projector case and a long tubular container for a screen. A single canister of film lay beside the other objects. Curse pulled the objects out of the container, overturned the crate, and set the projector case on top of it. His hands felt over the case until he was able to open it and expose an old-time projector. He then removed the film canister and worked feverishly to secure the film onto the projector's reels. A strange sense of magnetic purpose guided his actions with the projector. He knew that it was unwise to be spending more time in this place than he had to, but something possessed him to work the device.

"Curse, what are you doing?" Banshee's whisper sounded as loud as a shout in the silence.

"There's something I need to check out," he said simply. "You and Larry clear this hallway and come back to this room in a few minutes. I need to see something on this film . . ." With that, he gently shut the door in front of her and returned to his task.

The room was now completely dark, but it was small enough and Curse had enough spatial awareness that he could avoid the crate and find the screen canister. He deftly removed it from its case and expanded the frame on the back of it. Once everything was in place, he reached down and flicked the switch to start the projector.

Light flooded into the room as the projector wound the film with a clicking sound. The film quality was grainy, but it was in full color . . . the first thing in the Nightmarescape that had any color other than the ghostly lights in open eye sockets. Before him, Curse was watching what looked to be a home movie. It felt familiar . . . then he remembered. It was one of his own memories that he was watching.

He watched a former vision of himself standing beside the woman from his earlier dream. They were walking together in a park. He now saw both himself and the woman in full. They stood hand in hand. He had been a scary specimen even before the Nightmarescape had warped him into a monster. He stood at the same height, tight muscles rippling over his body. His hair was cropped down to his scalp, almost bald. Even though he was happy in the film with his love, he looked into his own eyes and saw an essence of repressed violence. He was young in the memory . . . late twenties. She was similar in age, but opposite in demeanor. Her face showed a beautiful smile that betrayed nothing more than happiness. Long, sandy blonde hair fell down over her back and around her shoulders. She was clothed in a simple black dress that came down to her knees. He was wearing a tight black T-shirt and camouflage shorts. Just barely, he could make out the outline of a pistol under his shirt. They seemed juxtaposed to one another as Curse stared at the film. He felt distant from it even though it played over in his own mind. He watched as he held the woman close and kissed her; it was genuine, but he now felt as though it was something he would not do at the present. His own memories felt alien to him.

Suddenly the film cut to a scene of an apartment. The same woman was packing a bag with clothing from a dresser. She now wore a loose white shirt and jeans. Tears streamed from her eyes.

"I can't do it anymore; I don't feel safe here." Her voice sounded far away as it echoed out of the projector.

In the memory, Curse found his hand reaching up for her without thought. He wanted to tell her not to go, but instead he sat back and said nothing.

"I still love you . . . I want the best for you . . . but I can't . . . can't . . ." She spoke in quick breaths.

"I understand," he found himself saying along with the projection, reliving the memory in his head as it played out before him.

The projection went white for a moment, and the next image was of his body lying slumped over, his head dripping blood out of one side. Where he had relived it through his own eyes the first time, he now saw it through a third-person point of view. It was as though he was watching crime scene footage of his own suicide. It felt empty to see. Most would recoil in horror and disgust, but he already knew this part of the story, and it only felt hollow and distant to him.

The projection went blank again for several seconds before leading into another memory. It was through his own eyes again, and he sat in the passenger seat of a vehicle. A voice sounded beside him, and he turned to see someone in the driver's seat.

"We know that he comes to this house; his girlfriend is in there with him now. We cranked on her earlier, and she told us he would be over. Whether she's tipped him off or not, I can't say," the man in the driver seat said.

Curse recognized him. James. They had worked together as bail bondsmen gathering fugitives. Curse remembered his work with James. He remembered when James died too. It now played in front of his eyes as the projector rolled the memory. Together they approached a door. Two local police officers had responded with them and were there to back them up. James knocked on the door. It opened, and Curse saw the same female from an earlier flashback. The same woman he had shot in the head with a shotgun.

She let James in first, and that was when Curse heard the gunshots. James fell back out of the doorway, several holes punched in his chest. Not a big deal, for his bulletproof vest would have stopped those. What was a problem, however, was the gaping hole in his neck that sprayed blood like a geyser. Curse grabbed the back of James's shirt and dragged him back out of the doorway. James left a slick trail of blood on the ground as he was dragged. Curse was fast enough to pull his comrade back behind their sport utility vehicle. Several bullets punctured the opposite side of the vehicle. Angry screams rang from the house before the door was slammed shut.

Curse reached into the SUV and grabbed the shotgun that he had left sitting across the front seat. The officers began yelling at him. He remembered the situation now. They were supposed to apprehend a male inside the location. He did not care to wait for the officers as they ran behind him yelling.

Gripping the shotgun in his hands, Curse charged for the door. He remembered the feelings well; violence and rage burned in his chest as he hungered for vengeance. As in his earlier memory, he blew the handle out of the door and then kicked it in. The man that they had gone to apprehend was standing behind the couch. His hands reached behind his back. He had tried to hide his weapon, but Curse's shotgun blew him off of his feet. The woman then shrieked and ran toward him. He remembered her words from his previous flashback, her anger and grief over what he had done. His rage would not allow her to live either. Her head exploded as he remembered, but this memory was not as dramatic as the last. She simply fell, her head hitting the floor with a wet thud. Curse slammed another round into the chamber of his weapon and remembered that another man had been in the room as well. He found the man standing with his back to the wall and his hands up. He was just a skinny redneck wearing baggy pants and a tank top. A feral growl grated from Curse's throat as he trained his weapon on the man.

"Take it easy, bro, you got me . . ."

Curse watched the film and a smile crossed his face.

"Indeed." The shotgun unleashed a final blast as the man's white tank top turned red. He was thrown against the wall from the concussive blast, chunks of plaster breaking from the wall and falling around his body. A fountain of blood bubbled from his mouth as he fell to the ground and bled out upon the floor.

Curse knew the rest of the story now. He had not simply killed in cold blood. He was fueled by vengeance. He had taken the life of James's killer, but he could not let the other two live. The rage that ate at his core had seen to it that would not happen. The shootings were deemed reckless but clean. He was allowed to walk away with no pending charges.

Mentally it had affected him in ways he had not comprehended. While he was vindicated, he struggled with losing James. What he could not have foreseen was how his lover would struggle with the killings.

While he felt justified, she thought him a monster. He knew that she could not understand, for she had not been there, but it hurt him all the same. He felt distant. His own emotions were spinning out of control. Often he would put holes in the wall with his fist for no apparent reason. She was afraid of him. He knew it, but he could not control it. That was why she had left. Already in a pit of despair and rage, her leaving pushed him over the edge. He had taken the gun to his head with a clear mind. He simply did not see another way out and no longer had the patience to wait until his soul healed.

Curse realized that the projector had been showing only light for a few minutes. He stood frozen for the moment, thinking about what had been his life. The power of the memories hit him, and his body felt heavy. It was time to move though; he had spent enough time here. So that nobody else could observe his memories on the projector, he picked it up from the crate and slammed it into the wall, sending a rain of metal pieces to the floor.

He turned around to see the door opening. Expecting to see Larry or Banshee, he was caught off guard when he saw an unfamiliar woman. Instead of Banshee's long dreadlocks, he saw straight dark hair that reached only the woman's jaw line. Instead of appearing as a typical resident of the Nightmarescape, she looked like a normal woman. There was no color to her being—she too existed in black and white—but she lacked the rotted appearance of most others. The only thing that marked her as a specter beside her lack of color was that blue lights burned in place of pupils in her eyes. In a heartbeat, he grabbed his revolver and raised it level with the woman's head.

20

"Who are you?" Curse growled.

She turned and ran. Curse bolted through the door after her. The once-silent corridor was now filled with the sounds of pursuit. Curse's heavy footfalls stomped after her while soft footfalls echoed in her wake. He wondered where Larry and Banshee were—surely they must have heard the chase. Perhaps she had killed both of them and then come to find him. She did not look like a dangerous adversary, but then again, that really did not mean anything. He followed at her heels as she rounded a corner into another hallway that was immersed in darkness.

The woman's footsteps still sounded directly in front of him, but he could not see anything. He ducked his head and kept his hands out in front of him should he collide with anything in the dark. The footsteps ahead made an abrupt turn, and he heard them moving to his left down another corridor. His reaction time in the darkness was hindered, however, and he felt his arms slam into a stone wall. After letting out a swear under his breath, Curse resumed his chase. She had gained distance in the brief seconds that the wall stopped him. Pumping his legs to move faster, he sought to close that distance. Longer legs giving him the advantage, he was back upon her in no time. Another abrupt turn—this time to the right—and Curse followed the sound without a moment lost.

There, at the end of the corridor, dim gray light shined on the walls. The woman's silhouette came into view as Curse pounded after her. The light was coming from a room off to the right at the corridor's end. The woman sped toward it and turned to run through the doorway. Curse was right behind her but stopped when he ran through the doorway to find himself on a narrow stone walkway surrounding a pit of opaque black water.

The walkway was only several feet wide and wrapped around the room. Connected stairways led up to other levels. The female was running for one of the stairways. Curse regarded the pit with due caution. It was sunken deep into the floor, mere feet of space existing between the edge of the walkway and the surface of the water. Decrepit ladders dropped down into the water from different points on the walk, and corroded chains hung down into it from somewhere up above. Dark streaking stains colored the stones between the edge of the walkway and the surface of the water.

Immediately Curse felt danger emanating from the liquid. Everything stayed quiet as he resumed his chase of the woman at a careful pace, but he could not help thinking of some unseen threat that was concealed beneath the surface of that dark quagmire.

It could have been a monstrous beast that existed from someone's fears, for the pit was almost an eighty-foot square if his eyesight judged correctly. Maybe it was just a hiding place for some massive weapon. Whatever was in there, he dismissed it from his mind and barreled after the woman. She was almost up the first flight of stairs when he reached the bottom. His legs took him up the stairs faster than hers could. She was only about a quarter of the way up the next set of stairs by the time Curse caught up with her. Not wanting to be foolish and wrestle with her on the stairs, he waited until they crested the weathered stairway and were on the walkway once more to grab for her.

His gun still in one hand, Curse reached with his free hand and grabbed the neck of her shirt. It was just a plain white button-down shirt, but it held when he grabbed her. The sudden stop to her movement jerked her off of her feet, and he used his hold on her to help guide her to the ground. Within a second's space, he had straddled her and put the gun in her face.

"Why were you watching me?" he demanded.

She was petrified. As he studied her face intently, he considered the fact that she looked more natural than any other denizen of the Nightmarescape he had seen so far. It crossed his mind that the decayed appearances of most in the Nightmarescape could take some time to manifest on a body. Then again, Larry said that Curse was brand-new, and he already looked like hell. There would be questions for this one indeed. She simply stared at him. Despite the fact he had only asked one question, he was already growing impatient.

"Answer me, damnit." He pulled her face close to his own, and brought the hammer of the revolver back with his thumb.

"I . . . I . . . am . . . ," she managed to stammer.

"Yes? Out with it," Curse demanded in an icy tone.

"I'm trying to study this place," she blurted out at last.

Now there was a surprising answer, but the Nightmarescape seemed to be full of nothing but surprises. This would be an interesting conversation; Curse only wished that Larry could be there to participate in it.

"Studying this place? What exactly are you studying? You look like you've been here a little too long to just be visiting," he goaded her.

She looked directly into his eye sockets, and he could feel that she was attempting to probe his intentions. They held their gazes locked on each other's faces until she finally spoke.

"If you put the gun away, I'll tell you," she said meekly.

"If I put it away will you run again?" he questioned.

"I will not." She continued looking at him. The slight tinge of an Eastern European accent rang in her voice. She was a beautiful woman despite the lights in her eyes and her gray skin.

Curse resolved in his mind to kill her if she tried to run again. He eased himself off of her and held his thumb on the hammer of the gun as he uncocked it and returned it to his waistband. He even extended his hand to help her sit up. She took it and crossed her legs Indian style to show him that she would not run.

"I was a student of parapsychology," she began. "I started having dreams about a place like this when I was a little girl." Curse listened and attempted to place her accent precisely before quickly getting frustrated and abandoning the endeavor.

Where she was from was irrelevant for now; he just wanted to know what she was doing and why she had been watching him.

"I went to university in my late teens and started studying psychology. Psychology led me to parapsychology, and then I wanted to major in that and physics. I started studying dreams and metaphysics because the dreams would plague me every night. I would see this place . . . this whole world and the people in it. It terrified me. I wanted to make them go away." She looked regretful; a full human face was easier to read than a skull or a rotted face.

"So what happened?" Curse had let the harsh tone of his voice dissolve into one that was level.

"I studied and worked on a project that could open doorways to unconscious realms. I began delving into metaphysics and learning about dimensions and things . . . then I built a device that could split the fabric of this realm and my own, and I went in and out a couple times. But the more I went in and out, the harder it was to return. I began to change and now . . . here I am . . . like this . . . a piece of this world now . . ." She sighed heavily. "I had so much waiting for me back home. Now I am trapped here."

"So if someone comes here, this place turns them into one of its own; what happens if you go back?" Curse rolled the idea around in his head.

"If someone who has been claimed by this place goes back and stays? It got to a point where when I returned after several days, I would begin to feel very weak . . . my consciousness felt like it was fading . . . I had to come back here to get rid of the feelings." Her head hung as she spoke.

"This thing you made . . . do you still have it?" Curse attempted to mask his excitement. Larry had told him about the device just earlier and now by fate he may have found it.

"I do . . . it's in this building . . . I'm going to use it for a little more research and then destroy it. It's dangerous . . . I didn't know who was in this place. If I'd known it was full of vengeful dead, I would not have allowed my studies to go on this long. I just want to do a little more research so this place is known and others don't try to open gateways. Imagine what could happen if so many evil presences poured into our former world . . ." She looked up at him with sorrow in her eyes. "I lost everything because of my research. I was engaged to be married, but how could a man marry a ghost?" Dark tears that resembled the ichor from Larry's eyes began to drip from her eyes.

"I had a lover too," Curse said sympathetically. "The difference between us is you got stuck here by accident; I killed myself and ended up here."

"Making you a true creature of this place," she spoke for him.

"I have a friend who has a theory about all this . . . he's been here a long time and was a psychotherapist when he was alive. He says that this place is made of negative psychic energy and that those who spend their lives in misery and anger end up here when they die. He also said that to come here, the place finds you, and you have dreams about it while you're alive, then you show up here after death. Not everyone who's miserable comes here—it finds you. It's like a hell to some, a heaven to others. I remember having dreams about it, even remember some particular ones. I'm still trying to re-member most of my life."

She nodded. "Your friend is wise. Yes, that's what most of my research finds. What's hard to gauge is what will happen to you if you go back."

"Only one way to find out: trial and error," Curse reached his hand to her to help her up. She was not someone who belonged here. She was not a psychopath or a fighter; she did not even seem predisposed to melancholic humor.

"I need your device . . . I want to find my love."

"You are noble, still reaching for her. Be prepared though, you will remain as you are. She will not recognize you at first . . . you'll be a monster to her," she warned him.

"I might not even contact her . . . I just want to see her and know she is all right."

She smiled. It was one of the few things in the Nightmarescape that Curse had found beauty in.

"What is your name anyway?" he asked.

"I am Aja."

Curse grinned. "My name is Curse."

She looked at him in puzzlement. "No, it's not."

"It is now," he countered. "Like you said, I'm a resident of this world, and that's the name I was given here, so that's what I'm going by now."

"If I was going to end up here eventually, I would have done it as you did, by dying. It hurts so bad to just be trapped here." Aja sighed.

"I hate not remembering my past, but given your circumstances, perhaps mine have been more merciful. Come on, Aja, your device has good to do yet." Being in her presence made him feel calm. She was a link to the world they had both come from, and she might be able to take him back there. She was a reminder of natural life in a strange and unnatural place.

"I will take you to it. I have hidden my things in this old castle," she told him.

"Whose castle was this?" Curse inquired.

She shrugged. "It was abandoned when I found it . . . I don't know whose it is. I can't imagine I've been here more than a month."

Curse merely nodded but said nothing. That meant this place could belong to anyone who would be coming back to it at any time. He did not mention the projector he had found or the decrepit condition of the place. He wanted to retrieve her device and leave before some ancient army returned and they were greatly outnumbered. He also wanted to get away from the damnable pit. Whatever was in there, he did not want to be around when it was summoned.

He followed her along the walkway as they approached the next set of stairs. They treaded carefully; he would ask her about the pit later but lost the thought to a sudden distraction.

"Curse!" A feminine voice sounded from below them, little more than a forceful whisper against the glaring silence.

Curse and Aja turned to see Banshee holding her rifle above her head at the bottom of the walkway. Larry stood beside her, grinning as always. They broke into a quick stride as Curse motioned for them to come to him. Their faces showed surprise as they saw his new acquaintance. As they approached, he stepped forth to meet with them.

"Larry," he spoke hurriedly, "she made the device we're looking for!"

Larry's eyes widened. "Ya don't say do ya, son?"

"She's getting ready to take me to it. You should come with us."

Larry and Banshee followed him; Larry was so excited he could barely contain himself. Banshee seemed unsure of the situation. Curse noticed her apprehension and decided to acquaint them.

"Larry, Banshee, this is Aja. She's a student of parapsychology and physics."

"HAHA! I used to do the psychology myself! You and me could be talkin' a storm on that. Did I tell you I used to make people commit suicide!?"

Aja seemed immediately terrified of Larry. "That's nice . . . I think . . ."

Curse placed a hand on Aja's shoulder and placed himself between her and Larry. "He's great once you get to know him," he reassured her.

She merely nodded. Banshee moved up alongside the girl. She kept her eyes on Aja; Curse was not sure, but he thought he might have detected a slight hint of jealousy that he was touching Aja.

Nothing personal, he thought to himself. He really had no interest in either of them.

He had a love already; she was just in another plane of reality. She was the one he wanted. Perhaps he would not be able to show his affections because he was a monster now, but if nothing else, he could at least see her and ensure her safety. He did not know what he would do when he found her, because he did not know how long he had been dead or how long it had taken his presence to manifest in the Nightmarescape. What if he found her, and she was with another? It was possible given the circumstances under which she had left. He did not know how he would handle that. Would he go insane and kill the new man? That was a possibility. For the time being, he dismissed thoughts of what could be and focused on what was at hand.

They moved quickly along the walkway and stayed quiet. Despite the warm greetings, the eerie silence had returned. It felt as though the cold and silent place carried a tension that would explode should they speak further. Curse wondered if Banshee and Larry had noticed the dark water below them and shared the same dread of it that he did. He thought that they had not really paid much attention to it seeing as how they ran up to him immediately. The whole place did not sit well with him, and he would be glad to be away from it.

Just get the damn thing and get out of here, he thought to himself.

Curse had already found enough secrets in the fort. Should it have more secrets that were not as helpful, he did not care to find them. The three followed Aja up the last set of stairs and into a doorway at the end of the walkway. The door opened into a small room that looked like a primitive laboratory from the Victorian era. Ancient glass beakers and flasks adorned shelves and tables stacked with various mechanical components. A small oil lamp sat burning a gray fire on one of the tables. The scene reminded Curse of *Frankenstein*, only there was no body to resurrect.

Aja made her way to one of the tables and picked up a boxy item made of wood and metal. Coils, wires, and vacuum tubes stuck out from the box. It could not have been bigger than a square foot. A strange satellite type device sat on the top right side of the box.

"This is it," she said, holding it up for the three of them to see. All three were unimpressed.

"That can open up dimensions?" Banshee's jaw hung low.

"It does not look like much, but you would be foolish to underestimate its power. I want to destroy it personally, but I want to research this place more so I can warn others of it and prevent them from coming here," Aja explained.

Larry began laughing. "Warn 'em and they're still comin' anyway!"

"What makes you say that?" she asked.

"Because, dear, people are idiots! Tell 'em not to stick their hand in a fire, and they do it anyway. Eventually some jackass is going to try to use it for power purposes."

Banshee sighed and spoke. "Even if this thing can do what you say it can . . . Larry is right. Destroying your device won't stop humanity from coming into this place and trying to fuck with it. This place has been around as long as humanity has, and I'm sure someone else with a similar background to yours will find a way in at some point."

Curse spoke next. "Why are we so terrified of letting this world overlap with the conscious one? We don't know what will happen, but a small-scale experiment could be what is in order to see how it will affect things. You've gone in and out several times, Aja, and now the Nightmarescape has turned you into one of its own. We came to the Nightmarescape as organically as it can happen. What will happen to us if we go back?"

Aja looked at him confused. "Nightmarescape—is that what you all are calling this place?"

"What were you calling it?" Larry asked.

"Hell." The tone in her voice spoke the truth of the statement.

She was clearly not happy to be there. Larry loved it there. Banshee seemed to survive all right even though she burned for vengeance. Curse had not decided if he was quite at the point where he would consider it a hell or not. He was feeling less alienated as time went on. He only wanted to go back to the other world to learn who he had been and see his lover once more. He wanted to communicate that he was sorry somehow. Maybe he could sneak in on her while she was sleeping and whisper in her ear. Just maybe she would process his words in her unconscious state and know he was still with her.

A sound from outside the room startled all of them. They were unsure what they heard at first, but then it became clear as a scraping and clanking metallic noise. Curse rushed to the doorway. The chains that led into the pit were moving.

The third level of the walkway terminated into the door they had entered. The chamber with the pit stretched up into darkness. He had no idea how far up those chains went. On closer inspection, they were moving downward. He could hear a strange cacophony of voices from above.

Quickly, Curse ducked back into the room and motioned for someone to turn the lamp off. It went out, and the room disappeared. Curse watched as the chains continued to move down into the water. The voices were coming closer, but it was hard for him to understand them as they echoed off of the walls and reverberated throughout the room.

Soon enough the sounds were decipherable. Curse could not believe his ears.

21

"The time has come for you to awaken from your slumber and follow your pastor into battle. There are those that would have us destroyed and eradicate the blessings granted to us . . . to stop us from fulfilling our legacy that has been destined since the dawn of creation!"

A strange sloshing sound caught Curse's ears. A sense of horror washed over him as he looked down at the pit and learned what had been lurking beneath the dark water. Emaciated and rotten bodies were climbing up the ladders and onto the stone. Gangling, atrophied limbs stuck out from under the surface as more of the corpse-like Plague Faction creatures crawled from the water. The scene was one of true repulsion. More and more bodies crawled from the water. They dragged the filthy liquid onto the stonework with them as well as detritus from the pit. The voice from overhead intensified as the chains descended. Curse looked up and observed a grated metal platform attached to the chains with several shadows on it.

He shrank back slightly into the darkness as the platform continued past his position. Four forms stood on it. Two stood silently in pitted plate mail armor, their faces invisible behind ancient helms. In their hands they gripped bucklers and spiked maces. The voice was coming from a creature wearing a monk's robe swathed about his frame. A patchwork leather hood was draped over his face, obscuring his identity. Curse saw why his voice had been so cacophonous; in his hand, he grasped a megaphone that he used to scream his litanies to the undead things below.

Curse instantly recognized the last figure from the British soldiers' descriptions. It was Pastor Nox. He stood at least two heads higher than the other three. His form was wrapped in a fetid black cloak pocked with holes and torn to threads in spots. Dirty bandages constricted his forearms, a thick gray liquid of a viscous consistency dripping out from the cracks between the wrappings. His head was adorned with a helm that at first seemed alien in design before Curse recognized it as the mask of a Black-Plague-era doctor. In one hand, the Pastor held a scythe that was taller than him. He was a vision of death made incarnate, the image of the grim reaper brought to life.

"And Hell followed with him," Curse mouthed to himself.

Indeed, Hell was climbing up out of a pit of filthy water just below him. The platform came to a grinding halt several feet above the surface of the water. Insane ramblings about plague and how disease was a blessing bounced off the walls from the speaker's megaphone. So far the only way out was through an entire army of shambling dead.

Curse moved back into the room and pulled both guns from his pants. He could not see his friends in the dark, but he knew they were just behind him. He could hear Banshee rummaging through her backpack.

"We're trapped in here . . . ," Curse informed the others.

"What ruckus is going on out there?" Larry inquired.

"It's the Pastor . . . he's got his retinue, and that water was full of Plague Faction corpses. It was almost like they were sleeping in that water, waiting for him to wake them up." Curse reached for Aja in the dark.

"Is there a way out of this room that does not involve us going back down past that pit?" he inquired of her.

He could not see her, but he knew that her face wore an expression of abject terror. Even if she did not know fully what the Plague Faction was or what they were doing, she got the message that they were not something to be trifled with. Her voice was hesitant as she answered.

"Not this room, no . . . this is a centralized chamber surrounded by stone on all sides."

"You know this fort—what is the quickest way out of here," Curse shot back at her.

"The way we came in . . . I've been here for what I can gauge to be a month in real time . . . I've never seen anyone else here . . . I just decided to use this room because it seemed the safest place . . ." She was on the verge of sobbing, fear taking her over.

A light flashed on in the darkness. Banshee cast the beam of a flashlight around the room looking for a way out. Even under the white light glow of the flashlight, the room was still dark gray and black. She began searching the walls with her hands, the light bouncing around as she did so.

"What are you looking for?" Curse asked her.

"A thin spot in the walls." She did not look away as she searched. "I have two grenades," she mentioned over her shoulder.

"HAHAHAHAAAAAA, good show, woman!" Larry was probably doing one of his psychotic dances as he said it.

Larry did love some carnage and would probably be happy either with an explosion or a fight. He just loved to be in control of his battles and not have infuriated military men trying to chase him down.

"If you can't make a hole, sounds like plenty of folks out there could use 'em!"

Banshee took a moment to consider which would be a better use: offense against the horde or an escape route. Curse weighed the options himself. What if the wall held against the blast? What if they wasted a grenade that could have been used to save them all? The little bit of light illuminated Banshee's face as she began to form an idea.

"We're going through them," she said. "I'll use one to take out a portion of them, and I'll detonate the other in that hallway and hopefully bring a good piece of it down, sealing them in."

"Let's do something before they all crawl out and we have to fight everyone who's ever died from a disease," Curse intoned.

Within moments, the four of them had formed up in a single-file line. Curse stood first, Larry was behind him, Aja stood behind him holding the device, and Banshee stood at the rear with her grenades.

"Curse, take this for the hallway." Banshee stepped forward and gave him her flashlight before hooking the grenades to her backpack and readying her rifle. Curse returned the Nambu pistol to his pants.

They charged out of the room and into the mouth of death itself. Bodies littered the first level of the walkway. They stood, crawled, shambled, and tripped over each other as they rose from the water. None moved to help each other; their deteriorated minds only felt hunger, hunger to do the will of their pastor. He was the driving force of their sentience in the Nightmarescape—without Pastor Nox to give them direction, they would likely be shambling and groaning idiots.

The speaker's rhetoric became more heated and impassioned as they descended the walkway. Curse reached the first tier of stairs and opened fire on the forerunners of the horde. Larry's shotgun boomed from behind him and several rounds snapped from Banshee's rifle. The preacher ceased his ranting temporarily as the gunfire cut him short. Several bodies were knocked back as the rounds struck them. Upon turning and seeing the interlopers, the speaker turned his fiery oration toward them.

"There! As I speak, our Lord has sent us infidels to prove the point!" His finger pointed toward the four of them. Immediately, the afflicted began clawing their way up the stone walkway, eager to destroy the intruders.

Curse fired several more rounds at the nearest creatures. One took a round to the shoulder and stumbled sideways. It gripped onto another nearby piece of flesh and continued its sideways drop. Rotten hands grabbed to steady their balance on one another as several of the things fell off of the walkway and into the water once again. Curse saw that knocking them back in was currently a better way to get by than trying to destroy each one in turn. The afflicted outnumbered them heavily, and they would surely be overwhelmed if they did not move quickly.

Curse's hand slammed the revolver into a nearby head. The crack of bone followed the thing off of the walkway. Another creature came after it and was met with a similar treatment.

Curse placed the gun and the light in his waistband and took to them with his hands. Their emaciated frames were light to him, and they were easily taken off their feet. Several would fall together at times as they clutched for something to hold onto and found their comrades.

He was creating a sizeable hole in their ranks, but as soon as some fell into the water, others were still climbing out to take their place. If they stayed here, being overwhelmed was inevitable. Banshee still had the grenades, but they were in too close proximity to use them right now. Curse hurled more decayed and atrophied bodies back into the mire, attempting to get to the doorway they came through. Larry and Banshee turned their weapons on the bodies that were climbing up the ladders behind them.

Throughout the combat, the four on the platform watched. The speaker with the megaphone screamed and gestured wildly, his words lost amidst the chaos. The Pastor stood watching calmly, his guards following his lead. Should they join the melee by leaping into the fight from the platform, the balance of the fight would quickly turn. A heavy glut of disease-ridden flesh had accumulated on the side of the walkway near the door. Curse almost wished Banshee would toss a grenade onto the platform and try to destroy the four standing on it. Perhaps that would end this nonsense for good.

The irony was that the Plague Faction did not know the device was walking out the door right in front of them in the hands of a scared woman. Or then again, perhaps they did. Maybe the Pastor knew and was simply waiting for them to escape with it so he could follow, with some unfathomable goal in mind.

Either that or he was waiting for them to become overwhelmed so that he could swoop off of the platform and destroy them himself. Curse wished that he had a bunch of

Nightmarescape

zombie-minded fools to command and pad the space between himself and his enemies. Larry's shotgun sounded behind him.

A slight movement of his eyes revealed that the Pastor was reeling on the platform, a ragged set of holes torn in the chest of his cloak. Viscous, black liquid poured from the wounds and dripped from the rotted clothing into the water below. The Pastor calmly regained his composure and stood at his full height again. The wounds began to seal themselves.

22

Banshee was occupied shooting her rifle into a press of bodies that were climbing out of the pit. She stood just before the nearest ladder and blasted the afflicted back down as they climbed up. After doing it several times, she became jaded, and fired at the metal ladder itself. The bullet made a clanking noise and a white spark, but ricocheted off the metal. In frustration, she slammed the butt of the gun into a skull that ascended the ladder and then attacked the ladder itself. One piece of metal holding the ladder connected to the stone buckled slightly—several more frantic smashes and it snapped. The ladder now hung by a single piece of metal. Several pairs of rotted arms reached out of the black water and gripped the rungs.

Banshee hoped that there would be enough bodies to aid the weight of the ladder in collapsing into the water. She watched as the things momentarily fought over the right to climb the dangling ladder. Three of them came up the corroded rungs, but their weight did not break the metal.

"Damnit," she hissed as she raised the butt of the gun again and prepared to attack the last piece of metal.

As she prepared to strike again, she was knocked off her feet, a hard blow landing against her head. One of the afflicted that the group had knocked down and moved past had regained its footing and pressed an attack from behind. She fell back and hit the wall before pitching forward onto her front. Her head hung over the side of the walkway, and she realized that she could see dark ichor pouring from above her eyes into the black water only several feet below. She was dazed from the impact and did not process what was happening just yet. She could only watch and try to comprehend her circumstances. The world seemed slow around her as she became aware of a splitting pain in her head. She moved her hand up slowly and felt her forehead.

Her skin burned as her fingers touched the freshly split wound. Her fingers came away wet with black fluid. Sluggishly, she pushed herself up with her hands. She turned to the side and before she knew it, the bodies that had been climbing the ladder were upon her. They clawed her with bony fingers, tearing at her flesh and hair. A ripping pain radiated through a different part of her head as one of the hands grabbed one of her dreadlocks and ripped it clean out of her scalp. A chunk of dark meaty flesh followed with it. They were weighing her down. Her senses were starting to come back to her after the impact, and she was panicking.

There were a bunch of them on her now, tearing at her. She attempted to reach for her pack, but realized in terror one of the things had pulled it from her back while she was down. Her hands searched the walkway for her rifle, but it was nowhere to be found. She struggled to push her body up against the weight bearing her down, but too many of the things were on her.

The boom of a shotgun shook the air above her. Larry was still shooting. She wondered if he was going to stay and fight for her. The thought was abruptly dismissed as she looked down at the dark water and two bony hands surged up from the ladder and seized the sides of her head. A face covered in filthy boils emerged from behind the hands and gurgled rancid liquid from its mouth.

That extra weight was the tipping point.

She felt her belly sliding along the stone toward the pit. Realizing what was happening, she willed her body to move again, but her hands were already over the edge as the thing that had grabbed her disappeared beneath the surface of the water. She kicked her feet out behind her, desperate to grab onto anything that she could with her legs. She only succeeded in smashing her bare toes on the stone, causing herself further pain. And then the surface of the water was rushing to meet her.

Inky darkness enveloped her as she broke the surface face first. The rest of her body followed into the mire. She opened her mouth to scream but could not make a sound as the foul-tasting liquid rushed into her mouth and nose. Breathing was not a necessity in the Nightmarescape, but having lungs and a nose full of water that held all manner of decay was a hideous feeling. She coughed and struggled to rid herself of the liquid. Her efforts merely created bubbles in the noxious fluid and allowed a way for more of the water to get into her windpipe. From all around her, sharp, bony fingers dug into her flesh and tugged her every which way. Pain rang in her head like a jackhammer, for those wounds had not yet begun to seal over.

This way and that they tugged her in the dark, liquid hell. She struggled to kick and swing her arms, but the gaggle of bodies hanging onto her like a grotesque mass of parasites weighed her down. As she broke one limb free and struck outward, the other was seized. Down she sank deeper and deeper into the darkness, the stench of decay and the feeling of drowning coursing through her.

She knew that she did not have to breathe, but the noxious liquid hung heavily in her senses of smell and taste. Her gag reflex overtook her, and she vomited in the liquid, her own acidic stomach contents floating into her face. As revolting as that was, her vomit was probably the least disgusting thing in the pit. Pain coursed through her as the things tore at her. She could not see anything with the water being so brackish and dark. Her mind began to resign itself to oblivion. She had been close to getting back to the real world and getting her revenge, but now that seemed a distant possibility. These things would rip her apart in the bottom of this watery hell. She opened her mouth to scream again; this time she was able to force the air into the liquid as the fetid water churned and bubbled around her mouth.

Curse's elbow flew forward and slammed into a brittle skull. The bone gave way against the force, and he felt the structure caving beneath his blow. He seized the body with the other hand and plunged his own bony fingers into the area he had crushed. His hand went through the soft and wet decayed flesh with ease as he attacked the thing's brain matter with his fingertips until its body melted into dust in his grip.

He had previously resolved himself to just knocking them out of the way, but they were pissing him off. Rage pounded through his being as he slammed both of his hands down on the next creature in a powerful hammer fist attack. It fell beneath the blow and another rushed forward to take its place. He landed a strong punch to the thing's jaw and knocked it off the platform.

Briefly he turned to survey his allies. Larry was shooting at the four on the platform. The speaker's jaw had been blown off, and he gurgled constantly through a bleeding ruin of a mouth. The Pastor was bleeding again from several more wounds, yet he stood watching the carnage before him as though nothing was amiss. One of the guard's helmets was pockmarked with holes, yet he stood resolute. Curse noted that his mace was missing from his hand. Aja was cowering between Curse and Larry.

He did not see Banshee. Her rifle was on the stone walkway a few feet from Larry. One of the rotten creatures was shaking her backpack. She had to be in the water. He froze amidst the carnage.

"Larry!" he bellowed over the fight.

Larry turned his head as he unleashed another shotgun blast that clipped the pastor's head, sending small chunks of his helmet flying away. He then took a moment to look to Curse. Had he not been distracted, the shot probably would have struck home and ended this mess.

"Banshee!" Curse screamed.

Larry looked over his shoulder for a moment and became aware of the things holding her belongings. He blasted the remaining piece of the ladder that she had been attempting to destroy. For Banshee, the ordeal seemed to have been an eternity; in reality, it was the space of only a few moments. It had been so fast after she fell and the things descended on her that Larry had not noticed her missing amidst the chaos.

Turning his shotgun to the side, Larry unleashed a blast into the creature holding Banshee's pack. The blast took the decrepit thing off of its feet, and it dropped the pack. Larry caught the pack by the straps before it hit the ground. He grabbed one of the grenades and ripped it from the pack, the pin staying attached to the strap.

Curse pushed Aja toward Larry as he primed the grenade. Without another moment's hesitation, Curse dove into the water. Sludgy darkness overtook him as he swam down through the liquid. He did not know how he would find her in the opaque fluid, but he could not leave her. Deathly limbs reached for him occasionally, but he took them in his hands and bent them back until they snapped against his strength. He swam downward, not knowing how much distance he had covered until he felt something soft and fleshy beneath him—a floor of bodies.

They lay at the bottom of the pit, some stirring and trying to search for a ladder so they could get up to the surface. Some came after him, for even in the dark water, his eyes were still shining blue lights. The plague afflicted knew that they did not have any eyes. His were a beacon to mark him as something different, something to be targeted.

The eyes. On the floor of rotten flesh several feet in front of him he could make out another pair of blue lights shining faintly through the mire. He powered himself through the water over to them, his fury rising as he swam. Reaching the lights, he found that a small mass of plague-afflicted bodies were swarming all over Banshee. He grabbed the first one his hands could find. Upon finding its head, he placed his hands on the top and bottom of the skull and gave it a violent twist. The thing sunk away in the darkness, paralyzed for the moment. He found an arm that had tangled its hand around her dreadlocks. Moments later, it was bending at the wrong angle, the fingers unable to grip. His foot found the next one, delivering a hard crack to its sternum despite the fact that they were underwater. A shock wave rumbled through the water from up above. Larry must have detonated the grenade.

Banshee felt the weight of her attackers suddenly being lifted from her body. Someone was fighting them off of her. She felt her own resolve strengthen as another bony hand was removed from her flesh. She added her own strength to the fight, no longer completely overwhelmed. She struck out at everything near her with her fists and feet. Several of the things were still on her back; she rolled her body violently and knocked them off balance before continuing her vicious assault. She struck out until something else grabbed her arms. It was not a creature of the Plague Faction; it was far stronger than they were. Her defensive frenzy arrested, she noticed two blue lights staring into her own eyes out of the murky dark. She threw her arms around Curse.

Despite the horror and hell of the pit, he had thrown himself into the crucible of death and decay to pull her back from the brink. She held him tightly as the two of them swam upward, both kicking their feet to be clear of the water faster. Banshee coughed and spat as she broke the surface. Her body ached in numerous places due to the wounds she had sustained on her head as well as the spots where bony fingers had dug into her flesh and torn pieces away from her. Curse pulled her through the water, occasionally giving a stiff downward kick as an errant swimming plague-afflicted reached for them from below.

They made their way to the nearest ladder, and Curse reached out to grab the skull of the creature trying to climb it. In a fluid motion, he slammed the thing's head into one of the metal rungs, and it came free of the ladder, sinking back down into the darkness. Banshee climbed out first; Curse followed. They were near the doorway now, and the grenade had cleared most of the bodies from the area.

Larry held Banshee's rifle in one hand and his shotgun in the other, pouring fire into anything that got near him. Aja stood behind him, moving with his body. Curse screamed for them to move while they had an opening. Banshee was on her hands and knees, coughing and sputtering vomit. The nauseous liquid had taken its toll on her. For the second time, Curse lifted her up.

"No time for exhaustion," he said as he pulled her forward into the dark hallway.

Larry and Aja followed in the same direction. Curse had already pulled out his revolver and the flashlight. The white light illuminated the hall and shined on the turns in the corridor. It did not seem as though any of the Plague Faction had made their way into the hall. Then again, that was logical seeing as how they wanted to be around the edge of the pit with their master. Just because they were not in there yet, though, did not mean they were not going to follow. Larry and Aja rounded the corner and tossed Banshee's rifle to her. Curse turned around just in time to scream a warning to Larry.

He watched as Pastor Nox began to leap toward them from the platform. His cloak billowed out around him, light shining through the holes and threadbare spots. Death was swooping down on Larry. Larry turned his head just in time to see the wraith descending behind him. Most would be horrified to see such a thing, but Larry's face wore a huge grin as he turned his body and fired buckshot from both barrels of his shotgun into the Pastor.

The large dark thing that had been flying through the air moments before was halted in its movement. The scythe fell from its hand and sunk into the water. The Pastor flew backward, smashing into the edge of the platform and then falling into the water himself.

"Gotta have the reflexes, son!" Larry beamed as he ran into the hallway.

A crowd of lurching creatures followed after him. Aja clung to his backside. Together they ran through the hallway, the creatures hissing and gurgling behind them. Larry released the last grenade and primed it briefly before dropping it in front of the creatures. Several made it past before the explosion rocked the hallway. The narrow confines magnified the shock wave from the explosion.

Curse felt himself pushed forward by the blast. The sound of the explosion died away as he heard the last remnants of stone falling upon stone. He did not stop to turn and look. To do so would cause all of them to stop, and the creatures that were following would easily catch up to them. A few of them would probably not be a problem for the four of them, but none of them felt like having more rotted corpses dig their fingers into their flesh.

The flashlight bounced off of the walls as they charged through the corridor, following each other around the turns. The things behind them lost ground as they slammed into walls and tripped over each other. Light bled together as the flashlight found the end of the corridor, and the four of them charged out into faint gray once more. Larry and Curse turned immediately and began pouring fire into the corridor as the last pursuers of the Plague Faction stumbled out after them.

Their projectiles knocked the creatures from their feet. One pitched over face first, its momentum carrying it to the ground with a fleshy thud in front of Curse. Curse brought his foot down on the thing's head, imploding its skull under the pressure. The weakened bone structures of these creatures made them easy to destroy, but there were just so damn many of them. They were enough on their own, but the fact that they had allies and organized leadership made them a dangerous foe indeed.

Larry vaporized another head in a hail of buckshot. Two more creatures stumbled from the dark hallway, having finally regained their balance. Curse leveled his revolver at the first one's head and blew a sizable chunk out of the thing's skull. It stumbled back with brain matter spilling from the wound.

Curse sighted the gun once more and took the rest of its brain apart with a final shot.

The body evaporated into dust. The other creature charged through the falling dust that was its former comrade. Larry met its face with the butt of his shotgun. It seemed unfazed by the blow and snatched for him with its long, bony fingers. He brought the gun up between himself and the thing. It grasped onto the weapon and struggled to pry it from his hands.

"No, you're not gettin' this!"

Larry threw his head forward and struck the thing's face with the top of his skull. It staggered back, black viscous liquid pouring out of a fresh split in its forehead. Several boils on the thing's head had popped as a result of the impact. It stood hissing and gurgling momentarily, waiting for its face to reform. Curse thought the thing was pathetic. Its mind was destroyed, and it followed a madman blindly. Not only that, but the thing's body had been reduced to a shell of what it had been when it was alive and healthy. Curse had no idea how long this thing had existed in the Nightmarescape in this condition. It could have lain in that pit for centuries for all he knew.

Larry wrestled the shotgun from the afflicted's hands and fired up under its chin, blowing a hole through the top of its head. The dark fluids pouring from the thing dried as it seized up and evaporated into dust.

"Well, that was interesting for a bit of sport!" Larry exclaimed.

Banshee was doubled over again, gripped by nausea. The filth of the pit still hung heavily on her. She and Curse both reeked of human decay. Curse came to her and held her up, but she was struggling against collapsing.

"What'd y'all find in that toilet, anyway?" Larry inquired now that the threat was gone.

"That pit was full of those things . . . they dragged Banshee down. The bottom was nothing but bodies . . . I don't know how many more there were down there. A bunch of them were waking up as I fought others off of her. That pit could be deep as hell and have dead from forever under that water," Curse spoke for the both of them.

"They're stuck for a little while now!" Despite the ordeal, Larry's spirits were high. At least one of them was enjoying this. Curse and Banshee had just swum through liquid decay and were shaking off the effects. Aja was visibly horrified by the whole experience.

"Who were they?" she whispered.

"That, my dear, was what people 'round these parts call the Plague Faction. That cloaked jerk I shot was their leader. You said you've been in this here fort about a month and haven't seen anyone?" Larry carried the conversation.

"When I first opened the way to this place, it was in that room. I'd seen that room and the pit in my dreams, so I knew where I was . . . but I didn't know what was in the pit or that the fort was still frequented by anyone . . . they were just lying there in that water the whole time . . ."

"Well, it's a good thing we got to you before them cuz they want your device too. They want it to get back to the other world and spread their diseases to the living. If they had begun stirring with you in here alone, they would have torn you apart and fucked around with that thing 'til they really would have done something crazy." Larry grinned.

Curse held Banshee up; her pack was still on Larry's back. He smoothed his hand over her hair to keep her calm. He thought briefly on why the incident troubled her so much and then remembered all of the bodies grabbing and pressing onto her. He weighed that against the circumstances at the end of her former life. His lips would remain sealed on the matter. True, she had been no innocent in her life, but he needed her now and did not want to alienate her by dredging up her traumas. He needed Larry too. Larry had proven himself incredibly useful as a guide and had connections. Aja was very new to the group, and he wanted to keep her around, but once she had shared the secrets of the device, Curse realized that she was expendable. He hated to think that way, but it was true. She was not a being geared toward survival in the Nightmarescape. He would protect her as best as he could for taking him back to the other world, but he wondered if she would be able to hold her own that long. Shaking the thoughts from his head, he helped Banshee up and turned to the others.

"Let's get moving—those stones won't hold them forever, and we don't know where that elevator goes. I don't want the damned grim reaper hopping down on us from the shadows somewhere," Curse said.

Larry let out one of his peals of laughter and held his shotgun high. They all laughed briefly about seeing the Pastor flying through the air, being the vision of death before being laid low into the filthy water by grinning Larry and his trusty old turkey shooter.

They followed the hallway back into the main chamber of the fort and out through the enormous doors again. Once outside, the overcast sky bathed them in its gray light. Banshee took a deep breath, inhaling the cool, clean air. Curse observed a hint of a smile cross her face as she did so. He could tell that she was deeply relieved to be away from the pit and its foulness.

24

They walked down the winding path back to the village; Larry stood in front with Aja behind him. Curse and Banshee fell in step together as he still held her up to keep her from doubling over. The stench of the pit was still fresh on their skin. It struck Curse as strange that nobody in the Nightmarescape smelled like a rotted corpse even though they looked the part. They had no smell for the most part. Then again, if they were made of psychic energy, they would not have much smell. The pit smelled because someone remembered it being full of decay and that manifested along with it. They would air out in the open and possibly find a place to wash off. Curse pushed the foulness from his mind so he could focus on Banshee.

"Why do you keep that barbed wire on your arms? You have enough reminders of what happened," Curse spoke softly to her.

She looked up at him, startled by the inquiry. Her eye sockets focused on him in a long measured stare as she thought about his question.

"The constant pain won't allow me to forget. It keeps me strong and allows me to focus my anger. When I'm in the heat of a conflict, I feel the pain and think of what those assholes did to me—it makes me fight much harder." She finished the statement with a grin to lighten the mood.

"We have much in common," he said to her.

She nodded as they ceased to speak any further. Larry was rambling his theories and thoughts to Aja, who nodded respectfully whether she thought he was full of shit or not. Curse and Banshee walked side by side, feeling an understanding for one another that had not existed before. He had not known her long, but she had proven herself to be a trustworthy and kindred spirit like Larry. He needed her as a reliable partner to watch his back. More than that, he had also come to value her companionship. Her presence kept him from feeling lost in this world. He knew that he would learn how she regarded him in due time. *Don't get too close just yet,* he thought to himself.

The whole point of him seeking passage to the former world once more was to see the woman he had loved. The more he considered the circumstances, he was struck with the realization that he most likely could not be a part of her life again. He just wanted peace of mind that she was safe. When that was done, he thought about allowing himself to feel closer to Banshee.

"Okay, where do we go from here?" Larry spoke back to them, Banshee in particular.

"Back the way we came," she stated bluntly.

"Back through the peanut gallery?" Larry raised his eyebrows with the statement.

He then looked to Curse, Curse looked to Aja. Curse did not know if she could deal with anyone else attacking her for a while.

"No way around them?" Curse asked.

"I personally want to go back to the house to mess with the thing," Larry offered.

Banshee and Aja had not been to the house yet. They regarded each other carefully.

Catching onto their apprehension, Curse spoke up. "He lives in an old farmhouse that's rigged up with traps. It's a fairly safe place, since it's far from most conflict."

Hesitantly, they agreed to go with them. Banshee trusted Curse now and knew he would not place her in danger. Aja really did not have much say in the matter; she was a sitting duck without the three of them.

Gunfire from the town's combatants became audible again. There was now a jeep sitting at the edge of the town. It was dark gray in color with an iron cross emblazoned on the hood. An air-cooled machine gun was mounted on the back of the vehicle.

"Hey!" Larry turned to the others, his face covered by a huge smile. Looking at the vehicle more closely, they observed smoke coming from the vehicle's rear exhaust. Quickly, they made their way to the side of the building. The fight had moved to another corner of the village. They could hear loud voices from inside the building, possibly an officers' meeting.

Larry and Curse rounded the corner first. Larry leapt into the driver's seat of the jeep, and Curse took the machine gun. Banshee ran close behind with Aja in tow. Banshee leapt onto the back of the vehicle with Curse and assumed a kneeling position with her rifle pointed toward the building. Aja sat in the passenger seat as Curse wheeled the weapon toward the building should anyone come chasing after them. Larry beamed behind the wheel of the vehicle.

"I'm a motorist!" he screamed.

Voices yelling in a foreign language sounded from inside the building before two soldiers in German uniforms rushed out to confront them.

Curse held down the machine gun's trigger and opened fire on the pursuers. They both fell as the hail of bullets took them off their feet. Nobody crumbled to dust, but the jeep was moving, and they could not catch up to it on foot. Curse swept the gun around the village for errant snipers in the buildings or a larger fight that they might pass through.

"Thanks, Jerry!" Curse yelled over the roar of the engine.

Larry steered the jeep through the village with reckless abandon. Curse assumed that Larry had learned to drive in the Nightmarescape and that he did not intend to slow down or let anything get in his way. Up ahead on the roadway, a soldier in a gray uniform ran out from behind a building and was raising his rifle to fire at an enemy combatant as the jeep barreled onward. The soldier turned just a moment too late, and before he could react, the jeep slammed its bulk into him.

Landing on the hood with a metallic thud, the soldier struggled desperately to hold onto the vehicle. His face slammed into the windshield in front of Aja, creating a large crack in the glass. She let out a brief scream.

"Get off, damnit!" Larry swung the vehicle hard to the right.

The soldier did not have a strong enough grip to hold on through the movement and was flung from the hood of the vehicle onto the road once more. Curse looked back and saw the man rolling in the dusty road. He had probably suffered broken bones and other trauma from the impact, but whether he would heal or not seemed irrelevant at the moment.

Bullets zinged past them as other soldiers began shooting from their concealed locations. Several struck the frame of the vehicle but did little more than cosmetic damage. The jeep was moving too fast for them to draw good shots.

Over the dusty ground the tires bounced as Larry drove into the forest once more. It was a long way back to Larry's farmhouse. Tires scrabbled over dead pine needles and leaves, kicking up a sizable debris trail in their wake. Larry swerved heavily from side to side, avoiding trees. Back past the cliff they went; Curse swiveled the machine gun and briefly stared at the spot where they had found Banshee. She was still beside him in the vehicle. It felt strange to see something of this place that he had formed into a memory.

Curse had come to the Nightmarescape with few memories of his past life, and even those were scattered and incomplete. Memories of the Nightmarescape were gelling with memories of his past life in his mind, creating a gestalt that existed in two worlds. Even though he wanted to return to the other world to see his lover once more—despite the fact she had left him—he knew that this was his existence now. He knew that Larry was the closest thing he had to family. Banshee was becoming more than a friend, and he dearly hoped to keep her close. He did not know if Aja would be around for long.

She seemed too scared and somewhat helpless. The Nightmarescape was a place of violence and carnage. She was an intellectual and lacked experience in physical conflict. She also did not seem to be a personality prone to melancholy or rage. This potentially made her a weak presence in such a world. Curse knew how to tap his anger and use it effectively. Banshee seemed to be able to do the same. Larry reveled in violent chaos and was perfectly suited to such an existence.

He let the thoughts roll through his mind as the jeep sped through the forest. The only thing he did not like about this mode of travel was that Larry was leaving an obvious trail that would allow them to be tracked. Curse made a mental note to learn his way around later. So much had happened that he had become disoriented and was relying solely on Larry and Banshee to get him around. Should he become separated or should either of them be killed, he would be completely lost in this unknown territory.

The plain where the battle had been fought loomed into view from between the trees. Larry made a hard right turn and drove alongside the edge of the tree line, staring out at the battlefield. Numerous craters pocked the surface of the ground. Soldiers from different time periods mulled about the carnage, picking up weapons that had been dropped in the conflict. The original group of British soldiers was still there. Several armored knights stood sentry in front of the gun emplacement. The tanks were parked flanking either side of the gun as well. Several soldiers from the American Civil War stood in a group talking. Curse could not tell if they were Union or Confederates. What seemed interesting was that their uniforms were definitely different colors. *Perhaps they had to set aside their prior conflicts and come together out of circumstance*, Curse wondered to himself.

Kitenge stood with several African warriors, possibly Zulus, and was pointing out at the battlefield.

The contingent left behind seemed smaller than the one that had arrived as relief. There was no sign of the Plague Faction or Japanese soldiers. Fine piles of dust littered the ground where they had been killed. Curse saw the Japanese officer's sword sticking out of one of the dust piles and

Nightmarescape

smiled to himself. Several moments later, one of the British soldiers plucked it from the earth.

Larry turned the jeep off and pointed toward the group of Civil War soldiers. "Those are probably some of his boys." Larry held a certain vehemence in his voice.

"Whose men?" Aja inquired.

"The colonel's, jackass," Banshee snapped at her.

Aja only looked confused. Curse smiled to himself, remembering the slight hint of jealousy that he detected from Banshee when she had seen him talking to Aja and holding her.

"What colonel?" Aja asked.

"Larry got himself into a predicament while he was living his past life and killed a colonel's son. Apparently it was a Civil War colonel, and he's here in the Nightmarescape as well," Curse explained.

"The what?" Aja's face held an expression of incredulity. Aja had already forgotten their previous conversation, her memory washed over with fear and adrenaline.

"Nightmarescape is what we call this fair land. Remember?" Larry reiterated. "How much talkin' have ya done here to these rubes?"

"I've interacted very little with anyone . . . ," she said softly.

"We came here after death. We remember our former lives through flashbacks, but not all at once. You came here in a different manner. You remember everything. It took the colonel a while to remember that I killed his boy. Then he actually recognized me, and he and his goons have been on my tail ever since. I'm gonna have a hootenanny on his hide when I kill him." Larry reached over and patted his shotgun while he spoke.

"I've got some friends in the Archaic Front, but many are friends of the colonel. I have to tread carefully when I'm around them. Never know who is one of his," he continued.

"The what?" Aja was completely lost, having been left out of prior conversations.

"We'll tell you later," Banshee chided. "Right now, let's keep going."

"We're takin' the scenic route," Larry declared as he brought the jeep back to life.

He drove the vehicle back into the forest and weaved in between trees with more caution this time. He was moving slower and trying to exercise some stealth for a change. The robust vehicle trundled over roots and rocks. Due to Larry's more careful driving, the vehicle left less noticeable tracks.

Curse knew they were going back to Larry's crumbling old farmhouse but had no idea how to get there. Larry apparently knew the woods, or he was acting like he did while trying to put distance between them and the Archaic Front.

While they drove, Larry filled Aja in on life and existence in the Nightmarescape. She seemed to digest the information and understand it the best she could. His information filled in a number of blanks for her. The two of them were having a good time talking about theories and existence.

Curse continued to swing the gun back and forth, being on guard for anything that may come their way. After some time, they drove past another cliff face. Several bodies wrapped in furs turned toward them as they approached. They grasped long wooden spears tipped with sharpened stone heads. Larry grinned and nodded his head to them as they drove past. They nodded in return. Curse assessed their demeanor. They seemed disturbed by his presence but did not move to do anything as the jeep passed them.

"Neanderthals?" Curse yelled to Larry over the din of the engine.

"Eh, some kind of tiki-worshippin' jerks!" Larry yelled back.

The jeep continued to weave between the trees, eventually coming to an open and arid plain where they drove for some time. Larry was definitely taking a much longer route than they had run on foot. Curse continued to survey the open ground from behind the gun. After a period of time crossing the plain, another line of gray trees loomed in the distance. Larry drove the vehicle into the woods once more.

Larry guided the jeep along the edge of the tree line to avoid being easily detected in open areas and passed several ruined and decayed structures along the way. None of them seemed inhabited, so they were able to continue past them without incident. After what felt like several hours of driving, Curse caught sight of the farmhouse in the distance. He recognized the location as the field he and Larry had run though just after his manifestation.

Curse allowed his guard to drop momentarily as he looked down at Banshee. He realized the moment he did so that he had made a grave mistake.

25

The jeep was struck with explosive force on the driver's side. A fireball erupted as the jeep was flung onto its side before rolling over onto its top, and all four of them were thrown from the vehicle. Searing pain tore through both of Curse's arms as he tried to push himself up from the ground. Looking down, he observed that both of his arms were severely broken.

"God damnit," he growled under his breath as the crushing pain of fractured bone rushed up into his torso.

He snarled as he looked the useless members over and saw a hint of bone pushing through his right arm, black ichor streaming from the wound. His teeth gritted to the point where they almost broke on each other as he attempted to gain control of the pain. He could feel his body healing the wounds with mental energy, but it was taking a fair amount of time to repair such damage.

Using his legs only, trailing his temporarily disabled arms, he crawled behind the wreckage of the jeep. Wild shouts and sporadic gunfire sounded from the other side. Curse placed his back against the wreckage and waited for his limbs to finish healing. The left one was the first one to finish.

Curse reached for his waist and pulled out the Nambu pistol. He only needed one hand to shoot it with its light recoil, and in such a scenario, one weapon was better than none.

Leaning his head around the back of the jeep for a quick peak, he observed three forms running toward him. They all wore cloth wrapped around their heads and screamed with harsh throaty accents. Two of them carried AK-47s that they fired indiscriminately while the other carried a long tubular weapon that he was attempting to load something into. Curse watched what he was putting into the weapon for a moment before realizing that it was a rocket-propelled grenade launcher.

Curse looked at the wreckage of the jeep. The back end was sitting high in the air due to the fact that it had landed on the machine gun mount. The machine gun itself was facing toward the attackers. Dropping his pistol, Curse maneuvered himself under the vehicle and struggled to get a hold on the machine gun's trigger mechanism. His left hand seized the control in a white-knuckle grip while he forced the fingers on his right arm to squeeze it as well. His right arm was still working to return to its original shape and reknit the fracture. He screamed as the pain from his fracture burned all the way through his arm. His scream intensified as the weapon began to kick, sending shock waves of pain down his injured arms. Roaring to life, the weapon spat its deadly payload in uncontrolled sweeps. Curse's broken arm and the compromised mobility of the weapon made accurate shooting almost impossible. Still, he persevered through the agony, gritting his teeth as the weapon rattled in his hands. Shooting a torrent of fire in their direction was better than nothing. Some of the rounds had to strike them eventually.

They kept coming. Curse kept his hands on the machine gun's trigger. The pain was going away as the fracture healed. When the sensation had subsided to a manageable level, Curse gained more control of the weapon and swept a punishing wave of fire over the attackers.

The three assailants were all knocked from their feet, their weapons still firing as they fell. One of the airborne bodies dried and crumbled, its former head now replaced with a gushing stump. Curse peered out from under the jeep and saw Larry charging for one of the downed bodies and then heard the trademark explosion from his shotgun several moments later. One of the bodies that was still lying on the ground maneuvered its AK-47 to the side and fired a small stream of rifle rounds into Larry's body. Larry was stopped momentarily by the trauma, but recovered and kept moving. The shooter screamed something up at Larry that Curse could not understand. Curse watched as Larry pinned the man's shooting arm to the ground and then placed his shotgun against the man's head. Another boom and the man's body became dust.

Larry turned for the other one but was met with a sharp kick to his kneecap that sent a sickening snap across the landscape. Larry fell screaming—the first time Curse had heard him scream. He previously thought Larry incapable of any pain, but seeing him wallow on the ground now, nursing a broken limb of his own, drove Curse into a fury.

Knowing that he would not be able to get a good shot off on a prone body with the machine gun, Curse charged toward the downed attacker. The man was up before he even got close. Curse stopped frozen as he saw that the launcher was reloaded and that the man was dropping to a kneeling position.

The world moved in slow motion as the small warhead flew from the launcher, riding a plume of white flame. Curse's head turned as he watched it fly and felt his insides shake with the scream that resonated inside him. The warhead shrieked through empty space before impacting with a sickening crack as it embedded in Aja's upper chest. Curse watched in horror as she was lifted from her feet and flew several yards through the air before the explosive detonated, sending gory pieces of her flying in all directions.

26

The last few bits of Aja's upper body rained down as a pair of legs topped with dark-colored intestines tumbled to the ground. Her remaining limbs flipped over each other as though they were made of rubber and dissolved into dust.

Curse felt himself howling with rage as he charged toward Aja's killer. He leapt upon the man with a heavy thud. The man yelled something in a thick accent that Curse could not place. Curse had no idea what he was saying, nor did he care. His fist hit the man's head with crushing force. The downed combatant attempted to put a guard up, but Curse landed another punch before he could and felt a snap beneath his closed knuckles. Curse's fingers dug into the cloth covering the man's face as he ripped it off with a single fluid motion. A gaunt, desiccated face covered by a slight beard stared back at him. Curse slammed his own head down into the man's face and pulled back to see it now a sludgy ruin. His headbutt had destroyed the man's nose and probably shattered one of his cheekbones. Still the man struggled and tried to fend him off while yelling.

Curse was gripped with a familiar fury. He had seen James shot and killed, and now he had seen Aja completely

Nightmarescape

destroyed. Rage pumped through his body as he placed both of his hands on either side of his quarry's temples. The man's hands came up to his wrists but did nothing to move them, for he was severely overpowered. Seething with hatred, Curse dug his bony thumbs into his enemy's eye sockets. An agonized scream sounded below him as he felt his thumbs dig deep into flesh followed by a visceral pop as black ichor began pouring from the fleshy matter. There was no mercy for this one. Curse assured himself of that as he dug deeper into the soft sludge inside the man's head. The screaming beneath him stopped as the body suddenly seized and then crumbled into nothing.

Curse threw his head back and unleashed a primal scream of rage, loss, and vindication all in one. He then sat on his knees and stared at the dusty heap that had been Aja's legs. Larry was struggling to stand back up now, his fracture mostly healed. Banshee came to both of them, her face showing only shock. Curse looked both of them over.

Whatever wounds they had sustained in the fight had healed. The physical wounds were not what mattered in the Nightmarescape. Those with a strong enough presence would regenerate to their former selves. The psyche, on the other hand, did not regenerate and would stay wounded.

Curse thought of how he had come to this place feeling nothing but loss and loneliness. It was amplified now that he had lost someone here as well. Aja had not been with him for long at all. Even less than Banshee, but the fact did not dim her loss any less. She was also one that he, Larry, and Banshee had saved. Had they not found her before the Plague Faction was reawakened from their dead pool, she would have been torn apart limb from limb.

The weight of the whole situation crashed into Curse, and he shrugged his shoulders into a posture of defeat. Though he had known that Aja might not survive very long in a place such as the Nightmarescape, he felt as though he had failed in protecting her long enough to even make it to Larry's house. All three of the companions were in a morose state. Larry's perpetual grin had changed into a scowl. Banshee hung her head low but held something in her arms. It was Aja's backpack.

Banshee looked up to Curse the moment she felt his eyes upon her. At least they still had the device . . . if it was not damaged. How would they get it to work though? Without Aja to show them, none of them would know what they were doing with it and could possibly cause catastrophic damage.

Curse brooded over the thought as he bent and collected the attackers' weapons. Two AK-47 rifles and a rocket-propelled grenade launcher. He then made his way back to the jeep and retrieved the pistol he left under it. He also worked to loosen the machine gun from its mounting to bring it with him.

After several minutes of working at it, he gave up. He could retrieve some tools from inside Larry's house and remove it later. Fury seethed through his being as he dropped the weapons beside the jeep's wreckage and walked over to the pile of dust that had been the attacker with the launcher. Banshee and Larry watched as he opened the fly of his pants.

"You god damn piece of shit," he rasped between clenched teeth as a stream of dark liquid left his body and soaked the dust into the ground.

When he was done, he closed his pants once more and kicked at the ground with a scream. Dust flew up from the impact to be blown all over by the wind. Curse then pulled the revolver from his pants and fired several rounds into the ground, sending more dust up into the air. When he had his fill of molesting the dust, he walked back to the jeep and hefted the weapons once more. Silently the three of them made their way to Larry's house.

When the grim march through the yard was over, they all stood on the porch. Curse and Banshee stood back as Larry unlocked the front door. As Banshee was about to step her bare foot onto the doormat, Curse grabbed her shoulder and pulled her back.

"Trapped," he simply stated.

Banshee gave him a hint of a smile and stepped over into the dark house. Immediately, Curse went into the living room and dumped the cache of newfound weapons on the floor. He had shot several AK-47s in the past, so he felt comfortable with those, but he had never dealt with a rocket-propelled grenade launcher.

The thing was just a tube with a trigger and no ammunition at present. Closed-chamber weapons in the Nightmarescape never seemed to need reloading as long as the wielder granted them enough mental energy, but this thing did not seem so simple. He tossed it aside for the time being and let it clatter off into the dark. He would look around where he had killed the weapon's owner later and see if there was any ammunition. He would also take the machine gun from the jeep. Right now it just did not seem to matter.

He positioned himself down on the couch and held his head by the temples. He was still losing people. Just earlier, he had been thinking about how he would protect any of the other three and now he had failed one of them. Even more, it might have been the only one who could get him back to his love. Despite Aja's brief presence, she had made an impact on him nonetheless. He felt even more protective of her as she had been vulnerable and out of place. Then he thought of the woman that he had seen after waking up at Larry's and about how he had killed her out of rage. He felt guilt now, guilt that hit him in the center of his chest like a sledgehammer. Leaning back against the decaying piece of furniture, he let out a heavy sigh.

"Fuck," he rasped under his breath.

Banshee sat across the room, watching him. It seemed as though she was almost trying to take cues from him on how to handle the situation. She still held Aja's pack in her arms. They sat together in the dark living room, just watching one another in silence. Larry could be heard elsewhere in the house crashing around. It was Banshee who spoke first.

"That's the second time I've seen someone die who did not deserve it. I've killed before, but it's different when you're fighting for something you believe in and have to do it. To see someone innocent die . . . it affects you on a different level. It's much more personal." She stood and came to sit with him.

"You're right," Curse nodded as he stared off into the dark. Banshee sat on the couch beside him and took his right hand in both of hers. He looked over to her as she offered a faint smile. It was not a one of happiness, but one of reassurance. She moved forward and wrapped her arms around him. He felt himself unconsciously returning the gesture. The barbed wire on her arms stuck into his bare back as she held him. He did not let it bother him. He instead took the physical pain and stuck it deep within his psychic self, allowing it to be a stimulus that would remind him of her should he lose her at any point. Together they sat in the dark room for a good while in their embrace.

They were interrupted some time later as Larry came into the room dragging a large box. "You two, none of that on my couch!" he bellowed.

"Just an embrace after losing a friend." Banshee regarded him with a smile.

"Well then, in that case, carry on, ya heathens . . . When you're done fondling her, Curse, I've got something here for you!" Larry gave the box a kick with his toe and a heavy thud sounded from inside.

"What is it you have there, Larry?" Curse asked. Larry's grin came back to his face momentarily.

"Stuff for your new toys!" His perpetually crazy eyes rolled down to the weapons Curse had dropped on the floor. He looked back at Curse and winked. A moment later, he left the room again.

Curse sat on the edge of the couch, eying the box. "Well, shall we?" he asked Banshee.

"Certainly," she responded.

Curse stood and went to retrieve the box. He brought it over to the couch so that he could sit beside her as he opened it. The box was a wooden crate that had the lid barely nailed in place. His bony fingers dug under the lid and ripped it off with little force. As he looked down and surveyed what was inside, he felt himself laughing. Two bayonets for the AK-47s sat on top of twelve rocket-propelled grenades.

"You have to admit, the crazy bastard knows when to give good presents," he said to Banshee. She returned a smile to him.

Larry became visible in the doorway again with a sack of tools slung over his shoulder. "Oh and I'll take care of the machine gun on the jeep . . . at least it'll make a good yard decoration! You two just rest now; I can give you some fancy head talkin' later if you like!" With that he was out the front door.

Curse and Banshee shook their heads. Larry was still upset even if he didn't show it. Curse lay back against the couch again and stared off into the darkness. He could feel his consciousness slipping from him. Another flashback was coming.

Suddenly he was sitting in a different living room. The woman from his dreams was sitting beside him on a different couch. This one was a light tan in color and very well kept in contrast to Larry's moldy dark-colored thing. Her eyes were filled with tears. Curse tried to understand what she was saying, tried to listen, but he was furious at her. He looked down and noticed his hands trembling. Willing them to stop, he was finally able to hear her.

"I'm sorry, I just can't go on like this," she said.

Curse felt pains in his chest from having to relive this again. He had already dealt with the aftermath of her leaving once—how many more times would he come back to it?

"I will always love you, and you will always be a special part of me, but it just won't be healthy if we keep going on this way."

Curse found himself nodding as she spoke but said nothing in return. She sat beside him and put her arms around him. He found that he could not consciously return the gesture. He then became aware of something poking him in the back. Numerous small points were stabbing into his flesh right where her arms were holding him. Curse awakened with a start to find himself firmly grasped in Banshee's arms once again. Upon coming back to consciousness, he let out a grunt, and she released him.

"I hate flashbacks from my old life," she told him.

"Yeah . . . same here," he agreed.

No more words passed between the two for some time. They simply sat together, trying to digest in their minds all that had happened. Curse later stood and walked over to a window where he could observe Larry in the front yard yelling at the jeep as he attacked it with a large wrench.

When he had his fill of watching Larry, Curse found the backpack with Aja's device inside and removed it. He sat staring at it and trying to figure out how to make the thing work. Thinking that there might be some writings or schematics in the bag, he set the device down on the table and began searching through the pack. Banshee watched from the couch. Reaching down to the bottom of the bag, Curse found several papers that had been crumpled when the device was dropped in on them. Rummaging through them, Curse read about physics and equations that made little sense to him. He also read several theories that Aja had hastily jotted down. Setting all of them aside, he found a letter buried beneath them. Curse sat down in a chair to read it.

It was a letter from Aja's fiancé describing how he missed her and how upset he was that she spent so much time buried in her work. The letter described how he saw her less and less as she delved deeper into her research. Curse grunted to himself as he thought of what had actually happened to her. The letter closed in saying that he wished that she would be done soon, and they could be together again. Curse assumed that the fiancé never saw Aja after she had begun turning into a creature of the Nightmarescape. Curse knew how it felt to watch someone drift away though. That old familiar ache never seemed to leave him. He grunted and set the letter aside as he thought of the situation.

His attention turned back to the device. He sat and stared at it, trying to make sense of the different parts. Several switches stuck out from the front of the thing. His fingers traced over them, trying to figure out what they might do. He turned the device around to survey for anything on the backside that could be a connection to the switches. Not finding anything, he turned it around again in frustration and decided to do some experimenting.

A moment of trepidation seized him, but he pushed caution from his mind and flipped the first switch. A strange mechanical whine began from inside the device. It sounded as though some wounded motor was trying to power the thing.

"Guess that's the power . . . ," Curse muttered to himself.

His fingers found the next switch and flipped it. The whining sound intensified and several tubes on the side of the device began to glow. As their glow became more radiant, he could feel heat coming off them. He then reached and flipped the final switch. The device screamed louder, and the heat became more intense, but nothing else happened. Curse surveyed the front of the thing again and found several small dials. He grabbed one and twisted it back and forth. The heat rose and fell with the dial. Returning it the way he found it, he grabbed another and tried the same thing. The light dimmed and then brightened. Repeating the procedure, he did the same with the final dial. The machine's sound grew to the point where it sounded like the scream of a dying animal. Curse quickly turned the dial in the opposite direction until the sound fell to near silence.

Curse flipped all of the switches off once more and thought about how to manipulate them for a result. Light, sound, and heat. He knew the thing operated on some wave frequency given those three variables, he just had no idea

Nightmarescape

how to manipulate them correctly. Fearful of damaging the device, he pulled his hands away from it and began thinking about how to make light, heat, and sound interact in a fashion that could split dimensions. Perhaps there was something missing or left behind that would amplify the device. The front door burst open, and Larry waltzed in carrying the machine gun that had been mounted on the jeep.

"HA! The bastard wanted to be stubborn, but I showed it!" He hefted the weapon in the air and brought it down on the table next to the device.

"You been playin' with that thing, son?" Larry inquired.

"To an extent," Curse asserted.

"Well, what does it do?"

"So far it's a fancy-looking heater." Curse shrugged. "I turn these dials, and it starts making noise, gets hot, and these tubes glow." He pointed at the tubes on the side of the device.

"And how does that do anything?" Larry furrowed his brow as he gawked at the device.

Curse shrugged again. "Not sure yet . . . I think there might be a piece we're missing that amplifies the energy or something of that nature. Just a theory so far though."

Larry rubbed his bony fingers over his chin. Something was brewing in his head. "I know a guy who might be able to figure this thing out some more. There are a number of engineers that were killed in combat. I know a few of them, but we have to get back to the Archaic Front." He paused. "I'm hesitant to do that though. I don't think we want anyone knowing what this thing is just yet. If we go handing it over to him, we might never see it again, and then you can't go back to your young lady."

"And I can't kill those bastards who murdered me!" Banshee interjected.

Larry and Curse turned and looked at her. The lights that had been her eyes seethed intensity. Both of them admired her drive for vengeance, but it would not help them figure out the device.

"My dear," Larry began, "there will be a time when you shall have your vengeance, but right now we have to figure out how to get you there."

"Who do you know who might be able to help us with this thing?" Curse asked.

"Well, we'll have to get back to the Archaic Front, and then we will give it to him in some discreet place. The guy was an engineer when he was alive, and he lived in your century after me so he will have more knowledge of this kind of science."

"And just how do we find him?"

"Going back to the Englishmen will be a good start. They know that group pretty well. They also know who's gunning for me and who's not. Even here, much like our previous world, constant power games are being played within factions. As many friends as the colonel has, he has just as many enemies. Many of them will be willing to help me because I am against him. At the same time, many would be just as willing to help him, so I would like to tread carefully in their ranks without a huge presence."

"So even politics never die," Curse snarled.

"Afraid not, my boy, but it's all in who you know, and I got some folks to know and those who know knows!" Larry gave another trademark thrust of his index finger with his proclamation.

"Right." Curse was not in the mood for Larry's word-smithery. "Let's go see if we can find this engineer."

Larry nodded his consent, and the three of them began collecting supplies to head back out into the chaotic world.

Curse hefted the launcher, and then slung an AK-47 over his shoulder. His trusty revolver and recovered Nambu remained in his waistband. Larry provided him with a simple pack, and he threw several rounds for the launcher in it. When done gathering the supplies, Curse affixed the bayonets to the ends of the assault rifles. Banshee traded her rifle for the remaining AK-47. She took several large items out of her pack before placing the device inside. Curse and Larry would entrust her with its safety. Larry took only his trusty shotgun and an old .45 caliber revolver. Even though he possessed many more modernized firearms, he was keen on the classic weapons he had used in his life. He wore the revolver in a worn leather holster while carrying the shotgun. The three of them set out again with Larry in the lead.

27

Larry guided them across the gray landscape to where the earlier battle had taken place. Curse still had not developed a cognitive map due to the fact that he had mainly been running behind Larry. Now he stayed cautious but mapped their footsteps at the same time. He had done it before, though he could not remember where or how. It simply came to him unconsciously, probably something from his former life that he had yet to remember.

How he did it was not important so much as that he simply did it. Banshee kept an even pace with him several feet away. They surveyed the landscape for any threats while Larry led them to their destination. Entering another forest of rotted trees and dried gray foliage, they all took their time to tread carefully. There might have been more hidden attackers nearby, and they did not want to immediately engage in another fight.

Rage flooded Curse's thoughts briefly as he thought about what had been done to Aja. He wondered why the attackers were there in the first place. Then again, maybe there was no reason. The Nightmarescape was a chaotic place full of chaotic minds. They could have been wanderers that were searching for a fight. They could have been crusading for some lost cause. Whatever their reason, they had killed one of his people, and they had paid the price.

Realizing that he was letting his anger distract him, Curse turned his attention back to watching the world around him. The three of them had moved a great distance through the forest. Hours, minutes, days, years, time did not matter here. It swirled and coalesced together like blood from a wound circling its way down a drain. There was no lifespan as far as he could tell. You lived again in the Nightmarescape until you were destroyed or your psychic energy became too weak. It had to be a symbiosis the realm had created for itself. The world needed the psychic energy of its residents to survive.

After what seemed like several hours of an uneventful trip, Curse caught sight of the crumbling village once again. More tanks were stationed around the gun emplacement. They were different from the two that had come to the fight. One was a Russian T-34. The other was a destroyer of some sort. Curse did not recognize it immediately because of the garish black and gray camouflage pattern that had been crudely daubed onto it. The remaining two were foreign tanks that Curse did not recognize. Several lightly armored personnel carriers and a half-track sat behind them.

A greater number of soldiers ambled about the village now. Larry signaled for Curse and Banshee to wait at the edge of the woods as he surveyed who had come to the village. Seeing no one who looked directly related to the colonel, he waved the other two on, and they approached. A large congregation of warriors was standing around a smoldering pile of ashes.

Several Vikings stood at the very center, resting their hands on their axes. Their skeletal faces grinned out from behind tangled and patchy beards. Several of the World War I soldiers that he and Larry had fought alongside stood laughing with them. They were joined by a group of men in full plate armor who stood weary guard, blades and bludgeons slung over their shoulders. One of the British soldiers looked up and signaled to the three of them as Curse and company breached the premises of the village.

Quickly they made their way over to the group. Larry and Curse were greeted with handshakes and warm slaps on the back. The warriors had not met Banshee yet but greeted her with all the same affection. Curse did not see any other women around and wondered how long these men had been stuck without women.

Even though he had gone into battle with the warriors, he did not trust them entirely and would maul any one of them that made an unwelcome advance toward Banshee. She was raped before her murder, and so he felt an overwhelming need to protect her from such things. Whether anybody even thought about sex in the Nightmarescape was a completely different matter. Larry had said that some people even lacked genitals altogether. Whether this was due to injury, decay, or whatever reason, he did not know. To Curse, being intimate with anyone that looked like anything from the Nightmarescape seemed to be a horrifying proposition. But then again, people had never failed to disgust him with their practices before.

He resolved to keep Banshee safe from anyone who might offer her such treatment and expelled the rest of the thoughts from his mind as he put a smile on his face while exchanging embraces with the warriors.

"And who's the bird you brought with you?" one of the soldiers asked.

"Let me introduce you all to Banshee," Curse put a hand on her shoulder and brought her forth. "She's a consummate fighter."

She smiled back at him for boasting about her. The soldiers greeted her respectfully.

"Wonder what else she's consummate at!" one of the Vikings chided.

Curse's smile widened, not because he found the joke funny, but because it was an opportunity for violence.

"Keep at it, playboy, and I'll do you like I did the pieces of shit these guys saw me kill earlier," Curse's mouth widened to show a big toothy grin.

"Yeah, this one here is a beast!" One of the soldiers slapped his back.

The Viking warrior stared at Curse with measured anger. Despite the warrior's countenance, his gaze left Curse and drifted to the ground. The warrior did not want to start a conflict here amongst the men. Curse would remember him for the slight, however. If there were further problems, he might even see to a combat accident should they both be together in the next engagement.

The conflict was momentarily forgotten as soldiers around them rejoiced at their presence once more.

"This bloke here . . . he killed about twenty of those plague boys, and he started out with his bare hands!"

"I saw him beat five into dust with the butt of a rifle!" They laughed and played up his deeds in the fight.

He returned their congratulations and followed Larry through the throng. Larry pulled one of the soldiers aside.

"Son, do you know where we can find Lieutenant Drake?" he asked.

"He's over here; I'll take you to him!" Larry and his crew followed the soldier over to one of the ruined buildings.

The officer that they had seen earlier was sitting at a table with several other soldiers. They looked to be from the World War II era, judging by their uniforms and the fact that one of them carried a Thompson submachine gun. Another warrior in full plate armor stood beside them. His sunken and corroded face was surrounded by a chainmail coif while a tabard bearing a large cross fell over his armor. All of them looked up as the three approached.

"Well met there, L. T.!" Larry yelled.

"Mr. Spectre." Lieutenant Drake nodded to him without standing. He seemed somewhat annoyed at the distraction but did not turn Larry away. The others around the table stared at them with irritated expressions. Curse recognized the lieutenant as the man who had directed the movement of the gun earlier.

"I'll be brief as you're busy, but is Nigel with you right now?" Larry asked.

"He is, Lawrence; he's near the rear of the village working on his tank as usual," the officer responded.

"Very good, I think we got something he might be interested in!" Larry exclaimed.

"Right, we'll talk more later; let me finish discussing strategy with these gentlemen."

Larry led Curse and Banshee away from the group of commanders. They followed him through the ruined buildings and moved toward a modified World War I tank sitting at the edge of the village. At least it had originally been a World War I tank. Curse recognized the slanted chassis and tread pattern. If his memory of military history was correct, it looked to be a British Mark IV . . . or it had been at some point. The vehicle had been heavily modified, many of its original dimensions and functions having been altered. Its blocky chassis was now covered in all sorts of spikes and blades. A lone body was walking around the vehicle, stringing razor wire along the sides. The figure seemed engrossed in what it was doing and did not notice their approach. A heavy coat hung down over its frame, and it wore a flattened helmet over a leather mask that covered the top half of its face. A thin chainmail veil hung from the leather. Curse recognized this to be the clothing of the original tank drivers.

"Nigel!" Larry boomed as they approached.

The figure looked up from its labor, a single hand reaching toward a pistol holstered at its hip. Upon seeing who was walking toward him, he began shaking his head and relaxed his hand.

"What in bloody hell do you want, Lawrence?"

Larry stopped in front of the tank driver, grinning like an idiot. His friend quickly embraced him with a hearty laugh.

"Right then, madman, what is it now?"

"Got an interesting piece of machinery you might want to look at," Larry's brow rose and fell as he spoke.

"And what might that be that's so interesting?"

"Got somewhere away from prying ears?" Larry's eyes shifted around deviously.

Nigel's gaze followed his, sweeping across the surrounding area. His chainmail veil flowed with his movements.

"Let's talk in the tank then," he said hurriedly before climbing up the tracks, moving around the razor wire and onto the top of the vehicle. He then disappeared into an open hatch.

Larry, Banshee, and Curse followed him. It was cramped inside the tank. The metal walls imposed on all sides, and they were stuck right next to the engine. The thing felt like a huge tracked coffin. Nigel leaned his back against the command chair of the vehicle. Curse could tell that the inside of the tank had been heavily modified as well. Most tanks reminiscent of the period barely accommodated two or three people, and yet all four of them had managed to squeeze into this one with minimal room to spare. The controls for all of the guns had been moved so that they were accessible by the driver rather than the normal crew positions. Curse believed Nigel was the sole operator of the vehicle.

"Well, what've we got then?" Nigel's voice snapped Curse out of his wonderment. Banshee reached into her pack and removed the device.

"And what the hell is that thing?" Nigel looked disappointed. "Is this another joke of yours, old man?"

Larry breathed a ragged laugh through his grinning teeth before explaining. "A little while back . . . earlier, maybe several hours ago, we went into that fort that sits next to the village . . ."

Nigel's eyes were gone, and hollowed out sockets with blue lights remained in their place, but Curse could tell that if he still had eyes, they would be bulging out through the holes in the leather.

"The Plague Fort?" Nigel asked with an air of incredulity.

"Ya see, the thing is we didn't know what it was at the time. I'd never actually been inside it, but Banshee here had been, and we were looking for a place to hole up in case the colonel and his boys showed their faces."

Nigel leapt up and grabbed onto the hatch of the tank and spit out of it.

"Pompous imperious bastard, I won't let the spit I throw at his name sully my machine!" he exclaimed.

Apparently this colonel did have more enemies than just Larry.

"Yes, that's the spirit!" Larry continued, "We got in there and found someone hiding . . . a woman. She told us that she had been studying at a university and had created a device that could allow people from the old world to transition into this one."

Nigel held his arms across his chest. "And this little piece of shit can do that?"

"So we're led to believe. She was killed while we were taking it back to my place."

Nigel placed a hand on his head. "And the ones who killed her, did they know about this?"

"I don't believe so; they were Arabs, I think. Looked to be just out to fight," Larry explained.

Curse gripped the weapons in his hands as he thought of Aja's killers.

"And is that where he got those things from then?" Nigel indicated toward Curse's weapons.

"It is," Curse spoke this time. "I took their weapons after I killed them." He hefted the launcher for Nigel to see. "They shot a rocket right into her chest and destroyed her entire upper half. They paid the price for killing one of my people and getting in my way." Curse's anger begin to show as he spoke about Aja's death.

"Easy bloke, no offense. What did they get in the way of?"

"I'm going to use that device to get back to my old life and see my wife, girlfriend, whatever the hell she was. Nobody will stop me now that I have a way," Curse's voice thundered off the inside of the vehicle.

"Admirable passion, but you got a perfectly good girl right there with you." Nigel nodded toward Banshee. "A woman in the old life won't recognize you with that corpse face you got."

"I know."

"How do you even know she's still alive? You're obviously new here, so I won't press you on how long you've been here, but you know how time works in these parts. The world you left could be a completely different place by now. I'm sure if Lawrence or I went back, we wouldn't recognize it," Nigel continued.

Curse sank back at his argument. What if that was true; what if he was trying to get back only to find a world that he no longer remembered?

"What do you think I can do with this thing anyway?" Nigel asked while he motioned for Banshee to hand the device to him.

"Well, you've always been mechanically inclined; Curse here tried to get the thing working but could only get it to glow and make noise. It's got something to do with waves and all that," Larry stated.

Nigel looked somewhat puzzled. "I know how to fix and build tanks, not how to manipulate bloody physics," he said flatly.

"Nigel . . ."

"What?"

"Nigel . . ."

"What!?"

"Nigel . . ."

"What in bloody fuckin' hell is it, Lawrence?"

"The world is a wide place, you can always do BOTH!" Larry's eyes beamed with the proclamation.

Nigel threw his head back and let loose a throaty laugh from beneath his mask. He took the device in his hands and began to look it over.

"The switches control heat, light, and sound. The dials adjust the intensity," Curse stated as Nigel listened intently. "I just can't figure out the frequencies we need yet."

Nigel nodded as he looked the device over with increased curiosity. "Gimme a few minutes with this thing," he said.

With that, they left him alone and climbed out of the tank. They stood beside the mechanized behemoth while the shrieking sounds of the device became audible from inside. The weird scream echoed off the metal walls and bounced around inside the vehicle. Curse thought to himself that Nigel's ears had to be killing him.

The scream rose and fell as Nigel tinkered with the dial. Banshee began moving away; the sound was bothering her. Curse followed. Larry stayed near the tank with his palm pressed flat against the metal. His head was nodding and bobbing to some strange tune that only he could hear. The shriek of the device rose and fell with his rhythmic movements. It reminded Curse of when Larry had been sawing on a fiddle some time ago. The thought made him laugh.

"What's funny?" Banshee asked.

"Larry . . . he's fucking nuts," Curse replied.

"Well, that's obvious. I would love it if the tank guy could get that device to work," she said matter-of-factly.

"Wouldn't we all?"

"I'll tell you why I actually keep this barbed wire on my arms." Fire burned brightly in her eye sockets. "I've kept it because I've been hoping to use it on those assholes who killed me. I want them to feel it digging into their flesh as I tear into them. I'll leave their corpses with the same scars they left me."

Curse nodded. He understood her drive for vengeance. He had not avenged his own life and really had nothing to avenge since he had died by his own hand, but he did know the feeling of needing to avenge another. He let his fingers dig into his palms as he replayed his friend's death in his mind once more.

Banshee was talking again, but he realized he had not heard anything she said for a few minutes because he had become absorbed in his own thoughts. Mentally he scolded himself, and resolved not to show her such disrespect in the future.

"I'm sorry, something was distracting me . . . what were you saying?"

"Ah . . . I was just spitting venom about those rednecks that put their knives—and their dicks—in me."

Curse studied her face. Determination and resolve were written on her features. Beneath the gray and white skin, her jaw was set, and the heat was still in her eyes. She was set in her course. He knew in his mind that he was set in his as well, and he saw a mirror of his own determination in her.

"You'll get them. I'll help you," he offered.

Her expression of determination slowly turned into a sadistic grin. "I would be honored for you to help me." She smiled.

"Then they will pay. I'd love to see the look on their faces when you come back for them." The thought gave Curse satisfaction.

She stepped close to him and placed her hands around his wrists. His instinct was to pull away from her, for he was on the cusp of making his way to his former life and seeing his love again. Even if his lover never saw him, he would see her. At this point in time, he did not want to let another woman show him such affections. He slowly began pulling his hands from hers. Her smile left as he did so. She took a breath.

"I know how you feel right now. It's okay. You're not rejecting me; you feel committed, and it seems wrong to let another close to you in the time being." Her voice was full of understanding.

Curse nodded but did not feel a need to speak. She had summed his feelings up well. Instead he just looked into her face for a long moment. He could tell that she had been beautiful in her former life. Her features were nicely formed and symmetrical. It was hard to picture exactly what she looked like staring into her undead face. He formed a mental picture in color of how she could have looked. He also thought of who she was as a person. He remembered her telling him that she was basically an eco-terrorist. How would that have affected him had he known her before the Nightmarescape? Context was an interesting device. Here she was a victim out for revenge. In their former lives, she had been a killer, and vengeance had been wrought upon her. Even vengeance had a limit though. Her killers had taken theirs on her to a level of outright sadism. They weren't just avenging a friend; they were evil men waiting for a reason to justify their intent.

Curse stood staring at her a moment longer until a shout from the soldiers took his attention away from her. A commotion was brewing up near the front of the village. Soldiers were scrambling. Larry had even turned from his moment of musical enjoyment and was facing the front of the village. He began rapping his fist against the hull of the tank to get Nigel's attention. Moments later, Nigel's head poked out of the hatch and then disappeared after a brief survey. The tank's engine roared to life, its tracks grinding across the earth as it maneuvered to the press of bodies at the front of the village. Larry hung onto a gun turret sticking out from the side of the vehicle. Curse and Banshee fell in alongside the machine in a brisk run.

"More incoming!" A voice was screaming above the chaos. The group of commanders had left their ruined building and were marching toward the front. Nigel's tank rumbled up behind the men at the front of the village. Curse and Banshee moved up from behind it. Curse had not noticed it before, but the soldiers had dug several trench lines in front of the village. Many of the World War I and II soldiers were dropping down into the trenches and sighting their weapons. A crew was moving a machine gun mounting into a makeshift nest. The howitzer crew was manning their position once more. Viking warriors and armored figures were falling in beside them. Soldiers with ranged weapons were preparing their guns while the Vikings and medieval soldiers would make for a devastating close combat punch when bodies began falling into the trenches.

Curse stopped beside the tank and began loading a warhead into his launcher. Banshee stood beside him, and Larry dropped from the turret to join them on the ground once more before he skittered up the tank's tracks and began screaming at Nigel down a small hole in the closed hatch. When he was done, he leapt off the vehicle once again.

"Had to tell him to be careful with the device!" Larry exclaimed. "Now let's have some fun before the colonel and his jerks show up!"

Curse and Banshee moved forward and fell into the trenches beside the soldiers. A British soldier turned his attention from his bolt-action rifle and slapped Curse's shoulder.

"Good to have you aboard for another go, Major!"

His accent made Curse laugh a little as he prepared for battle. Beside him, Banshee readied her weapon. One of the Vikings beside the soldier turned toward Curse and brandished his axe with a grin spread across his face.

"Should be a good romp!" he yelled.

Curse nodded his enthusiasm before another voice sounded behind them.

"Quiet, you lot!" All heads turned to see Lieutenant Drake standing behind the trenches. "Remember my signals! Wait until they are close and you can hit them well. It does no good to fire wild shots. Artillery and tank fire will rain down upon them to soften them up before they reach the lines. All at the ready!"

Momentarily Curse turned his attention back to the open plain ahead of them. He could see the enemy in the distance. The gray landscape was being slowly overrun by a dark tidal wave of bodies. Not only bodies this time—enormous metal behemoths towered out of the sea of flesh. Some were even covered with more bodies, creating the illusion of huge moving walls of flesh.

Curse had been in fights during his life. He had been shot at and had shot people in return. He had been in plenty of fistfights and stared directly into the eyes of people with no trace of humanity. He knew that he had been hard in his former life. He knew he was hard now, but the sight of a massed charge made him want to shit himself. He looked over to Banshee. Although she did not show it overtly, he could detect the same trepidation in her movements and her subdued facial expressions. Trying to take his mind from the coming onslaught which could lead to the final moments of existence, he grabbed the nearest soldier's arm and pulled him close.

"What are the signals?" he asked in a low voice.

He did not feel ashamed to ask. He was an outsider aiding in a fight and had not been trained the same as those he fought alongside. Banshee cocked her head and honed in on the conversation as well. The soldier nodded and began to speak in a voice so that only the two of them could hear.

"Lieutenant gives the signals with his saber. The first one will be when he drops the sword, and the artillery and tanks shoot heavy fire into their ranks. The second, he will thrust it back and forth a couple of times. That's when machine guns and the like will open up. A couple of the old-timer boys even have a catapult somewhere near the tanks that they'll use too. The third one he'll slide the blade up and down; that's our cue to quit watchin' him and open fire. We keep our fire on them until they reach the trenches. Then just before they hit, he gives the last one and draws the saber along his throat. The close combat guys hop out and engage as they're hitting the trenches, and then we keep up our fire support. Y'all got it?"

Curse and Banshee's heads nodded in unison.

"Right then, get ready, the first signal is coming."

Curse turned his head so that the officer was visible out of the corner of his eye. The Lieutenant raised his saber high into the air and held the stance for what seemed to be a small eternity. The tip of the blade looked as though it might reach the gray sky and cut a hole in the clouds. Everyone in the trench felt the tension building. The officer's body strained at holding the pose. The men were bristling for the fight to begin. Many of these warriors had been in the Nightmarescape for the better part of a century, some longer. The Vikings had been there almost a millennium. The medieval soldiers had been there for hundreds of years. Some had adopted newer technologies. One of the armored knights was wielding a small submachine gun in one hand and a bladed mace in the other. Whatever the weapon was, it looked suitably archaic—possibly something form the early twentieth century. Curse did not dismiss his embracing new weapons. He did however admire that most of the warriors fought as they had in their lives and survived here so long. He knew that he would survive with them if he just kept his wits about him.

He had to survive, for he had made a promise to Banshee. He also felt as though he owed Larry something for having introduced him to the Nightmarescape and taught him so much that would have taken him many years to learn on his own. Getting killed did not seem like an adequate repayment for such knowledge. Curse looked back at the lieutenant . . . it was time.

The saber fell. As the blade sliced the air, everyone could feel the tension being cut with it. Explosions shook the ground as the howitzer launched its heavy payload into the air, and the tanks opened up with their main guns. The air was filled with the sound of flying munitions. High up into the gray sky the howitzer's round flew before entering its lethal dive bomb. The noise of the shell falling stirred the men's morale as the tank rounds hit home in the mass of advancing foes. Limbs flew in all directions from the initial bombardment. The howitzer shell followed, adding its own deadly toll.

The eruption that came upon its fall created a large hole in the mass of flesh. Still they came. Another volley quickly followed. The attackers kept coming. Momentum carried them. Enormous blossoms of light and smoke threw more bodies into the air. Still they came like a dark tide of flesh preparing to break upon the shore of the trenches. Curse looked at the warriors around him. They had steeled themselves with resolve to meet their enemy head on. They would show no fear. They would not back down. The attackers were getting closer now. Curse could discern individual shapes across the expanse of land.

More Plague Faction were charging at the fore of the assault. It was not just the Plague Faction and a few Japanese soldiers wrangling them this time however. There were all sorts of sordid characters charging this time. Nazi soldiers, plague-ridden bodies, heavily armored warriors, deviants, and derelicts of all sorts, they all charged together brandishing weapons of myriad varieties. Some carried guns from the primitive to the advanced, others carried hand weapons such as blades and clubs, most of the plague-afflicted ran forth with nothing but their bare hands and rabid instincts. They were hungry, and they were getting closer.

Another battery of artillery fire belched into the air and fell for the attackers. They closed distance before the rounds hit home. The Lieutenant thrust his saber forward and brought it back twice. The air was filled with the rattle of machine-gun fire as the smaller weapon emplacements began to fill the space with their devastating barrage. For every body that fell, several more clambered to take its place. Worse still, few killing shots were landed.

Those that fell were overrun by their comrades until their own wounds healed, and they were able to get up and rejoin the charge. Some were trampled by the weight of the horde and did not get back up. They still came closer despite the heavy volume of fire. The lieutenant gave the third signal. Curse, Banshee, and everyone in the trench who had a firearm took a strong firing position and let loose with their weapons. Curse used his rifle to fire measured shots. The weapon allowed for quick sighting and then a strong burst of fire. He was pleased with himself as several of his targets turned to dust upon his shots striking.

He only took a few bodies out of the tide however, and they were still charging at full momentum. Over the chaos of battle and the roar of the guns, a new sound presented itself. It grated the nerves somewhat like the shriek from the device, but it came from the sky. Those in the trenches turned their eyes skyward just in time to see several Nazi war planes screaming down toward them. The half-track and several other vehicles behind the trenches began to adjust their guns moments before the air was filled with antiaircraft fire. The flak guns rumbled and rattled on their metal carriages as the gunners attempted to rake the incoming aircraft. Machine-gun fire fell upon the trenches from above as all heads ducked behind cover. Explosions stitched the ground and the trenches, sending showers of dark earth into the air wherever they hit. The scream of the aircraft behind the machine guns was absolutely chilling. Curse made a mental analogy to angels of death swooping down for them from the gray sky. He then thought of the famous quote about death flying down from Heaven once more.

". . . and Hell followed with him." Perhaps they would see Pastor Nox again soon. He could have very well been in the horde.

The planes continued in their course as they flew directly toward the trenches. The machine guns ceased firing as a chill coursed through Curse's bones. The guns had stopped firing because the planes were about to drop their bombs. Curse dropped his weapon and grabbed Banshee, forcing her down to the bottom of the trench as he put his weight on top of her, covering her with his own body.

"Stay under me," he commanded her.

She did not argue or resist. He believed that she knew what was going to follow. All the soldiers in the trenches were down now. They were prepared for what was to come. The Doppler noise of propellers sounded directly above them. An explosion sounded high up in the air. Some of the antiaircraft rounds had hit home. There were still planes coming though, and they were right over the trenches.

All braced themselves for the impact as an ominous screech filled the air. The planes had dropped their payload. The bombs screamed toward the ground for several seconds before the inevitable impact.

Curse wrapped his arms around Banshee's torso as he pressed down on her. He locked her in his grip beneath him. Should she want to protest, she would not even have been able to get the air into her lungs to speak. Curse kept her down as the first of the impacts shook them.

An intense blast of heat blazed over them as the earth around them was loosened by a shock wave. The airborne earth rained down on those in the trenches. Curse lost his bearings as the remaining explosives detonated and shell shock overtook him. His consciousness was buried under a dark onslaught of ground.

The shock into unconsciousness jolted him into his memory once more. He was a child again. Sitting in an older woman's lap, he was looking at an ancient photo album. She was showing him some photos that were shades of yellows and browns. Curse found his young finger pointing to a strange-looking character in one of the dingy old photos.

"Who's that?" he asked.

He found himself studying the picture and taking the portrait in. The man in the photo wore a loose-fitting brown suit reminiscent of the early 1900s. His eyes carried a strange air of wiliness to them. His face was gaunt and clung tightly to his facial bones. The man's hairline was far receded except for a line of distended scraggly hair that hung around his head in a horseshoe.

"That was a great-great-great-grandfather of yours . . . he was not very close to our family. We don't speak of him very much . . ."

"What was his name?"

"Lawrence Spectman."

Larry. So that's why Larry had gravitated toward him. They were distant kin.

The memory faded from his mind as another one took its place. He was in an office with James.

"Take a look at this—she's not in custody yet, but apparently this woman is wanted for questioning about several murdered hunters in the area. They were hunting deer and someone stalked them and killed them. This girl might know something about it."

James handed him a flyer. It was a police sketch of a female in her early adulthood. Her features were quite beautiful and symmetrical. She was very familiar. Her hair hung down around her face in dreadlocks. Curse could recognize the features and bone structure anywhere. It was Banshee. Though he had never seen her in his previous life, he had taken in enough of her to recognize her anywhere.

It was interesting to him that two people he had found in the Nightmarescape had intersected his life at some point in time. They were not major players, but he had known of both of them in some capacity before finding them in the Nightmarescape. His mind swirled through a torrent of chaos as he spun back to consciousness.

A war was raging around him. Gunfire sounded from all directions. He was covered in loose dirt. He realized that Banshee was screaming beneath him. She was trying to force herself up and remove his weight from her. He established control of his body again as he sat up and moved back off of her. She was unscathed. The thought relieved him. He reached for his weapons; they had not gone far. His hand found the launcher first and then pulled the rifle close. Acrid smoke burned upon the air as he peered his head over the edge of the trench ever so slightly.

Through the thick smoke, ghostly figures ran toward him. Leveling his launcher on the edge of the trench, Curse sighted a tangle of bodies coming in his general direction. Curse fired the weapon and watched as the warhead streamed toward his targets. It flew at them through the smoke; they never had time to see it coming. The warhead struck the group of rushing attackers and immediately destroyed several. Others were thrown in all directions from the explosion. He momentarily thought of Aja's body and how her upper half had been reduced to nothing by the launcher he carried now.

He reminded himself that he was using it as an act of hatred for her killers.

A burst of rifle fire sounded beside him. Banshee was up and shooting now. With measured precision, she picked targets and unleashed bursts of fire into them. Curse was too busy raising his own rifle and finding targets to notice her success rate. All around them guns boomed. The Lieutenant would not get to deliver the final signal because nobody could see him, and the attackers were almost upon them.

Curse immediately wondered how many men had been killed by the bombs. There was still too much smoke for him to take a good measure of the trench. Explosions of dirt leapt up in front of him as bullets struck the ground before him. Who was firing at them from within the smoke, he had no idea.

"Two can play that game, you damn krauts!" Curse looked to his right to see that the soldier he had been next to was still alive.

That was something small to be thankful for. The other thing to be thankful for was that the soldier had a primitive telephone unit that he had pulled off a fallen comrade and was cranking it up to communicate with someone.

"They hit us hard with an air attack—get us some damned air support!"

Curse hoped that the air support would make haste in its arrival. He knew that even though the Axis planes had turned around and that the fighting had closed almost to hand to hand, they would be circling for another pass.

Curse returned to firing at the rushing attackers. They were mere yards from the edge of the trench now. The medieval warriors and Vikings leapt from the safety of the trenches, rushing to meet the enemy in brutal close combat.

Axes and maces met flesh; bullets ricocheted off of armor. Rounds from the trenches knocked bodies off of their feet, and the melee fighters ensured that they never got back up. More explosions thundered from the tanks. The smoke from the bombs was beginning to clear. Curse took a measure of who was still in the trench. Their numbers had been thinned significantly by the bombardment.

Curse heard a creak of metal behind him and turned to see the half-track rumbling up to the rearmost trench. The gunner swiveled the turret and fired rounds of large caliber ammunition into the charging mass. Bodies exploded under the onslaught of the guns. The punishing volley could not hold them off forever though. Still they came en masse. Supporting fire could be kept up as long as they were not overrun. Tracer rounds continued to rip bodies asunder as the charge rolled along on its momentum.

They were right on top of the trenches. The warriors who had leapt out to fight were on their own. Curse rattled off an automatic burst into the charging bodies as they surged forward. The first one dropped down into the trench next to him, and within a heartbeat they were engaged in mortal combat. The frenzied warrior hacked at him with a knuckled trench knife in one hand and fired wild shots from a broom-handled Mauser with the other. Curse blocked the swings of the blade with his rifle. Several stray rounds from the pistol punctured his abdomen. Grunting with pain, he swung the rifle around and struck the attacker's face with the butt of the gun. Bone splintered and cracked under the weight of the wooden stock. The soldier dropped to the floor of the trench. Curse wanted to follow him down and finish the job, but another body tumbled through the air and landed against him. This body was much lighter than the soldier he had just fought. It was one of the plague-afflicted. Its sharp, bony fingers dug into Curse's arms as he placed the rifle between himself and its slathering jaws.

The soldier with the knife and pistol was back up. Curse swung his attacker into the path of the soldier's blade. The blade fell in a strike intended for Curse, but instead impaled the bony torso of the afflicted. A sickening gurgle escaped the thing's mouth as a stream of dark froth bubbled up from its throat. Curse pulled his weapon back and kicked the afflicted in the chest. It stumbled back into the frenzied soldier. Curse brought the rifle to his shoulder and fired a heavy stream of rounds into the two of them. The afflicted took several rounds to the head as the rifle bucked in his grip, and the thing's body quickly crumbled to dust. Several rounds from the pistol flew in Curse's direction. Curse closed the distance, ducking the swinging blade. He brought the butt of his rifle into the bone of the man's sternum. A crack resounded, and the soldier doubled over. Curse fired a brief burst from his rifle into the man's head, and he ceased to exist.

The soldier's weapons dropped to the floor of the trench. Curse quickly snatched them and threw them into his backpack along with the rocket-propelled grenades. He then turned his attention to Banshee. She had been overwhelmed. She had been knocked to the ground, and two German soldiers were slamming the butts of their rifles into her. She covered her head, but her face was a bleeding ruin. The din of battle roared, yet he could hear her screams of pain. Rage exploded from within him. He surged for her with his gun blazing. Bullets struck the assailants' upper bodies and abdomens. Momentarily, they fell off of her, but there was no relief as Curse crashed into them.

He was a whirlwind of violence, slamming the butt of the rifle back and forth into the soldiers. After a particularly hard hit, his foot slipped from under him, and the rifle fell from his grip. Momentarily disarmed, he reached into his pack and retrieved the new knife and pistol. The pistol spat rounds into both bodies as he brought the hilt of the blade down on the first soldier's skull. A spike on the end of the handle made a sizeable chasm in the man's head. Curse shifted his grip and slammed the knuckled handle down into the man's skull. The soldier fell to the ground on his knees, and Curse executed him with a round to the forehead.

The other was still reeling. Curse brought the blade down into the back of his neck. The man attempted to scream through a tortured gurgle as his throat filled with his own ichor. Curse ripped the blade from the man's neck and pressed the barrel of the pistol to the side of the man's head before pulling the trigger. A star-shaped wound ruptured where the weapon had been pressed against his skull. The wound only showed briefly as his being disintegrated into nothing.

Banshee was sitting up at this point. The wounds to her head and face were beginning to heal. Curse helped her to her feet and retrieved both of their weapons. She smiled briefly to thank him. More attackers were coming. Their screams and gunfire echoed throughout the air. Out of nowhere, the noise was eclipsed by a sonic boom from above. Together, Curse and Banshee turned their heads skyward to see a jet screaming overhead. Within a heartbeat, the advancing mass of enemies was lit up with enormous explosions.

White flames erupted from within the seething sea of flesh, sending bodies skyward. Moments later, the jet was gone, and a buzzing noise took the place of its sonic boom.

The gray sky became dark with planes. Curse threw his head back and let out a guttural laugh as the planes soared closer. The mass of air support passed over the trench and flew out over their attackers. Gunfire and explosions were replaced with the screech of falling bombs as the planes disgorged their payloads. Gray and white fire surged skyward from the impacts of the bombs. Armor and bodies were thrown into the air atop the pillars of flame. Burned metal and bodies fell back into the mass. Some were crushed into the ground beneath the weight of the falling armor.

More planes were over them and began dropping their payloads. The ground shook as more explosions rattled the earth. Fire exploded from numerous sites, flinging even more bodies and machines across the battlefield. For a moment, the assault was halted as the horde began attempting to seek temporary cover from the rain of dirt and shrapnel. Then the napalm fell.

29

Burning walls cascaded from where the napalm bombs landed. Planes crisscrossed above the mass of charging attackers, dropping fire from above. Many were incinerated instantly by the intense heat. Others were burned all over their bodies and fell to the ground as charred flesh sloughed from their bones. For the first time, battle cries were replaced with screams of pain. The stench of burning flesh permeated the air as thick black smoke rolled from the burning bodies. The stench of burned flesh combined with the gray and white fire and the screams of burning pain, turning the world into a colorless hell.

All the while, Curse and Banshee stayed down in the trench. The soldiers around them had bunkered themselves as best as they could. The ground still shook as the thick, opaque smoke billowed down into the trenches. Some removed gasmasks and placed them over their faces to keep the stench from affecting them. The fighting had been brutal and inhuman, but the smell of burning flesh made the whole scenario even more abominable.

Burning napalm had settled onto the earth between the trenches and attackers. Tortured forms rushed from within the flames, casting them in the image of demons surging from the fires. Some of the Plague Faction did not even attempt to avoid the fires and charged straight through them. Their fanaticism was strong enough and their senses so dulled that they became little more than running incendiaries. The attackers who still had more of their faculties rolled on the ground screaming in a vain attempt to extinguish the napalm flames. Medieval warriors were completely confounded by the rain of fire and more modern soldiers quickly learned that little could be done to quench such flames.

Curse eased himself up and let his eyes barely crest the trench. The sight of flaming bodies lurching and charging forth greeted him. Grating screams of pain emanated from the line ahead of him. The gut-wrenching stench of burning flesh permeated the air in thick dark smoke. As Curse saw the fiery attackers charging, he drew a breath and growled to himself.

"You've got to be shitting me."

Quickly he dropped back into the trench and retrieved his rifle. Banshee was moving to her feet.

"They're on fire, and they're still charging us," he informed her.

She was at his side as they both took position on the edge of the trench and began firing at the burning bodies rushing toward them. The soldiers that were in the trench were up with the two of them and firing as well. Several bodies slowed and toppled beneath the flames and gunfire.

Deprived of the bodies as substrate, the napalm simply fell to the ground and burned where it landed. Everyone in the trench wanted to stop as many of the burning attackers as they could before the fiery bodies dropped down into the trenches. The sounds of battle reached their crescendo once more as the machine guns and artillery opened fire again. Burning bodies were scythed down by the rapid fire, but even as they fell, more were surging forth. Charging plague-afflicted and various warriors had comprised the first wave, but now it seemed as though they were facing an enormous army of well-armed attackers. Dirt flew up from the trench's edge as rounds impacted across the earthwork. Curse found one target after another and felled each one with a short burst from his rifle.

"Come on, I can handle all of you," he snarled.

Curse unleashed as many shots as he could as the next wave of attackers crashed over the top of the trench into the defenders. A heavy form slammed into Curse and knocked him from his feet. A soldier wearing a spiked helm of the German World War I army held his bayoneted rifle aloft and prepared to drive it down into Curse, but in the blink of an eye, Curse struck his foot out in a bicycle kick and smashed the attacker's lower leg bones. A screech of pain resounded from the soldier as he lost his balance and fell forward, his weight coming to rest upon Curse's legs. Curse used his legs to ensnare his attacker's torso and then steadied his upper body so that he could unleash a stream of point-blank gunfire into the soldier's face. As the rifle kicked in his hands, Curse watched his adversary's head disintegrate into chunks of dark flying matter. The body clutched between his legs then gave way and crumbled to dust as the soldier's essence was extinguished.

Curse snatched the man's archaic rifle as the body became insubstantial. As he hurried to his feet, another form was barreling into the trench toward him. On a reflex, Curse's arm grasping the rifle shot upward, and the bayonet met with the flying body. Having only one hand on the rifle, Curse almost lost his grip on it as it was knocked toward the ground beneath the attacker's impact.

A scream sounded over the din of battle and a splatter of black ichor splashed into Curse's eyes as he attempted to look up at who he had impaled. Bringing both hands to the rifle, Curse slung the weapon and the attacker backward before beginning to wipe the ichor away from his eye sockets with his free hand.

The battle raged around Curse as he attempted to remove the foul viscous liquid and return to the fighting. Gunshots, screams, and melee combat surrounded him, but he was disoriented amidst it all not being able to see. Memories of his first moments in the Nightmarescape came crashing back to him. He felt as though he were trapped again with unseen forces swirling around him. A sense memory of being dazed and helpless returned to him, and he screamed as he began tearing away at the tissue around his eye sockets with his fingers.

Staggering, he found himself falling to his knees as he slipped in the muddy earth. His weapon . . . where was his rifle . . . his fingers worked feverishly to pull the blinding ichor away from his eyes, but he was panicked, and his skeletal fingertips tore his flesh, allowing his own dark fluids to spill into his eye sockets as well. In the murky darkness, he felt something slam into him and then the earth on the side of the trench coming to meet him.

"Get the hell off him!" A familiar female voice rang through the gloom.

Curse steadied himself against the trench wall. A burst of gunfire followed Banshee's scream before something fell beside him in the bottom of the trench. His flesh was beginning to regenerate itself after several moments, and he realized that most of the ichor in his eyes had become his own. More gunfire sounded beside him. Banshee was still shooting at something. As the dark oily film receded from his field of vision, Curse's sight returned. The first thing he saw was a medieval peasant soldier attempting to regain his footing. Curse was briefly consumed by another flashback.

He was a young boy again, probably early adolescence. He was on the ground outside of his school, and a foot was slamming into his midsection.

"Yeah, that's right, what're you gonna do, bitch?" A voice boomed from above him.

Curse felt so small and weak against the larger aggressor. He attempted to use his body as a shield against the blows, but in the process, he turned his head and glimpsed his attacker. The attacker's features were obscured into a shadow, and Curse could not make them out at first, but then he realized that he was no longer a child living his old life. He was in the Nightmarescape staring at the face of a man who had attacked him while he was blinded. The momentary disability had brought back memories of bullying and beatings from when he was a child.

Recovering himself, Curse snatched the peasant by the sides of his head and proceeded to throw his own skull forward into the man's face. A mighty crack resounded over the chaos as Curse's skull delivered a devastating blow. Dazed, the peasant fell to the ground once more, and Curse descended upon him, his hands a blazing fury of fisted blows. A bloody rage surged through Curse as he pummeled the peasant over and over. The man attempted to block his blows, but Curse continued his assault. Facial bones cracked and snapped beneath his knuckles, flesh broke, and ichor bled freely from contusions on the man's head.

Curse was jolted out of his frenzy as a sudden shock of pain tore through his chest. Impalement was a horrid sensation indeed. Curse felt his skin and muscle tissue splitting as something ripped its way through his back and thrust out the front of his torso. His flesh ruptured in a spectacularly gory fashion, and he sat momentarily feeling the dark ichor bleeding into his internal spaces and out of his skin. The pain knifed its way through his torso and entire body as he was paralyzed by it. More of his flesh was rent as the blade was pulled out in a violent jerk. He fell over and struggled to gain a hold of his body once more. Then the endorphin rush hit him, and the pain was forgotten as his bloodlust took over once more. Throwing his body to the side, Curse heard the blade crash down into the ground where he surely would have received a killing blow. Wheeling around on his knees, Curse faced his assailant. Another flashback and he was a kid again. This time, instead of being beaten, he was being threatened. Curse shook the image from his head as it took shape and continued his fight.

Curse turned to the new attacker and lunged forward, throwing the lightly armored warrior off balance. The warrior's short sword stained with Curse's fluids fell from his hand and clattered to the ground. A chainmail coif adorned the warrior's head to protect from bladed attacks, but it was of no defense as Curse brought a crushing blow of his elbow down into the man's skull. Curse followed up with another blow from his other arm. The warrior attempted to roll out of Curse's reach, but his attempt was futile. Curse reached back into his past and summoned memories of abuse and violence to power his rage. Raising both of his hands high in the air, Curse clasped them together and brought them down upon the warrior's head. A sickening splat resounded as bone gave way, and Curse's hands embedded themselves in the mush of what had been the warrior's face. Several heavy punches followed, and the warrior was no more. Curse reached down and retrieved the sword that had impaled his torso.

Still stunned from Curse's blows, the peasant was recovering and regenerating when Curse approached and slashed the sword toward his face.

The blade severed both flesh and bone with a resounding snapping sound as it was buried into the side of the man's skull. Curse kept his hand on the hilt of the blade and pressed downward, using the flat of the blade as a fulcrum. The peasant's skull snapped further, and more brain tissue was destroyed from the force. Curse jerked the sword back as the peasant's being withered and disintegrated before him.

Anger and bloodlust pumping through his veins, he turned as Banshee screamed from nearby. One of the zombie-like plague-afflicted was forcing her up against the back of the trench. She held her rifle between her body and the thing, but it was stronger than her and was snapping for her face with its rotten jaws.

Curse surged toward it and in one swift movement brought the sword down on the thing's neck, sending its head toppling from its body. The headless body became nothing, with no psychic energy attached to it, but the head itself was already starting to regenerate a body as it lay on the ground with its jaws still snapping. Curse brought the point of the blade down through the thing's skull, and the head became nothing as well.

No sooner than he stood upright, a crushing force slammed into the back of his torso.

Curse felt himself go airborne before connecting with the side of the trench. His body throbbed from the immense impact, and he was stunned, bringing the momentum of his frenzy to a crashing halt. From above him he heard a deep growl over the raging conflict. The utterance disturbed the air around it as Curse noticed a large shadow looming over him.

Automatic gunfire sounded from nearby, and the shadow receded. Curse used the opportunity to get to his feet and come face to face with his attacker. Even though he was still slightly dazed, the sight of his assailant almost made his jaw drop off of his head. Staggering backward was an enormous specimen of a primordial human. Thick splotches of body hair hung from gray and cadaverous skin. The man's face was sunken with hollow flesh clothed in a heavy beard. Primal hatred burned in his eyes as he recovered from Banshee's shots and swung his club once again. Curse dove out of the way just as another gunshot exploded from Banshee's rifle. The burst of fire was cut short and replaced with a sickening thud as the club connected with Banshee and threw her across the trench.

Curse recovered his footing and, now unarmed, went to meet the brute in hand-to-hand combat. The man unleashed a roar and swung his club once more in a wide arc, but the heavy weapon made him clumsy. Curse ducked deftly under the swing and then brought his shoulder up into the man's belly. The blow caused a lightning bolt of pain down through Curse's shoulder. Not only did his body still ache from the forceful trauma of the club, but the primitive creature before him felt as though it were made of hardened muscle and concrete. Nonetheless, Curse knew he had struck a firm blow as a pained grunt came from his foe. The impact behind his weight forced the warrior backward, and his club fell from his hand. Satisfaction was short-lived, however, as the warrior roared once more and raised his fists before bringing them both down in a hammer-fisted blow right between Curse's shoulders. The strength of the impact knocked Curse to the ground.

The warrior was strong, but his fists did not pack the same power as the club. Acting without pause, Curse flipped onto his back once more and rolled out of the way as the warrior brought a crushing punch down where he had been lying. Missing the attack threw the warrior off his feet just long enough for Curse to get to his feet and deliver a strong punch to the warrior's skull. The blow sent the warrior reeling despite his size. As he staggered back, Curse noticed a stone dagger tucked into his adversary's loincloth. Immediately he seized the blade and plunged it into his foe's neck. The howl of a wounded animal echoed from his enemy's throat as the warrior sank to his knees and began attempting to remove the blade from his neck.

Curse set himself to finishing the opponent off just as a rattle of large guns threw earth up from around the sides of the trench. The primal warrior lurched forward as the heavy weapon fire raked his body and threw him to the ground. He continued to reach back for the blade once upon the ground. With his immediate threat downed, Curse looked up to see a ragged half-track rumbling toward the trench. Its rear-mounted gun turret sprayed the trench with another volley of indiscriminate fire. Plague-afflicted, Archaic Front soldiers, and all others were taken off their feet by the punishing hail of bullets. Some heads exploded from the impacts, and their bodies quickly dissolved into dust.

Curse threw himself to the floor of the trench and began reaching around frantically in an attempt to find his rocket-propelled grenade launcher. Several feet away from him, the primal warrior was still attempting to pull the blade from his neck. Curse observed the tube of the launcher sticking out from underneath him. Another volley sounded from outside the trench as the half-track continued to rake the earthworks, indiscriminate of friend or foe. Curse's hands and knees carried him over the trench, and he quickly reached the warrior. Digging his skeletal fingers into the warrior's flesh, Curse pushed upward with his whole body, flipping the warrior onto his back. Another pained scream rose from the warrior as the blade was pushed farther into him. Curse retrieved the launch tube, then found his pack laying on the ground and removed a grenade round. After quickly locking it into place, he crested the edge of the trench and found his target. The half-track was currently spraying fire toward a far end of the trench, giving Curse an unobstructed chance to sight his weapon on the vehicle's front. When he felt he had found a good shot, he let the grenade round fly towards its target.

Unlike many of the tanks and vehicles that both sides fielded, this vehicle had almost no additional armor or other ramshackle components added over the long years it had been in the Nightmarescape. The grenade round punched through its front armor, and the vehicle juddered to a grinding stop. Moments later the thing exploded in spectacular fashion. First the front end and the engine blew skyward upon a plume of gray and white flames. Then the turret and machine guns were carried off of the vehicle by a plume of flame and flew through the air.

Curse's success was short-lived as he became aware of an awful reality. A huge chunk of the turret was flying directly toward him. In a moment of self-preservation, Curse sought to throw himself out of the weapon's path. He realized too late that the world around him was moving faster than he had perceived. It was as though everything moved in slow motion as the thing hurtled through the air, and he felt his feet barely start to move. Within the blink of an eye, the flaming piece of machinery impacted the front of the trench right before his face. He was thrown backward once more, heavily striking the other side of the trench. On his way down, he noticed that Banshee was still lying on the trench floor unmoving. That was just before his perceptions were obliterated in a dark landslide of ruined earth.

30

Darkness once again. Buried under the landslide, Curse attempted to move, but found that the weight of the displaced terrain prevented his body from doing anything. He thought he could feel the gritty texture of soil against him, but it somehow felt insubstantial at the same time, and he could not tell if he was conscious or not. The muffled sounds of battle filtered down through the cover of ground but reached his ears in distant and distorted tones. The world still trembled from trampling feet and heavy gunfire. Reality was a distortion. A war was raging on above him while he was buried and could not move to act.

A sudden panic swept over him as he thought of Banshee. She was out in the trench, possibly being attacked again. He remembered seeing her laying limply on the trench floor just before the shower of debris took him. His body strained against the burden pressing down upon him, but it was to no avail. He could not move himself or the matter around him. A defiant howl welled up from inside him, but upon exhaling it, he realized his mouth was full of dirt. Not needing to breathe, unable to die, immobilized, screaming on the edge of consciousness, he fought within his dark and claustrophobic purgatory.

He shook with the ground as a violent rumble sent tremors down from above. The next thing he felt was an immense heaviness above him. Something huge was moving over him. Curse struggled to vocalize again as the weight pressed down on his body. Pain surged through his bones and muscles as the mass continued to bear down upon him. His skull was on the verge of popping at any moment beneath the crush.

That would be it. He would not be able to regenerate. He would be destroyed along with his psychic mind and would crumble to annihilation. The others would never know what happened to him. Banshee and Larry would be without him. He had already lost one ally against this insane world, and he was about to follow her, not with a bang but with a whimper. Dust beneath the earth and nothing more. He would never see his lover again. The thoughts weighed upon his mind as heavily as the earth weighed upon his body. Rage began to burn inside of him again.

This heated anger was unlike any he had felt so far. It literally set his body and mind ablaze. Against the dirt in his mouth, he unleashed his breath in a tortured bellow. Sound waves pushed through the dirt, forcing a minute amount of it out of his mouth. Hot air circled up around his face, bringing with it stinging particles of grit. His head was pounding, not just from the external compression above, but also from what he exerted from inside himself.

His fury was born of defiance against an inevitable end. He forced his rage out into his extremities and strained with his muscles, pushing back against the density around him. He defied this ending. With every ounce of strength he could muster in his confinement, he pressed outward.

As hard as he pushed, however, he could not keep the oppressive weight from bearing down further. His body felt as though it were imploding as the rubble pushed down heavier. Pain radiated throughout his flesh and bones. His head pounded as though a jackhammer was attempting to smash its way out of his skull. Another scream of indignation and defiance worked its way up from inside him to the same result as before. When the breath left his mouth, the darkness took him. Feelings of pain and pressure both ceased as a nebulous oblivion took their place.

31

All suddenly became quiet as his consciousness disappeared. Awareness became nothing. Then after lingering in the dark space for an unknown time, Curse became aware of a faint gray light. Slowly the gray bled its way through the black until his mind could see only shaded gray, similar to the first time he had seen the sky of the Nightmarescape. Somewhere in the gray, a high-pitched wailing began to gain volume. The sound built until it reverberated throughout the gray space and emanated from all places at once. As it grew, it became painful.

From the inside of his head, the ache radiated outward as a dull sensation. Whereas before he had felt as though a jackhammer was working its way out of his skull, he now felt as though his brain was swelling in accordance with the volume of the strange sound. The gray solidified into a vision.

He was in the bed again, slumped over to the side. The gun was still in his hand. It was the ringing in his ears from the gunshot that he had been hearing, but the pain was dull at this point, almost gone. His mind itself was fading away. Was this how final death in the Nightmarescape took place? With a return to the end of the previous life? No . . . it was another vision. After floating in the dying body and mind for an indefinite span, the door to the bedroom opened, and the woman that he had seen in his visions so often walked in, her face red and puffy, her head hung low.

"I forgot . . ." She choked on her words as she became aware of the sight of her former lover laying on the bed with a spray of cranial gore blasted across the walls and sheets.

Her mouth dropped open as she sank to her knees and began to weep. "I never wanted this . . ."

Curse remembered wanting to speak and say something to her, but his nervous faculties were no longer working. He existed only long enough to see her reaction to his suicide. He thought she had left. He had not expected her to come back and actually see the aftermath. The expression on her face told him all he needed to know. He was now struck by guilt, for he still loved her even though she had left, but he had taken his actions to remove his own suffering. He never intended to scar her in such a way. He thought briefly of the bedroom they had shared, where he lay. Since she had declared her intention to leave, it would no longer be a sanctuary, yet she would remember it not for the good times they had shared in the space, but as a tomb for the man she had once committed herself to. The room had become a cold place where their once-shared emotions of warmth would hold no purchase. He knew that with his last act, in an attempt to escape a tortured existence, he had robbed much of her soul. Even though she was no longer his, he had wished for her to live her life and prosper. Despite the fact that he did not want her gone, he understood why she felt the need to be away from him and did not fault her for it. Now though, his actions had dealt her a psychological wound that would remain open forever.

The guilt he felt in those moments was worse than any physical pain he had experienced in his life or the Nightmarescape. His thoughts were consumed by hate and self-loathing. Having actually seen his beloved's reaction to his death, he thought of the consequences of his actions.

With the most recent revelation, Curse wished that his flashbacks would cease. He did not want to know any more about his former life. Attempting to vent his rage and sorrow at what he had seen, Curse tried to scream, to move, to vindicate himself in some way at all, but he simply remained trapped as a consciousness in a dead body, unable to respond. After lingering in the body, wishing he could be away from the hellish scenario, his mind melted into the gray once more. Curse was thankful for it as the pain of guilt still stung and burned. At least in the gray purgatory he could be alone with his thoughts and not be trapped in the worst memory imaginable.

The gray embraced him and pulled him back into a fog where he felt himself beginning to numb again. Whereas the guilt had gripped him previously, he felt nothing in the empty gray space. His enjoyment of the emptiness was short-lived as another flashback came to him. He was in the house once more where he had shot the two men and woman with his shotgun. Shouting sounded from outside the door as he looked around at the three downed bodies.

He remembered. The local police had screamed for him not to go back near the house once James had been pulled away. Curse remembered however that once he knew that James had passed on, he could not contain his rage and would vindicate his friend. Fuck taking them to jail.

Curse looked at the three bodies. He detected ever so slight movement. It was not just an involuntary reflex from a dying body. The male who had been standing against the wall reached his arm behind a chair and sat up. A pistol came up in his hand. The pistol belched forth several rounds as Curse threw himself sideways and racked another round into his shotgun. He then watched as the man's face exploded in a gory ruin. The man's body fell to the ground once more and ceased moving. Curse turned and looked to the female's body. She stared back at him, the chasm that had been part of her head continuing to dribble its contents across her face. Seeing her like this pulled him into another vision.

He was reliving his brutal attack on the first woman he had encountered in the Nightmarescape. His focus centered on her face as she looked at him so full of sadness. That was just before his fist had connected with her the first time. He burned the face into his mind even though his interaction had been brief, and then he flashed back to the dead woman on the floor once again. He pictured her features grayed and dead, as a creature of the Nightmarescape. It had been the same woman. In the vision, he found himself studying the downed and bloody woman. Sure enough, she was wearing a white sundress.

Even though he was reliving memories and not actually inside his body, he felt a sensation akin to a lump in his throat. So it had been the same woman. That was why her presence had enraged him so much. The guilt of slaying an innocent woman in the Nightmarescape dissolved from him. He had killed her twice. He wondered if that was enough vengeance for James. Even if she had not been the one pulling the trigger, Curse did not feel sorry for her. She was guilty by association. Curse briefly wondered if the two men were also in the Nightmarescape somewhere, but the thought was short-lived as the gray pulled him away from his thoughts and into its numb embrace once again.

For a long while—or maybe only a few moments—there was nothing but gray, until the universe slowly faded to black once again, and Curse was left alone in the oblivion. It was then that he realized he could feel his body once more. Something was scraping along his back—something sharp.

The dirt was still covering most of him, keeping his senses trapped in darkness and distortion. Another impact against his back, and he felt a scraping of something metal across his flesh. Then something else scratched through the dirt and clawed at him—fingers. He felt the cold air of the Nightmarescape rushing against his exposed skin.

Whoever you are, let me out of this hell, Curse thought to himself.

More earth was being pulled away from his person. The metal tool continued to scrape against him, and whoever was digging with their fingers did a fine job of digging them into him, taking a fair amount of skin along with the dirt. He began trying to move, to work more of the dirt around him loose. No sooner than he began moving, he felt himself being yanked backward by two hands that gripped his exposed shoulders. Being jerked out of his earthen tomb, he fell backward. Whoever had pulled him out wrapped their arms around him from behind and held him up. He could see the battlefield once again.

The soldiers in the trench were still fighting furiously as more attackers were coming. Curse turned his head to see that one of the Englishmen was setting down a field spade and picking his rifle up once more.

"Seems like your boy's good to go," the soldier said to someone behind Curse before rejoining the fight.

A familiar boom sounded after the comment. Larry's shotgun.

Curse became aware of the arms holding him. They held him in a firm grip. He knew that whoever they belonged to would not let him go. They would not let him fall over again. In addition to their strong grip, Curse became aware of a stabbing sensation digging into his skin from the arms.

The stimulus reminded him that it was Banshee. He remembered sitting on Larry's couch and having a flashback then awakening to her arms being wrapped around him as her barbed wire dug into his back. Here they were again with her holding him. Though her hold was strong, it was simultaneously gentle. It served to tell him that she would hold onto him, but that nothing would take him from her again. He felt safe there in her arms for the first time since he had been in the Nightmarescape.

The irony struck him. They were probably in one of the most dangerous places imaginable: a trench that was being assaulted. A number of attackers could overwhelm them or a shell could explode and obliterate them all, but despite the obvious dangers, he felt safe simply because of the way she held him. He was lost in the thought as her voice sounded in his ear and stirred him to action.

"I've got you now, but we have to get back in the fight," she said gently. "Come on, wake up, come back . . . I can't do this without you."

At her last statement, Curse forced himself to move. He still felt sluggish as he always did after a flashback, but he began to stand. She moved with him and helped him to his feet before reaching down and retrieving his rifle for him. Without him realizing it, she had forced the weapon into his hands before he could even take a step.

"Thought you were getting away from me so easily?" He turned to see her smiling at him.

Despite her smile, he could tell that she was shaken at the possibility of having lost him beneath the earth. Not wanting to be responsible for the bereavement of two women, Curse silently thanked his circumstances for being able to return. He would tell her what he learned while buried in that tomb, but for now they had to fight if they were to be around to talk later.

"You were the last thing I saw before that dirt buried me, of course I couldn't leave so easily," he reassured her. "Now back to business."

Curse felt his faculties returning to normal as he and Banshee flung themselves against the wall of the trench once more, aiming their weapons out into the charging attackers. Their numbers had been thinned significantly, but they were still coming undeterred. Larry had now joined their press as well and was firing rounds from his shotgun at scattered bodies.

"Good to see you back, son!"

"What happened while I was buried?" Curse screamed to Banshee before unleashing a short burst of fire on a charging plague-afflicted.

"Another air strike," Banshee answered.

Curse wished to have seen that. He had felt the world shaking as he lay beneath the earth, but it was no substitute for seeing it with his eyes. At least there had been some good fortune.

"The air attack gave us some pretty valuable time to get you out from under all that dirt. If the bombs hadn't cleared a good bit of space, we would still be holding them off, and you'd still be buried. The attackers in the trenches were cut off, and we've been finishing them, but there are more coming," Banshee informed him as more bodies came rushing toward them.

They unleashed their weapons on the charging bodies and another wave fell. After their own weapons filled the air for a brief period, they became aware of the planes passing over their heads again. This time there would not be another immediate bombing—the aircraft overhead were now engaged in a high-altitude fight to the death.

Machine guns sounded from high above the fighting as the planes engaged in a massive dogfight. Phosphorescent tracer fire cut the gray sky as pilots trained their guns on each other. Many of the propeller-driven aircraft were able to engage each other and follow, but the single jet they had seen strafed through the aerial carnage before turning off in the distance for more passes. As the massive aircraft guns delivered their payload to their targets, fiery explosions erupted in the clouds, and flaming metal fell to the earth. Curse and Banshee both dropped for the meager cover the trench could afford them as a flaming chassis zoomed down and crashed into oncoming attackers.

The burning piece of machinery hit the ground with a jarring impact that they felt through their legs before it bounced up into the air several feet and then dragged its bulk through the earth, plowing numerous bodies with it as it skidded along. A long corridor of destroyed earth, wreckage, and burnt flesh was left in its wake.

Danger was mounting for all on the field of battle as the planes overhead found their targets and sent more fiery wreckage streaming down into the combatants on the ground. Curse focused through the rain of fire and metal as he found a charging enemy soldier in his sights. Just before he could shoot, an arm snaked around his torso and jerked him to the side as a flaming piece of scrap impacted where he stood moments before. Banshee held him for just a brief second longer before releasing him.

"Looking after you is getting to be a full-time engagement," she joked before turning back to the charging attackers.

In addition to the dogfighting overhead, planes were still diving and strafing the battlefield. After loosing several shots, another fiery piece of wreckage fell not too far from their position.

Curse became aware of something that unsettled his gut. The attackers on foot were backing off. It was not because of their numbers. A sea of plague-ridden bodies and soldiers still littered the landscape like a huge moldy carpet. The German and Japanese soldiers were marshalling the plague-afflicted to hold tight. From the sea of bodies, the armor rolled forward. Tanks, half-tracks, and other armored vehicles moved to the front of the advance and began rumbling across the blasted no-man's-land. After the armored vehicles had moved out to the fore of the attack, they waited as other vehicles joined them in serried ranks. After idling for a period, the armored company began to move forward in earnest as the attackers began an assault to break the trench line.

As the war engines kept their steady advance, the throng surged forth behind them. The mechanized assault unleashed its guns on the entrenched defenders. All around them, colossal explosions erupted. Curse heard a high-pitched noise behind him. Turning, he observed that Lt. Drake was blowing a whistle. At the sound, the soldiers in the trenches were abandoning their positions and falling back. Curse snatched Banshee by the arm as they ran away from the trench to seek cover behind their own thin line of armored vehicles. Larry was close on their heels.

The remaining tanks and artillery stationed on the edge of the village unleashed a barrage of their own into the advancing armor. The planes continued their lethal fight overhead, and the world was covered in a storm of bullets, artillery shells, and fiery metal. Back behind the line of vehicles, the camp was turning into chaos.

"We need to get out of here!"

"They'll overrun us soon!"

"Fuck stayin' here!"

The voices melted into a slur of shouts and yells.

The leadership moved in amidst the chaos and attempted to restore the men to fighting order. Lt. Drake and the armored warrior stood upon a small crumbled wall and began shouting.

"We're in a dire position," the lieutenant yelled. "Our adversaries are rushing us with their armor, and we do not have the artillery to fend off such an assault. We will fall back in good order. To stay here and occupy the town and trenches is sui—"

He dove to the ground as a chunk of smoking wreckage fell from overhead and crashed into the wall where he had been standing. The other soldier that he had been standing with was thrown from the wall upon the impact. Both of them quickly recovered and got to their feet.

"Our armor will stay and hold them off as long as they can. The rest of us will fall back in disciplined order. If you have a gun, stay near the back to provide covering fire for the escape."

With that order, the warriors armed with only hand weapons led the retreat. The commanders followed behind them, and the soldiers armed with firearms brought up the rear. Curse looked to his companions and moved to follow the soldiers and warriors. He felt his arm being pulled back as he started moving.

"Hold on, boy, we've got to find Nigel!" Larry exclaimed.

"Oh shit . . . the device . . ." Curse had forgotten about it in the ruckus.

"Well . . . where's his tank?" Banshee asked.

All three of them surveyed the line of vehicles along the rear of the trenches. More tanks had moved up to reinforce the line as they had been fighting in the trench, but they did not see Nigel's archaic chassis among them. As they moved closer to the line of tanks, a large smoke cloud that had been created by an artillery blast began to clear, and they observed Nigel's tank stationed on the far side of the rearmost trench. Several flaming pieces of wreckage fell out of the sky and clattered off of the hull. Nigel's guns boomed, launching shells into the advancing assault. The three of them did not look past the tank far enough to see their result. Together, they climbed up the hull and track of the stationary tank, careful to avoid the blades and spikes that adorned the chassis. Larry slammed his knuckles into the top of the vehicle.

"Lemme in, damnit!" he hollered as he banged on the tank. Another volley from the tank's guns shook the vehicle.

Curse and Banshee held onto each other to keep from being thrown off balance. The hatch opened, and the three of them dropped into the vehicle. Curse jerked the hatch shut and spun a wheel lock to secure it.

"Lawrence, I'm a little preoccupied. What's the meaning of this?" Nigel asked as he prepared his guns for another volley.

"Nigel, where's that thing we gave you to mess with?" Larry inquired.

"Back there somewhere . . . it's not really important right now . . ." Nigel motioned over his shoulder.

Larry reached out and grabbed Nigel by the shoulders. "Nigel, we've been friends for a good while. I wasn't messing around with you when I told you that thing can do what I said it could."

The tank rocked from the force of a nearby explosion. A noisy disturbance rang through the vehicle as the vibrations shook through the hull. Nigel grunted in frustration.

"Then take it and go, I'm sticking here to carry the fight," he stated.

"We need your help with getting the thing to work!" Larry exclaimed.

A cacophony of noise rang through the inside of the vehicle as machine-gun fire rattled off of the tank. Somewhere nearby, another explosion sent shock waves through the ground.

Nigel peered out of his narrow vision slit and took a query on the battle outside. From the little bit he could see, he did not feel optimistic.

"One of you open up that hatch and tell me what's going on out there," he instructed.

Curse opened the hatch again and looked out on the panorama of the battlefield. The nearest tanks had been reduced to smoldering wreckage. Enemy armor was moving in rapidly. The vicious aerial fighting resumed in the sky, with bits of wreckage continuing to fall. The trenches were entirely deserted, and the line of tanks was largely decimated.

Another enemy shell impacted against the hull as the tank shook. Curse held on to the edges of the hatch as he struggled to keep from falling from the opening. Nigel's modifications and extra armor kept the tank from bearing the brunt of the impact and held the chassis together. Had the round been a larger one though, they probably would not have been as lucky. Curse took another brief glimpse at the world around the tank.

He watched as another one of the defending tanks exploded. Gray and white flames leapt from a huge hole in the vehicle's front, and then the turret exploded and fell away from the hull. Watching the smoke and fire stream into the gray sky cast an overly depressing pall over the whole situation. Curse sank back into the tank and closed the hatch once more.

"Nigel, the line is almost entirely destroyed. The Axis tanks are closing in. Soon they'll all have a clear shot on the last few vehicles here and behind them will come all the guys running on foot. I know this thing is sturdy, but it's a needless sacrifice to stay here," Curse said in a cool tone.

Nigel reached behind his veil and rubbed his chin as he weighed his options.

"Not to mention . . . what could happen if the Plague Faction and Axis actually got their hands on the device . . ." Banshee trailed off and went silent at her own statement.

A sigh escaped Nigel as he grabbed the tank's control levers and removed the brake. "All three of you are right," he concluded. "It's worthless for us to stay here with that thing if we're only going to get overrun and killed. I was ordered to stay and hold . . . but the outcome could be far worse."

Nigel was a soldier, and all three of them read the burden they were placing on him by pushing him to go against his orders and abandon his position. They knew however that he also understood the greater picture and would not sacrifice himself without merit in the face of such circumstances.

The old tank growled through its modified engines and took off with a jolt. Curse and Larry were holding on to the sides of the vehicle, but Banshee was caught off guard and fell, her butt landing right next to the device.

"It also won't do us any good if anyone crushes it," Larry peered at her through his big wild eyes before breaking into one of his trademark peals of insane laughter.

Larry's high-pitched cackle echoed off the inside of the tank, making it sound more distorted and demented than it actually was. Curse found himself laughing along with him. It was good to hear his laugh again. He had not heard him let out one of his crazy laughs since they had lost Aja. Banshee reached over and grabbed the device before pulling it to her chest and letting out a relieved laugh of her own.

"We're not out of it yet, you bloody cretins," Nigel intoned as he drove the tank forward and over the first trench.

He would have to clear some ground by moving toward the enemy in order to make a turn and head in the opposite direction. His point was driven home as several bullets bounced off of the tank's hull. The three of them continued to laugh for a short time afterwards regardless.

"Damnit, Lawrence, your insanity has infected both of them as well! Can't you touch anything without fucking it up?"

Curse reached forward and snatched Nigel's shoulder, giving him a start in the driver's seat. "Hey, man, if we could be blasted to oblivion at any second, I'd rather go out laughing amidst the carnage with my favorite people than cowering in the back of this iron coffin whining."

Despite the terror they had all just endured in the trench and Curse's near brush with destruction in the landslide, the three of them could now breathe relief. They would survive for the time being. Banshee and Larry were still at his side. They had endured a fight worse than Curse could have conceived of in his imagination, and all three of them had survived the horror. Nigel had made it out of the maelstrom with them and would possibly be able to help them decipher the device when he wasn't driving the tank. Things were finally looking up again after losing Aja.

Nigel strained as he pulled back on the right control lever, and the tank began to turn. Curse moved himself to sit next to Banshee. They continued to laugh softly to one another while Larry echoed his own laughter at a higher volume.

"Brilliant, I have to maneuver this behemoth through hell and high water with three lunatics in the back!"

The turn ended, and the tank rolled forward. Nigel flipped a switch, and the vehicle began to move faster than anything from its time should have moved.

"What did you do to this thing anyway? Tanks from your era are only supposed to go about four miles per hour." Curse was curious.

"Just little bits and things from here and there . . . put a new engine from a much newer vehicle in it, for one. Added a booster line to it, obviously added armor and the like on the outside. It's a bit of a kitbash, this one." Curse could tell from the inflection in Nigel's voice that he was smiling behind the chainmail veil.

"If we get out of this, can you teach me to drive one of these things?" Curse asked.

"Damnit, Lawrence, you know how to keep me busy, don't you? Figure out this damn dimensional portal thingy, save our non-armored asses, teach me to drive your tank! Can't you all let me get out of this mess before throwing more on my plate?"

More bullets zinged off of the hull. The mood inside the tank had been cheerful for a few minutes, but the sounds began to remind them all of the danger they were still facing.

"I think the machine guns are hitting us at random. I wouldn't worry much about anyone picking an accurate shot from a tank cannon at this distance and speed. We're almost at the edge of the village ruins anyway," Nigel told the others.

Curse stood and opened the hatch once more so he could look back toward the aftermath of the fight. The trenches were completely overrun with plague-afflicted and Axis foot soldiers. The last few tanks were now nothing more than smoking wrecks as the enemy armor rolled in and over the trenches. Above the field of battle, several planes were still engaged in a heated combat, but aircraft from both sides were peeling off and leaving with smoke trailing from their wings and tails. Wreckage from downed aircraft littered the ravaged field as though it had grown out of the ground itself. A mass of gray flesh and uniforms swarmed over the wreckage, obscuring it from sight.

Curse turned his head in the other direction and observed the retreat of the Archaic Front Soldiers. They were falling back in good order as they had been instructed, but the opposition was moving in fast. He hoped that they would be hasty enough that most of them would be away before the attackers were upon them. Curse dropped back down into the tank and secured the hatch.

"Where are they falling back to?" Curse asked Nigel.

"There's an outpost a little bit back this way. They should have sent more damn reinforcements . . . communications must have been cut off pretty early on after we got our first wave . . ."

"I saw a guy in the trench calling the airstrike with some kind of old telephone. I think he was killed in the fight," Curse stated.

"Nelson," Nigel responded. "That was one of our communications men . . . good man . . . I'll be missing him." Nigel dropped his head and breathed a soft prayer for his departed comrade. "I'll miss all the boys we lost in this fucking mess."

32

The elation and relief from earlier lifted as the somber reality sunk in for Curse and Banshee. They became quiet and introspective. Larry stayed quiet with his own counsel for some time. He probably had been involved in such situations before, having been in the Nightmarescape so long.

"I'll miss them too, Nigel," Larry spoke up first. "I've known your unit for some time. Longer than these two misfits even." He indicated Banshee and Curse with his hand but smiled at them to show he was attempting to soften the mood. "The men you lost today will be remembered."

"Yes. They fought valiantly." Curse let his appreciation for the soldiers out.

Banshee nodded solemnly, not knowing quite what to say.

"The three of you did too." Nigel broke off their grieving for his comrades. "You weren't a part of our fight to start, but you stayed with us through the whole thing and refused to back down. Even as the shadow of the last hour fell . . . the three of you stayed with us. Thank you so much. Even though I may act pained by the things you've asked me for, I owe all three of you far more than anything you have sought of me."

Larry slapped a hand to Nigel's shoulder.

"And even though you're a peculiar loon, Lawrence, you're no slouch on your friends. You've taught these young bloods well."

Curse took pride in Nigel's words for his actions. He could not imagine that Larry and Banshee felt any different. The four of them rode on in silence for a time, pondering their deeds in the battle as well as the enormity of loss.

It was a feeling Curse knew all too well. He had lost one close friend in his former life while he was in combat. In the Nightmarescape, he had lost Aja. He had not experienced losing multiple people at once the way Nigel probably had in his time fighting. The pain of losing Aja, a new friend, stung enough. He thought of the bond he had forged with Larry and Banshee. Losing either of them would take any grip he had left on his mind. Curse could only imagine how Nigel felt losing the men he had been fighting alongside since the First World War.

The tank rolled on as they pondered. The sounds of battle were growing faint outside of the tank. Curse pictured the image of the monstrous tank rumbling over the colorless landscape. After they traveled for some time, Nigel leaned forward and squinted through his viewing slit.

"There we are up ahead," he informed the others.

Curse opened the hatch and looked out at their destination. To his surprise, they were approaching a large field encampment, not just another small outpost. This one appeared to be centered around a wooden fort. Temporary structures such as tents surrounded the fort, and the whole site was ringed by a fence of wood, barbed wire spools, and rampart stakes. Several machine-gun nests and cannon emplacements watched the perimeter. Two Gatling guns flanking the front entrance turned their barrels on the tank as it approached. Nigel slowed the tank so they would not perceive the entrance as hostile.

Curse felt the tank slowing to a crawl as one of the gunners stepped toward them. The man's outfit looked to be from the Spanish-American War. Curse was still surprised every time he saw a warrior from another time period. From beneath a wide-brimmed hat, glowing blue lights shined out of sunken sockets in a skeletal face.

"Who goes there?" the sentry inquired.

Curse felt himself being jerked down from the hatch as Nigel took his place. "It's me and several fighters from the line—let us in, nimrod," Nigel commanded.

The sentry grinned beneath his hat and motioned for the others to let the tank inside. The other gunners moved forward and opened a gate in the fence that was broad enough for the tank and another small vehicle. As soon as the tank had lumbered through, they quickly secured it once again. Curse crawled up to the hatch again and pulled himself up onto the roof. Banshee followed, and together they sat on top of the armored vehicle while looking out upon the camp. Bodies began leaping up from in front of the tents as the tank rolled along a central path leading to the fort. Curse saw more Civil War-era soldiers mingling with several other American soldiers carrying tommy guns.

They all nodded as the tank rolled past. On the side of the path opposite them, a cadre of armored warriors raised their weapons in salute. Rolling on along past them, several African men stood at the vehicle's approach. Curse believed that they were some of the Zulus he had seen earlier, and then he saw Kitenge sitting on his jeep behind them.

"Kitenge!" Curse called.

Seemingly startled, Kitenge rolled forward and leapt off of his jeep. He looked at the tank and the form on top of it for a moment before realizing who it was and acknowledging with a wave. Several men in rotted military fatigues came to stand at his side while the tank rolled past.

The tank's treads began to slow as they approached the front gate of the fort. As the tank rumbled to a halt, a soldier wearing a breastplate and armed with a halberd approached. Nigel and Larry clambered out of the hatch and dropped to the ground. Curse and Banshee followed suit.

"Where's the rest of your company?" the sentry inquired through a French accent.

"They're on the way now. We were overrun. The others are making their way back on foot. What happened to the communications?" Nigel spoke for everyone.

"Don't know about that. The commander might," the soldier replied.

"If he's in, I think I need to see him," Nigel said flatly.

"And what of them? They're not of our camp."

Nigel seized the soldier by the edges of his breastplate. "Listen to me, you clod, these three fought valiantly alongside all the men that we lost in that fudged mess back there. On top of that, they have brought important technology and information with them. You will afford them the same respect you would any of this company. Am I understood?" The words rolled out of Nigel's mouth with particular venom, for he was not in the mood to be trifled with by one who had not participated directly in the fighting.

"Clear, sir," the other responded.

"Very good then. We need an audience with the commander." Nigel spoke in an upbeat voice, masking his restrained fury from a moment ago.

The soldier turned and opened a small door next to the front gate. Nigel followed behind him, the other three close behind. They walked through the central plaza of the fort. It was nothing fancy. Logs embedded in the ground made up the bulk of the structure, with stacked sandbags reinforcing behind the wood. Several platforms created a sort of upper level. Gunners turned from machine gun and mortar nests on the platforms to survey the new arrivals. Passing through the plaza, they arrived at a small wooden building near the back of the structure. The Frenchman knocked at the door and then took a step back. Several seconds later, the door opened.

"Commander, one of the tank drivers and some new arrivals to see you, sir."

A man wearing a rotted yet still regal uniform stepped from the door. Blue lights shined intensely from behind a pair of spectacles that sat on the bridge of his nose. He stood with his hands clasped behind his back.

"Well met, Corporal. You are back from the front before anyone else . . . ," he began.

Even though his features showed him to be of African descent, he spoke through an accent that rang of both Italian and Somali dialects. Curse made a mental note to ask his story later.

"Indeed, Commander Mudhei. The position was overrun by a superior force of men and armor," Nigel explained. "My tank was the only one to survive. The remaining infantry are returning on foot now, still running from the foe. They might be followed here. My tank moves faster than they can run, so I returned to warn you."

The commander digested the news and considered his options. "I see ..." He spoke slowly, the weight of the situation settling on him. "How many are they in number?"

"I could not tell you, sir. They covered the landscape with their numbers. It was hard to see a spot on the ground. Not only that, but they had a large armored detachment with them consisting of all kinds of vehicles. The men in the trenches held out after the airstrike and fought valiantly, but then the armored company rolled in and decimated our tanks with a superior force of cannon. The men in the trenches continued to fight until the retreat was given. I don't know what happened to communications."

The commander nodded as he took the news in. "And who are these three? They did not leave with your company." He regarded Larry, Curse, and Banshee with suspicion.

"They are dear friends now. Of myself and our company. This is Larry Spectre."

Larry stepped forward with his grin stretching across his face. As Commander Mudhei reached to shake Larry's hand, he was met with a vice-like grip and boisterous greeting. "Mornin', Commandant!" Larry exclaimed.

Commander Mudhei smiled. "A spirited one you are."

Nigel continued the introductions. "Curse here is a terror on the battlefield from what everyone can tell."

Curse stepped forward and shook hands with the commander.

"Well met, sir," he greeted.

"Much so indeed," the commander responded.

"And certainly not least, this is Banshee."

Banshee stepped forward and nodded. The commander looked reluctant to touch her. "We do not often have women alongside our forces . . . ," he explained. "I can tell, however, that you are not a typical lady."

Banshee's head went back as a wicked cackle echoed from her throat. "Far from it, sir," she stated through a smile.

Nigel spoke next. "Sir, the three of them joined up with us and fought with the utmost of valor in the trenches alongside our boys. Larry and Curse met up with some other members of the company earlier as well and aided in the first defense of the position. They're actually the ones who convinced me to turn my tank around even though it was the last. I realized it was sage advice because I could relay a warning sooner, and the threat wouldn't be at the doorstep without time to prepare."

"Sage advice indeed. How many of our number remain?"

"Hard to tell amidst the chaos. We lost a good number in the trenches, and there will be no other armor returning," Nigel told him.

Commander Mudhei nodded again. His shoulders slipped slightly at the news, but he recovered himself and resumed his commanding posture. "Very well then. We will prepare to meet the threat at our gates and offer what protection we may to those returning."

"Yes, sir. One more thing. These three have something that we must protect with our very lives," Nigel stated.

Curse began to open his mouth, but Nigel spoke before he could. They had wanted to keep the device a secret, but it was also important that someone know what it was should they perish.

"What is that, Corporal?" the Commander inquired.

"They may have found the rumored device that splits the realms and return us to the former world," Nigel told him before an uneven silence settled over them.

"What?" The commander was flustered by what he had just heard. "Seriously?"

"Yes, sir, they asked me to work on it and figure it out, but I can only get it to make noise so far."

"Well, Corporal, you are one of the most mechanically adept in this camp. I'd imagine it would not be beyond you." The commander had regained himself. "The word shall be spread that our own are retreating and that attackers may follow. After we have this settled, I would like to see this device."

Nigel saluted as the commander retrieved a large archaic radio and began issuing orders. The four of them left the small building and returned to Nigel's tank. The camp was becoming a hive of activity as warriors were moving to take up positions around the fenced perimeter.

"Where do you all want us?" Curse asked Nigel.

"Not more than five feet from me," he responded.

With that, Nigel climbed up along the tracks of his tank and dropped inside. Curse and the others crawled up onto the top of the tank and watched the camp. With a growl, the tank's engine roared to life, and they began rolling toward the front of the camp to meet the coming threat.

After some time, the retreating company became visible across the field. They ran for their lives as shouts went up from inside the camp, and the soldiers readied themselves for an inevitable combat. At the front gate, guns were trained out on the field.

Curse briefly wished that he had been able to retrieve the grenade launcher from the trench, but he believed it had been buried in the landslide. He took an inventory of what weapons he still had. The pistol and revolver were still tucked into his waistband. He also had the AK-47. They would have to suffice. He looked back to see that a group of defenders were now almost at the gate. Nigel's tank rumbled forward to be closer and provide precious fire support.

The sentries at the front were opening the gate for their retreating brethren. There was not a great number of them. Lt. Drake ran at the head of the retreat, the armored leader beside him. Behind them were many of the medieval and Viking warriors; the rearguard, however, had taken significant casualties along the retreat.

Outriders of the plague-afflicted and Axis charged behind them, refusing to allow any stretch of ground to exist between them. Those in the advancing horde with guns unleashed wild shots as they ran. The unlucky few that were taken off their feet by the rounds were swamped by plague-afflicted as their comrades continued the retreat. The situation was brutal and inhuman, but all knew the price they would pay if they stopped.

An explosion sounded off in the distance as the enemy armor became visible once again. Following the explosion, a shell whistled its way high into the air and came down right in the middle of the retreating soldiers. They had been so close to the gate, but the blast destroyed some immediately and scattered most of the others. A very lucky few ran through the aftermath of the explosion and into the camp.

Then the fight was right on top of them again. Machine guns and cannons opened up into the charging horde, scything many presences out of existence. A low rumble sounded from the rear of the camp, and Curse turned to see a wave of friendly tanks moving to the front. These were not typical battle tanks, however; they were all super-heavy vehicles with enormous cannons mounted upon their hulls. It would have taken the lumbering behemoths a great deal of time to

Nightmarescape

have reached the previous front. Fortunately, their lack of mobility forced them to stay put, creating a powerful protection for the camp.

Upon rolling to a halt at the front of the camp, the ground shook as the heavy tanks unleashed hell on the attackers. As much as it pained the defenders to fire outward when their friends and fellow soldiers were out among the enemy, they knew them to be lost. Enormous explosions jettisoned earth and bodies into the air as the heavy tank rounds dug holes in the advancing wave of flesh. Several enemy tanks in the distance became victims of the superior firepower.

Machine-gun fire and explosions filled the air. Curse aimed his rifle at the mass of charging bodies and opened fire. As long as he shot at chest level, he would hit something. The horizon was awash with bodies. The tank shook as Nigel fired its main cannon and caused a small explosion in a tangle of plague-afflicted trying to get close to the gate.

Another salvo from the heavy tanks shook the ground as a curtain of detonations leapt up in front of the enemy advance. Earth and body parts rained freely across the landscape.

The entire encampment rocked as the enemy tanks responded. Tents went up in eruptions of dirt and flames. Several of the machine-gun and cannon emplacements were consumed by voracious blasts. The firepower in the camp was not terribly diminished by their loss.

The tanks traded off again, the super heavies within the camp exacting another toll upon the attackers. The response was devastating. A line of concentrated explosions rippled up at the front gate. The explosions decimated the only line of defense that kept the attackers from pouring into the camp. Curse gritted his teeth as he saw the sentry gunners crumbling to dust and their mighty weapons broken into pieces.

Then they were charging into the camp. A steady line of warriors who had been at the front of the retreat rushed to meet the intruders. Vicious close combat ensued. Axes and blades hacked flesh from limbs as the press of firepower aided their struggle.

"You two come with me!" Larry leapt off of the tank and sped toward the fighting.

Banshee and Curse followed him. As they neared the melee, they began unleashing everything they could from their guns. Curse and Banshee utilized the automatic fire of their weapons while Larry used his shotgun to deathly effect on the closely packed attackers. Their efforts felled some of the enemies, but the troops were still fighting a desperate battle. An engine roared nearby as Kitenge and his contingent rolled to the front line. The tribal warriors leapt from the vehicle and added their own vicious assault to the fight. Kitenge left the jeep with a grease gun in his hands and began dumping gunfire into the mass.

The ground continued to shake under the barrages of the super heavy tanks. Mammoth explosions separated the attackers in the field from those who had made their way into the camp. Another sound joined the machine-gun fire and cannon retorts. Curse looked skyward to see a thin line of planes flying up above the attacking horde.

They were all heavily damaged but able to stay airborne. He could not tell if they were friendly or not at the outset, but that was answered promptly as bombs began falling from the aircraft the moment they were over the attackers. A hearty cheer rang up from the besieged defenders as the ground shook. The planes then flew over the fort and turned for another pass.

Looking out past the fighting in front of him, Curse observed that the bombing run had put a significant dent in the advancing armor. This was largely due to the fact that the armor had been bunched together in an advancing line rather than randomly spread out as it had been at the beginning of the previous battle.

Bodies were crumbling to dust at the front of the camp as the deadly fighting took its toll. More reinforcements were rushing from other parts of the camp to hold what had been the gate. Curse focused his own firepower into the press as a tank came rolling past him. He craned his head briefly to observe the strange vehicle. It was a standard Sherman chassis, but the turret had been modified so that the gun was more of a nozzle than a cannon. Several large drums were secured to the vehicle's back. Curse realized the vehicle's intended purpose as a bright gout of white flames sprayed out of the turret and swept across the attackers.

The effect was similar to the napalm strike from before but on a smaller scale. Small arms fire erupted from just outside the camp and zinged off of the tank's hull. Curse began to move away ever so slightly just in case an enemy cannon struck home on the flamethrower tank.

A commotion sounded overhead as the planes rounded to make another pass. They strafed the blasted landscape of flesh with their guns before opening their bomb bays for another deadly delivery. More enemy armor and bodies were sent skyward from clustered eruptions on the ground.

The heavy tanks added their ferocious onslaught to the death falling from above. Such a deadly toll hindered the attackers severely as the remaining pieces of their armor were destroyed from the combined bombardment. If they were going to continue the assault, they would have to do it through strength of numbers alone. Given the monstrous firepower that was in the fort, such a task would be next to impossible.

Curse surged forward and added his strength to the carnage at the gate. Banshee ran with him. Larry called out to stop them but found himself moving as well when they did not respond.

First Curse came upon an armored warrior who had fallen and was being assailed by plague-afflicted. A hail of fire rattled from Curse's gun as he shot several of them off. The butt of his rifle connected with a skull and sent its owner reeling back. Curse lashed with the bayoneted barrel and ripped a steaming pile of dark ichor and rotten intestines out of another of the afflicted. The creature screeched in pain, and Curse fired several rounds into its head. It ceased to be. His foot reached out and connected with another afflicted that was charging him. A snap behind the thing's leg muscles sounded as it toppled over. Curse impaled his bayonet through the back of its neck and fired into its skull, treating it to a fate similar to its predecessor.

Curse found himself lost in a nirvana of adrenaline and violence. Impaling a nearby afflicted, he ducked as another adversary attempted to close grips with him. He dropped down and hurled the new arrival over his shoulders with a fireman's carry. As soon as the impaled afflicted hit the ground, Curse delivered a sharp kick to the back of its neck and watched as the head fell limply to the side. He dispatched both downed attackers in turn with a headshot for each.

Banshee fought right beside him, creating a destructive hurricane of her own. Curse looked up briefly enough to see two afflicted assailing her from both sides. With one arm she

Nightmarescape

struck out in a backhanded swing, delivering her barbed-wire-wrapped forearm into a diseased face. With the other arm she fired her rifle from a single-handed grip into the second thing's head. When it was dust, she finished its companion off in a similar fashion.

Larry was felling several of the things at a time with blasts from his shotgun. At such a close distance, he could aim between two of the creatures and send hefty amounts of pellets into both. The concussive blasts from the shotgun tore heads apart and knocked bodies off their feet.

The warrior Curse had helped was on his feet again, burying an axe into the nearest enemy head he could find. All of the melee fighters at the front were whirling dervishes of death. They fought with the strength of several men each as they swung their weapons and shields into the seething horde. Every so often one of the men would tire and become overwhelmed. Some were lucky enough to have comrades close at hand to beat their attackers away; others, however, were dragged screaming into the horde where they were ripped apart by bony hands and slavering jaws.

Thick, disgusting smoke curled into the air as the flamethrower tank continued to immolate bodies. Some of them screamed; others hissed and continued charging until the flames burned their bodies to dust.

The ground trembled under another battery from the heavy tanks. Each blast they released sent shock waves through the enemy advance, exacting heavy casualties. If the attackers continued the assault, they would surely break their own backs upon the fort's defenses.

Cheers began erupting from the men around the fort. Curse looked out past the immediate fighting and observed that the back of the assault was peeling away from the advance.

It was their turn to retreat now. Most of the Axis soldiers had stayed near the back and let the plague-afflicted carry the brunt of the assault due to their overwhelming numbers and expendability. Some had surged forth to press the fight, but those of strategic mind saw that the engagement was going badly. Not wanting to waste their numbers any further, they had seen to break off the attack and leave the remaining plague-afflicted to occupy the defenders while they retreated. It was a good move, for the press of bodies at the gate was still too great to send anyone out in chase.

Curse laid admiration of strategy aside as he returned his attention to eradicating the remaining attackers. They were so mindless that they did not process why the rest of their fellows were leaving. Their minds only knew hunger and the orders of their beloved Pastor Nox.

Several emaciated gurgling forms came at Curse. He was able to slay one with his rifle before the others grabbed on to him. One fell about his legs and began biting at his calves. Its jaw could still exert a lot of pressure for something so gaunt, but his pants prevented its teeth from digging into his flesh. Curse grunted as rotten teeth bit at his legs while he grappled with the other afflicted. The zombie-like creature's jaws snapped at his face as he shoved the rifle up and smacked it in the chin. With his enemy momentarily stunned, Curse pressed the advantage to fire down into its fellow. When the one on his legs was dust, Curse returned his attention to the remaining afflicted. As it lunged for him once more, he prepared to finish it off just before a gunshot snapped from nearby, and an eruption of gore sprayed from the side of its head. Moments later it became dust. Curse looked to where the shot had come from and saw Larry grinning at him with his old revolver smoking in one hand.

"I was just about to do that myself," Curse yelled to him over the chaos of combat.

"Son, you're hoggin' all the good fools! Let the rest of us have fun too!" With that, Larry let out a rip of laughter and unleashed another blast from his shotgun into a nearby afflicted.

Almost all of the attacking soldiers had fled the scene, leaving behind a dwindling number of the afflicted. The heavy tanks had ceased their explosive batteries due to the fact that most of the fighting had become so centralized that their blasts would hit their own. Machine guns still mercilessly ate apart those on the flanks as the melee fighters hacked and slashed to their last. They were on the point of exhaustion, but they would be free of their burden if they could just hold out a little longer.

Many of the plague-afflicted were crumbling as the defenders poured on punishment. The Axis were off of the field now. Curse hoped that the planes would follow them and continue to harangue them on their retreat, but he assumed that the aircraft were too damaged to continue a pursuit and would have to touch down soon.

Several warriors fell at the gate, past the point of exertion. Plague-afflicted bodies swarmed over those who fell and began to tear into them. Curse and Banshee rushed forward to meet the voracious ghouls but stopped as the ground shook beside them. Nigel's tank was rumbling toward the spot that had been opened by the fallen warriors. The metal behemoth collided with brittle-boned bodies, heads and limbs clunking off of the reinforced hull. A screech went up from the afflicted that had been knocked down as the tank's tracks ground their bodies into the earth. Limbs and body parts popped beneath the grinding tracks. A number of nearby plague-afflicted leapt onto the vehicle's hull and became entangled in the blades and razor wire that Nigel had added to the vehicle. The tank continued to crush through the throng of attackers, a gangling mass of emaciated bodies hanging off its hull.

Nigel's insane gambit opened up a huge column of ruined flesh and dust in the attackers' midst. Curse and several other defenders from inside the fort rushed forth to fill a space that divided the remaining attackers. The fighting was fierce as the fresh defenders added their force to the fight. Fists, blades, cudgels, and firearms all struck the dwindling number of afflicted. Curse met with Kitenge in the crucible of battle once again as they waded into the fray.

Ichor poured freely as they sprayed gunfire into the closely packed afflicted. Several bodies before them crumbled to dust, but a wave of flesh surged forth from within the ragged mass as the afflicted seemed to be energized by the impending end. Bodies fell about Curse and Kitenge. They were both knocked from their feet as a swollen and corpulent body lunged its way out of the ranks of afflicted and crashed into them. Curse's rifle fell from his hands as he hit the ground, and a mass of the afflicted descended upon him.

Before any of them could touch him, Curse snatched the pistols from his waistline. Indiscriminately, he fired into the bodies that were bearing down on him. Smaller rounds from the Nambu pistol and the powerful punch of his revolver repelled many of the attackers.

A spray of automatic gunfire sounded over him, and several more were knocked away from him. Larry's shotgun boomed as well. Banshee and Larry freed Curse of his last attackers before shifting their attention to the remnants of the afflicted. Curse leapt up and saw that several afflicted still assailed Kitenge on the ground. He was wrestling with two, a head caught under each of his arms, but others were falling about him, gnashing at his flesh with their teeth.

Curse punished them with a barrage from his pistols. His legs kicked out as the soles of his boots struck into the bony bodies. Curse placed one of the pistols against one of the heads that Kitenge was holding and snuffed it out of existence with a single shot. With the weight of attackers off his body, Kitenge shifted his weight and slammed the remaining creature's head into the ground. Dark ichor oozed from numerous bite marks on his hands and legs as he forced the brittle skull into the dirt. A screech sounded from the rotten throat as Kitenge finished the afflicted with a flurry of fisted blows.

"Thanks for earlier." Curse grinned as he helped his friend up.

"Ha! Thank you for just now!" The tears in Kitenge's flesh were regenerating.

Curse returned his attention to the fighting and observed that there were only a handful of afflicted left. The zealous rage of the defenders made short work of them. Within minutes, their desiccated bodies were reduced to nothing.

The camp shook once more, but this time it was not due to the shock of an explosion or cannon. A rousing cheer was ringing from the throats of the defenders. They had repelled a force of superior numbers and come through as victors with a minimal number of casualties. The lost would be mourned in due time, but for the moment, the soldiers were caught in the relief of victory.

The battle over, Curse bent to retrieve his rifle from the ground. Upon standing again, he was almost taken off his feet by something crashing into him. He caught himself with a reminder that the battle was over just before he engaged in a defensive reaction. Instead, he reached his hand up and rubbed it over a mass of dreadlocks as Banshee's arms tightened around his shoulders. Reactively, he felt his other arm snake around her torso and pull her close.

His devotion was still to the woman of his former life, but he and Banshee had been through hell together, and he would not ward off her happiness in the moments of victory. As he held her, he felt hands slapping him from behind while offering thanks and compliments on his fighting prowess. He half-heartedly acknowledged them, as his concentration was focused on Banshee's embrace. After holding him for a while, she pulled away slightly and smiled up to him. Despite her ghoulish appearance, the smile warmed him. They had both survived together. Someone else had survived with them, of course, and they were reminded of it as a grinning, snickering face appeared between them.

"Y'all know we gotta have a hootenanny after this!"

Both of them were taken with laughter as Larry interjected into their private victory moment. Kitenge appeared next to Larry and congratulated his old friend as well.

"You can bring your friends to my fight any time, Mr. Spectre," he said through a laugh.

"I know how to pick 'em, eh?" Larry's eyes lit up as he began laughing to himself and then launched into a victory dance, clicking his heels against the ground as he whirled around in a circle.

Nigel's tank rumbled back to the group, and his head became visible from the hatch. "Didn't I tell you lot not to get more than five feet from me?" He shook his head. "And there you went hopping off the tank and charging into the fight head on. Ah well, hop in—we have business to attend."

33

Curse and Larry told Kitenge they would catch up to him and leapt onto the tank. The sides of the vehicle were streaked in the gore of their enemies. Chunks of gray and black flesh hung off of the blades and razor wire. Nigel would leave the remains on the vehicle as a grim reminder of what would happen to those who advanced against him and his men.

Nigel steered the tank back toward the center of the camp. When he found a suitable place to park the vehicle, he turned his attention toward the device.

"Close the hatch," he instructed. Larry complied. "I don't want others to hear or see what we're doing and ask questions. The only reason I told Commander Mudhei is because I had to have a good reason for leaving the front when the armor was ordered to hold."

"Understood," Curse responded.

With that, Nigel turned back to the device and began working the knobs once again. The high-pitched wail returned, ringing throughout the enclosed metal. All of their ears throbbed under the sonic assault. The light followed soon after. Lastly they all became aware of a strange heat emanating from the boxy device. The three energies coalesced into a strange mess of screaming light and warmth.

Curse looked downward and put his hands over his ears. The light and the noise were turning the inside of the tank rather inhospitable. The heat from the device joined with the already overwhelming exhaust and burn of the tank's engine. Nigel turned the dials back to their starting positions and flipped the power switch.

"Fuckin' hell," he snarled to himself. "I really don't know what to do with this thing . . . it makes no sense . . . she didn't leave you any notes or anything?"

"Nothing useful, from what I can tell," Curse told him.

Nigel reached under his chainmail veil and rubbed his chin. He then shifted his head to stare at the device for a long while.

"It seems so simple . . . but its activation is perplexing beyond all hell . . ."

The quiet and Nigel's thought process were disturbed as Larry reached out and slammed the grip of his revolver into the top of the device.

"What the hell are you doing, Spectre!?" Nigel exclaimed. Curse and Banshee were momentarily taken aback by Larry's irrational behavior.

Larry simply shrugged and explained himself. "Sometimes hittin' stuff makes it work!"

"I don't think it did much this time." Banshee smirked.

"We need a better place to work," Curse spoke up.

"Agreed, and I have a spot," Nigel said. "It'll be a small drive though . . . I'm going to take a few folks with us in case those Axis boys are still nearby."

All three consented. With that, they exited the tank once more and followed Nigel as he made his way to Commander

Mudhei to request an escort. Banshee loaded the device back into her pack so they could keep it with them.

Once more, they entered the small door leading into the fort. Commander Mudhei was standing in an open part of the fort speaking to several soldiers who hastily departed to carry out his orders. Nigel approached as the others left.

"Sir!" he announced himself.

"Yes, Corporal?" the Commander asked.

Nigel dropped his voice as he explained the circumstances. "We have the thing we spoke of earlier . . . ," he began.

"Let us step away from prying eyes as we discuss this," Commander Mudhei stated as he entered the small building again.

"You wanted to see it?" Banshee asked once they were inside.

"I do, if you would be willing to share, ma'am," he invited politely.

She promptly removed the device and set it upon a table of rotten dark wood. Commander Mudhei stared at it momentarily. He did not seem impressed. Curse began to laugh a little at his dismayed expression.

"Don't let the appearance fool you—it's all business," he stated.

"I can see that," the Commander responded. "What does it do?"

Curse made a demonstration by turning the device on and then manipulating the dials until the thing was radiating at full capacity. The Commander still seemed unimpressed by the glowing and screeching thing.

"And how does this do anything?" Commander Mudhei was now looking at Curse in dismay.

Curse sighed in frustration. "I'm not sure yet. The girl who made this thing was going to show us how to use it."

"And where is she now?"

"She was killed by some lunatics while we were trying to get this thing to Larry's house." Curse's face became somber and stony as silence fell among the group.

"I see. I am sorry, but so far I cannot see how this . . . box . . . will do what you claim it shall."

"That, sir, is why I came to ask you for an escort," Nigel interjected.

"An escort!?" The Commander's hands flew up. "Corporal, I barely have enough men here to hold the fort in case another attack is mounted against us. I would need reinforcements before anyone leaves."

Undaunted, Nigel continued his argument. "Understood and appreciated, sir, but would this not be a matter worth investigating further? Access to our former world is something that has been strived for in this realm for centuries."

"Indeed it is, Corporal, but I cannot sacrifice the men in this fort by diverting man power that is critically needed here."

"I understand, sir, but if I could get these three into the city with this device and work with some of my contacts, we could unlock the secret to working it. Then there would finally be a doorway that so many have been looking for."

Curse imposed himself in the conversation. "Would you allow Nigel to take us?"

"I would, but you must assume the risks on your own if you want to leave the protection of the fort at this point. If you can wait a while, some reinforcements may be able to bolster our defense, and it would be a more plausible request."

"How long?" Curse asked. He was growing very impatient having the device in his hands and being so close to using it to return to his former love, but not being able to do so.

"Not sure . . . they get here when they get here. I've sent word to other outposts, and they have been willing to spare some of their forces, but they will only provide small numbers from each. Also understand I would prefer that you stayed here and waited for them because if you are killed the device may be captured. We do not want the Plague Faction or the Axis obtaining this thing. I'm sure you have been informed that they are aware that it exists," Commander Mudhei spoke through measured frustration.

"We have," Curse stated flatly. "I don't know who knows what about it or where they may be thinking to look, but I would doubt they know we have it. The girl who invented it said that she hadn't talked to anyone."

"But that doesn't necessarily mean anyone knows anything . . . they could be operating on rumor alone," Banshee spoke.

"Very good, my dear; idiots will believe anything!" Larry let his opinion into the conversation.

Commander Mudhei let his brow furrow. "That's speculation. Chances are the woman you speak of did tell someone. It's too coincidental that there is suddenly a huge commotion over this thing and then you three show up holding it."

"Well, word has been traveling somehow," Curse grunted. "When I first met your soldiers, one of them told me about the rumors and said that he wasn't sure what the Plague Faction and Axis wanted with this thing, but that you all were intent on stopping them from getting it. What did your forces know of it?"

"The rumors and nothing more. Think though of the carnage that they could bring upon the former world should they get their hands on it. The thought fills me with dread to think upon." Commander Mudhei looked off and pondered.

"All right then, we'll wait for your reinforcements to arrive, but do us a favor and don't tell anyone what is going on," Curse said in a gruff voice.

"Indeed, Mr. Curse, you have my word on that. I also do not want word getting out within the camp that the device is right here under our nose. Word would travel, and before you know it, someone would tell the wrong person, and our enemies would be back at the doorstep."

"All right then." Curse nodded. "Thank you for working with us, Commander."

"My pleasure. Hopefully you will figure that thing out."

"We will take leave of your presence, sir, as we wait for the reinforcements," Nigel informed his commander.

With that they were dismissed and left the fort once again. Banshee carried the device as always while they made their way back to the tank. It seemed as good a place as any to bide their time. Banshee climbed into the tank to secure her pack once more while Curse sat against one of the treads. He was getting anxious. As he sat, he thought of the woman from his dreams. His woman. Or she had been. A blizzard of emotion raged through his mind as he began to think again about what would happen when and if he found her.

There was a high probability that he would not even let her see him. *Maybe I could just whisper in her ear while she's sleeping . . . but how different is everything going to be?* Curse thought to himself.

And what about Banshee? Curse could tell that her fondness for him was growing by the moment. While he did not see a strong lustful component to any relationship in the Nightmarescape, he realized that he was starting to care for her in a strong companionate fashion.

Not that it made a difference, but he wondered how she felt about his quest to find his love. She had told him she understood, but he doubted that for the moment. He remembered her brief moments of jealousy when his attention had been focused on Aja. He knew however that Banshee would support him in his wish to see his love whether she wanted him to return to the woman or not. Perhaps her motives were split. Maybe she wanted him to get it out of the way so that he could have closure and know that his lover was all right, then she would capture his attentions for her own.

What the fuck is wrong with you? Don't do her like that. Curse shook out of his brainstorming and admonished himself by throwing his head backward, slamming his skull into the side of the tank. *How dare you think of her in such a way.* She had saved him several times and put herself at great risk to do so. He had done the same for her. Yes, she had made her affections known, but he could not fault her. He knew that in going to find his lover, he was chasing a ghost. He could find her, but he could not do much once he did.

Banshee had told him she understood his need. Questioning her motives was not a worthwhile endeavor because her actions had already backed her words. He had also made a pact to aid her in her quest for vengeance against her rapists and murderers. Each of them would work to fulfill a desire for the other.

The tank shook as Curse slammed his head into the armored hull again out of frustration. His vision became blurry as he saw Larry's fuzzy silhouette walking into his frame of view.

"What is the need for that now, son?" Larry asked as Curse felt himself passing out from the impact.

The darkness was a welcome relief from the thoughts that had been tearing his mind. He floated in that space for some time in an oblivion that had become so familiar. He had been in that space many times recently. He held it with both a certain appreciation and disdain. Ultimately, his feelings about the darkness varied with circumstance. At the moment, he found it to be a release from his thoughts. When he had been buried under the earth, it had been damnation.

He attributed his varying degrees of welcome to what he had been doing at the time. At this point he had knocked himself out, and the escape from his frustrations had made it wanted. When he had been in the battle and ended up buried, he was fighting and had things to complete. A double-edged sword indeed.

He allowed himself to drift in the darkness a little longer before another memory began to take form in his head. He was reaching into his deepest self to grasp onto a former reality. He remembered his love again. It was a happier time, not one of the recent memories of his death traumatizing her. He merely remembered her for who she was. She came to him now as an image, and his mind raced with excitement to see her once more. His thoughts were subsumed by the idea of crossing into her present world and finding her.

Let me stay here for a while until it is time to find you, his mind echoed.

Curse felt his chest fill with a fluttering feeling as he remembered her in various outfits and stages of undress. It was the feeling of a lover who was about to return to their mate's arms after a long separation. He did not even know how long the separation had been. The gulf of time felt as though it had been forever, but could have easily been yesterday.

The positive emotions washed over him for a little while longer before he realized that doubt and uncertainty were creeping into him again. Given the last conscious memory he had of her, how would she respond to his return? He remembered his first flashback in the Nightmarescape in which he had been in bed with her and become a horrid monster right before her eyes.

Visions of his lover disappeared from his mind as he was pulled back into darkness. He thought about that initial vision. In the dream, he had been interacting with her. That seemed strange because everything else had been a straight memory. He had interacted with her and changed into what he was in the Nightmarescape from his human form. Perhaps she had been asleep and dreaming and his astral self had crossed her, depositing them both into a lucid dream. Perhaps more likely, his mind was working off of memory and guilt to give him a vision that informed of his past.

It was plausible that his unconscious had formed the vision for him and incorporated elements of his missing her with guilty feelings he had yet to understand. If he could find her in the other world and ask without terrifying her, he would.

A hand shaking his shoulder slowly rocked him back to
consciousness. A voice that sounded far away at first but
very familiar resonated in his ears.

"The reinforcements are here, son; let's get ready to go
for a ride!" Larry's hideous skeletal face materialized into
view.

"Okay, Grandpa," Curse responded.

"Come now, just because I've got a hundred years or so
on you doesn't mean you can throw lampoonery at me!"
Larry began pulling Curse to his feet.

"I'm not making fun of you . . . it was in a flashback I
had back in the trenches."

Larry's eyes widened like saucers. "WHAAAAAAA . . ."

"In the vision, I was looking at a photo album with an
older woman . . . there was an old-fashioned picture in there
of a guy with your hair and grin wearing a suit from the turn
of the century . . . she said it was my great-great-great-
grandfather who they didn't like to talk about . . ."

"HAHAHAHAHAHA!" Larry's laugh boomed like
thunder. "You mean you and me are distant kin? Ain't that
somethin'! I knew there was a reason I found you just after

you manifested! Maybe the Nightmarescape picked up on our thread of kinship, and your psychic energy reached out and found mine as a nearby beacon or something . . . hmmmm . . ." Larry pondered while wildly gesturing with his hands. "You know . . . it makes sense . . . even though I never married, I did put my seed in a woman I was quite fond of . . . our courtship fell apart before she had the child though, and she moved to another part of the Union . . . my blood passed down over several generations. Remarkable!" Larry seemed quite ecstatic at the news as he and Curse climbed up onto the tank.

Nigel's head poked out of the hatch as they mounted the vehicle. "Look around, Curse, they gave us quite the escort for this little errand."

Curse did as advised and saw several lightly armored vehicles flanking the tank. Kitenge and two of his warriors sat in his jeep on the right hand side of the tracks along with a half-track and a pickup truck with a machine gun mounted in the back. Turning his head in the other direction, Curse noticed a light tank from the World War I era and two Humvees with machine guns mounted on their roofs. Each vehicle was cast in the gray and black pallor of the world and showed signs of corrosion on the paint. Some of them wore crudely daubed black and gray camouflage like the first tank he had seen in the Nightmarescape. He knew they were all sturdy despite their appearances. The sight of the vehicles caused Curse to throw his head back and laugh.

"An escort indeed . . . do they know why they're escorting us?"

"No, Commander only told them it was a mission of importance he could not reveal to them. They are soldiers by nature and were inclined to follow the order," Nigel responded.

Curse nodded as he eased himself down into the cabin of the tank. Banshee was already inside, clutching her pack to her chest. She had stayed out of sight with the thing. She looked up and smiled as the other two entered.

"Y'all want to know something funny?" Larry boomed over the growl of the engine.

"Maybe . . . who knows with you," Nigel cautioned.

"Curse here and I are distant kinfolk!"

Banshee laughed. "And how do you know that—were you working on a family tree while you were knocked out?"

"A memory," Curse explained. "I was looking at a photo album with my mom or grandmother or someone and saw a picture of him from when he was alive . . . when I asked who he was, she said he was my great-great-great-grandfather, Lawrence Spectman, who they did *not* like to talk about."

"Surprise, surprise there . . ." Nigel shook his head.

"I knew of you too . . ." Curse pointed at Banshee.

"Me? How?" Her expression was one of shock.

"I worked in bail bonds before I died and ended up here. A flyer with a photo of you on it was circulated around a lot of agencies . . . I think you were wanted for questioning in the disappearances of some hunters . . . we know how that turned out . . ." Curse trailed off.

Banshee displayed an expression of shocked incredulity. "How . . . nobody knew anything . . ."

"Someone did," Curse informed her. "It was just a picture of you, like a sketch, not a mug shot. I'm assuming you had friends in the underground when you were engaging in your activities . . . well, one of them must have given you up under questioning of some sort."

Banshee looked as though she had just been slapped. She sat in stunned silence for some time.

"Were you looking for me, Curse?" she finally asked.

"I don't believe so. Like I said, it was just a notice that was circulated in case we came across you. I just remember it because it came to me in a flashback, and I could recognize you . . . in the former world. I recognized your hair and facial structure . . . you were very beautiful in life."

Her expression softened at his compliment, but she still seemed hurt by what he had told her. She did not know anything about her likeness being passed through law enforcement channels. Curse knew someone had to have given up information on her. That was how the game worked. She seemed to be deeply hurt by the revelation that someone she had trusted betrayed her.

"Look, Rayna . . . Banshee . . . getting upset over it now is not going to change anything. You were killed before any agency could pin anything on you. You should focus your energy on getting through to the former world and getting vengeance on the assholes that killed you. Your personal reputation in environmental circles is irrelevant now." She nodded as Curse spoke, but he could tell his words were having little effect.

Instead of continuing his speech, he simply sat down beside her and wrapped an arm around her shoulder. Her head fell to the side and rested against him. Silence settled among the group for a time, as no one was quite sure to say amidst the revelations.

"So, Nigel, where are we going exactly?" Larry ultimately broke the silence.

"A bit of London," Nigel replied.

"There's an actual piece of the city here?" Curse inquired.

"No, that's just what I call it. It's a huge chunk of city from the late 1800s . . . the cobbled streets and nasty brick buildings just remind me of old London. The residents of this place call it the City of Despair, and they're from all around Europe in that time period. There's a couple actual engineers there and whatnot who might be able to help us."

"So we get to see a real old-time city?" Curse asked.

"HA! Old-time only by your standards!" Nigel responded.

Larry leaned in toward Curse. "If his city is old, what about my rickety-ass house? That thing was a pride of the 1890s, son! You gotta respect antiquity, boy!" A trademark peal of laughter rolled out of his throat and echoed through the tank.

Curse withdrew himself as Larry and Nigel began talking to each other. Banshee had sat silently while the others spoke. Curse could tell that she believed he was lying to her. Though he had been truthful with her, her trust in him seemed shaken nonetheless. She displayed the slightest hint of betrayal as she turned toward introversion. Turning her head, she became silent. She seemed to make a faint effort to pull herself out of his hold, but he tightened his grip and would not let her go anywhere. She sat still, choosing not to fight in such close quarters. After he sat holding onto her and listening to Larry and Nigel's voices for a time, he could not stand the silence between them any longer.

"When we get to wherever we're going, I want to be alone with you for a while. We have some things to discuss."

She turned her head and stared directly into his eye sockets. He admired the determined glow from within the spaces where her eyes had once been. She simply acknowledged him with a nod. Curse let her be and moved to the front of the vehicle with the others so Banshee could be alone with her thoughts. He sat behind Larry and Nigel so he could listen to Nigel's description of the city.

"I don't know . . . it's like the London I remember, but slightly different. It takes from the architecture of the time, but appears in dilapidated and rotten condition like everything else here. Another thing, there are civilians here too . . . people who died of cholera and the general squalor of the city—not everyone's a soldier like the last few places you've been."

"As long as there's a place for me to have a good drink and shoot 'em up, I'll be content," Larry chimed in.

"Tell us about these engineers you know of," Curse said.

"Ah yes, men of science and design each. They did things such as work with electricity and build railroad tunnels back in their former lives. If anyone can help us with this puzzle, it would be them," Nigel boasted.

Curse nodded to himself.

Nigel and Larry resumed the conversation for some time. Curse looked back to Banshee to see if she was paying attention. She was slumped over with her back leaning against the wall. At once he knew that she had lapsed out of consciousness and was probably having a vision of her own. She lay there limp with her weight resting against the metal hull of the tank. Her head hung loosely from her shoulders as her body moved ever so slightly with the motions of the vehicle.

That must be how I look when I pass out too, Curse thought to himself.

Seeing her in this state of vulnerability granted him a new appreciation for having both her and Larry to watch his back when he passed in and out of consciousness, for she appeared completely helpless. Curse thought about all the times he had phased into his unconscious mind to learn of details and memories relegated to his former life. Had the two of them

Nightmarescape

not been there to watch him, he would have been a sitting duck to anyone nearby.

While he was thinking about the loss of consciousness, he remembered that a string of memories had been revealed to him on the old projector back at the fort.

"Larry, I have something to ask you," he spoke up.

"What is it, son?"

"I haven't had a chance to talk to you about it yet, but back in that fort, I found an old projector in one of the rooms and watched the film reel. It showed me a couple of memories from my old life . . . are you aware of devices like that? Things that can show memories here in addition to the flashbacks?"

Larry considered the question for a moment. "They do exist, but I don't know much about them or how they work. Projectors, things called television sets, something called a computer, they all show you things, and when you find them here in the Nightmarescape, they can show you memories. In the old life they were just for watching things, but when you find one here, it can show you pieces of your subconscious."

"Well, nobody's going to be watching their memories on that one again," Curse said through a grin.

"Now why'd you go and do that?" Larry shook his head.

"I smashed it when I was done watching it. It was weird . . . I felt really drawn to the container it was in, and then after I pulled it out and watched the film, I felt compelled to destroy it because I thought it was only showing my memories, and I didn't want anyone else to see them." Curse kept his grin as he told Larry this.

Larry sighed. "My dear boy, the projector wasn't someone who looked at you the wrong way or badmouthed your friend there . . . I know how you love smashing everyone, but those artifacts are quite rare and useful. I would have loved to have it, but now that's not possible. I suppose you didn't know what you were handling . . . just don't do it again."

"All right then, I'll give you monopoly over all the projectors, TVs, computers, and other media devices we find," Curse joked.

"It's not so much that I want to remember more than I do—I think I remember everything at this point—but those items are rare, and I could trade them for great things!" Larry's voice rose in excitement.

"You know something, Larry, I don't want to remember any more of my former life." Curse's mood suddenly changed.

Larry met his pessimism with a shrug. "My boy, I think you have a great story you're following, but how you pursue it is up to you. I have helped you unlock a great deal of potential so far. You could be a titan here in this realm."

"That's the thing . . . I'm in this world now—how relevant is the last one?"

"Well, we are trying to go back there so you can see your lady, right?" Larry asked.

"We are . . . but once I know that she's all right, what ties do I have left there? Here I have you and Banshee and all these guys we've been fighting with. I'm part of something here, and my existence is now here on this plane," Curse explained.

Nigel had withdrawn from their interaction and was concentrating on steering his tank. Curse briefly thought of Kitenge and the others who comprised the escort. They had all volunteered to escort them despite the danger to their own selves. They did not even know what they were escorting. Curse acknowledged their fierce dedication and loyalty as soldiers.

He turned back to look at Banshee again. She was still lost within the folds of her own consciousness. Her body had not moved a millimeter, yet trembled with the vibrations of the tank's engine. Curse considered how time might be passing for her in her unconscious revelry. He wondered if his visions had lasted the entirety of unconsciousness or for mere moments, much like a dream. Though some may seem to last forever, in reality dreams only occupy the space of several seconds. Curse questioned what she was seeing in her dream state. He did not want her to hate him after revealing his prior knowledge to her.

"She's fine, son." Larry's voice broke Curse's ruminations.

"You think?"

"Yes . . . she's just . . . being a woman. She will come to her senses after she wakes up from whatever she's remembering and sees that you're still at her side. And be at her side you will . . . I've seen the way you two interact when you think I'm not looking. Keep in mind, I wanted to shoot her when we found her! You've had thoughts for her since you first saw her. You just haven't moved on how you feel because you still have what's-her-face waiting in the other world."

"Damn, you're good," Curse attested. "Just do me a favor . . ."

"Anything, my dear boy."

"Whatever happens . . . don't convince her to commit suicide."

Larry's eyes grew large as he began cackling. "Son, you're too much! She's too strong and smart for that." Curse nodded. "But let me tell you something . . . she feels the same way you do, probably even stronger. The fact that she can't be yours yet makes her desire more pressing. Understand this though, she will not put her feelings above your desire to be with your old lady. Morally, Banshee is set in her grounds."

Curse moved back to Banshee and ran a hand through her hair while she was unconscious. "She is someone special indeed," Curse conceded. "How does romance . . . work here . . . ?" he asked.

Larry guffawed again. "Unless you're into necrophilia, it's really more of an emotional connection than a physical thing for right-minded folks in these parts. Some folks do still give in to their . . . shall we say, 'carnal' urges. Lots of folks who are lacking in impulse control engage in such activities."

"You're both bloody disgusting, talking about fucking anyone in this world," Nigel interrupted. "If you're done being whackin' perverts, maybe one of you should stick your head out the top and see what we're approaching."

Curse followed the advice and stuck his head out of the hatch. He was greeted with a black and white vision of a rotten city from the end of the 1800s. Several vehicles from the escort moved in front of Nigel's tank as he followed them onto a dirt path. The others fell in behind. A raucous noise rose up from the path as the tank's treads met the beginnings of a cobbled street.

35

A garrison of soldiers standing around the outskirts of the city glanced up at the advancing column. Several large guns stationed on rooftops and in emplacements were trained on the vehicles. As the column rumbled closer to the city's outskirts, a group of soldiers approached the lead vehicles. Seconds later after a brief consultation, the guards were waving the column into the city. Curse dropped back into the tank and observed Banshee groggily awakening from her unconscious state. He snatched her hands and began pulling her up.

"Come here, you have to see this . . ." She followed without question. "Larry, are you coming up with?"

"I've been here before," Larry answered without interest. "You kids go enjoy the fancy big city."

Curse hurried up through the hatch once again with Banshee in tow. Upon climbing out onto the top of the tank, they were exposed to the inside of the city. As the tank and its escorts rolled down the street, they saw enormous buildings of gray color and crumbling brickwork. People of all sorts clung to the sides of the streets as the military vehicles rumbled along. Curse and Banshee saw women wearing hoopskirts and large hats, children wearing breeches, gentlemen in suits and top hats, and soldiers carrying muskets walking alongside those carrying modern polymer rifles and others. All of them stared up at the vehicles from their gray and eyeless faces.

As grandiose as the sensation of anachronism and discovery was, Curse could not help but feel sorry for all the regular people who had suffered the grip of the Nightmarescape. It did not surprise him however. Larry had said that people who were exposed to hardship and strife in their lives were more likely to find the infernal realm in their dreams. Life up until the mid-twentieth century had been hard for everyone all around. Even in the modern unindustrialized areas of the world that Curse had left, hardship and pain were still rampant. Hell, even those living in civilized and industrialized locales still endured their share of strife.

In his life, he had never known what it felt like to starve or live in a war zone, but he still had encountered enough horror and suffering to put him in touch with the Night-marescape. He thought of Banshee too and the way her life had ended. Though he did not know all of her experiences, he could guess she had her own share of demons. And then there was Larry and his set of rather unique circumstances from the turn of the twentieth century. There was no telling what drove that man to his mental state.

Perhaps things did not change that much over time after all, and he had more in common with people of different time periods than he initially thought. He studied the residents of the city as the tank rolled further into the archaic metropolis. His vision found its way back to Banshee. She was watching the world passing around them with intent interest. The movement of the city began to slow as the tank ground to a halt. Nigel and Larry joined the two of them on top of the vehicle. Several men were working their way back from the vehicles at the column's front.

"You men stay here," Nigel commanded.

"Yes, Corporal," a spectral soldier acknowledged. The soldier crossed his bolt-action rifle over his chest and moved back to guard his vehicle.

"You three come with me," Nigel motioned for Curse, Banshee, and Larry.

They followed as Nigel made his way down a winding, grimy alleyway. The group passed numerous open doorways as they walked. Banshee tightened the straps on her pack to pull the device closer to her body. Curse watched as she deftly pulled her pistol from her backside and concealed it behind her right thigh. In a haste to be out of the tank and join Curse, she had left her rifle within the armored vehicle. Curse carried his weapon with him, but they were not expecting to encounter a fight within the city. It seemed to be at least a neutral ground where many of the residents were not engaged in the eternal combat that seemed to consume most areas of the Nightmarescape.

Curse moved closer to her in case he would need to protect her. The two of them walked side by side behind Nigel. Numerous pairs of glowing blue lights stared out of the doorways at their passing. Several deathly creatures wearing filthy rags looked up and moved to the side of the street as they approached. In their lives they had most likely been beggars and street urchins. Nigel continued past all they encountered, his head held high with martial bearing. They continued to follow him until he led them to a rather nondescript door in the dirty street.

Nigel stopped at the door and knocked loudly before stepping back and placing his hands behind his back in a parade rest. Several seconds later, a viewing port opened at eye level, and two shining blue lights peered out.

"Who goes there?" a raspy voice inquired from behind the door.

"I come to seek aid in a research project of sorts," Nigel spoke coolly and with a crisp English accent.

"I see . . . password," the voice demanded from the other side.

"If you don't let me in, you bloody twat, I'm going to go get my tank and drive it through this door," Nigel continued without raising his voice an octave.

A coarse grating laughter echoed from behind the metal door as the viewing port slammed shut and the door flew inward. Standing in the doorway was a disgusting sight indeed.

A sunken and skeletal face grinned at them from atop a white lab coat streaked with black and gray grime. Like Larry, the thing had no lips, but it seemed to have a strange face composed of gray flesh that transitioned to bare bone below the cheeks.

"Nigel, so good to see you. Do you want to make that rust bucket of yours go faster still?" the scientist inquired.

"That might be interesting in due time, but as of now, I think I have something of much greater import . . . something I could use your help with."

The scientist's eyes surveyed the others with him. "A nasty bunch of malcontents you got with you there, Nigel . . . but the girl's as beautiful as they get around here . . ."

Curse stepped forward in front of Banshee to remind the scientist of his manners. A low growl rumbled in his throat as his muscles tensed. He towered over the gangling scientist's form in both height and girth. Whether the wretched thing could help them with the device or not, Curse resolved to be severe in discipline if the creature overstepped his boundaries again.

"No offense there, big guy . . . didn't know you two were an item . . . just a gentlemanly compliment to a lady," the scientist attempted to ward him off.

"We're not 'an item' as you put it, but overstep your bounds with her again, and I'll give you a gentlemanly compliment against the side of your head," Curse warned.

Nigel came between them. "Forgive the slight, Curse old boy. Doctor, Curse is protective of his friend Banshee. He does not appreciate when men speak to her in such a manner. He's also got a bit of an explosive temper he can't seem to help, so I'd stay on his good side were I you."

A chuckle arose from the thing in the lab coat. "No harm done. Chivalry and willingness to defend the honor of a lady are admirable traits. Come in, you lot."

The new arrivals filed in with Larry bringing up the rear. As he crossed the threshold into the building, his eyes met with those of the scientist. The scientist met him with a strangely transfixed grin. Larry answered the expression with a high-pitched shriek from his own grinning mouth as he brought his revolver up to the scientist's chin. For the first time, the scientist's face betrayed a hint of fear. Larry's gaze held him momentarily until another ghastly cackle rolled out of his throat.

"You should've seen your face." He laughed again. The scientist eased at his laughter and accompanied him with a sickening gurgled chuckle of his own. "But seriously . . . don't mess with my great-great . . . great . . . something grandson," he hissed. "Now, who really runs this lab, Igor?"

Nigel had turned and was watching the scene unfold before him. "I can't take you anywhere, Lawrence." He shook his head. Larry merely responded with a breathy laugh as the group moved deeper into the building.

The ragged lab-coated creature led them past numerous tables littered with mechanical items in various stages of assembly. Several other rotted creatures in lab-coats and aprons sat at some of the tables tinkering with the items. One looked up from behind the white-hot flame of a soldering iron before raising its welding mask and coming around the table to meet the group.

"Who have you brought in to see me?" a Germanic voice asked from a gaunt face featuring blue lights glaring out from behind thin-rimmed spectacles and a bushy gray mustache.

"The tank driver."

"Ah, Corporal, so nice to see you again! Is your rust bucket not moving fast enough?" Nigel relaxed his military bearing as the mechanic spoke to him.

"No, Doctor, it is running just fine. It actually saved our asses not too long ago. Our business here is to seek your assistance in figuring out the function of a particular device."

"Is that so? What kind of device?" The scientist's mustache rose and fell as he spoke.

"Well . . . these three claim that this thing they have found can split the fabric between this world and the former. Try as we have, we have not been able to get it to do anything," Nigel briefed.

The bushy eyebrows behind the glasses raised up at Nigel's declaration. "I see . . . and just who are these friends of yours?"

"May I present to you Mr. Larry Spectre, Curse, and Banshee." The three of them each nodded at their name.

"Greetings to you all. I am Dr. Alman. I have spent much time working on machinery and design. I must admit rumors of a device such as yours have persisted within this realm for as long as I can remember. What makes this thing capable of doing what you claim?"

"Beyond what its creator told me, I have no idea," Curse stated.

"Here, have a look at it." Banshee removed her pack, and set it upon a table in front of Dr. Alman. The mechanic opened the pack and removed the blocky device from inside. His brow promptly wrinkled in frustration.

"Not much on the outside, but appearances can be deceiving . . . ," the doctor said gently. He found the power switch and turned it on. His hands moving deftly, he began to experiment with the dials. "Light, sound, and heat," he stated to himself.

"Well, we figured that much out," Curse responded.

"Give me a little time with this thing." Dr. Alman issued the statement as both a request and an order. He turned away from the group and focused his attention on the device.

"If you two want to see the city a bit, Lawrence and I will stay here and guard the device," Nigel offered to Curse and Banshee.

Banshee smiled and nodded for Curse to follow her as she moved back toward the door. He determined that she welcomed Nigel's offer so she could speak with him alone.

"Leaving so soon?" The greeter's demented voice called to them as they approached the door.

"We'll be back," Curse said as they left.

Out in the street, they walked at each other's side for a while. They followed the alleyway in the same direction they had been traveling before stopping at the lab. The dirty street eventually opened out onto a wide thoroughfare of cobbled road. The road was situated on the edge of a river of dark water. Curse followed Banshee as she observed her surroundings and then headed for a small waist-high wall at the edge of the river. She turned and placed her lower half against the gray bricks before reaching out for Curse's hands.

Curse shouldered his rifle and placed the skeletal tips of his fingers upon her palms. Where the ends of his fingers had been eroded away to expose bony digits, her hands had been left intact as they were in her life. The palms of her hands felt worn but still smooth and fairly soft. She wore her nails at a short and functional length. Banshee had not been one in life to desire typical feminine adornments. He admired her for that. Her existence had made her emphasize practicality over appearance. It spoke of her pragmatic sense to him.

Her hands reminded him of the rest of her. Besides her face and deathly pallor, she seemed to be almost perfect compared to other residents of the Nightmarescape. Yes, her skin was still gray and unnatural, but she lacked much of the signs of rot that permeated many other bodies. Whereas he was a heavy slab of muscle, she was lithe and taut. Her muscles rippled tightly beneath her skin. Indeed, she had been slightly younger than him when she ended up in the Nightmarescape, but given the fact that their new home could be an eternal realm, that seemed of little consequence.

Curse looked into Banshee's face and found himself thinking of the way she had looked in the former life. In his mind, the beautiful human face took the place of her spectral reality. When he saw her now, that was usually the way he thought of her. He felt himself sighing as he thought of his former lover. He longed to be back in her presence, but he felt a strong draw to Banshee as well. His head hung at his conflicted desires.

"I have to apologize for doubting you," Banshee spoke up.

"Huh? Oh, it's nothing . . . don't worry about it."

"No, I had a memory vision while we were in the tank. You know we actually did cross paths in person at one point," she continued.

Curse's vision leapt up from the ground to meet hers once again. "What? Why don't I remember this?"

Banshee met his surprise with a small smile. "Why didn't I remember until now? This world lets us see what it wants from our former lives. Do you want to know what I remembered?"

"Yes, please tell me."

"We were in a diner . . . somewhere in the sticks. I was with a female friend who was eating. Being vegan at the time, I didn't find anything I could eat there. I saw you . . . well, I hadn't met you, but I knew it was you in my vision. Kinda the same way you knew that you saw me in your vision. You were sitting on the other side of the dining room. I sat with my friend, talking while she ate. Some redneck guy came up and started bothering us. He was preaching to us and giving me crap about my hair. I saw you look up. He kept on me, and I told him to fuck off. He became belligerent and started screaming in my face and shaking the table. That's when you came to me, Curse. You snatched him by the collar of his shirt and threw him to the ground. He yelled and tried to shelter his head, but you landed several really hard punches against his face. I think you knocked him out because he quit moving. Then you asked if we were all right, paid for your food, and walked out."

Curse found himself laughing softly at her story. "Yeah, that sounds like something I would have done."

"You protected me then as you protect me now . . . and I doubted you." Her smile left. "I never should have."

"I probably saw the picture of you after that run-in. That's why it seemed familiar before I knew it was you."

Banshee's arms were wrapped around him before he could object. She placed her head against his chest and squeezed. He sighed and somewhat reluctantly placed his arms around her as well. Her want for him was getting stronger. They had bonded very significantly through their new existences. Their bond was strengthened by the fact that they had faced hell together numerous times and persevered through one another's aid and care.

Indeed though, he still had feelings for his former lover and wanted desperately to see her once again. But Curse could not deny what he was feeling for Banshee. As he considered his predicament, he held her and stared out at the black, rushing water. The sight reminded him of the vile, dark pit in the fort. He remembered his panic when he realized that Banshee had fallen into the disgusting fluid and dove in to find her struggling against the plague-afflicted. His memory was flooded with the rush of needing to protect her as he surged toward the tangle of flesh at the bottom of that abyss. Soon after, he remembered the sense of relief that had come to both of them upon breaking the surface, and he allowed himself to revel in that sensation for some time as he gave himself over to Banshee's embrace. In this state, he allowed his mind to return to thinking about his former lover. He thought of her face and what positive memories of their relationship had been revealed to him. He wanted to be back with her . . . he also wanted to hold Banshee and accept her. Another sigh worked its way from his chest.

"I know . . . you still want to go back to her," Banshee's voice echoed against his chest cavity. Curse found his hands gently pushing Banshee away from his body.

"Nothing against you . . . I still have a strong loyalty to the woman I committed my former life to . . ."

Banshee smiled to him again. "Your devotion is so admirable. She was very lucky to have you while she did."

Her words were well meant, but they struck a sorrowful chord within him. He remembered the horror and pain he had caused his love when she saw the aftermath of his suicide. He had scarred her through the ultimate act of his own selfishness. The sting of responsibility ate at his psyche. He had not told Banshee about any of those memories yet. He did not know how he would be able to communicate them.

Banshee looked at him while he held her at a short distance. He could tell that she could sense his guilt and pain, but she was cautious of approaching it. Eventually she offered a simple statement.

"You can tell me anything."

He only returned a nod to her as their attention was suddenly snatched away from each other.

"HEY! Y'all come back this way!" Larry was standing at the edge of the alleyway and waving them back toward him.

"Good Lord, what now . . . ," Curse grumbled. Banshee smiled to him.

"We'll talk more later."

Curse dropped his rifle from his shoulder as he and Banshee followed Larry back into the laboratory. They were readmitted by the wretched little scientist thing without hassle. Inside they were greeted by a frowning Dr. Alman with his arms crossed over his chest.

"This box is nothing but a loud flashlight," he informed them.

"Is it?" Curse asked. "Trust me . . . the woman who made it used it to come to this realm. She did not come here like most of us . . . she was a living person who stepped through using this thing."

"And where is she now?" Dr. Alman inquired.

"Dead. Caught a rocket in her chest," Curse said in a cold tone.

The doctor shook his head. "You're playing me for a fool . . . Nigel, I welcome you here, but please do not bring such theatres of absurdity to my laboratory."

The device was still screaming softly upon the table. Curse lowered himself and turned the dials to their furthest positions. Once more the scream increased, the light grew in intensity, and heat began radiating from the device. Curse gripped the top of the thing in his hands and snarled at it.

"Work, damn you," Curse growled under his breath as he tore at the knobs in a panic.

He thought of his lover in the other world while his fingers dug into the wooden furniture of the device. The thoughts of her overpowered his mind . . . he was so close to having her back in his presence, even if only for a few brief moments. His attention focused on her as his desire and need grew. The frustration built within him as the thoughts seemed to come as a mockery of what he could never have again. Still, he kept his mind focused on her. He could not give in to his frustrations.

He was too close.

Dr. Alman opened his mouth to say something as Curse let out a scream and in front of them all, the fabric of reality itself split in an ugly black gash. A thunderous noise accompanied the ripping of dimensions as the device sent out its infernal signals and blasted a tunnel between realms. Every mouth dropped open as Curse staggered back from the device and stared at the gaping hole in reality.

"Son . . . you did it . . ." Larry's voice was barely above a whisper.

36

Curse stood back staring at the rent in the universe's fabric with astonishment. What had he done exactly? All he could remember doing was turning the dials to their furthest and thinking about his lover. Maybe that was it . . . turn the signals to their maximum and think about where you wanted to go . . . potentially the psychic pull could have done the rest. The Nightmarescape itself used psychic energy to pull presences into its grip. Somehow Aja had figured out how to manipulate that energy with this device and thoughts. Not just thoughts though—feelings, desires. Just as the Nightmarescape used negative energy to pull those who had suffered into its fold, the device used memories and wants for the former world to open an avenue between the realms.

"Aja, you genius . . . ," Curse said to himself upon the revelation.

"Where's it going to take us?" Banshee asked.

"No clue . . ." Curse still could not believe he was staring at a rip in reality. With luck, his lover would be somewhere on the other side. He maneuvered himself so he was standing in front of the tear.

He growled to himself as he stared at the portal. It was wide enough for two bodies to move through. He steeled himself as he prepared to step into the unknown. Just before he moved his feet, he felt something grab his wrist. Turning his head to the side, he saw Banshee standing next to him. She offered him a reassuring smile as her hand moved down and took his. Using his other hand, he hefted his rifle to a position between his arm and side so that he could fire off hip shots should there be a rude greeting in the other world. Though Curse believed he was going to go to see his love, he would not be caught on the other side unprepared. He also thought of the fact that he was holding Banshee's hand on the way to see his love. Normally the thought would give him conflict, but he put it in his mind that her touch was a reassurance for now and nothing more.

Thinking of encouragement, Curse turned his head to his distant relative Larry. "Are you coming with us?" he asked.

Larry shrugged. "This is what we've been going through all this trouble for, right?" Larry assumed his position behind Curse and Banshee, loosing a strange chuckle.

"Nigel, are you coming?" Curse asked.

"No, my friend. I'm going to stay here . . . we'll make sure that the portal remains open so that you may have an avenue of return. We don't quite know how to turn it off yet you know . . ."

"Well, don't go tinkerin' with it while we're in there!" Larry warned.

"Safe return, my friends," Nigel nodded to them.

Curse assented to him and turned his head to gaze upon the portal once more. It merely sat there as a dark chasm ripped in the world in front of him, a void in both the conscious and the physical. His hand gripped Banshee's as he took short, slow steps forward. The two of them moved together into the void. After several steps, they were overcome with darkness. The world disappeared from around them, and they were suddenly floating in an empty space.

Larry readied his shotgun for whatever might be on the other side before turning to Nigel and a dumbstruck Dr. Alman and throwing an exuberant wave to them.

"Gentlemen!" With the exit greeting, he stepped into the portal behind Curse and Banshee.

At first the darkness seemed as though it were the beginning to another unconscious vision. The void was short-lived however, and almost as soon as it had taken over their minds, Curse's vision was suddenly assaulted by a world of color.

Having become accustomed to the monochromatic Nightmarescape, Curse's senses were taken back by the riot of shades and hues. After several moments of adjustment, he began to process his new surroundings. The sun was down, and the blanket of nightfall had spread across the sky. It was a partially cloudy night watched over by purple clouds gently floating above. Several open spots in the clouds revealed the dark curtain of space and the occasional star. Seeing the night sky for the first time in ages was a beautiful thing. Curse found himself momentarily lost in the shades drifting softly above him as though they were almost alien now.

After a few moments with his head craned skyward, Curse turned his attention back to the earth. Underneath the soft darkness of a cloudy night, Curse could tell that they were surrounded by grass and trees. Even in the subdued shades of night, he could tell that these plants were green and thriving as opposed to the black and gray dead fauna of the Nightmarescape. There was so much contrast to be held between the two worlds. He turned momentarily and surveyed his companions.

Banshee and Larry were just as they had been in the Nightmarescape. Being transplanted to the current plane of existence, they looked downright horrifying and ghoulish against the living world. He knew that his appearance was no better. Personal appearances were forgotten as he observed the black rip in the universe still sitting behind them.

Confident that the others were still with him, Curse turned his attentions forward once more. The backside of a small house stood before him. Curse felt an immediate pull as his subconscious mind drew him toward the building. It felt to him as though he were following something predestined rather than moving on his own as he approached the rear doors. Yes, he could feel it, his prize, his former love was in there somewhere.

Silently and under the cover of darkness, he made his way onto the house's back porch. Banshee and Larry followed him, not making a sound. They both seemed confused by what he was doing, so he drew them close and spoke to them in a low whisper.

"She's in this house . . . I don't know how I know that, but my gut is screaming at me . . ." They both nodded in response.

Curse lowered himself and peered in through a window. The inside was engulfed in darkness. It had to be late in the nighttime hours, probably well after midnight. Exercising extreme stealth, Curse made his way over to a windowed back door. He reached out and took a firm grip on the doorknob before attempting to give it a twist. It did not budge.

Curse let out an almost imperceptible grunt before turning to Larry and Banshee again. Their gazes could not stay in one place for very long. The world seemed so fresh and vibrant to them even under the fall of night when compared to the drab shades of black, white, and gray that composed the palette of their former realm.

"I need to get in there," Curse spoke softly to them.

"Try some more doors and windows before you go breaking anything," Banshee whispered back.

Larry said nothing but grinned widely and hefted his shotgun toward Curse.

"Only if we have to," Curse replied before moving off in a crouch to try several windows on the back of the house.

Not one of the windows budged. Curse found himself hoping that the residence did not have an alarm system. If anyone was alerted to their presence, the circumstances would become very strange indeed. He also hoped that no residents of this world would find their trans-dimensional highway to the Nightmarescape.

Pushing the thoughts from his mind to focus, Curse moved around the side of the house to try several more windows. With due caution, Curse's skeletal fingers felt along the bottom of each window for an opening. Several tries at different windows left him frustrated and near the point of trying to quietly break glass for an entry. There was one window left before he was around the front side of the house. Hoping against hope that this one would grant him access to the inside, he dug his fingers under the window's frame and found that it moved slightly at his touch. Pressing his hands farther under the frame, the window moved upward.

It was loose in its movement, and he wondered if the lock had been set or not. Either way, he was glad it was him entering the house of his former lover instead of someone intent on harm.

With the window up all the way, Curse eased his body across the window frame and into the garage. He moved with stealth and grace in opposition to his usual crashing movements in the Nightmarescape. Once inside the garage, he continued to survey the world around him. Two medium-sized cars were parked in the garage. Two vehicles sent a warning through Curse's mind.

Perhaps they both belonged to his love . . . maybe she was doing very well for herself and purchased two cars . . . or one of them belonged to someone else. He had to remind himself that he had no idea how long he had been away from this world. Fear and apprehension were beginning to creep into the back of his mind. If he found someone else in the house with her, he did not know what he would do. Whether he had been gone several months, a year, or a decade, he did not know if that was a reality he could handle.

A gentle scraping noise distracted him as he turned to see Banshee lithely slide across the window frame and onto her hands and knees before moving in a half crawl step to meet him. They both watched as Larry first set his shotgun down on the interior side of the window, and then hoisted himself up to climb inside. He made it halfway before losing his balance across the frame and tumbling face first into the garage.

Curse and Banshee stepped back slightly as his face hit the concrete. A thin trickle of dark ichor bled out from his forehead and onto the ground near one of the cars. After they left, it would look just like oil under one of the vehicles. Curse and Banshee watched him for several moments as he regained himself and stood. There was something that was strange about the injury. In the Nightmarescape, the ichor would have evaporated within minutes of hitting the ground, and the wound would have resealed itself by now. Larry caught on to their surprised expressions even in the dark.

"What?" he mouthed softly.

"Your forehead," Curse whispered back.

Larry reached his bony fingers up and felt his forehead for a moment before bringing them back in front of his face and seeing that he was still bleeding. In the dark and silence he emanated a subdued chuckle.

"Looks like we ain't so indestructible here!" he whispered in a mirthful tone. "Here we bleed just like anyone else . . ." He looked down at the small pooling of dark ichor that had come from his head. "Something to remember us by, eh? I think we should call this crap nightmareplasm!" He followed the whispered comment with another subdued chuckle.

"Yes, Larry, nightmareplasm . . . try not to get it all over her house when we go inside." Curse's irritation was apparent even through his hushed tone.

He had much more important things to pay attention to at the moment.

In the darkness, Curse made his way over to a door in the garage that led into the house. With extreme caution, Curse gripped the handle and gently turned it. The door was unlocked. *Not good security, my love,* Curse thought to himself.

He put the thoughts aside as he slowly opened the door to avoid causing any creaks. It opened smoothly with no resistance. Without hesitation, Curse made his way into the house. Banshee and Larry were close on his heels; one of them closed the door just as silently as he opened it. Once inside the residence, Curse continued to follow the strong pull from inside his mind. It guided him through the house. He had no idea where he was going, yet he had no doubt about where his subconscious pull was taking him.

Curse led the way into a living room area. Taking care not to disturb anything in the room or trip over stray furniture, he continued his advance through the residence. Once clear of the small obstacle course, he stopped at a doorway on the opposite side of the room. There he turned to Larry and Banshee.

"You two stay here," he commanded them.

"Ahhh, my boy, you'd separate us from sharing in your most precious moment?" Larry asked in a low whisper.

"I want to have a few moments with her alone . . ."

"Understood, son. We'll sit on this here fancy sofa."

"Just don't make a damn mess," Curse grunted.

"Be truthful with her, Curse," Banshee advised.

"I will," he responded before handing his rifle to Banshee.

With that, the two of them retired themselves to the living room as Curse moved into a hallway. Away from Banshee and Larry, Curse felt his thoughts drifting to trepidation once more. He could not even remember his name from this life. He had not been able to recall his love's name yet either. She was an image and a presence to him, but he could not put a name to her. Desire took him over and he gave himself to the unconscious urging that pushed him to move onward. He passed several doors that he knew not to be of importance in his quest. Though he had no idea what was behind them, the fact that his urging did not make them of note was enough to ignore the doors and keep moving.

He followed the hallway further and rounded a corner. Carefully placing his feet to make soundless footsteps, Curse followed his mind's direction and continued straight on down the hallway before he came to stand before a final doorway. His mind screamed to him that beyond this door lay his lost love. He could not explain how he knew that. In some sense, his former relation to her may have formed a psychic bond that threaded the two of them together. That thread now pulled him along toward her, having led him to this final barrier.

38

His mind screamed at him to just throw the door open and rush in for her. He obtained a grip on his id and reminded himself that he was not the man he used to be. Despite the fact that he was so close to his heart's desire, his insecurity in his new appearance was giving him second thoughts. His hope was that she would be asleep when he entered and that he would be able to whisper softly into her ear.

A tremble overtook Curse's body as he pondered his own fear of entering the room and being confronted with a reaction similar to the one from his first flashback. A moment that should have been sweet was rapidly becoming painful and fraught with fear. His body shook as he reached down and placed his hand on the doorknob. Catching himself before opening the door, he looked sideways at his own reflection in a mirror hanging in the hallway.

In the dark, he made out the silhouette of his reflection. The blue light in the back of his eye sockets shone out at him balefully. The cold glow seemed to mock him as he stood at the threshold of what should have been considered a triumph.

And despite his appearance, why should he not have felt triumphant? He had crossed the fabric of the universe itself to transcend two planes of existence in order to find her. His actions had bordered on the impossible.

"Thank you, Aja," Curse mouthed silently, for he would not have found himself here had it not been for her device.

And then he thought of Aja and how she had lost her life while attempting to teach him about the device. He owed it to her to master his apprehensions and fulfill his quest. To abandon his pursuit right upon the threshold of attainment would be a detriment to her memory.

With these thoughts in mind, Curse took a firm grip on the doorknob once again and ever so softly pushed the door inward. Beyond the door, he found himself in a dimly lit bedroom. A digital clock sitting upon a table cast its red glow across the space. Curse checked the time and noted that it was 2:58 a.m. That likely meant several hours before she would wake.

Then Curse centered his vision on the bed. There she lay. Curse slowly and cautiously padded his way over to her. Although he was able to obscure his footfalls, his steps and movements felt heavy. Still he forced himself toward her. In the soft light of the cloudy night and the red glow of the clock, he saw the full detail of her beauty. She was laying on her left side, one half of her face obscured by the pillow she pressed her head against. Her soft dirty-blonde hair trailed behind her head and rested on the bed. Curse found himself reaching for her. He knew that he could disturb her, but he was powerless to resist his instinct to feel her once again.

His skeletal fingertips found their way to the supple skin of her shoulder. He let his fingers slide down until the remaining flesh of his fingers graced hers. A shudder went through him as he touched his long-lost lover. At last he was in her presence once again. He let his fingers squeeze her shoulder gently. She flinched at the touch and rolled over onto her back. Curse pulled his hand away and stepped back should he disturb her further. It was at this point he heard something else moving in the bed.

Curse froze. Dare he believe that another may have been in her bed? In his haste, he had not taken a full view of the bed before approaching. He suddenly felt all of his emotions being replaced with the familiar rage that had burned through him so often in recent times. Now trembling out of anger rather than fear, he rounded the bed and stopped on the other side when he saw the outline of another form under the sheets. Immediately he felt the urge to reach down and attack the sleeping form. If he did that though, he would startle his love to a truly nightmarish scene. He had already traumatized her enough with his own self destruction. He did not want to cause her further pain, but his compulsion to harm the man sleeping in his love's bed was overpowering him unlike anything he had felt until this point.

His hand reached to his waistline, and he found the grip of his revolver. Within a brief space of time, he had the gun out in his hand and was pointing it at the sleeping man's head. The hammer cocked back as Curse's thumb pulled it down. He stood there with his finger on the trigger, ready to depress it for an uncounted time span. His heart was pushing his body to act in one way, but his brain was straining against his muscles to keep an inevitable devastation from occurring. One more urging, an ounce of impulse was all it would have taken, and the weapon would have snuffed the man's life out.

The duality of Curse's intentions froze him in a temporary state of inactivity. His burning rage made him want to kill the man, but his compassion for his love prevented his body from completing the action. *What will happen to her if I do this . . . ?* He felt trapped in his predicament and found himself trying to find a sign or justification for whether he should act or not. One came from behind him.

"Curse, don't." Banshee's voice was a soft whisper.

He was surprised he even heard her given the intense struggle inside his head. "Why?" Was all he could ask.

He noticed that a light was shining from behind him. She still had her flashlight and was looking at things on a dresser.

"Look at this," Banshee approached him and held a framed photograph out to him. Her light illuminated the picture inside.

Curse reached down and took the picture from her. It was of his former self and the woman in the bed. They were standing outside during the springtime. He was positioned behind her with his arms crossed over the top of her chest. Her hands were wrapped around his forearms. Both of them wore huge smiles. Gentle rays of sunlight shone down through the treetops. The whole picture radiated life. It was beautiful and came to him in a brief memory. He remembered the sensation of her hands holding onto his arms as her body snuggled against his. He committed the memory to his mind forever to never be lost again. Cherishing the memory as it was etched into his mind, he turned to Banshee. He continued to hold the gun where it was.

"I thought I told you to stay in the other room," he whispered to her.

She ignored his statement. "That was on the dresser . . . there are pictures of him and her too . . . but, Curse, turn the picture over."

Curse did as she instructed and flipped the picture in his hands. The back of the frame was open and showed the back of the photograph. In a gentle feminine scrawl, something was written on the back.

Jenna and Damien . . . April 3, 2004 . . . Curse read the inscription to himself.

"Larry found a calendar on the table in the other room . . . the year is 2010."

"God damn . . . six years . . . I've been dead for six years . . ."

"Apparently," Banshee said gently. "But she still remembers you . . . she holds love for you in her heart . . . time has passed. She is still here, but you have been gone for a long time. Her life has changed in your absence, but not in spite of you."

Curse looked at the man in the bed through the sights of his revolver. Banshee's words had touched him. His existence had changed. Jenna's existence had changed. She had even seen him dead.

A love for him still lingered in her after his death. Up until just now, if anyone had told him that someone could come back from the dead in some sense, he would have believed them to be stark, raving mad. Jenna could not have known that he was in another dimension trying to find her again. He knew that he had wrecked her life once and felt the horrendous sting of guilt from doing so. How could he exist if he destroyed the life she had found for herself?

Curse's thumb gripped the hammer of the revolver as he slowly depressed the trigger and guided the hammer back into a resting position. A sigh escaped him as he set the photo back on the dresser.

"Speak to her—let her know you're here," Banshee urged him.

Curse nodded and moved back to Jenna's side of the bed so he could kneel. Softly, with no intention to bother her, he reached and gently placed his hand over hers. He paused, momentarily petrified before he found the words and began to whisper softly to her.

"Jenna . . . ," he began. "It's Damien." *Yes . . . that was my name.* He had not been able to remember that fact until seeing the back of the picture. He did not know if he would want to remember it any longer after he was done here.

"Damien . . . ," Jenna spoke softly in her sleep.

"Yes, dear?"

"I miss you . . . ," she murmured.

"I know, and I you. Know this though—I still love you. I've never stopped loving you. Six years beyond this world and I still love you, and I will forever. I'm all right, I'm in a . . . good . . . place, I guess, with people who care for me."

There *were* people who cared for him, but he did not want to tell her that he had been in a hellish place that they called the Nightmarescape. She did not need to hear such details.

"I love you, too," she spoke again in her sleep.

"My dear, don't worry about me. Know that, beyond this world, I still love you and think of you. I see that you have found another mate . . . your life has changed, and at first I was livid, but a close friend put things in perspective . . . I'm in another place, and you're still here. I don't blame you for moving on . . . I'm actually proud that you've had the strength to keep moving on without me."

He paused, waiting to see if she would respond. She merely slept. He continued speaking to her.

"I also want to apologize . . . I never meant for you to see me after . . . well . . . when I shot myself. Know that the guilt stings me deeply still to this day. You never should have seen that . . ."

"Damien, I forgive you," Jenna spoke through her unconsciousness.

He felt lightened as she said those words. Knowing inside that the scar of the incident would be deeply carved into her soul forever, he did not expect his mere apology to alleviate the pain of the past, but knowing that she had found some peace made him feel less absorbed in the guilt. He moved his hand from over hers. A gentle smile spread across his lips as he reached and delicately trailed the tips of his fingers over her face.

"My love, it's time for me to leave you again," he whispered.

"Don't go." Jenna readjusted her position on her back as she spoke with a sleepy voice.

"I have to. Just as you have a new life here, I have a new existence I must return to. You rest, my love. I will always cherish you." After several moments, she did not respond. Curse watched her chest rise and fall before he shifted his body so that his face could reach hers.

With the utmost care, he moved his head down and pressed his lips to her forehead. He left her with a gentle yet heartfelt kiss. "Sleep tight, my love."

A smile spread across Jenna's face after he touched his lips to her head. She looked safe and content there in her bed. Curse did not bother to look further at the male in the bed. The man's existence was inconsequential to him at this point. He had to let go and move forward. His wish to come back and make his peace with her and know that she was safe had been fulfilled. Now he had Banshee and Larry to look after. After they returned to the Nightmarescape, they would rearm themselves and set out to seek Banshee's vengeance.

Curse stood and turned to Banshee once again. She was smiling at him. He turned his back on the room and motioned for Banshee to follow him out. Silently, they made their way back through the dark house into the living room. In the darkness, they were met with Larry's insane grin once more. He was holding a paper towel he had gotten from somewhere against the bleeding gash in his head.

Curse turned to Banshee. "Damien, Rayna, and Lawrence Spectman are the names of dead people. Curse, Banshee, and Larry Spectre are their current incarnations," he declared. "This was my life once, but now I have another existence. It is an existence where you two are the closest people to me. I do not belong here any longer. Let's go back where we belong."

Banshee smiled and wrapped her arms tightly around him. He returned her embrace now without guilt or hesitation. After holding her for several moments, she pulled back and looked up into his eye sockets.

"I'm proud of you," she told him. "You came across the entire universe in an act of love, and you've made a certain measure of peace within yourself."

Curse grinned sadistically. "Don't think that's going to calm me down . . . I'm still mad as hell about this whole business . . ."

"That's the spirit, my boy!" Larry was up on his feet now and making little effort to subdue his voice.

"Larry, shhh . . . we're not out of here yet . . ."

With that, Larry silenced himself and took one of Curse's hands from around Banshee to give it an aggressive shake. Yes, he was distanced from his old life, but he had two people now that had taken him as their own and would stand beside him. The thought gave him a degree of comfort.

"Let's get out of here before they wake up," Curse said to the others.

Quietly they agreed and with deft silence made their way back to the garage. As swiftly as they had entered, they exited through the open window back out into the night. Larry was more coordinated this time, making his way out without falling again. Curse thought of Larry's injury once they were outside.

"Larry, your head still hasn't closed up . . ."

"I've noticed, son—kind of a bitch I must say! I guess we don't heal here like we do back home. Maybe the psychic residue that sustains us there doesn't follow us into this world."

"That would make sense. Aja told me that when she came back to this world after being in the Nightmarescape for a while, she would get extreme headaches and feel like she needed to go back . . . maybe the presence the Nightmarescape creates for us won't last forever in other places . . . remember how you said it was a form of symbiosis?"

"Indeed, son. It must be a link that we don't have here. We should be getting back anyway though. We'll return to this world again soon enough to get Banshee's pound of flesh!" Larry spoke normally now that they were no longer in the house.

In agreement, the three of them moved through the backyard once more. The black void in reality was still there gaping out as an opaque shadowy gash in the darkness. It looked as though something had sliced a blade through the flesh of the universe and then pulled it open. Curse found himself staring into the ugly portal. Slowly unease was creeping into the back of his mind.

Something was telling him that an unseen danger was lurking somewhere near or in the portal. He steeled himself against the rising dread in his gut and moved toward it. His time here was over. His quest was completed, and there was nothing more for him here. The Nightmarescape was where he belonged now. With this in mind, Curse moved closer to the gateway. His mind screamed to him at the last second to move away, but it was too late.

39

A huge corroded blade swung out of the portal and caught Curse directly in the chest. He was thrown back with the force as the blade continued its sweep with his weight added to it. Banshee let out a scream as she saw Curse lifted from his feet upon the rusty thing, a trail of nightmareplasm spurting from his wound and bubbling out of his mouth. As the blade held him high in the air, the disgusting form of Pastor Nox stepped through the portal, his red eyes burning hatefully from behind the mask he wore. As his form moved into the world, a cadre of gangling plague-afflicted lurched out from behind him.

Banshee was the first to fire with Curse's rifle, taking two of the afflicted off their feet and stitching a series of gory eruptions across the Pastor's chest. A gravelly grunt sounded from behind the infernal mask as the Pastor shook Curse on the end of his scythe.

Agonized grunts escaped from Curse's throat through the bubbling stream of nightmareplasm that poured from his mouth. As he struggled to free himself, he realized that he could not find purchase on the long scythe. The blade continued to rip through his tissues, sending piercing waves of pain throughout his body.

The situation was ironic to Curse, for he remembered his first battle with the plague-afflicted and the Japanese soldiers. His memory replayed for him the sensation of holding the Japanese officer aloft upon a rifle, a bayonet impaled through his lower jaw and into his cranium. Curse remembered how he had held the man there until he was satisfied with his agony and finally granted him release. Now Curse was the one on someone's weapon with his body being torn asunder. Pain lanced through his entire being from the traumatic shaking of the scythe. Banshee was able to land several more rounds in the Pastor's chest before plague-afflicted swarmed her and she and Larry were engaged in their own battle.

Through the ripping agony, Curse's memory of the officer gave him a slim glimpse of salvation. The officer's pistol and his revolver were both tucked into his waistband. Mustering all he could through the pain, he reached down and pulled both guns from his pants. The Pastor's hideous red eyes held him transfixed as he did so. This was a being who possessed no soul. Curse knew of his hideous plans, and now his demonic presence was right on the doorstep of the woman he had spent his life loving. Not if he could help it.

Curse swung the pistols down toward the Pastor before the retort of the weapons filled the air. Eruptions of flesh and nightmareplasm exploded from the Pastor's upper body and head as round after round struck home. The solid mask upon his face cracked and splintered under the impact of the bullets. Pieces of the mask fell away from the Pastor's head, and for the first time, his truly gruesome visage was displayed to Curse.

Residents of the Nightmarescape were hideous already, and the plague-afflicted were horrific even by those standards, but they did not compare to the visual essence of death that had been concealed behind that mask. Pastor Nox was a true creature of decay and damnation.

Rotten bits of stringy muscles and gristle clung to a largely bared skull with several chunks of bloated flesh obscenely patched across the head. Beneath such decay, blood-red lights still burned out of his empty sockets. His mouth opened in a hideous gurgled scream as Curse's rounds struck him, and the scythe fell from his hands. Curse crashed to the ground with a heavy thud. His entire being shook as he was reminded of an awful reality. He would not heal as he would in the Nightmarescape. With the pain of his wounds making his arms shake, Curse moved his body as best he could and fired the pistols into Pastor Nox again. Several of the rounds caused grazing damage as the Pastor lurched over to Curse in a strange unnatural gait.

Looking up, Curse could see the Pastor's full height. The rotted cloak and bandaged arms coupled with the face of death itself sent a wave of preternatural dread through Curse. He had seen and lived through hideous things in both his former life and the Nightmarescape, but having this being of pure ruin tower over him shook him to his core.

It was then that he saw a form crash into the Pastor's enormous figure. The Pastor was knocked back, sending his filthy cloak flowing out to his sides as Curse saw a mane of dreadlocks trailing behind his rescuer. Banshee had saved him again. He thanked her under his breath as he struggled to work his way upright. His body convulsed with pain as he stood and began to work the scythe out of his midsection.

Dropping the guns momentarily, he attained a firm grip on the wooden shaft of the weapon and pulled. The blade stayed lodged within him. Banshee's struggle with the Pastor continued as Curse watched her land several backhanded blows with her barbed-wire-laced forearms against her adversary's head. As formidable as the blows had been, the Pastor merely staggered back and came for her.

Banshee struggled as the rotted and disgusting creature took her arms and lifted her into the air. Curse pulled at the scythe with all his might, but the wound was holding the blade in a vacuum. He screamed as he pushed harder against the weapon in a vain effort to rid his body of it. Just as his strength was about to give out against the pain, a tearing agony surged through him as the blade was jerked out of his body by unseen hands. Instead of joining the fight immediately, he fell to his knees screaming.

"Come on, son, plenty of time for that soon enough!" Larry was attempting to help Curse to his feet and support him.

"Larry . . . Banshee . . ." was all Curse could say.

Larry looked back to Banshee's fight just as the Pastor slammed her to the ground and a sickening crack resounded from her fall. Banshee let out her own scream to accompany Curse's.

Her cry of pain cut him deeper and sharper than his debilitating wound ever could. Curse quickly shaped the agony into rage. The violent pounding of anger thumped through his head as he forced himself to his feet against the protests of his body. Lights were on in the house behind them now as well as several other surrounding buildings.

Curse found his guns and lurched forward as the Pastor now loomed over Banshee. Just as Curse was about to open fire, two armored forms clanked their way through the portal. They were the two retainers that had stood at the Pastor's side upon the platform. Curse snarled under his breath as he unleashed a torrent of fire from his pistols into one of the newly arrived threats. Larry added the retort of his shotgun as he fired into the other.

"I handled these fools once—I can do it again!" Larry yelled as he charged forth and sent another cloud of projectiles into the armored warrior.

The sound of buckshot crashing into armor rang out with a metallic clang as the warrior staggered back from the force.

Curse noticed that no more plague-afflicted were running amok at this point. Larry and Banshee must have dispatched them all. He was never aware of how many there were—there might have been as few as five—but he could not tell amidst the pain of impalement. The Pastor and his two guards were enough to keep all of their hands full though. Curse continued to pour fire into the armored form nearest to him. The warrior staggered backward under the onslaught and disappeared into the portal. Once he was gone, Curse did not wait to see if he came back. He pressed himself on toward Banshee and the Pastor's melee. Each movement and contortion of his muscles sent shock waves of torture throughout his being. It was very possible that his injuries would prevent him from being much help, but he urged himself on despite the grievous wounds.

Larry fired two more blasts from his shotgun. The plate armor afforded the bodyguard an extra layer of protection against the shotgun blasts, but the pitted metal was weakening and buckling under the repeated shots. Several pellets had struck the warrior's helmet as well, creating numerous small dents and holes. Despite the damage to his armor and body, the warrior continued to advance toward Larry. His distraction allowed Curse to move ever closer to Banshee and Pastor Nox. As Curse staggered forward, he watched as the Pastor raised his huge hands and began to pummel Banshee with a series of crushing blows.

The sight drove Curse beyond determination and into frenzy. He stumbled against the weight of his injuries and raised his guns to lay down a curtain of fire as he lurched forward. The tear in his midsection was making his movements more and more of a struggle with each passing moment. He was also starting to feel weak under the strain of losing so much of the nightmareplasm that gave him a corporeal form. Despite these things, he soldiered onward, continuing his attack. Several rounds shot forth from his guns and struck the Pastor in various areas, causing him to fall backward and momentarily abandon his attack on Banshee. She used the time to recover quickly and retrieve her pistol.

Just as Banshee turned to fire at Pastor Nox, however, the second bodyguard reemerged from the portal and raised his mace high above his head in preparation to strike her. In a desperate effort, Curse lurched forward, firing his weapons at the warrior. He was on top of the melee now. He forced himself forward as several rounds punctured his enemy's armor. The bullets seemed to have little effect as the warrior prepared to swing the mace in a deadly arc. At the last moment, the warrior became aware of Curse's threat and turned his trajectory slightly so that the mace swung toward him instead.

Curse struggled to move himself in time, but the injuries from Pastor Nox's scythe had crippled him to a point that his movements were greatly hindered. The flanged weapon collided with the front of his skull. A jarring impact traveled down from the top of his head and radiated throughout his entire body. In brief nanoseconds before the inevitable crack, Curse felt his skull fracturing under the intense impact.

The impact continued to transfer its force from the strike as metal pushed further into bone, and Curse's skull began to give way. The mace traveled downward through the shattered bone and into the brain matter that gave Curse the psychic energy to sustain his body. With the trauma still shaking him, Curse fell. On the ground, he struggled to make sense of what was still happening around him. A vicious fight was ensuing, but his senses were falling into groggy distortion once again. A crushing ache radiated throughout his head from where the mace had struck him. He fought the shock of the injury while attempting to process the fight. Awash in a choppy sea of agony, Curse worked his head up so that he could see.

Gunshots sounded from nearby. Banshee was holding her ground now against the armored warrior as she blasted several pistol rounds into him from point-blank range. Then the Pastor was on her again as the two engaged in a deadly close combat. Larry intercepted the other guard as he staggered away from Banshee.

The remaining armored warrior focused his attention on Curse once more. Looking upward in a daze of pain and disorientation, Curse saw the warrior raising his mace again. Time seemed to slow to a crawl as the weapon swung downward in a wide arc once again. Curse attempted to will his body into action but was unable to make his limbs move as the weapon fell toward him.

Another crack against his skull, and he felt more of its bone structure give way under the brutal impact. His head bounced off the ground from the force of the strike. His

Nightmarescape

senses began to fade due to the trauma. He had to hold on. Summoning the last reserves of strength that his body could muster, he raised his ruined head once again. If he could have seen himself, he would have known that a huge chunk of his forehead and the top of his skull had been caved in by the repeated mace strikes. Chunks of gray pulpy matter were pouring out of the hole in his forehead along with a voluminous flow of nightmareplasm. The black fluid trailed down his face in thick drips. The wounds were too much for his body in this world. He would give what he had in a final expenditure of effort.

By sheer strength of will alone, Curse focused his perceptions the best he could. The armored warrior no longer perceived him as a threat and turned to join his master in combat against Banshee. Curse forced his hand forward in an attempt to crawl and catch the warrior's legs, to do something to stop him from adding his attack to the fight. As Curse reached, his hand fell upon something. His fingers gripped the object that had been laying on the ground as his mind rushed groggily to figure out what he was holding. After a brief period of feeling the object, Curse realized it was his revolver. He forced his fingers closed around the large frame of the firearm as he watched Pastor Nox pin Banshee to the ground as the armored warrior raised his mace once again. Banshee normally had no difficulty in holding her own, but the Pastor possessed a strange and supernatural strength.

Curse's mind processed what was happening as the warrior's mace began to fall again, destined for Banshee's head. With what little willpower remained, Curse raised the revolver and fired a single shot. The shot had not been aimed very well as Curse's vision was fixed on the falling mace. The mace had begun to fall in a heavy downward motion, but after his shot, it faltered in its course as its wielder seemed to suddenly lose his balance. Curse looked down from the mace at the armored figure and realized that he had shot straight through the back of the warrior's knee. A small entry wound was visible through the mail under his greave. Curse could process however that a ragged tear of muscle fibers and tendons had erupted on the other side of his leg. The warrior swayed for a moment, his balance having been centered on his now ruined leg. Curse watched as the armored form pitched forward and then threw itself backward in an attempt to regain its footing. Upon moving back, however, any semblance of a stance was lost, and the armored warrior staggered backward for several steps before crashing down on top of Curse.

More damage was done to his body, but his senses were so eroded and there was so much pain coursing throughout his being at this point that it did not matter anymore. Just as soon as the form had landed on him, it was removed once again by a violent upward jerking. Curse heard a loud noise right above him. Larry's shotgun retorted through the fog of disappearing perception. Curse was able to lift his head and see a blast exploding into the armored warrior's face. Pieces of armor splintered and flew away as the buckshot struck them, tearing a huge hole in the warrior's helm.

With the majority of the warrior's cadaverous face now exposed, Larry unleashed another blast from his weapon that caused the warrior's head to implode.

The warrior fell back, and his body began to melt into black ichor. Curse became aware of a seemingly distant voice yelling down to him.

"Curse! Get up, boy!"

In response, Curse could not find the strength to speak. He meekly raised his hand and pointed over to Banshee's embattlement. Larry took the cue immediately and fired a blast of buckshot into the Pastor's twisted form. The force of the blast knocked Pastor Nox backward off of Banshee. She was quick to get to her feet as Larry aimed his shotgun at the now kneeling pastor. Curse thought it strange that Pastor Nox had suffered as much damage as he had and still was able to fight like a demon. Perhaps it was his diluted pain tolerance. He seemed more than just another resident of the Nightmarescape. The Pastor was already regaining his footing and preparing to attack once more but never got the chance.

Another explosion shook the air around Curse as Larry's shotgun blasted forth another cloud of buckshot at point blank range. The cloud had little time to spread out before it collided with Pastor Nox's head.

Bits of skull, brain matter, rotten flesh, and black viscous nightmareplasm flew away from the Pastor's shoulders in a gory spray. Pastor Nox's body continued to stand for a moment before it lost the last vestiges of nervous control and fell lifelessly to the ground. Upon hitting the ground, the entire body seemed to melt and become a dark puddle.

Despite the absolute agony that wracked his body and his dulled perceptions, Curse felt an overwhelming sense of triumph. He had pushed himself to his last in order to protect Banshee from a fate similar to his own. His actions had given Larry enough time to eliminate the threats assaulting them. Curse knew that his final moments were upon him as the darkness of the night began to encroach ever further on his vision. He felt distant and far away from his own body.

Now his head lost the last reserve of strength holding it up. He fell back to the ground and noticed something a little strange. The black ichor that had been pouring out of him was trailing its way back into the portal, almost as though it was moving with its own sense of purpose. He watched his own essence flowing away from his body and back to where it had come from.

His attention was quickly snapped away from the fact as he felt his head turned in someone's grip. His face was pulled upward to stare into Banshee's. Her expression was one of shock and horror. Curse looked up to her as she cradled his head in her arms.

"Don't you do this . . . don't you leave me . . . ," she hissed. Another voice came from near her.

"Get him back to the portal! Get him up now!"

It's too late for me, Curse told himself.

Instead of fighting any longer, he continued to look up at Banshee. The intense blue lights in her eye sockets held him, almost as though her gaze alone would prevent him from fading away. As he looked into those lights, her features changed before his eyes. Her ghostly appearance began to fade as her former living persona took over his vision. He saw her now as he had in his memories. She was a living, lush, and beautiful creature. He studied her face as his senses became ever darker. The all-consuming pain subsided at the sight of her. He wanted to stay in this state a little longer before the inevitable claimed him.

It hurt him to see her face so agonized over his grievous wounds and circumstances, but he took comfort in the thought that he had allowed her to carry on. He wanted to speak to her, to tell her not to worry, but he could not find the strength to do so. Her lips trembled as she looked down at him. He attempted to reach a hand up and stroke her reassuringly as he had done when she told him her story of abuse.

He wanted to reassure her and let her know that everything was all right. He did not want to leave, but there was little choice in the matter now. He savored the sensation of her hands holding his head as his vision became dark to the point where he could no longer see her face. After several close calls and escapes, death had finally come for him. He felt something touch his cheek just as the darkness claimed him.

It was something wet. A teardrop. He knew that she would miss him horribly. He did not know what—if any—existence would await him after this. In her arms and in the gentle darkness though, he ultimately felt a sense of security. Only in this disappearing space of consciousness did he allow the terrible wounds upon his body to claim their full due. His essence faded with the gentle whisper of a night breeze as his consciousness quietly passed into nothing.

Banshee watched in abject horror as the icy blue lights in Curse's eye sockets faded and disappeared. She and Larry had begun to lift him to his feet and move back to the portal. They never had the chance, however. Curse's body melted into a puddle of nightmareplasm as they held him. Banshee screamed in torment as his being liquefied in their grip.

It was not just any scream of anguish. Larry remembered the shrieking she had emanated when he and Curse had first jumped her. This one disturbed the air around them and shook the earth as she wailed a note of pure misery into the night. Larry felt the intense vibrations shaking through his body as he placed his hands on Banshee and began to pull her away from the scene.

"Young one, we will mourn him, but we cannot stay here." Larry felt the sting of Curse's loss as well. They had been distant relatives, and Larry had been quite overjoyed to have a young member of his bloodline to teach and nurture. That had been taken away from him. He had killed the Pastor for taking his great-great-great grandson, but a rage was building inside of him that rapidly replaced his sorrow. That was one of the characteristics Larry had developed in life and passed down through his blood, the ability to turn despair into destructive anger. Yes, he may have cut the head off of the serpent, but that meant that there was still a length of serpent to punish. When he returned to the Nightmarescape, he would find every last one of Nox's disgusting minions and make them pay as well.

A strange high-pitched noise was drawing closer in the distance. Banshee recognized the noise as police sirens, but Larry had never heard them before. Nonetheless, he recognized the fact that they were something he did not want to deal with. He pulled Banshee, ushering her toward the portal. She felt heavy in his arms, as though she could not will herself to move. She just continued staring at the dark puddle that Curse's body had become.

Larry resorted to dragging her toward the portal. His foot slipped in something wet as he moved on. Looking down, he realized that the black ichor that Curse, Pastor Nox, and the others had become was flowing into the portal, almost as if under its own sentience.

"The Nightmarescape reclaims what is its own," Larry said sadly as he continued to drag Banshee.

Moments later, they were through the portal and back in the laboratory again. A scene of carnage greeted them.

Plague-afflicted were running rampant through the building attacking the scientists. Nigel and several other soldiers were fighting a valiant effort to hold them off, but numbers were weighing against them. Putting their grief aside for the time, Banshee and Larry added their own violence to the counter-attack. Larry sent a cloud of buckshot through the close confines and blew a small gaggle of the shambling creatures off their feet. He then leapt over to the table where the device was situated and switched the thing off. Banshee threw herself into combat with reckless abandon.

Holding only the pistol now, she put rounds through the skulls of several charging plague-afflicted before one got close enough for her to bring the gun itself into the thing's head. Several times she slammed the weapon into the creature's cranium, until the thing's skull gave way entirely, and it crumbled to dust.

Several of the things were holding Nigel down in a corner. She threw herself into his fight, wildly firing rounds from her pistol and backhanding her barbed wire into some of the creatures. Startled by her sudden onslaught, they abandoned their attack on Nigel. They focused their attention on her, and she was quick to dispatch all of them with pistol and brute force. In her haze of enraged anguish, she could not have counted how many there were. Several more bodies came charging at her. Chaos ensued.

An emaciated body crashed into her, and she took it to the ground. Larry's shotgun boomed somewhere nearby. Nigel threw himself into another melee. Banshee easily overpowered the nearest plague-afflicted and worked her pistol up against its skull. The thing hissed as it tried to pry her away. Its struggle ceased as she unleashed a single shot that blew out the opposite side of its head. The thing's body crumbled to dust in her grasp. Freed of its burden, she raised her weapon and fired into the remaining bodies. Some seized and disintegrated; others fell.

She stood once again to see Larry blasting one of the creatures into nothing at point-blank range. Several soldiers that she recognized from the convoy were in the laboratory as well, beating down plague-afflicted or shooting them at close range.

"How in the hell did they find this place?" Banshee growled under her breath.

It was at that point she observed Dr. Alman's decrepit assistant crouching in a corner, occasionally turning his head back to survey the carnage with an odd chuckle. She crossed the room toward him, blowing a hole in the head of a plague-afflicted along the way. A small shriek emanated from his gangly frame as Banshee snatched the back of his lab coat and jerked him around to face her.

"You let them know the device was here," she snarled through clenched teeth as she placed the barrel of her pistol under his chin.

The wretch trembled in her grasp as she held him with a measured stare. "I haven't told anyone . . . anything . . . I don't know what . . . you're talking about . . . ," he stammered.

"Of course you don't," she pressed her weapon deeper into his flesh. "It seems funny to me though that we disappear for a little while and when we try to come back, the very people who were chasing us come into the other world and kill one of ours . . . and now here we are in the midst of all this fighting and you're just sitting in a corner laughing . . ."

"They came on their own accord . . . I had nothing to do with it!" he protested.

"You're full of shit," Banshee retorted as she began to depress the trigger of her pistol.

"Pastor will protect me!" the dreadful little assistant screamed as the pistol sent a round up through his cranial cavity.

Banshee stood unmoved as a shower of brain matter and nightmareplasm splattered down on her and the crumbling body. Rage trembled through her being. There would be a time to mourn her loss of Curse, but now she had to avenge him. She did not know the exact connection between the wretched assistant and the Plague Faction, nor did she care. His scream for the Pastor was admittance enough. It was because of him that Curse had perished. The thought caused her to tremble as she snapped her head around the room, looking for another target for her rage. She was struck with disappointment when she saw that there were none.

Larry was helping Dr. Alman to his feet. Banshee immediately rushed over and seized him by the collar.

"You and your fucking assistant brought them here!" Her voice rose to a screech as she howled the accusation.

"Nay, my dear . . . he did it himself." Dr. Alman's hands were up in placation as he made the statement. A voice sounded from behind her.

"I think you should listen to him before you do anything rash, Banshee." Nigel was now standing not far behind her.

"Allow me to explain, please . . . ," the scientist pleaded.

"And why should we believe him, Nigel?" Larry joined the interrogation.

"You weren't here when they first showed up . . . he fought with us—the other guy just went off in a corner and sat there chuckling. He would not have been fighting with us if he had been part of drawing them here," Nigel responded.

Banshee had a moment to reclaim her lucidity from the blinding rage. "Why would he have called them here?" She asked, the composure in her voice cracking.

"I don't know . . . Edward was always a little mad. I never thought it to be anything too much worth time or thought. I don't even know when he would have had contact with any of the Plague Faction . . . he was here the whole time," Dr. Alman explained.

Banshee relaxed her grip momentarily and let the pistol move away from the scientist. Her rage was beginning to be replaced by a profound sadness and sense of loss.

"I think we have some things to look into," she merely said as her resolve seemed to falter, and she moved away from Dr. Alman.

An arm was suddenly wrapped around her shoulder. Larry was beside her now. She remembered Curse saying that Larry was a distant relative. It was not much of a connection to have someone's great-great-great-grandfather with you, but Larry had proven himself to be a very valuable friend, and under the circumstances, he was the only connection she still had to Curse.

"Yes, my dear, much to investigate and many who we'll make pay," Larry stated bluntly.

Larry's usual cheerful demeanor was gone. His face had changed from a perpetual grin to a strange flat expression that betrayed little emotion. She knew that the change in his demeanor meant that he would be even more dangerous than usual. Larry had a sworn enemy now in every single presence associated with the Plague Faction. That included all of the Axis forces that were assisting them. Larry had a wealth of enemies before, but now he would destroy the entire world if he could.

Banshee thought of her own scores to settle. Yes, she still had business in the other world, but she wanted to avenge Curse's slaying. Her personal retributions could wait. She would make a wealth of entities pay until she felt satisfied in her vengeance. At least the damned Pastor was gone now. The lack of his leadership would most likely cripple the remaining creatures in the Plague Faction, as they would fall into mindlessness.

And yet amidst all her burning desire for revenge, she could not displace the bereavement she felt. Curse had accepted and understood her. He had never judged her. He had promised her his hand in attaining her goals. He had selflessly thrown himself into great risk protecting her. She had helped him attain his goal of seeing the love of his former life, but she had not been able to protect him in the other world. The pain of loss ripped through her much like a blade. Her insides physically hurt from the grief she felt. She wrapped her arms around herself and squeezed a little to help alleviate some of the pressure she felt mounting in her torso. And then she became aware of another sensation. Something was gently dripping down her face. She reached up and her gray fingers came away with a clear liquid on them. The liquid was slowly pouring out of her eye sockets. Tears.

How in the hell . . . Since her rebirth in the Nightmarescape, she did not think crying to be a physiological possibility. However, things often thought impossible in the Nightmarescape had a way of becoming reality. Larry squeezed his grip around her shoulders as he watched the tears stream down her face.

"There will be a time to weep," Larry told her. "Do as you must now, for soon we will put ourselves knee deep in the innards of those who have wronged us."

Banshee could only nod in response. She did not want to open her mouth, knowing that she would sob if she did so. Despite the fact that she was torn with grief on the inside, she did not want to betray the full extent of her emotions in front of Dr. Alman and the soldiers. Surely she and Larry would have a discussion in due time about their feelings on Curse's loss, but now was not that time.

A commotion sounded from the front door as Kitenge came rushing into the room. A clear look of worry was spread across his face.

"We have fought enough of them away to get the vehicles moving again, but we must go now to take advantage of the window!" he yelled to them all.

The group did not need to hear any more as they followed him out of the laboratory. Larry moved to the back of the room and returned the device to its pack before chasing the others out. Nigel stood before Dr. Alman.

"Doctor, are you coming with us?" Nigel asked.

"No, my old friend. I am going to stay here and defend what is mine," Dr. Alman responded, a fierce blue intensity burning out of the lights behind his glasses.

"Very well then. Take care, Doctor," Nigel offered a salute, unsure of whether he would see his friend again or not. Dr. Alman returned the salute.

"And you, Nigel."

The entire group was in the street by the time Nigel charged through the doorway. The city was a scene of pandemonium. Plague-afflicted were running rampant in the streets. Every member of the group began firing their weapons into the emaciated and desiccated frames that lurched through the alleys.

Larry grabbed onto Kitenge and yelled above the chaos. "Where in the hell did they all come from?" he screamed.

Kitenge pointed to a drain in the side of the street. A diseased and rotted face was staring out of the opening, hissing through a frothy stream of bile. One of its gangly arms snatched out for anything that might get too close. The thing seemed stuck in the drain.

"What the hell?" Larry began. "What are these idiots doing?"

"They came out of the sewers all over the city at the same time. We were back at the vehicles when they just started crawling out and attacking everyone. Our guns cut down quite a few, but they kept coming. Soon after, we came to retrieve you all . . . where is Curse?"

The mention of his name stung Banshee even in the midst of the fighting. She channeled the anguish with her pistol as a howling plague-afflicted lurched toward her with its thin arms outstretched. After dispatching the creature, she looked back to Larry momentarily to see how he would respond.

"Curse won't be joining us, my friend . . . it's a long story. Let's get out of here and I'll tell you everything," he explained.

Kitenge responded with a solemn nod. "My condolences, Lawrence." He then unleashed a hail of bullets from his grease gun into several diseased bodies.

Hisses and screeches followed the afflicted as they fell. The group continued to press on toward the vehicles, trampling the fallen creatures underfoot.

As they charged, Banshee focused her mind on the fight at hand. The combat helped her channel her emotions for the time being. Her finger squeezed several more rounds out of her pistol into a mass of attackers. After several of them fell, she began to notice something. This attack consisted of Plague Faction only. There were no Axis soldiers or any other allies fighting along with them.

"They don't have any allies with them!" she yelled to the group.

"Indeed, dear," Larry responded. "Looks like the Pastor raised his last cause on his own."

Nightmarescape

Black ichor slicked the streets as they pressed onward toward the idle tanks and other vehicles. They were laying so many bodies to waste. Some crumbled to dust quickly, others absorbed more trauma and put up a harder fight. All of the city's noncombatant residents had abandoned the streets under the attack. Only fighters and plague-afflicted filled the roads and alleys now. Whatever weapons were at hand were used to combat the menace from below. Swords and axes hacked at flesh with sickening sounds as muscles were torn and bones were broken. Gunfire erupted from all directions, ringing off the sides of the buildings and echoing down the narrow alleys. Carnage ensued on a grand scale, and though the afflicted lacked the intelligence to realize it, their numbers were slowly being whittled down.

Larry and Banshee had fought their way back to the main road with their group of soldiers. The vehicles stood before them idling. The men who had stayed to guard the vehicles poured punishing volumes of machine-gun fire into the afflicted from roof-mounted weapons. Under the cover of the guns, Larry, Banshee, and the others made their way to their respective vehicles. Engines rumbling, the column roared to life as their wheels and treads began to grind across the cobbled street again.

Banshee found herself mounting the top of Nigel's tank just as it began to roll forward. Seconds later, she had dropped into the metal behemoth and jerked the hatch shut behind her. Nigel concentrated on driving the tank. Larry crouched near him, trying to stare out of the driver's viewing port as well. Outside the vehicle, Banshee became aware of the grotesque sounds of screams and bones snapping as plague-afflicted charged the rumbling column, being ground into sludge beneath the girth of the vehicles or impaled on blades that had been fixed to the exterior armor. The noise of machine guns still echoed outside as their users had no intention of letting up on the lethal barrages that kept the rest of the afflicted at bay.

Wearily, Banshee asked a question of the other two. "We could kill them all off if we stay and help defend the city. Right?"

Nigel responded first. "Our responsibility is to get that bloody portal generator of yours out of here right now before one of those things gets a hold of it. There are enough soldiers here to deal with the rest of these sickly cadavers."

Larry turned with a menacing grin on his face. "Yes, I think Nigel's right, but also think of how many of these bastards we'll crush beneath this tank on the way out! The rolling column will attract them and kill many! If I had some of my damn dynamite with me . . ." He trailed off as Nigel spoke.

"What happened after the Pastor chased you all through that portal?" he inquired.

Larry began to tell Nigel the tale of how the three of them had crossed into the other world and lost Curse. Banshee did not want to hear it. She moved to the back of the tank once more where the noise of the engine drowned out most of their conversation. There she meditated for a time on how she felt. She wanted to be alone now in this space so that she could grapple with her feelings of loss. Nothing came to her. She felt more exhaustion and emptiness than anything. Admonishing herself for not being able to mourn, she found that her consciousness was slipping away from her. She was so tired. Her head felt heavy under the weight of her mind. The emptiness sat inside her as a dull ache. Outside, the sounds of combat began to fade.

"We're out of the city," Nigel called.

Banshee did not respond. She sat with her back against the hull of the tank and her legs out before her. It was not that she did not want to answer, but she found that she could not. All thoughts passed from her mind as her body became limp, and she felt the burden of consciousness slipping away from her. Then as Curse had done many times, Banshee embraced the darkness that she was swept into. There in that peaceful oblivion, she allowed herself to hang. There were no feelings, there was no sorrow, no ache, no anger, just a temporary nothing. It was a welcome rest.

How long she floated in that dark space, she could not say. She merely allowed her mind to exist in the oblivious state until a memory began to shape itself out of the nothingness and play before her eyes. It was one she had seen before, the exact same memory she had seen in the tank on the way to the city. She remembered herself in the diner once more, seeing Curse in his human form.

Her heart warmed as she saw him there in that memory, and she watched it play out, him coming to her protection once more as she knew he would. And there she stayed for a while, locked within the beauty of her memory, away from the ebb and flow of time, away from the turmoil that assailed her, away from the forsaken world that she now belonged to. The tank rolled onward toward a destination that she neither knew nor cared of in this state. She would take this time to rest and remember. Larry and Nigel left her to be at peace inside herself while Larry finished recanting Curse's tale. Nigel sang Curse's praises to Larry and swore to remember and honor him. Then they rode on in silence. It was a time for reflection as the only noise became the engine of the tank and its treads carrying the three of them across the gray landscape.

41

Jenna and her husband stepped out onto the back porch with several police officers. The officers had swarmed the residence after receiving several complaints of gunfire and a large fight in the backyard. Strangely, there were no shell casings or other evidence of a struggle even though the 911 calls had claimed there were multiple people fighting and shooting.

Jenna remembered waking up to the chaos and finding her backyard the scene of an intense struggle between numerous bodies after a strange dream about her former lover Damien. Gunfire sounded over shouts and smacking sounds. She could not place just how many combatants had been fighting, but she estimated well over ten at one point. She could swear that some of them had glowing blue lights in their eyes, but she dismissed the idea as a trick of the light. The shock of waking up to such a scene on her property had distorted her perceptions, she told herself. But just what had she perceived, and what had actually happened?

The officers told her that several of the neighbors spoke of ghosts shooting weapons at each other. Jenna assumed that they had simply been roused from their sleep and had not been able to recover their senses yet. The shadowy forms in the rear of her house must have been human beings . . . what else could they have been?

Then she thought back to the dream she had about Damien. She dreamed that he had entered the bedroom and placed himself next to her as she slept. He then began talking to her about how he missed her after being away for so long. He apologized for the way their relationship and their lives had gone. She told him that she had forgiven him. That was true . . . for all the pain that had occurred between them and as a result of his final act, she still held him deeply in her heart and could not stay angry at him forever. Despite the trauma of seeing him after his suicide, she remembered him for who he had been before all that ugliness. Though the scars were still entrenched in her mind, she preferred to remember him for being the man that she had loved.

She had been on her own for three years after Damien's death, coming to terms with losing him. The realization finally had come to her that she needed to move on with her life, and she had found a suitable person to do so with. She had carved a niche in her mind for Damien and posited her love and positive memories for him there to hold forever while she continued her life.

The thoughts in her mind now made her want to weep. She was a survivor, yet she had lost so much and been so traumatized by Damien's suicide. Alone now, with the officers having taken a report and left, she thought of him. She thought of life and love, of death and loss, of existing and surviving. Tears began to roll down her cheeks as she bit her lip. Despite even the greatest tragedy, the world continued to move on implacably. One may die, yet be survived by others. Whether the ripples of disturbance caused by their death were known to them or not, their indelible impact would live on with those who still survived. A lost loved one could live on indefinitely in the memories of a survivor.

Jenna looked out upon the backyard through teary eyes at the only visible disturbance she could see: several dark puddles of an oily black liquid resting in various places. Any bodies or objects from the struggle were gone, and the dark liquid was the only thing that had not been there the night before. She wondered if there was a connection between the liquid and the fighting that had taken place.

Then she remembered again that she thought she may have seen blue lights shining from the eyes of several combatants. It was significant at the time because in her dream with Damien, she remembered rolling over at one point and seeing him above her. He was surrounded by shadow, so she could not make out the details of his person, yet she knew it to be him from his voice and his words. When she turned and saw his form enshrouded in darkness . . . she remembered seeing two blue lights peering at her from his shadowy silhouette.

My emotions are getting the better of me, she thought as she turned and entered the house once again.

42

Back in the Nightmarescape, a presence was awakening. At first, he did not process his surroundings. Everything was dark. The world slowly began to take shape as the darkness receded to a shade of gray. Groggily, his senses began to reveal the world to him. Forms began to solidify out of the gray as the overall surrounding became a shade of darkness again. There were shapes in the dark, inanimate objects were spread around the room. Small holes in the wall allowed a soft gray light in to reveal the room in detail. It was a moldy old place cast in hues of gray and black. The furniture was clearly old in its construction and decoration. The overall condition of the room was one of musk and decay. Despite the fact that it was a disgusting place, an air of familiarity surrounded it. Familiarity surrounded the entire situation.

At first he was only able to process through his senses, then slowly, his mind allowed his muscles to move. He righted himself, placing his hands at his sides on the moldy old couch where he sat. His mind was actively thinking now.

Who am I? The thought echoed in the back of his brain. It warranted consideration for a moment before the answer came to him. *My name is Curse.*

That question answered, another thought came to him. *Where am I?* He looked around momentarily before recognizing the room he was in. *I'm in Larry's house . . . his filthy old dilapidated house.*

Curse threw his head back and laughed at the thought. He was back in the Nightmarescape. Feeling his hands over his body, he learned that he no longer bore the hideous wounds inflicted by Pastor Nox and his goons. Reveling in his good fortune, Curse pondered how exactly he had come to be where he was. Was it possible that he had dreamed the whole thing, having never left Larry's living room after passing out for the first time? No . . . that seemed too implausible. The Nightmarescape showed memories, not entire dreams of what could happen. Confused momentarily, he wondered where Larry was as the story of recent events played itself out in his head.

No, it was not imagined. It had actually happened. How he had come to exist again in the Nightmarescape vexed him until a certain phrase from Larry came to his mind. "When you're alive, somehow your dreams can get in touch with this place . . . and then it has you. When you die, it wrangles you in, and you manifest once more . . ."

Curse briefly remembered the sight of his vital fluids pouring out of him and flowing back into the portal . . .

Curse had traveled back to his former plane of existence and died once again indeed. Then he must have materialized again in the Nightmarescape. This time, in contrast to his previous reincarnation, he remembered all the events of his former life that had been revealed to him along with all the events that had happened after he came to the Nightmarescape.

He remembered the people he had found too . . . Larry, Banshee, Nigel, Kitenge . . . they must have all still been off in another part of the realm fighting. He also remembered his mortal encounter with Pastor Nox in the former world . . . if the Nightmarescape had pulled him back in after being slain in the former world, the Pastor was back in the Nightmarescape somewhere as well.

A sadistic grin split Curse's face. He had accomplished much, but there was still more for him to do. He had completed a goal of returning to his lover to speak his peace with her. Now he had matters of vengeance and retribution to think upon. First he would use the device again to return himself, Larry, and Banshee to the former world so that they could extract Banshee's revenge on her rapists and killers, then they would return to the Nightmarescape, his new home, and he would make Pastor Nox pay for attempting to destroy him. Yes, there was much to do indeed, but he knew that he could not do it without Larry and Banshee, so he resolved to wait for them in Larry's house until they returned.

Curse threw his head back as he reclined into Larry's moldy couch. His existence was far from over. The Nightmarescape had reclaimed its own from the former world and would see to it that its children continued to play out the everlasting drama that created enough energy to sustain the insatiable realm of the lost and damned.

ACKNOWLEDGMENTS

T. S. Dann would like to thank all family and friends both living and passed on. You've all been sources of inspiration to me, and you know who you are.

ABOUT THE AUTHOR

Nightmarescape is T. S. Dann's first book in a series. Before his writing career, he spent five years at Georgia State University earning a dual degree in psychology and sociology. After this, he spent several years working as a police officer in the Stone Mountain area. He currently resides in the outskirts of Atlanta where he rabidly works on the Nightmarescape series. His attitude toward all of his work is "If you hate it, perfect, fuck off," so don't direct your complaints to him, save them for the Internet.

Find out more about the author and upcoming books online at www.morbid-publications.com.